THE FAVOURITE

THE FAVOURITE

S.V. BERLIN

First published in 2017 by

Myriad Editions
www.myriadeditions.com

Registered address:
Myriad Editions
New Internationalist, The Old Music Hall,
106–108 Cowley Rd, Oxford OX4 1JE

First printing
1 3 5 7 9 10 8 6 4 2

A CIP catalogue record for this book
is available from the British Library

ISBN (pbk): 978-0-9935633-8-6
ISBN (ebk): 978-0-9935633-9-3

Designed and typeset in Palatino
by WatchWord Editorial Services, London

Printed and bound in Great Britain
by Clays Ltd, St Ives plc

Sign up to our mailing list at
www.myriadeditions.com
Follow us on Facebook and Twitter

About the author

S. V. Berlin was born and raised in London. She has worked as a copywriter, facilitator, speechwriter and wilderness search-and-rescue professional. She lives in Manhattan.

For Anne

I

House

1

White Galoshes

She was in New York when it happened, on the way to a party, laughing and joking in the back seat of a cab. Now, in the grey light of an English morning, she followed her brother along the hospital corridor and wondered how she had got here. She could remember almost nothing of the last twelve hours – the message that flashed up on her phone, stark and to the point, the mad dash back to her apartment, the journey to the airport and the flight itself. And yet, there remained the simple fact of being here, which felt inexplicable and unexpected, and in that way had all the hallmarks of a dream.

As they continued through another pair of swing doors and down several flights of stairs, she listened to their shoes squeak on the linoleum like footstep sound effects. Ever since she was a small child she had mentally rehearsed for this event, but today those careful scenarios had vanished, the reality flat and unreal against its surroundings – the plain red bricks of the hospital building and the ordinary tone of their voices – while that other voice, the constant observer developed through therapy and other American pastimes, the voice which analysed and commented, had today been utterly silenced.

'They really do keep these places in the basement,' she murmured to her brother as they descended the stairs. He looked tall and remote – and much older, of course, since the last time she had seen him. He acknowledged her with a slight, not unfriendly shrug, while his girlfriend – a timid-looking person who had scarcely uttered a word – continued to follow a few steps behind them. A minute or two earlier she had found herself trying to make small talk with Peter, the attendant who had met them at reception. Now she heard him clear his throat. 'I know it's a cliché,' he said, 'but she really does look very peaceful.' This disclaimer was clever of him, she thought. He had taken the measure of his visitors, calculated perhaps that despite the circumstances they considered themselves cynical and knowing, above common displays of hysterics or emotional outpourings – and adjusted his words accordingly. They reached the bottom of the stairwell and entered a dim passageway. *Not long now*, she thought.

They arrived in a furnished waiting area, where Peter opened a side door. 'We're just in here,' he said in a low voice, and ushered them through into some sort of anteroom. She saw a large interior window and beyond this another, smaller room, carpeted and softly lit, its walls swagged in a thick curtain material. In the very centre of this room was a bed, and on the bed was a person who was clearly fast asleep.

Her brother was the first to speak. 'She looks asleep,' he said.

'Yes,' she said. It was true. You could see breath in the rise and fall of the sheet, even at this distance. A memory came to

4

her, like an object thrown up by a wave – of *King Lear*, how the king thought he saw Cordelia's breath upon a mirror – and she turned away from the window and saw that Peter the attendant was waiting, with his discreet shop assistant's air, a little behind and to one side of them.

'Please,' he said, motioning towards the little room, 'take as long as you like.'

She glanced back through the window, at the figure on the bed.

'I brushed her hair,' he added nervously, 'the way I thought she might have liked it.'

'Thank you.' She didn't know what else to say, struck again by the immense tact and complexity of his words, and overcome by an almost unbearable feeling of gratitude for this person, whose voice was full of kindness and apology, who had – as the duty nurse had pointedly informed them – left his own family and come into work on a bank holiday for the benefit of someone else's.

Peter gave her a wan smile and excused himself

'Do you mind if I go in alone first?' she said, turning to her brother. He shrugged.

'I'm not going in, thanks,' he said.

The room felt hushed and separate. And friendly, she decided – definitely friendly and warm, like a friend's sitting room. She was relieved to be allowed to make her approach gently and from a distance, rather than having it sprung on her as she had always feared. She had always imagined that when the time came she would be met by an officious and indifferent man in white overalls and brought into somewhere clinical and cold. Their shoes would echo off steel and tile and she would be marched up to a metal trolley where he would whip the sheet off with a magician's flourish and no warning. Slowly she neared the bed and noticed that her mother's face was framed by a kind of white ruff or flouncy Elizabethan collar – a gesture that showed care and thoughtfulness. Edging closer, she stood motionless for several seconds, waiting. The room was silent. Her mother's head was turned slightly to one side, to the right, and her eyes were closed. *She looks exactly like herself*, she thought gratefully. If her features looked wispy and indistinct, incidental in some way, this lent her the careless look of a sleeping figure in a painting – a Pre-Raphaelite Ophelia, hair fanned out in the water. In a crack of her mother's lips there was a fleck of dried blood, and she had the urge to dab it off, as her mother would have done for her at one time, with a scrap of licked tissue that held the faint odour of lipstick.

She leant down and gently kissed her forehead. It was something she had never done before, and doing it now felt artificial and faintly dishonest. Her mother's skin was very cold – or rather she assumed it was, because, as she straightened up, the sensation, or the memory, seemed to vanish. She wondered how you were supposed to say goodbye. Were you to say it out loud, the way people did in films? Or were you to quietly think it to yourself? She murmured it under her breath, feeling foolish and fraudulent, the word inadequate and not enough. Last chance for everything, she thought: to see her mother's hands, which really were those of a pianist – the first part of 'Für Elise' anyway, and most of the difficult second part, long, tapering fingers moving rapidly across the keys. Effortless.

On top of the sheet someone had placed a blanket, as if to provide warmth. It was a pretty and thoughtful thing, brushed cotton like a baby's blanket and covered in tiny flowers – speedwells, perhaps, or daisies. Gingerly she took hold of one corner and lifted it and saw beneath the bars and wheels of a metal trolley. There was only the outline of her mother's arms, bound to her sides by a cotton or linen winding sheet, the length of her body wrapped entirely. She drew the blanket back up, as for a moment the sheet's crisscrossing weave seemed to stand out in great detail, making her think briefly, guiltily, about thread count. There was one last thing, she decided, and she felt a frisson of wrongdoing. Her mother, of all people, would have had no objection to it. In fact her mother would have approved. *Would have.* Impossible words. She pushed them away and reached into her coat pocket. Her camera was an out-of-date contraption, the film having to be schlepped to the photo store to be developed every time. But it gave the taking of photos the satisfying surprise factor that was so rare these days. Leaning in close, she pressed down on the shutter. The click, normally imperceptible, felt jarring and irreverent in the little room as a fraction of a second later the flash illuminated her mother's face.

Out in the corridor her brother and his girlfriend were speaking in low voices. Once more, Peter seemed to appear from nowhere, a few steps behind her. She remembered another mystery she and her mother had speculated about, but for some reason, once the internet arrived, had never got round to looking up.

'I was wondering,' she asked Peter, 'what temperature you keep them at.'

She glanced across at her brother, who continued to stare ahead, unfazed – but she saw his girlfriend's head snap round. They had discussed the particular horror of mortuaries, she and her mother. They had wondered about what went on in them, and where. And this was their chance. Her chance.

'We keep the temperature at four degrees,' Peter replied, in a matter-of-fact way that did not surprise her.

'This place ...' she said. She felt the need to acknowledge the room behind them, its soft lighting and comforting fabrics – and Peter's kindness. 'It doesn't look how you'd expect.'

'Well, we try,' Peter answered with a far-off smile, as if recalling something lost and long ago. 'It's a difficult time. And I always think ... if it were *my* mother, one of *my* family ...' He cleared his throat. '*Well*,' he said, 'it wouldn't do to see men walking about in white galoshes, would it?' He smiled more broadly at this, as if making a little joke. *White galoshes!* It was true, then. Of course it was – if not here, then somewhere the public never saw, in a room farther back, or one level down. But, as her brother stood up and frowned at his watch, she realised that there was no one to tell.

'It was kind of him, wasn't it?' she remarked to her brother as they all walked up the stairs.

'What was?'

'How he tried to make Mum's hair look nice and everything ...'

'It's his job, Isobel,' he said flatly. 'Anyway, she went to the hairdresser's on Friday.' A pause. 'She would have hated it brushed back like that.'

It was true that her mother always liked to prepare for her visits – everything perfect and polished and scrubbed – clean sheets on all the beds, grass freshly mown, the house aired and welcoming. Her hair was always an issue – *too fine, too flyaway* – so that whenever Isobel was coming her mother had it washed and set specially, proudly informing the hairdresser (so she imagined) that this was in preparation for her daughter who would be coming to see her all the way from New York. Today's visit was unplanned, booked last night at the last minute, the actual last plane out of the airport, the one you heard about in all the movies. As they went through the lobby and passed the white hospital clock,

8

she was astonished to see that only twelve minutes had passed since they arrived. She turned to comment on this to her brother, but he was walking quickly ahead, pushing his way through the revolving door, his girlfriend at his heels. The nurse at the main desk had not looked up this time, or even seemed to notice them.

'So I was thinking,' she said, and leaned forward slightly into the gap between the front seats. They had been driving for several minutes and the silence was beginning to weigh on her. It was like coming out of a movie with someone who had nothing to say. '*I was thinking...*' she repeated, having received no obvious response, 'that, if you like, I don't mind taking Mum's room? Then you guys can take the big bedroom in the front.' In the circumstances the prospect of sleeping in her mother's room was both comforting and discomfiting, but it would show good faith to offer up the larger room, which had been hers when they were children.

Her brother didn't reply and she took this as tacit agreement. 'Should we grab something to eat on the way back?' she asked. She hadn't eaten since dinner last night, and wasn't the least bit hungry, but she felt the need to say something, to offer practical suggestions. She turned to her brother's girlfriend. 'What do you think?' she asked. The girl stared back fearfully, like a small animal deciding whether to cross the motorway.

'I think we'll just drop you off, if that's all right,' her brother cut in.

Weren't they going straight to the house?

'Drop me off where?' she said.

'At Mu...' Edward cleared his throat. '*At the house*,' he said. 'Unless there was somewhere else you'd like us to drop you?'

9

The question hung in the air. Clearly she had missed something, some errand or work commitment her brother had mentioned earlier – though surely his workplace, whatever it was, would be closed today? The last remnants of the town flowed past in a grey-brown smear of identical terraced houses. She heard the shift of the gears as the small car began the steep climb up on to the Downs.

'I'm sorry,' she said, 'but I'm really confused. Where are you guys going to stay?' Hadn't their mother once let slip that her brother lived at least an hour from Danecroft Road, even without May Day traffic?

'Rather sleep in my own bed to be honest,' her brother replied. His tone suggested that the matter was settled. He murmured something to his girlfriend, who reached behind her seat for the white plastic carrier bag that had been handed to him at the hospital. It contained their mother's belongings – her clothes and jewellery. He gestured, and she pushed it under her seat without looking at it. 'We didn't get much sleep last night,' he said.

This sounded like a reproach. Did her brother think that she had somehow contrived to absent herself from the hospital and from their mother's bedside? To be with someone during their final minutes and at the moment of their death was a precious thing, a privilege. Edward was lucky to have shared this time with their mother.

'Your place is such a long drive, though, isn't it?' she said, determined not to take the bait.

'We'll make a start on the house first thing in the morning,' her brother continued, ignoring the question. 'There's a lot to take care of. I expect there's some food in the kitchen. Or we can let you out at the supermarket.' The town's only supermarket stood on the site of what had used to be its only cinema. Their mother had taken them to see their first ever film there, *101 Dalmatians*. After the building was shuttered and demolished, she and her brother had spent a whole summer playing on the site – digging up fragments of old glass and pottery and lengths of twisted rusty iron from what, she learned later, were the 'footings' – the very foundations of the structure. She was amazed the place hadn't fallen down. 'Up to you,' her brother prompted. But it wasn't up to her at all, Isobel thought. He had made the decision for her in the hollow, yet supremely reasonable, policeman's voice she didn't recognise, as if threatening her with arrest or a misdemeanour fine. When had Edward turned into this stuffy, uptight person? How different he was from the young man she used to know, with his open face and earnest questions. Then again, he had seemed different the last time they met, hadn't he? Then, too, the severity and unfairness of his words had shocked her. After that came his silence, and her unanswered letters, and the great span of years, until his text last night, more than nineteen years later. Aptly, his number had come up on her phone as 'Unavailable', and this lack of caller ID had provided an interval in which she had been able to dismiss the message, whose news was grim and unlikely and suspiciously unsigned – *Mum in hosp. Call if you like* – clearly a bad joke or a miscommunication. She had spoken to her mother earlier in the day, and she had been in good spirits, looking forward to doing a bit of spring cleaning, she said, about to make a start on the garden and tackle all the weeds. Then the second message arrived, signed this time with her brother's name, and she had gone straight to the airport. His next was reassuring, oddly jovial and affectionate – *Yes, of course we'll collect you! xo*. If there was one paltry shred of silver lining in this, Isobel remembered thinking as the cab lurched up Third Avenue and into the Queens Midtown Tunnel, it was that they might

11

now reconcile as their mother had always wanted. Until this moment she hadn't questioned the idea. She had taken it for granted that an event of this magnitude would unite them, that it would eclipse their estrangement completely, rendering it a petty and trivial thing. That it couldn't fail to. They would stay at Danecroft Road, enclosing themselves in the house for the last time, and get through it together as their mother would have wanted. Now, she watched her brother's face, austere and impassive in the driving mirror, and knew she'd been mistaken.

'Supermarket's fine,' she told him.

They drove on in silence, up towards the high road that crossed the Downs, past the greenish-silver tufts of grass, blown flat by the wind, and the familiar white dots of sheep scattered among patches of scraggly yellow gorse. Soon the lighthouse would flash by, still in its losing race with the sea. In a recent letter, she remembered, her mother had mentioned that money was being raised to repaint 'La Jolie Dame', as it was known in the area, and restore its smart red and white stripes. *They've moved it – again!!* her mother had written; they had set the structure farther back from the crumbling chalk edge of Beachy Head. She tried, and failed, to catch her brother's eye in the driving mirror. 'Anyone jumped off recently?' she said, as they passed the turn-off. The cliff was notorious. As bloodthirsty little children they had gobbled up news of each new suicide. 'Throwing themselves off it since the seventh century,' their mother had had no qualms in informing them. Though occasionally someone's dog went careening over the edge, and this had seemed to all three of them far more tragic.

'Not too bothered about that sort of thing to be honest,' her brother replied.

'Got it,' she said. She turned her attention back to the window and watched the river come into view, looping its way back and forth across the marshy valley to meet the sea – in its own good time, as their mother liked to say. One more hill and they would be in sight of the first rooftops and chimneys of the small seaside town where they had grown up – and, after that, the inconceivably empty house at Danecroft Road with its fridge full of food their mother would never eat and the bed she would never sleep in and the rooms she would never walk through again.

Taking out her phone, she typed out a text. She and Martin had been best friends all through secondary school, losing touch only when she'd had to drop out, in the first year of sixth form. In recent years they had struck up a friendship again, and since last night Martin had messaged at least three times. Why didn't she stay with him and Sean? They were practically next door, he pointed out, just a few stops inland on the train. An hour ago she had thanked him again but said that she'd be more than fine staying at Danecroft Road with her brother. The car reached the top of the hill and the sea appeared and spangled for a moment, shifting and congealing into the distance as Martin's reply lit up her phone. *We're so pleased!! Your bed all made up in your room.* Isobel stared at the eleven words, filled for the second time that day with a stupid gratitude.

Sunday

A Simple Fool

Leaving the pub, Edward was momentarily flummoxed about what to do next. It was a good twenty minutes' walk back to Danecroft Road, but hanging about for a minicab would take even longer. If he wanted to get to the house before his mother and Jules left in the ambulance he'd have to leg it.

As it turned out, he managed this not too badly. He had weaved with a spastic half-trot on his dodgy knees through the packs of whooping, binge-drinking teenagers, up on to the high street and into the twitten, to limp out, finally, on to Danecroft Road just in time to see the ambulance pull away.

'Bugger,' he said, stopping to catch his breath and pat himself down for the car keys. Was this what he got for claiming a few hours to himself? For having the gall to slink off to the pub for once? Earlier, when Jules had offered to stay at the house and help his mother finish the weeding, he had experienced a rare burst of optimism. Who would have guessed, he had thought happily, on his leisurely saunter down, feeling pleasantly full after an early lunch, that after all this time his mother and his girlfriend were finally warming to one another?

The ambulance was disappearing up towards the main road and, as he patted himself down again, Edward tried not to count how many times he'd instructed his mother not to use the stepladder in the garden. The bottom rung was dangerously loose, and the ladder would undoubtedly have had a hand in the fall or whatever mishap his mother had managed to bring on herself. 'This is why we have to keep an eye on her,' he had informed Jules recently: not because Mary was Grandma Buggins – some wobbly old dear who threatened to keel over for no reason – but because she was obstinate and refused to take his advice. She had declined his offer of a trip to the unfeasibly cavernous and depressing Home 'n' Wear to buy a new ladder, claiming the old one simply wanted repairing, and that *furthermore* – according to her – this was a simple task she could *manage perfectly*

14

well myself, thanks all the same. Edward sighed. Duct tape, he thought, locating the keys in a trouser pocket he could have sworn he'd already searched at least twice – *that* would be the culprit. His mother's make-do-and-mend attitude was admirable, but still an infuriating holdover from World War Two. Not that he'd thought, when Jules had rung just now, to ask precisely what happened and whether the stepladder was involved and whether his mother had sprained a wrist or twisted an ankle or whatever – there'd been no time for all that palaver – but knowing his mother it wasn't hard to guess.

By an unusual piece of luck he'd found a parking space yesterday right outside the house, so now, with some crafty manoeuvring round traffic, he managed to catch the ambulance up and get himself wedged in right behind it. It was frowned upon, speeding along in the wake of an ambulance – *a bit of a sneaky*, his mother would say. No doubt she'd tell him off about it later. And normally he would agree with her, but it wasn't as if he were some oik late for a football match; he only wanted to save his mother and his girlfriend the stress of arriving at the hospital alone, not to mention dealing with all the bumf they handed you – more and more of it these days. Farther along the main road a line of cars had pulled over to make way, and, as they hurtled past, Edward glimpsed two pedestrians hovering uncertainly at a zebra crossing. How fast they were going, he thought, astonished to see the last of the houses vanish, replaced by the soft green blur of the Downs, driving like the clappers towards the hospital in the larger town further along the coast – a bit over the top, really, for a sprained ankle or bruised hip, but he wasn't complaining. With the road clear ahead, the ambulance accelerated, and as the car's speedometer edged past seventy-five miles per hour Edward fixed his focus on the Christmas-tree flash of the ambulance lights and tried to ignore the guilty exhilaration of driving drunk, and way over the speed limit.

By the time they reached the town and Edward found himself in a hair-raising slalom along its busy main road, the thrill was already wearing off and he found himself pondering other things, such as what they might all have been doing now if his mother hadn't been so careless. It had become a tradition of sorts for him and Jules to spend at least one night at Danecroft Road each week. *Caregiver Weekend*, his mother labelled it, the joke being that she was fit as a flea and hardly in her dotage. At this time of year they both looked forward to the growing daylight hours and being able to potter in the garden until late – his mother with her secateurs, daintily snipping the dead-heads off the early geraniums, while Edward pulled on his heavy-duty gloves to yank up great patches of brambles, propelling them on to the grass behind him with the speed and efficiency of a human combine harvester – or so he liked to think of it. 'It's peaceful, I suppose,' he had explained to Jules, who Edward could tell thought it looked anything but. Gardening, Edward decided, as he joined the ambulance in a wide racing turn and barrelled down a side street, was one of life's great pleasures. Not the only one: this evening, before he and Jules made the journey back home, they had planned to go out for a well-earned Chinese. Although he was just as happy to eat dinner on his lap in front of the TV as he had when he was a child. He still enjoyed the familiar ritual of taking his plate into the front room to sprawl out on his grubby orange beanbag and hearing his mother say, 'Oh, Edward, let me give it a wash!' She'd been saying the same thing for twenty years, and for twenty years he'd been saying no, and by now the exchange had taken on the predictability of an amateur comedy skit – but it made his mother laugh. Later on, a bit drowsy after dinner, he often found his attention drifting from the television to the photos arranged on top of it – a faded yellow world of long-dead pets and waterlogged camping holidays, of windy days at the beach and cheese and pickle sandwiches gritted with sand. Recently, he had begun to notice that in many of the pictures his mother was not that much older than Edward was now, while their few relatives – people he remembered as biblically ancient and decrepit – now appeared as fresh-faced as policemen.

By the time he parked the car and had fiddled about with the Pay and Display and located Jules in the hospital's busy reception area, pale-faced and anxious, his mother had been whisked away into the bowels of the hospital. 'I doubt they'll keep us hanging about for too long,' he told Jules, who shook her head tearfully; he was touched by how distraught she looked on his mother's behalf. The duty nurse appeared to say they were doing tests – X-rays, he supposed – and they were sent to wait in a room with a low, saggy sofa and boxes of children's toys. *Pain in your arm?* offered a nearby poster. *Slurred speech? Call 999.* After about thirty minutes he'd had enough of looking at it and stood up to stretch his legs, but found the straight line of his pacing interrupted by a grey, floppy-eared rabbit. 'For fuck's sake,' he said to Jules, flinging the toy into a nearby box, 'what sort of parents don't teach their children to clear up after themselves?' It was intolerable, he said, being kept hanging about like this for the sake of a broken wrist.

As time dragged on and no one came, it occurred to Edward that perhaps he was being rather selfish. His mother would be frustrated herself – not to mention injured and in pain. She would be well aware that he and Jules were out here waiting, and be mortified about all the trouble she was causing. First thing tomorrow they'd take her over to Home 'n' Wear, he told Jules, and replace that ladder once and for all. Then he had an idea. 'Has she got her mobile with her?' He could have kicked himself for not thinking of this before.

'I don't know,' replied Jules uncertainly. 'I don't think so ...'

He tried the number just in case. It rang and rang before he remembered that hospitals made you turn your phone off in certain areas.

'She hates this place,' Edward said, letting himself half perch on the arm of the sofa. He didn't trust his knees to propel him back up if he sank into the sofa's depths again. *God's waiting room.* This was the name people gave to the town and its hospital. He looked at his watch. Ten o'clock. He couldn't stop his mother fretting about the inconvenience – *on your one night out, too,* she would apologise. Once they saw her he would brush this off in no time with a joke, Edward decided, and later they would have a good laugh about the whole thing.

Some time later yet another white-coated lackey arrived, clipboard in hand, to interrogate Edward about his mother's recent medical history. Any complaints? Dizzy spells? He went over it all again as patiently as he could. Look, one of your colleagues took all this information down two hours ago, he told the man. Nosebleeds? Anything like that? Come on, Edward said, I went through that at the main desk – don't you lot talk to each other? I told you, headaches, blood pressure, *no* and *no* – but I'm not a bloody doctor, am I? In fact, could we please *speak* to the consultant? Edward looked pointedly up and down the empty corridor. They appeared to be the only ones in the hospital. The real doctors would be all off playing golf for the long weekend. He was starting to lose his patience. Look, he said, trying again, why can't you just ask my mother for this information? The man looked away for a moment with an odd expression Edward couldn't quite place – embarrassment or confusion – and quickly down at his notes. Agency contractor, Edward decided – paid sod-all, piss-poor training, and ashamed of his own incompetence. Why can't you get all this off the computer? Edward asked him. My mother's information should be in there. System's down, replied the man. *Of course it is*, Edward thought. Well, in the meantime we'd at least like to see her, he said. The man eyed him warily. If it's not *too* much bother for you, obviously, he added, with maybe a bit too much of an edge. He was aware of Jules at his side, and her growing discomfort. Look, he said, I'm sure it's not your fault, but it's late and we'd like to get her home. The man nodded and scurried off. *The fucking nerve of it*, he told Jules.

Someone must have got the message, because shortly afterwards a real nurse appeared. They followed the efficient squeak-squeak of her sensible shoes down the corridor and through a darkened ward of sleeping, coughing people, and he was pleased to see that they seemed to be heading for a separate, more private-looking room at the far end where light spilled out dimly from under the door. 'Doctors,' he muttered to Jules, 'they think they're gods in white coats,' but at least his mother had some privacy. The nurse showed them in and he was surprised to see that the bed nearest them was empty, stripped so very thoroughly, it was as if its occupant had upped and died in some particularly messy and inconvenient manner. This brought to mind an excellent if spectacularly tasteless joke about haemorrhagic fever, although he knew better than to share it with the nurse, who was, if possible, even more humourless and po-faced than the one they'd dealt when they first came in. He'd save the joke for his mother instead. Her bed was discreetly curtained off, though whether through carelessness or a cost-cutting lack of fabric there was a large gap where you could almost – but not quite – see inside. As he went over the nurse called out something after him, but he was not in the mood to hear her excuses. He would poke his head through the curtains in some vaguely comical way, Edward decided, all the better to defuse his mother's stream of apologies.

Was this a joke? The person in the bed looked ill in such a blatantly grotesque way that Edward wanted to laugh. *Too much slap*, as his mother would say. Adding to the Hallowe'en effect was something stuck in the person's mouth, an object that resembled a pair of plastic novelty shop lips from a Christmas cracker. Freshers' Week prank, Edward thought, and the unwitting nurse had walked them right into it. Except Freshers' Week wasn't for months, was it? He turned to the nurse to demand an explanation, but she spoke over him. I do understand, she said. I know it's terribly distressing for you, she went on in a vaguely rehearsed way, but it's to keep your mother's airway open. What was she talking about? The nurse gestured towards the bed like the Ghost of Christmas Past. Her blood pressure, it's falling rapidly, I'm afraid, she said, ninety to fifty in the last twenty minutes. He followed her gaze and, for the first time, took in properly the pitiful figure in the bed. His mind reeled, weightless like a lift dropping. *No*, he told her, there's been some mistake. He watched her take a step away from him, as if trying to back out of the room, and part of him found this hysterically funny – a scene from a *Carry on Nurse* or *Carry On Dying*. Her eyes skittered away for a second, but he'd caught it – a micro-expression – what was it? Shame? Embarrassment? Confusion? They were standing right under the overhead light and he could see now that she was young, the skin on her face acne-scarred, artlessly blotched over with some thick, orangey powder which had sunk into the pores. *In the middle of a long and thankless shift*, Edward thought, *and too tired to know what she's doing*. They stared at each other. I'm afraid there simply isn't any more we can do at this point, Mr Vernon, except to make your mother comfortable. There has been some mistake, he insisted. My mother fell, it was a fall. Was she not hearing him? He was surprised to hear his own voice, pitched too high, querulous and pleading like a child or an old man. The nurse stared back at him, blank and implacable. My mother, she had a fall, Edward repeated, swept back for a moment to his schooldays, his French verbs. She had a fall. She fell. Past imperfect, past perfect. The air around him felt fuzzy, the few colours in the room too vivid, and he thought he might be sick. His hands were sweating, and he went to wipe them on his trousers but they were quite dry. Somewhere outside the room, a steady hammering noise started up. *A bit late for workmen*, he thought, and realised that the sound was his own heartbeat, the blood pounding through his ears. He tried again, sounding each word for her. Maybe she was hard of hearing, Edward thought, or from overseas, though he had not detected an accent. A simple fall, he repeated, which if she *was* from overseas, Edward realised, might sound to her like *a simple fool*. But for the first time, the nurse appeared to waver. Mr Vernon? she said. Haven't they spoken with you? Who? Spoken to who? he started. We've been kept waiting a very long time. They stared at each other for a long second. I'm so sorry, I thought you had been made aware. Who … he began again, but the thought was lost. There was a sharp pain behind his eyes and his vision felt thick and blurry. I'm sorry, he said, I just want to know what's going on. And what your treatment plan is, he added, in case she thought he was stupid. Treatment plan? Mr Vernon, as I tried to explain …

Did she have to speak so quickly? Edward thought. She was pouring words into his ears all at once in a clattering handful of Scrabble letters. He had been trying to sort them into some semblance of order, but he couldn't keep up. Haemorrhage … catastrophic bleed … her words went on, farther away now, and it occurred to him that she might have been saying them for some while, because they had the cadence of a chant. *A stroke*, he thought. *Am I having a stroke?* If not, why else would this have come into his head? Could his speech be slurring? This would explain why she couldn't grasp what he was saying. Wasn't there a video somewhere, on the internet, of a woman who had a stroke? She tried to dial for an ambulance but couldn't understand the numbers on the phone. This would account for the misunderstanding, the cognitive impairment, he thought. It was Edward who was ill, not his mother. And yet – there was something, in what the nurse said, a word or a sentence that had given him the sense of being within reach of something significant. If only he could pin it down and decipher the meaning. He could feel it, the existence of it, through the clamour and confusion in his head, and beyond that some part of his brain trying to get at it, scrabbling away furiously without him.

'I'm sorry,' he said, 'could you repeat that last part?'

'I was trying to tell you that your mother had a fall, Mr Vernon, caused by a brain haemorrhage, but that she is not in any pain.'

Now she was confusing his mother's fall with his stroke, Edward thought. They were descending into parody. Where was the man from *Candid Camera*? Surely he was going to leap out from behind the curtains – or indeed his mother herself would appear, arm in a sling, laughing heartily – it would be just like her. *Lost the plot*, Edward thought. *Lost the fucking plot somewhere, silly old git.*

'No,' he said. 'No, I don't think…'

The nurse appeared to gather herself and regard him evenly, as if weighing up whether to take a different line of enquiry or try a different tack. He noticed for the first time the name on her coat: *Park*, the name appearing to zoom into focus with great clarity because it was preceded by the word 'Dr'. *Doctor* Park, not Nurse Park.

'I am so *very* sorry, Mr Vernon,' she said, taking a step towards him. 'I truly thought they had spoken with you first.' Very gently she placed her hand on his arm, and it was this, this quiet gesture, that made him understand, finally, that her manner was not that of an overworked amateur but the professional deliverer of bad news. 'Mr Vernon, I'm so sorry,' she repeated, as the insistent ringing and the muffled jet-engine roar in his ears was joined by another sound, like the menacing woop-woop of a ground proximity klaxon, a warning of terror rising up from beneath. For a fraction of a second he felt it, the sheer terror, and himself balanced precariously on the nose-down edge of it, and knew that he had a choice, as with an almost physical effort he wrenched his mind up, and out, and felt himself gliding into an immense calm. 'I understand,' he said, and he saw that the doctor believed him. He felt in his pocket and found the car keys and held them out to Jules, who was standing immobile, half in and half out of the door, staring at the bed with a dumbstruck expression. 'I said can you please wait for me outside, Jules?' he repeated, rattling the keys at her.

'In the car?'

'Whatever you like. I'll meet you outside.'

He knew he was being unreasonable, but there was nothing else for it: he needed to be alone. He needed to clear his head.

He had been studying her face for some clue, some betrayal of consciousness. Her features appeared to be sinking, spreading and melting into the pillow, so rapidly that he wondered if it was a hallucination. Her eyes were shut tightly, as if concentrating on some difficult puzzle, and Edward wondered if this reflected some conscious effort, or merely his own wishful thinking. Her breaths had become laboured, with long periods, up to fifteen seconds at a time, when she appeared to stop breathing altogether and Edward would think, *this is it*, and push the button for a nurse – only for the breaths to start up again, with a ragged, choking rasp. It wasn't like the moment you got in films – though God knew he couldn't imagine what he would say and what sort of conversation you were supposed to have if you got one. The sound was like listening to someone being strangled. He shut his eyes and tried to imagine that she was dreaming – sprinting up flights of Penrose Stairs, trying to find the way out. Ascending and descending. Going nowhere forever. Closing his eyes made the sound louder, swelling the space around them, curtains blown outwards, furniture sent flying across the room like a nuclear blast in slow motion. He opened his eyes and took hold of the chair and moved it closer to the bed, wincing at the rude scrape of its legs on the floor. *If you don't have anything nice to say, come sit next to me*, his mother liked to quote. The doctor had suggested he say his goodbyes, and Edward had a sense of being affronted by this, because it was the stuff of soap operas and cheap fiction, self-dramatising and mawkish. An idea came to him, some inane thing people said, that *hearing was the last thing to go*. Was it true? What must it be like, trapped inside your own body, unable to communicate, only to hear the people closest to you filing solemnly into the room to say goodbye? And if you were past hearing, Edward reasoned, what, then, was the point? There was nothing to say. Instead he needed a gesture – one that was infinitely human and kind, ambiguous and – crucially – not final-seeming. They had never been a touchy-feely sort of family, but Edward hoped he could lay his hand on his mother's cheek without it seeming unusual if by some perverse quirk of neurochemistry she had an awareness of what was happening to her. Mentally he tried to absorb the planes and details of her face, to remember her as she was just hours ago, and commit that – not *this* – to memory. *Goodbye*, he thought stupidly, and didn't believe it for a second. As he extended his hand towards her cheek he was surprised to see his whole arm trembling. And then his fingers made contact with her skin and he recoiled, unable to help himself, drawing back his hand as if it had touched a flame.

He found himself outside, doubled over outside the hospital's main entrance, hands on knees, retching. In his head was a memory of running through the darkened ward, back past the sleeping coughing people, along empty corridors. How had he even found his way out? Some post-detonation whine was singing in his ears, and as he waited for it to die down a taxi pulled up in slow motion and disgorged a well-dressed couple arguing in a guttural foreign language. He watched their shoes as they edged past him. The man glanced down at Edward and said something in a low, disapproving voice – Farsi or Arabic. There was fear, Edward thought, in the coldness of her skin, and the fear was still down there, he could feel it, in the deepest corner of the brain where his amygdala remained on high alert, like a monkey that shrieked from a high tree, long after the leopard had passed. His neocortex had control now, he told himself, and gradually, through the noise in his head, he was able to discern it, calmly unscrolling its long litany of excuses and self-serving, subjunctive-tense bromides: *She didn't know if you were there or not. She wouldn't have wanted you to go through that, would she? Wouldn't she have wanted you to remember her as she was?* – weak, wheedling thoughts that disgusted him. What his mother *would have wanted*, Edward thought, was to not die. *Catastrophic*, the doctor said – like an earthquake or flood. He pictured the intricate structures of the brain, containing within them seventy-five years of memories – her hopes for her children, her plans for the future, the mundane considerations about what to wear or what to eat for breakfast – being pulverised under a tide of blood and swelling tissue as he crouched here uselessly heaving up puddles of beer.

Jules was waiting, Edward remembered, but just now he couldn't think where he'd parked the car. His mind felt like an immense blank, half buried under a thick layer of white noise. Next to the entrance he spied a bench and he went over to sit for a moment to collect his thoughts. A nurse and a frail, eighty-something woman leaning on a walking frame crept past him, and out of nowhere the memory came to him of a man he'd sat next to once on the night bus in London. He'd been a student at the time, and the man – Edward had assumed – was suffering from a bad cold, hunched protectively over a white plastic carrier bag, sniffling at odd moments. He had wondered what such an elderly person was doing on the bus at 3am, a lonely figure among the groups of raucous students. And then Edward had happened to make out the word printed on the bag in stark black capitals – BELONGINGS – and with a horrible lurch of comprehension he'd realised that the man was crying. Embarrassed, he had got off at the next stop and walked the rest of the way home. Would it be possible to decline his own bag when it was offered? Like the gift bags they foisted on you at charity dos, it would be full of things you never wanted – and in this case, Edward thought, would rather do without. It would mean losing the bracelet his mother always wore, engraved DNR in bright red letters. It had not been needed after all. She had sent off for it in the post after that American case that was in all the papers, the brain-dead girl whose parents were 'too hysterical with religion to pull the plug out', as his mother had noted at the time. She had been so proud and pleased when the bracelet arrived, showing it off and turning her wrist this way and that. On her it really did look like an expensive piece of arty jewellery, rather than an item from a catalogue that cost £19.99 plus £3 postage. The bracelet was not some morbid indulgence on his mother's part, but practical and a matter of pride and independence. She had that uniquely English fear of being a nuisance, of being *a burden* – to her children, especially.

Of course, his mother's anxieties had been completely wasted on his sister. Isobel had happily upped sticks and run off to New York years ago without a moment's thought for anyone. *Bloody Isobel*. At least *he* had been here when it counted. He would have to find her now, Edward supposed: call the long, overcomplicated American number he had never looked at, least of all dialled, but which was buried somewhere in his phone, and only then because his mother had begged him to take it years before. 'Just for emergencies, Edward,' she had assured him, understanding that he would never use it otherwise. And he never had – he was proud of that. He took out his mobile and scrolled through the short list of names, and found the number under *Mum – Emergency Contacts*. He punched in a short text message, and set off to find Jules and the car.

Sunday

Wishes

'It's not your problem she picked the wrong time to have her brain haemorrhage, is it?' the voice was saying. Julie shivered, swapped the phone to her other ear and ran a hand under the front seat for a second time – searching for a scarf, an old jumper, anything to fend off the chill in the freezing car. It had been a mistake, she thought, calling Lorraine – but she'd been so frantic with worry and, after the scene in the hospital with Mary, ready to be sick with it all. She'd had to tell someone, and as usual that someone was her sister, Lorraine.

'Asking for it if you ask me,' Lorraine observed tartly. 'Didn't they say it was an accident waiting to happen? Well, *didn't they?*'

'Yes, I suppose so,' Julie replied. The doctor hadn't put it quite that way.

'Problem solved, then! You've got nothing to worry about,' said Lorraine. 'So, what are you going to do about her house?'

This was another concern, the idea of going back to Danecroft Road tonight – she couldn't face it, though her toothbrush, her pyjamas and all her toiletries were still sitting in her overnight bag in Mary's spare bedroom. 'I expect

Edward will just drive us back to ours,' she told Lorraine hopefully, though this wasn't certain at all. In fact, ever since the ambulance had appeared outside Mary's house earlier, everything had felt decidedly *un*certain.

'No, I mean will he sell it or what?' Lorraine persisted. 'Must be worth a packet, in that neighbourhood.'

'Lorraine, could we not talk about it just now?' Julie whispered. At any minute she expected to see Edward's face appear at the window. Of course, Mary's house *was* in a very nice area, with the park just down the road, and all the shops right there on the doorstep – but it would be highly inappropriate to discuss all of that now – *a bit premature*, would be Edward's phrase.

'*Whatever*,' said Lorraine with a loud huffing noise. 'As per usual I was only thinking of you, and as *per* usual you have to be weird about it.' Her sister returned to her latest marital saga – her husband, Declan, and the woman she suspected him of having an affair with. This afternoon Lorraine had confronted the woman in Burger Tree. At home afterwards there had been threats of divorce – though it was unclear who had made them, and Julie was careful not to ask. 'A slag, *basically*,' Lorraine was continuing. 'It's no secret that she puts herself about. Trowels it on as well. Face full of make-up. Did I say that?'

'You did mention it, yes,' Julie replied. As it happened, Julie knew her – the *home-wrecker* – or knew her by sight, because she worked behind the counter at Julie and Edward's local post office. She spoke nicely, and was known for being good with the older people – patient if they were a bit slow counting out their money, always ready with a kind word or a helping hand. You didn't have to be a man, either, to notice that she was very pretty, but in a natural way – which for some reason made it difficult to imagine

29

her carrying on with someone's husband. And certainly not with Declan, who had married Lorraine right after they left school and had three children with her and who treated her like gold. Not that she could say any of this to Lorraine, Julie thought, squinting through the dark windscreen. Her sister wasn't shy with her opinions, and she wasn't one to mince words – but, as even their own mother admitted, woe betide anyone who tried to tell *Lorraine* anything. With its slammed doors and dramatic twists and turns, her sister's life was like something on TV. Her problems sounded so much bigger and more important than Julie's own, which according to Lorraine were *pretty pathetic seeing as you don't have kids to worry about.*

Today was an exception, though – surely, her own predicament happening now and yet to reach its conclusion, like something live and important on the news, while Lorraine's story was not that different from all her other stories. Still, in a peculiar sort of way this did make them quite soothing, the familiar words and phrases, the way they never varied, how they lulled you into a feeling of calm. Maybe this was why their grandmother liked church…

' …*listening*?' said Lorraine.

'Yes, sorry, I'm here!' Julie answered quickly. She must have drifted off for a second. Mindful of brain cancer, she swapped the phone back to her other ear and was just in time to catch Lorraine say, ' …like I said, *vile. Vile and disgusting* and I'm not having it…' knowing that shortly afterwards her sister would pause and say, *I ask you, what's she bloody got that I haven't?* and that Julie was not expected to supply an answer.

She leant forward and wiped the heel of her hand across the windscreen. Earlier, instructed to climb into the back of the ambulance behind Mary's stretcher, she had had no time to fetch her coat or her glasses. For the last half-hour she had been anxiously scanning the same anonymous, intermittent blur of people moving in and out of the hospital's main entrance. Lorraine's opinion – *What's your problem?* – was that if Julie was so concerned she should go back in, or get closer by parking in a disabled space. But she didn't dare, and it didn't seem right either. Edward had been very *definite* about waiting outside, and he would have his reasons. It was hurtful, though, being sent away and excluded at a time when Edward should need her the most. And yes – as Lorraine suggested – Julie supposed part of her *was* relieved, not having to sit there watching it all play out. But the doctors had led them to believe it would all be over very soon, so that now, the longer Edward was in there, the more she feared that this wasn't the case at all. Had Mary, by some terrible miracle, woken up? The idea had been going round and round in her head. *I doubt she'll be saying anything*, Lorraine had offered, nastily. *Though she is his bloody mother, so it'd be a bit funny if he left before she did – ha ha!* This idea – the more obvious explanation – had given her hope. Lorraine could be a bit sharp if you got her in the wrong mood, but her sister was always so *certain* about things – and then there was the *way* she spoke about them – with such confidence, as if what Lorraine decreed couldn't possibly be otherwise. She watched a nurse and an elderly woman on a walking frame pick their way across the car park, and then there was a pause on her sister's end and the unmistakable click of the cigarette lighter. She decided to take a chance.

'I know I'm being silly,' she said, 'and worrying too much, but you did say it would be a bit funny if Edward didn't stay with Mary, didn't you?' She waited, hoping this wouldn't be dismissed as a question they had already settled.

'I didn't say that,' said Lorraine croakily, through what sounded like a great lungful of smoke.

'Sorry?'

'*I didn't say that*,' her sister repeated. 'I didn't say it was *funny*. Why would I say something like that?' This was the other Lorraine, the one who changed sides without warning or misunderstood things that to Julie seemed obvious. *Boom, click – done!* Lorraine was fond of saying, snapping her fingers, when some niggling problem was dispensed with.

'I meant funny as in *strange*, not comical,' Julie explained.

'Why?'

'Pardon?'

'Why?'

'Why what?'

'*Why* do you think it's funny?'

This was the other problem: her sister's tendency to say one thing, and then, a week or a day or even a few minutes later, to swear up and down that she hadn't said any such thing, or insist that she had said the complete opposite.

'But I don't think it's funny...' Julie began, beginning to feel slightly light-headed.

'You just *said* you thought it was *funny*. There's nothing *funny* about being in hospital, Julie, I can assure you of that. What's *really* funny, if you ask me, is that you're always moaning on and on and on about his mother not liking you and how confused you are, when maybe you should take a look in the mirror and ask yourself *why*.'

How did this always happen? Julie thought. 'I was just agreeing with you. About Edward,' she said. 'And Mary.' She was starting to feel a bit deranged. Lorraine had got them completely off the point, while Julie was feeling so flustered that she couldn't for the life of her remember what that was in the first place. On the other end of the phone Lorraine was silent. 'I expect he just wants to be there for when … for when Mary …' She couldn't think of the appropriate word. 'For when she *passes*,' she said. *There*, she thought, *I've gone and answered my own question*. This wasn't what she'd wanted at all.

'*Dies*, you mean?' Lorraine said in a bored voice. 'Sounds to me like she's circling the drain.' This was a phrase from *Smash-up Saturdays*, a reality show about ambulance drivers in Glasgow that Lorraine and their father followed obsessively, and it conjured up unpleasant images.

As Lorraine returned to the subject of Declan, Julie looked for something to distract herself with and remembered the book sitting in the glove box. She'd come across it last week in the staff-room wastepaper basket, its spine broken and pages splayed open like the victim of an unspeakable sex crime. Feeling sorry for it, she had fished it out, brushed off the crumbs and bits of ash, and put it in her bag for later. Looking back, this might have been a mistake, because, as she traced the book's textured cover with her fingers, a horrible thought occurred to her.

'*Lorraine*,' she whispered, before she could stop herself, 'I just thought of something …'

'I can't get a word in edgeways with you tonight, can I?' snapped Lorraine. Julie had an image of her sister sitting in the kitchen with her feet up on a stool, examining her nails and glancing impatiently at the clock on the microwave. She felt a sickening sense of urgency, as if a stopwatch was running, counting down the seconds, faster and faster, to the exact moment when her sister's patience ran out.

'I know it sounds a bit funny – *strange*, I mean – but what about *Pathways to Possible*?'

There had been nothing out of the ordinary in not wanting to traipse over to Mary's this weekend, and, if once or twice

Julie had wished desperately that she didn't have to, this wasn't unusual either. The only difference, she had realised only a moment ago, was that this time, after all these years, her wish had come true – and it had done so in the worst way possible. Not only had her wish *literally* come true, Julie thought, it had come true within days of reading *Pathways to Possible*. Lorraine had mocked the book and its ideas. Yes, Julie had admitted at the time, her sister wasn't wrong, it did *sound* a bit like 'the sort of rubbish only hippies and nutters believe'. But once you read it for yourself it did make a funny sort of sense – she couldn't say why exactly. She had tried to put across the book's basic idea: that thoughts were made out of energy which rippled out into the universe as *intentions* which themselves *manifested* as actual *reality*. It sounded ridiculous. 'Too fucking complicated for me,' had been Lorraine's verdict. Julie couldn't blame her for that.

'Pathways to *what*?' said Lorraine.

'That book I told you about,' she replied. 'It's all about having positive thoughts, but what about the negative ones…?' She paused to let the word *negative*, and its implications for Mary's accident, sink in. The book had been very clear about what could happen if you sent negative thoughts out into the universe. Not that she had wished Mary harm, she continued. Not real harm anyway. But what if your negative thoughts really did affect your choices and what you did – or what you didn't do? And, if so, had they been *manifested* this afternoon? On the other hand, would it really have made a difference? Both Lorraine and the doctors had agreed it was an accident waiting to happen. Hadn't they?

'What's your point?' said Lorraine through a clatter of what sounded like taking dinner plates out of the dishwasher. 'You're just making excuses. Either way it's going to look like your fault.' And then the noise stopped and to Julie's astonishment Lorraine simply continued on where she left off, with her Declan story.

She held the phone a few inches away from her ear and let the voice recede to a faint chirrup. Lorraine was right, of course, and now she felt twice as bad as she had five minutes ago. Somehow, in the space of a few hours, Julie's whole life – her future with Edward – had become hinged on Mary. Then again, Julie thought, maybe it always had been. On television people were always waking up just long enough to point out the guilty party and have them handcuffed and marched off to prison before falling away again. In her mind's eye she saw Edward leaning over Mary's bed while Mary whispered weakly and urgently into his ear. If she had ever dreamed of life being more exciting – and she certainly hadn't – she was now faced with what Lorraine would call a real *situation*.

'... *listening*?' said a tinny, distant voice. Quickly she pressed the phone back up to her ear.

'Lorraine? Sorry, I couldn't hear you for a sec.'

'I *said*,' Lorraine hollered into the phone, '*she's the kind of woman who keeps a spare pair of knickers in her handbag!*' It was hard to know what to say in response. '*Well?*' demanded Lorraine. Were they still talking about the woman from the post office? Or had Lorraine moved on to someone else? She tried to think. 'You *weren't* bloody listening, were you?'

'Lorraine, I'm sorry ... I'm just so worried ... please, don't be like that ...'

'DON'T TELL ME HOW TO BE! You know what your trouble is? You're *selfish*! You think it's *all about you*.'

'I don't think that. You know I don't. *Please* ...'

'I'm tired. I have to go to bed,' Lorraine announced abruptly.

Not five minutes later Edward appeared, striding out of the darkness towards the car. 'They said they'll ring,' he said uninformatively as he did up his seatbelt. He drove them back home in silence. She didn't dare ask what had happened in the hospital. Then, about halfway back, somewhere on the dark coast road, Edward's mobile buzzed softly and he pulled over. 'Okay. Thank you,' he told the person on the other end. 'I appreciate that. Yes, I shall. First thing. Goodnight.'

She looked across at him questioningly.

'Have to call the duty nurse in the morning,' he told her. And, as if in an afterthought, 'Lot to do this week.'

She glanced at his face, trying to gauge his feelings, and understood then that Mary had gone. It was over.

'I'm so sorry, Edward ...' She tried to take his hand.

'Thanks, Jules.' He gave her hand a brief squeeze and let it go. They set off again, as almost immediately, next to her, the phone purred again – just once, for a text message.

'Jesus, who is it now?' sighed Edward. 'It's after midnight.'

Edward refused to use a smartphone, or text while driving. Julie picked it up. *Poss to collect me 2moro?* said the message.

'Who is it?' said Edward.

'I don't know. It's says it's ...' She squinted at the tiny letters – she was hopeless without her glasses – and then she held it a bit farther away and nearly screamed. '*Mum?*' she managed to squeak, as a recent episode from *Smash-up Saturdays* flashed through her mind, about a man who woke up in the mortuary in a body bag. 'It says *Mum ...*'

'Oh,' said Edward nonchalantly. 'That'll be bloody Isobel again.'

Isobel? For the second time in the space of a minute, relief flooded through her. 'Your *sister* ...?' Edward hadn't mentioned that his sister would be in touch, though it was only natural that she would be, thought Julie, at a time like this. Edward kept his eyes on the road ahead and didn't respond. 'Is she coming here tomorrow?' she asked.

'Unfortunately,' Edward replied. 'Look, I'm driving, can you take care of it?' He nodded impatiently towards the phone in her hand. 'Text her back or whatever.'

In all their years together this was the first time Edward had mentioned his sister. The only reason she even knew he had a sister was through Mary – although Mary had been oddly evasive. With Mary gone, and Isobel on her way, Julie realised, she would finally meet Edward's only other family member. She felt herself quite looking forward to it. Not only that, Julie thought, but by asking her to reply to Isobel's message Edward was trusting her with something important. She took a moment to think about what to say, to carefully compose the right words. *Yes, of course we'll collect you!* she typed. Then for good measure she added an *xo*.

It was only after they arrived back at the flat and were on the settee going over the arrangements for the next day that she realised her mistake. When Isobel had asked to be collected, Julie had assumed she meant the local train station.

'Hang on, you told her *what*?' said Edward. 'You do realise she's arriving at the airport?' She opened her mouth to speak, but Edward hadn't finished. 'Great, bloody marvellous, cheers, thanks a lot, Jules!' He slammed his mug down on the coffee table with such force that she thought the glass would crack. Did he think she'd texted Isobel the wrong thing on purpose? She'd never seen him like this.

'Gatwick isn't too far, is it?' she offered hopefully.

'*Heathrow*,' said Edward. '*West fucking London*. Look –' he thrust his phone at her ' – it's here in the message.'

She stared hopelessly at it. *LHR arr. 0932 hrs.* It said nothing about an airport – at least, thought Julie, not in words a normal person would understand. Should she have been paying more attention?

'I really am sorry,' she repeated. 'I should have thought, especially with her living in New York and everything.'

Edward shot her a look, and she felt herself reddening. *Another wrong step*. Of course it was Mary from whom she'd picked up this precious snippet of information. He paused, then continued, '*Look*, I really don't care where she bloody lives. The point is, she expects to be picked up in a few hours and chauffeur-driven through bank holiday traffic because she's too high and mighty to take a bloody train like anyone else – *end of*.' He paused to rub at something, a speck of grease perhaps, on the side of his mug. She frequently saw him inspecting items that she'd already washed up, running a finger over the edge of a plate or the prongs of a fork, or scrutinising the cuffs of a freshly laundered shirt. Meanwhile, she was in everyone's bad books this evening – Edward's, Lorraine's, and most of all Mary's, Julie remembered, if Mary but knew it – which, as Lorraine had pointed out rather harshly earlier, Mary *certainly wouldn't*. She watched Edward drain his mug in one gulp and was struck again by how handsome he was. He had already refused her offer of an omelette, but still she wished there were something she could do to put it all right. At that moment he leant over and gave her a quick peck on the cheek. 'I'm sorry, Jules,' he said. 'I'm being unfair. You weren't to know. It's her fault, not yours.'

'I could text her back if you like?' she said.

'No, leave it,' said Edward. 'Spilt milk. Anyway, no point in setting her off.' He yawned and looked at his watch. 'S'too late, she'll be at JFK by now.'

That must be the airport in New York, Julie thought – she was a quick learner – and wondered what Edward meant by 'setting her off'. She tried to picture what Isobel would be like in person. Was she like Edward? Or would she be more like Mary...? Best *focus on the positive*, she decided, as *Pathways to Possible* advised. 'Are you sure I can't make you something to eat?' she asked, feeling quite on edge from hunger herself – but you could hardly gobble down toast when someone had just lost their mother, could you?

'No – thanks, though.' He smiled wearily. If Isobel was more like Edward, she thought, why did Edward never see her? And why did he seem to hate her so much? *What had his sister done?*

Edward called to the cat and it emerged from under the armchair and came scampering over to him. 'I think I'll just get some kip here if it's all right with you,' he said. 'If I'm not up, give me a shout about six.' He swung his legs up on to the settee, made a space for the cat behind his knees and, before she could object, put one of her best cushions under his head and rolled away from her.

She couldn't recall a single night they had spent apart. But then, she had heard grief did funny things to people. For a minute or two she remained where she was, squeezed next to the cat on the edge of the settee, listening to Edward's breathing. Once she was sure he was asleep she got up and made the rounds of the flat's doors and windows to check they were properly locked and closed. Edward was strict about security, and this checking of everything was normally his job. As she double-locked the front door she tried not to let her imagination get the better of her – the intruders lurking outside, or the ones at this very moment locked inside the flat with them, men in masks who had crept in earlier while she and Edward were at the hospital and were now lying quietly in wait in the wardrobe or under the bed. Why did she think these terrible things? *Always project a positive mindset, for negatives are opportunities in disguise, waiting to be transformed into positives.* She tried to keep the book's advice in mind as she brushed her teeth with a spare toothbrush and examined her face in the mirror. *'Visualise and project positive thoughts,'* she whispered to her reflection, though none came to mind, and she soon found her thoughts returning to Mary – Mary, flat on her back in the garden, feet splayed out, a handful of wilting flower petals in one hand ... Mary, propped up in the hospital bed like a hideous rag doll ... *Not* thinking about something, Julie realised, going to fetch a clean pair of pyjamas from the airing cupboard, was so much harder than she had imagined. There were *all the words of loving supportiveness* offered by the closest people in your life, and imagining these *as a warm bath* – but this was even more of a challenge. She really would need to devote a lot of practice and a lot of *self-work* – as the book put it – if she had any hope of discovering her own *soul path*, let alone constructing the *internal emotional cathedral* that was crucial – so the book said – to a healthy relationship. She felt exhausted just thinking about it all and instead she imagined Isobel, sitting on a plane high up in the clouds surrounded by strangers. Was it really so much, Julie wondered, for her to ask her own brother to collect her from the airport? She was still annoyed with herself for the whole mix-up with the phone and Isobel's message. Lorraine would say she had been too busy thinking about herself. And yet, when she thought about how many weekends she had sacrificed cooped up at Danecroft Road with Mary, this did feel a little bit unfair. For years, Julie had sat politely on the sidelines as Mary and Edward discussed geranium cuttings and politics and obscure foreign countries and a thousand other subjects that she herself had little interest in. And where had it had got her? *Nowhere*, Julie realised, as she set the alarm clock for 5.45am. Mary had simply kept up that disconcerting manner of bland, artificial friendliness, like someone in a washing powder advert. Sometimes, if Julie attempted to contribute to the conversation, she would catch Mary glancing across at Edward with an expression of puzzlement. *Who is this person?* it seemed to say. *And why do you keep bringing her into my home?* Edward never remarked on this or even seemed to notice, leaving Julie to wonder if she was imagining it. Was Mary the only one who deserved Edward's loyalty and devotion? He was protective towards his mother – Julie understood that; it was only normal when a woman lived alone without a husband, wasn't it? Although Mary herself appeared unaware of her predicament. In her way Edward's mother was one of the most self-contained and confident people Julie had ever met. Did this mean that Mary was in denial as well? It was Lorraine's view that Mary was 'a bitter saddo who failed with men and doesn't want anyone else to have one either'. Edward's mother, Lorraine had suggested, was the reason Edward was so cagey about marriage and had still not proposed to Julie, a full eight years and ten months after they started going out. Was this true? And, if so, what would happen now that Mary was gone?

She got into bed and pulled the duvet up and lay with her arms relaxed by her sides, palms facing upwards. She would practise *positive projections* and *calming breaths* exactly as *Pathways to Possible* described them, and wake up tomorrow feeling much better – more *positive* – about everything. She took one deep breath – in, and slowly out – and then another, but even as she did so she could already feel her mind wandering. It wasn't easy to *shout yes to happiness*, Julie thought, when your bed was freezing cold and your boyfriend was curled up in the other room with the cat. Wide awake, she got up again, intending to retrieve

Pathways to Possible from its hiding place in her knicker drawer. And then she remembered that the settee was right under the window. When it was chilly outside, as it was tonight, a nasty draught blew in under the windowsill where the landlord had still not repaired the rotting frame. What Edward needed was a hot-water bottle.

Going out into the corridor, she passed the door to the lounge, and stopped. An unfamiliar noise was coming from the other side of the door, the sound so faint, and so unlikely, that she stood completely still for several seconds to make sure it wasn't just the wind. There it was again – a low, intermittent whimper. The sound gave her an uneasy feeling that she couldn't quite place. Maybe this was a positive sign – proof that Edward was vulnerable and needed her. He had made some derogatory remarks about *Pathways to Possible* last week, but the book promised that, if you followed its instructions, anyone in your life *could, and would, change*, whether they wanted to or not. For now, she would visualise and send out a positive thought on Edward's behalf. Alone in the dark hallway, she did feel a bit silly – but overcome too by that strange-yet-familiar feeling, an odd pressure or weight in her stomach she had felt conscious of earlier. She considered what a positive thought might look like – would it be grey and black, like newspaper print? Or warm and pink, like a baby? Carefully she formed an image in her mind, a tiny pink parcel with tissue-paper wings. How funny, Julie thought: she could almost see it, a butterfly emerging from her body to cross the space between herself and the next room, squeezing itself under the door and fluttering over to land comfortingly on Edward's shoulder.

In the kitchen she ran the tap and settled herself at the kitchen table to wait for the kettle to boil. She had opened her book to a chapter called *Productive Grieving – 10 Top*

Tips for Moving On Effectively, but she couldn't seem to concentrate on the words. She thought about Edward and their future together. Edward was the one truly *positive* thing in her life, the best thing that had ever happened to her. If Julie had to sacrifice another few days stuck at Danecroft Road to sort out Mary's belongings and sell her house, she was happy to support him. Mary, after all, would not be there. There would be no more wasted weekends, no more having to watch TV programmes she had no interest in, and no more walking on eggshells. Now, with Mary gone, there was no one standing in the way of their happy future together. *Pathways to Possible* didn't believe in accidents, and it certainly didn't believe in luck – but after over eight years, with her clothes nestled in the wardrobe next to Edward's, with their toothbrushes sitting side by side, with next morning's coffee measured out into the coffee maker and the question of whether they would drink it peacefully together already decided, Julie could hardly believe hers.

2

Fish Fingers and Chips

'We're going to cook you a dinner just like your mum would have!' Martin announced brightly when Isobel arrived at their house, which bittersweet promise turned out to be fish fingers and chips. Normally she would have wolfed them down. Today, she couldn't seem to chew them into small enough pieces to actually swallow. Martin and Sean didn't notice – or were being polite and pretending not to. Sitting round their kitchen table, Martin had commenced his usual monologue, bemoaning Americans and the way they pronounced words like 'mirror' and 'oregano'. It was a relief, Isobel thought, to be still for a moment, to do nothing and be nothing – like lying on the bottom of a swimming pool while voices busied themselves on the surface, their owners appearing as indeterminate shapes that had little to do with her. Although this did mean, she realised as she retrieved the limp remnants of a fish finger she'd attempted to hide under a pile of chips, that she was being a horrible guest. In the few hours since she'd got off the train there had been a number of gaping holes in the conversation, places where she'd been asked this or that question – what she thought of the kitchen renovation or why Americans insisted on thinking, doing, saying or voting for certain things – when perhaps she had not answered properly or with her usual speed. There were odd spaces in her thoughts. She would reach for an answer and find an unexpected hole where before she might have plucked a particular word or clever fact. Now, she found herself surfacing into the midst of a tense exchange between the men. Martin, a bit tipsy, was pressing his point. 'Well actually I don't care what you think,' he was telling Sean, 'I just know my dad and Isobel's mum are up there right now having a natter. Am I right?'

He looked over at her with an expression of confident appeal, and she smiled in a way she hoped came across as polite, but weary. 'See?' said Martin, victoriously. 'Heaven exists! I know it does.' Right now, Isobel thought, heaven existed right above their heads, in Martin and Sean's guest room, where she would crawl gratefully into bed if only she could think of a polite way to excuse herself.

My mother is dead, she thought dully. The words rang a false note. The fact could not seem to fit itself into her mind. It was like the day she first moved into her apartment, how the movers had stood outside and discussed among themselves the likelihood of getting her desk through the narrow hallway, and then up and round the sharp twist of the stairwell. Couldn't they take it up through the window? she suggested. The men shook their heads and sucked their teeth. *My mother is dead*, she thought. *She died*. The idea was so unlikely, and so stupid – possible, yes, but only in theory, and then only partially. The rest of the thing jutted out into darkness, unseeable and unknown.

'You know, Martin, it's really quite tedious that you even come out with this stuff,' Sean was saying, lighting a cigarette from the end of his last one. She didn't smoke, but it struck her then that after so many years in America there was something civilised about someone lighting up at the dinner table. 'Not to mention your timing,' added Sean, exhaling luxuriously. 'Take my parents,' he said, turning to Isobel and eyeing Martin warningly. 'Well, I suppose they both were taken,' he said with a thin laugh.

'I'm so sorry ...' she told him. 'When?' Was this a rude question? Though they had met on several occasions, she had managed to miss this crucial fact about Sean.

'Five years ago now,' he said. 'One after the other.' He flicked some ash on to his plate. 'And that's just that,' he said. 'Although I wish it were different, obviously.'

'Can't you use an ashtray?' said Martin.

As a child she remembered seeing people wearing black armbands. This tradition was long gone, but until now some unconscious part of her must have thought that orphans – for want of a more grown-up term – were in some way identifiable, like Harry Potter with the scar on his head. But the death of a parent didn't mark you out at all. Sean had got up and was busying about with treacle pudding and she thought about all the other things she didn't know about him, or Martin – or, for that matter, anyone else in her life.

'Let's have another glass of wine!' said Martin, opening the wine fridge.

'Maybe in a while ... ?' she said. 'But you guys go ahead.' She felt almost comatose, at that particular point of exhaustion where you could feel all the cells in your body jiggling about in protest. Martin insisted she eat pudding, so that by the time she got upstairs to unpack it was already half-past eight. For some reason she had agreed to go back down for a nightcap and now wished she hadn't. She sat down on the bed and stared at her suitcase. A pair of brand new, silver-embroidered hotel slippers – 'St Regis Rome' – had been placed neatly next to the bedside table and she put them on. A glass flask sat on the bedside cabinet and she poured some water into the little tumbler that fitted on the top. If she took half a pill now, she thought, and went down for one glass of wine, she could take the other half before she went to bed and rely on getting some version of sleep tonight.

The mere act of pouring, and then the swallowing of the little pill, made her feel instantly better – or slightly less worse. Raised voices floated up from downstairs – what she knew Martin referred to as a *heated discussion* and Sean called *getting cunty*. In calmer moments both maintained that this acted as a steam valve that made their relationship healthier. She closed the bedroom door anyway, and wondered again why she had promised to join them for another drink. What had she been thinking? Now she had to stay alert and find a way to distract herself until the row died down and she could, like a regular houseguest on a normal evening, walk back into the kitchen as if nothing had happened.

To kill time, she decided to call Chris. Since she'd left last night they'd had a brief phone conversation on her way to JFK and exchanged only a couple of texts after that. Chris picked up after two rings. 'Hey,' he said. 'I was about to call you. How you holding up?' His voice, after not even twenty-four hours away from New York, sounded to her ears so confident and American.

'Okay, I think,' she said. She'd been surprised to get a flight out at barely three hours' notice on a Sunday night.

'So, where are you, at your mom's?' His wording was unfortunate, she thought, suggesting that her mother was nearby – busy in the kitchen, about to call *Dinner's ready!*

'I'm staying with Martin and Sean,' she told him, though she was pretty sure that she had texted Chris earlier with this news. 'They're being lovely, actually.'

'Okay.' Then after a pause. 'So they're your *gay* friends, right?'

'Yep,' she said. 'That would be them.' She didn't really think about what she said next. 'So, I have a question for you ...'

'Sure,' said Chris. 'Shoot.'

'You have a bunch of vacation days, don't you? I was thinking, if you could get off work later in the week...' She hadn't planned on asking. And, if she and Edward had been staying together at Danecroft Road, Isobel thought, it probably wouldn't have occurred to her. As it was, the idea seemed to just slip out.

On the other end Chris said nothing for a moment. 'Off work?' he said, finally.

'Yes, if it's not too much hassle.'

'This week?'

'Well...yes.' She felt awkward at having to spell it out. 'For my mother's funeral,' she added, and instantly regretted it. That the words 'mother' and 'funeral' should live in such juxtaposition felt utterly wrong. And she didn't blame Chris for hesitating. It *was* a lot to ask, even from someone who always complained about not taking any time off. 'Chris?' she said, wondering if they'd been disconnected.

'Sorry. I'm here. Lost you for a second.'

'Okay...'

'Bad line.'

'Sure.'

'Give me a sec, just figuring it out...' She had an image of him scribbling sums on a piece of paper and frowning.

'It might be just for the weekend. We haven't made the arrangements yet.' *The arrangements*. It felt very strange to hear her own voice, these euphemisms tripping from her tongue. 'You can say no, Chris, if it's not a good time.'

'Yeah, I mean work has been, like, totally crazy...' agreed Chris, as if latching on to the idea and running with it. She noticed how he left the sentence unfinished, as if considerately leaving space for her to insert her own, negative conclusion.

'Look, don't worry about it too much,' she said. 'If something changes, you can let me know. Good?'

'Of course. Sorry, Izz,' he said. 'I get that it's tough. It's a bummer I have to work. I wish I could be there for you...'

'Please, it's totally fine.' At this point the whole conversation was faintly embarrassing, Isobel thought; it felt like begging. Besides, it would be easier to get things done on her own. Asking someone to use their vacation days for a funeral was a bit of a liberty. Christ, they'd only been dating for two months – what was she thinking? Was she hoping a virtual stranger would drop everything and fly over here to act as a human shield? Some kind of flimsy bulwark against her brother and his offputtingly laconic girlfriend? Now that she thought about it, that was exactly the reason.

'Shit, hold on, I got a call coming in,' said Chris. As he crossed to the other line she experienced a tug of nostalgia for the old days of long-distance calling, when every second felt precious and even the fact of them an obscene luxury, allowing you to feel in some dark and romantic way as if something was at stake.

Waiting for Chris to come back, she took the phone over to the window. The scene outside was the very opposite of her own hectic street in New York, with its shops and frenetic activity and honking cabs. The road was deserted and dark, with not a dog-walker or a car alarm to break the silence, just the clock on the bedside table ticking quietly. 'What about the Sunday papers? Marmite and Marks & Sparks?' Martin had asked her a few years ago. 'Don't you miss any of it?' The question had bemused her. 'No,' she had told him, 'I really don't.' She hadn't told him how much she loved New York City, the feeling you had of being simultaneously with and not with people, the freedom to walk everywhere on an island with rivers close on either side, and the ocean not far away. Or that she even loved the subway, which she would take over a taxi any time and at any hour because it was faster and had better stories. And that most of all she loved the city's utter randomness – how one moment you could be trapped underground in a smelly train listening to a homeless person's pitch, and at the next stop Gloria Steinem would get on. You could find yourself standing in a bathroom line chatting to Robert de Niro or plopped in some rock star's hot tub downing cocktails with the future US ambassador to the UN. She could only imagine how obnoxious she would sound, explaining this to Martin or anyone from her old life.

She listened to the silence on the line and went over to the bookcase and tried to guess which books belonged to whom, Martin or Sean, but it wasn't as easy as she thought. There was something soothing, Isobel thought, in being surrounded by the men's domestic paraphernalia – the Penguin books and stacks of dog-eared magazines and meticulously labelled box files – *Tax Returns* and *Gas Bills*, *Insurance Papers* and *Bank Statements* – their contents typed on their spines, this organised quality a counterpoint to the raised voices downstairs. Or was it? Her own belief was that this *merging*, this blurring of people's separate selves was what lay at the root of the problem. It was too much to ask, she thought, to be cooped up with one person your whole life.

'Hey, Izz. Sorry about that.' Chris sounded out of breath. 'Arbitrage opportunity. So what were you saying?'

What was there to say? 'Nothing, really,' she said. 'We have to start on clearing Mum's house tomorrow. I guess I'm not looking forward to that too much.'

'Will you sell it?'

This was an abrupt and very forward sort of question, Isobel thought, and it took her aback slightly. 'It's rented,' she told him.

'Oh, okay,' said Chris in a tone that was difficult to decipher. 'Anyway, I could get there next week, maybe?' Or how about the week after? Does that work?'

'I'll be back by then,' she said. 'Chris, honestly, it was just a thought.' And at this point, Isobel realised, one she had totally gone off the idea of.

'Yeah, I should let you go,' said Chris. 'I know you have stuff to do.' Downstairs, either Martin or Sean slammed a door. Raised voices were coming up now only sporadically.

'Sure. Of course.'

'Okay, well, you take care.'

You take care? Did she sound that bad? It was what you said to an old lady after you'd helped her cross the road. 'I'll check in later.' *Later*, Isobel thought, being a fungible concept in Chris's world, meaning some time loosely in the future, and later rather than sooner – but almost certainly not the same day.

'I miss you—' she started to say, but he was gone. Why had she even asked? She'd always done better on her own, even as a child. *Childhood.* The word seemed to shimmer with happiness. And then she remembered the unsettled feeling that Sundays used to bring, after about four o'clock when the threat of Monday morning and double maths could no longer be ignored. And that, as of now, she was no one's child.

Downstairs, someone laughed and she heard the television go on. A good sign – the *All Clear*. In a few minutes

51

she would go down, have her nightcap, and say goodnight. She stayed sitting on the bed for a moment to collect her thoughts. She felt very strange, as if at a great distance from everything, as if her real self, her own day-to-day aspect that she was used to, had been cast on a long line out to sea while the rest of her stood patiently on the shore. From there it was almost possible to convince herself that this was someone else's life, someone else who had got on the plane, who had gone down into the hospital basement, someone else who now sat here in Martin and Sean's immaculate guest bedroom – so that one day in the future she would be able to ask this person, *What was it like?* – and they would be able to tell her.

Monday

Thousands of Moving Parts

'You can blame Isobel for this,' Edward told a bleary-eyed Jules when at 6.15am he went to wake her up.

'I'm really sorry,' said Jules for the umpteenth time as he nudged the car into the thick sludge of traffic that was crawling past the end of their road. 'I just thought—'

'*Jules! Stop saying sorry,*' he said. 'I told you it's not your fault. It's just her taking advantage. It's how she is.' He was trying to sound matter-of-fact, and failing. Last night, despite making the longer drive back to their flat rather than staying at his mother's house, he had tossed and turned all night on the uncomfortable sofa. Now exhaustion had settled over him like a waterlogged blanket, its damp and shiver seeping into his bones.

'I just thought,' Jules said, 'since she's your sister and everything...'

'Look, there's absolutely no reason she couldn't take the train down, same as anyone else,' he said. He commuted up to London by train every day and it took barely an hour. 'I mean, can you give me one reason,' he went on, 'why that shouldn't be good enough for her? *Can you*?'

'It is the weekend...' Jules began.

'Engineering works. Yes. I know.' A juggernaut barrelled through the intersection ahead of them and he slammed on the brakes. *Death* right there, Edward thought, on eighteen wheels. He leant his hand hard on the horn. There was simply no point in hashing it all out again, he told Jules, this crap with the airport. He was too bloody aggravated. As well as knackered. 'It's amazing, isn't it,' he continued. 'She's not even here yet but she's already being a fucking nuisance.'

They reached Heathrow with only minutes to spare, just as Isobel texted to say she had her 'baggage' – as she put it – and was on the way out. He spied her as she came out of the doors and headed rapidly towards them along the pavement. She looked older, though not by much, and she'd had something arty and grown-up done to her hair – subtle streaks or strips or whatever it was women like her wasted their money on. By now she was probably some sort of feminist. Was his sister happy with her life? Edward wondered, and immediately dismissed the thought, which he hadn't asked for and which was of no importance. He simply didn't care what Isobel thought or felt. He watched her stop to fiddle with something on her suitcase, and took a furtive glance in the driving mirror, conscious of the salt-and-pepper hair that had appeared recently at his temples – 'distinguished', Jules called it – observing the faint lines extending from the side of his nose which were gradually digging their way down to meet the ones at the corners of his mouth. Any day now, he'd wake up to find that his face matched his passport photo, a document whose purpose was presumably to identify you after five days floating face-down in the sea. As time went on, the lines would become more pronounced. They would join forces to make brackets on his face, until his mouth was contained within parentheses, as if his words no longer mattered. When would it happen? Ten years? *Five*?

He saw that Isobel was on the move again, and walking towards them at a good clip. She looked healthy, he'd give her that, if a bit too well-slept, considering. Yet even at twenty feet he felt that familiar and oppressive sense of his sister's will, almost space-distorting in its intensity. The things she wanted, no matter what the consequences for anyone else, she would do regardless. She must have spotted him because she waved and increased her pace, bearing down now on the small car, almost upon them, so that he found himself counting down the seconds, fighting the impulse to jam his foot on the accelerator and drive away.

Beside him there was a flurry of movement and he was startled to see Jules's backside disappearing out of the passenger door.

'What are you doing?' he hissed.

'I thought I'd let your sister sit in the front...' she said, as she slid into the back seat. 'Or...?'

'Too late,' he muttered, as Isobel opened the door and pushed her face into the car. Now he'd be stuck in the front with her, listening to her prattle at his elbow all the way down to the hospital, waiting in vain for the comma.

'Hi!' she said, grinning as if she'd just arrived at a party. 'Can you pop the trunk?' He resisted the urge to correct her.

'*Wow*,' said Isobel. Mere seconds after he'd pulled away from the waiting area, Edward thought, and she was pointing in apparent wonder at a helicopter hovering somewhere overhead. 'You know helicopters aren't allowed to land in Manhattan any more?'

Thousands of moving parts all trying to get away from one another. How very fucking apt. Edward tried not to focus on the fact that Isobel had once again managed to be conveniently absent when being present mattered and was now making her presence felt a day late and at a time and place of maximum inconvenience. He felt his resentment and stress levels ratchet up a few more degrees. His hands on the steering wheel started to ache, the knucklebones showing white as if about to burst through his skin.

'In New York, I mean,' Isobel went on, turning to Jules. 'Since that crash? Do you remember? At the old Pan Am building?'

'Oh. I remember something about it...' he heard Jules reply. As it happened Edward recalled the incident well, a fantastically grisly tale involving a mechanical problem right as the helicopter took off. As the aircraft faltered, one of its blades had detached and spun down off the roof, landing on a woman who had the bad luck to be coming through the revolving doors hundreds of feet below, and instantly decapitating her. He couldn't care less about this either – or, as Isobel would probably say now, 'could care less'. And there was the way her voice rose up at the end of a sentence – admittedly, only the hint of an intonation, but all the same it put his back up. 'Uptalk', they called it. Some of the kids here these days spoke in a more exaggerated version, but in the States even the grown-ups did it.

As they rounded a bend in the road he caught sight of the long tailback of traffic ahead of them. How long would he have to be in the car with her? He could have done without going back via the hospital as well. He had not enjoyed fielding Isobel's questions about it – ones that came as soon as she got in the car, about their mother and what happened and why, and which he'd managed to brush off with a brief overview. She seemed satisfied with this, for now at least. He had no intention of reliving it all – not with Jules, and especially not with Isobel, who was once more peering out of the window, craning her neck at some other *unbelievable* sight on the London skyline as if she had not actually been born here just as he was. Did she have to comment on every sodding thing, like some fat American tourist declaring everything 'inneresting' and 'quaint'? Why did she have to batter them with this incessant rat-a-tat-tat, this unstoppable mania of words and asinine remarks? *Bloody Isobel*, Edward thought, taking up all the space and all the air – too vivid, too animated, too bloody *everything*.

He felt Jules's hand on his shoulder. Did he looked as pissed-off as he felt? A new anger hit him: fury with himself that he was allowing Isobel to wind him up so easily – and letting it show. Thank God for Jules. So far she had fended off his sister quite deftly, with vaguely interested noises that saved him the trouble. He watched Jules's face in the driving mirror for a moment. She looked drawn and tired. He could only imagine – though he had chosen not to – what it must have been like for her being at Danecroft Road yesterday when everything happened – though he was thankful that she had been. He had been careful not to press her for too many details about what would have been a traumatic experience, and in return Jules had been considerate enough not to burden him with any. 'I'm sure you'd rather not talk about it all at the moment,' he had told her – insurance against being dragged into some deep discussion. Jules seemed dismayingly prone to these recently: he had a vague memory of some book she had mentioned last week, which had sounded a bit 'woo-woo' and he'd told her so, but she'd seemed unusually taken by it. Of course Jules would never behave badly; she would never make everything all about her. *Unlike some people*, he thought, glancing at Isobel.

'At this rate,' he observed to no one in particular, 'we'll be lucky if we make it past Brixton by noon.'

'I always forget how big London is,' remarked Isobel dreamily. 'Manhattan is so walkable, so much smaller...'

His first thought was how different the hospital looked in the daytime. For a moment he wondered if it was the same place.

'Looks like the *Mary Celeste*,' he remarked to Jules as they walked into the lobby. Jules looked at him blankly. 'The ship,' he added, as Isobel chimed in with, 'It really *does*...' *No one was talking to you*, he thought. Every time she spoke he felt overwhelmed by a sense of outrage and injustice. At the front desk he gave his name to the lone duty nurse. As she clicked through her computer, he was conscious of an odd prickle of apprehension or anxiety passing between the three of them like an electric current. Even Isobel seemed to have burned through her repertoire of tedious observations and had fallen silent. They were like strangers in a lift, he thought, unsure what to say or where to stand. The hospital had a dormant air, vacant and smelling of nothing, as if the ill and the dying, and the hapless people who tended to them, had all taken the bank holiday off and gone down to the seaside for the day, taking their buckets and spades and their respiratory ventilators with them. He listened to the automatic doors, swooshing open and shut for no one, and it occurred to him how eerie the sound was and how it made the day even stranger and more bleached of colour.

A minute or two later a sandy-haired man appeared and introduced himself. He had a doleful expression, and

Edward wondered whether this was part of the man's personality or if it was a special skill acquired on the job. Pinned neatly to the left lapel of his white coat was a plastic name badge. *Peter Mort*, it said. Well, you had to laugh at that, Edward thought to himself, as the man led them across the lobby and through a series of smash-proof glass-paned doors. He was unsurprised to see that Isobel had perked back up, sailing ahead of them in her inappropriately bright red coat, her voice echoing down the corridor, chattering on to the unfortunate Peter Death in a way she presumably mistook for charming or socially winning.

He had not expected the mortuary to smell of new carpet. Preferable to the alternative, he thought, and tried to picture the bored and bossy surgeon's wife who'd likely had the place tarted up. Peter Death had brought them into a room that resembled a dentist's office, everything wincingly twee and 'tasteful' in that *phone for the fish knives* way his mother made fun of. He imagined the surly workmen cracking crude, nervous jokes as they rolled the synthetic plush over the cold tiles. *Sweeping it under the rug*. Even the walls were not immune, plastered with the standard cheap prints – depressing ones, naturally, like Lowry, with his lines of factory workers and smokestacks. Against one wall three strategically placed armchairs were aligned at perfect OCD intervals, while opposite sat an atrocity covered in a purple mock-velvet – a chaise-longue of some description – useful for dramatic types to faint in, Edward thought, eyeing Isobel, who was still circling Peter Death, yapping away like a terrier worrying sheep. Only then did he register that they were standing in front of a large, observation-room-type window – and he realised that in this way, perhaps the hideous interior decorating had provided a distraction and served its purpose.

Looking through the glass, he experienced a sick, falling sensation. It was like the dream where you stepped off the kerb only to find you'd walked straight off the edge of a cliff. For a second he feared his legs would buckle and he had to look away. He felt Jules – standing beside him – recoil with a small intake of breath. What had he expected? That the dead didn't look dead? He felt the need to focus intently on something – anything – else: a patch of wall, the fainting couch, or even Peter Mort's hair, which was thinning and combed lovingly across his pate. He felt desperate to fill his eyes with something unremarkable and ordinary.

'She looks asleep,' he said. *If you were completely blind.* What on earth had made him say such a thing?

There was a short silence, which he had no desire to fill, and then Isobel said, 'Do you mind if I go in on my own first?'

There you go again, he thought, *pushing in front.* 'I'm not going in, thanks,' he told her.

For some reason his answer seemed to take her aback. Was it so important to 'view the body'? He couldn't imagine putting himself through it all again. When you considered it objectively, the whole exercise was bizarre – not to mention pointless. Isobel hadn't moved. Instead she was staring up at him with the dazed look of a lost tourist, as if asking for directions. He took a reluctant step forward, closer to the window. They stood there for several more long moments while he made a perfunctory effort, a pretence really, of looking through the window with her. Was she going in or not? Peter Death was hovering again, like a guard in a safe deposit vault, which precipitated more unnecessary chitchat with Isobel until, finally, she went in. He watched her from behind the security of the glass. There had never been any point in trying to dissuade his sister from anything, and certainly not anything foolhardy. In fact he had the malicious desire to give her a little wave of encouragement. If Isobel insisted on seeing, as he had been forced to see last night, then by all means 'let her have it', he thought. But he had no need to watch her doing it, to witness the shock and awe or whatever hammed-up farewell process his sister had in mind. Weeping and theatrics – he didn't need it.

As he turned away from the glass he had a sudden memory of the interior window at Danecroft Road – the 'ghost window', as he and Isobel used to call it. It was years since he had thought about it, a pane of glass built into the wall between the sitting room and the dining room, to let in more light. These days it was more or less obscured by his mother's collection of books and knick-knacks, but when he and Isobel were children it had still been possible to see straight through to the sitting room from the dining room. More than once, Edward was sure, he had glimpsed someone – or something – some movement on the dining room side of the glass. Watching *Doctor Who* or *Top of the Pops*, he would find himself keeping the window in the corner of his eye, drawn to it without wanting to be. He said nothing to his mother, and didn't want to frighten Isobel, who was prone to nightmares. The knowledge of the apparition had felt like a responsibility, a weight on his small shoulders. And then, one day, Isobel had brought it up herself. He was astonished. 'What do you think it is,' she said, 'a ghost?' He had felt both disturbed and deeply relieved that his sister had seen it too. 'Maybe it's an optical illusion?' he suggested hopefully. He had got a book about them for his birthday and they fascinated him – pages and pages full of pictures and perspectives that played tricks on you. They had discussed the window at some length and reluctantly he had had to agree with her that they weren't imagining it. The ghost had appeared to both of them, independently and on separate

60

occasions, and in exactly the same way – a small flash or blur, like someone or something drawing back out of sight and hoping not to be seen.

Outside, he found Jules in the corridor sitting on an upright wooden chair. She looked stunned and pale.

'You all right?' he said, taking the seat next to her. She nodded. They were both ready to drop. Like him, Jules would be wishing Isobel would get a move on. They sat peaceably together for a minute or two, and then he said, 'Can you believe that coat?'

'What coat?'

'*Her* coat. Isobel's.' Wasn't this obvious? 'Bright red or international orange or whatever it is. Hardly appropriate for here, is it?'

'Didn't she have to pack in a hurry, though?' said Jules. 'I think that's what she said in the car. She went home to get her passport and got to the airport just in time.'

'Still no excuse.' He felt mildly irritated at Jules, who was being unusually obtuse. 'She should have made the effort.'

He looked around them, at the walls painted to waist height in a queasy institutional green that reminded him of split pea soup. Here and there the baseboards were scuffed and he wondered if people came out from the awful room where Isobel was now and kicked at them in grief or anger. More likely the perpetrator was some careless porter wheeling the trolleys through out of hours.

'It's weird, isn't it?' he said to Jules. 'All this. I can't get my head round it at all.' Weird too, he thought, this sudden compulsion to babble. He could feel it rising up in him like bile.

'Is it funny, seeing your sister?' asked Jules.

'It's like ...' He gestured for a moment towards the doorway, to the room beyond. His hand fell back into his lap.

'I suppose that's one word for it,' he said. 'Anyway, the main thing is to keep my temper until she pisses off back to where she came from.'

Jules looked at him, and he realised how angry he must have sounded. He had been sharp with her earlier and he felt bad about it. Really, she was being incredibly good putting up with Isobel. He attempted to backpedal with some humour. 'Pack her off again like a baggage,' he said in his funny Monty Python voice.

Jules smiled, but he could tell her heart wasn't in it either. 'So she'll go back to New York after this?' she said.

'I don't see why not. It's where she likes to live, apparently.'

'She was born here, though, wasn't she?' said Jules.

'Not that you'd know it.'

'Why do you say that?'

'Come on, she's so *American* ...'

'Is she?' said Jules.

Why was Jules sticking up for her? 'All that bloody smiling,' he answered. 'Anyway, let's not delve into it all now.' He sensed a tiresome conversation coming on if he started trying to explain anything at all about his sister. He gestured towards the door. 'I do wish she'd bloody get on with it.' He hoped his girlfriend hadn't suddenly acquired a fondness for answers and details. Women were enthusiastic vivisectors, picking things apart until they died. They were natural scientists. Jules was different, though, and unique in that way. She neither dramatised nor overanalysed, never pestered him with questions or interfered with his decisions. She trusted him to do what he thought best. Most importantly, she was able to let things – including him – just be. Now and then she might push him a bit about what he was thinking or feeling, but to some extent all women were like that, weren't they? It was written into their DNA and you had to live with it. But, when she did, he knew that only a word or two from him was sufficient. He reached across to give her hand a conciliatory squeeze and trusted that this too would suffice, but at that moment he saw that Isobel was coming towards them and self-consciously he withdrew it.

His sister didn't appear to be crying or openly distressed. She looked calm, almost serene. Someone less charitable, Edward thought uncharitably, might say this proved how little she had cared about their mother in the first place. And look, Edward thought, there was Peter Death, pale-eyed mole person, obsequious and right on cue, trotting obediently a few metres behind her like a lapdog doing its best to keep up. He felt a grim sympathy for the man, having a job where his customers were always at their lowest ebb; where he got lumbered with people like his sister. He stood up to indicate they were leaving, but to his irritation Isobel took this as a sign to press the hapless man with bizarre questions about fridges and temperatures. Mortuaries and their dubious accoutrements, he recalled, were one of his sister's and his mother's macabre pet obsessions – flimsy totems against the inevitable. Of course, people in Peter Mort's line of work were trained to be non-reactive. He glanced over at Jules – what must she think? It was the dreadful simpering that really got up his nose – another American tic that his sister had picked up along with the glib overfamiliarity and fake niceness and incessant smiling and the tendency to appear communicative when you had nothing actually useful to say. Because being American, these things meant nothing at all.

Outside in the car park he fended off Isobel's attempts to pay the ticket. For the second time that day he nosed the car out of the hospital car park and went through the pitiful to-do list that he had been compiling in his head since last night: *undertaker, call landlord, call caterers, empty house, return keys, funeral, friends afterwards*... They were tasks and errands that would have been unthinkable twenty-four hours ago. How would he possibly get it all done? And with Isobel in tow? He might as well add *avoid heart attack* to the list, Edward thought, as he narrowly missed hitting a pedestrian who had paused in the middle of the road to stare down at their phone. He counted himself lucky that there had been no outbursts yet from Isobel. No sobbing or histrionic rending of the curtains – although it was early days, he remembered, and best not to count any chickens. He glanced at his watch. Two o'clock already. Ideally he would have had a proper night's kip under his belt before they started on the house. If he could just manage to close his eyes for fifteen minutes he might be able to clear the fog from his mind. If he could only go home now, Edward thought, and crash out in front of the television – but it was impossible, there was no time. Then he remembered that it was Bank Holiday Monday. Nothing 'official' could really be achieved until tomorrow, could it? They could drop Isobel off at Danecroft Road, get a proper night's sleep at home, and come back first thing tomorrow and make a start then. Small mercies.

Once they were through the shopping centre, he drove them quickly through the town, only slowing his speed when the last of the houses had disappeared. At the top of the hill his favourite view waited. From there you could see clear across the Downs, to the lighthouse, and the gentle green slopes that led to the sea, shining far below. On the way up to London Jules had suggested – kindly but naïvely – that they might have Isobel to stay with them in their flat. He had assured her this was not the best idea in the world. His sister was like a loud and selfish cuckoo, he had explained, claiming more than her own share, taking up space and pushing everyone else aside. To himself he'd thought that he could just picture Isobel, barging into their flat, imposing her opinions, going through his bookshelves, banging on endlessly about her travels to obscure non-Interpol parts of the world nobody had the blindest bit of interest in. If Isobel had her way, they would wake up tomorrow morning to find she'd rearranged all their furniture. It was best for all concerned, he told Jules, if Isobel stayed at Danecroft Road – which was where she usually stayed, wasn't it? Jules had not mentioned it again. *Bloody Isobel.* He watched her in the driving mirror, glowering at a passing farmhouse. *Was she sulking?* Isobel, never satisfied, turning and restless, all sparks and pyrotechnics, burning like a Catherine wheel, and like a firework perpetually threatening to come spinning off the fence. She wasn't volatile, not exactly that, Edward thought, more like sodium, a fundamentally unstable compound, and this made his sister unreliable and deeply selfish. And this charade she was proposing, he thought, what was all that about? This flummery involving the three of them staying at his mother's house like some jolly camping holiday? Really, it was hard not to laugh. Still, after everything that had happened, how typical that his sister would expect something more.

Tuesday

Grief – Opportunities

Julie lay in bed sleepless, staring at the dingy bar of orange street-light that poked out from under the bedroom curtains. Next door in the lounge the TV chattered. For the second night in a row Edward had taken to the settee with the cat. In three hours' time they had to drive over to Danecroft Road and start clearing out Mary's house and she had still not got the story of Mary's accident worked out in her head. She switched the bedside lamp on and felt around under her side of the bed for the book.

She turned to the introduction. *If you are reading this,* it said, *you are only one step away from achieving the life you deserve simply by thinking from a higher, more evolved self. The door of possibility is always there. All you have to do is choose to walk through it.* In later chapters, the book promised, they would reveal what this *evolved* self was. There was an asterisk next to the word, she noticed, so she went to the bottom of the page and read: *Tip: This has nothing to do with the so-called theory of evolution!* She skipped forwards a few chapters. *'Victim' is a word, a word you choose, a word you will learn to break free of! In reality, everything that happens to you is not 'happening' to you. YOU are the one with the power to make your own reality.*

The idea made her head spin – *Pathways to Possible* was full of them – and she put the book down for a moment to think about it. The clue, Julie felt, was contained within the inverted commas, much like the sarcastic remarks Edward came out with. She read on. *To achieve your new authentic self and the successful life that goes with it, you must become the magnet that attracts the RIGHT things – NOT the WRONG things.* Was she a magnet attracting the wrong things? And had she inadvertently attracted them to Mary? This seemed to confirm all her worst fears. Confusingly, a little further along, her fears were put to rest. Individuals, it said, brought misfortune on themselves. Helpfully, it then listed all the ways this could happen. People ate the wrong foods, it said, or drank their wages away and mistreated their loyal spouses, only to wonder why they ended up unhappy and alone. To Julie this made complete sense. It was so easy to turn round and blame other people for your misfortunes. *Whether wealth, cancer, or a beautiful and more spacious home*, the book went on, *you have the power to manifest your destiny by your thoughts and intentions.* Seen this way, she thought, Mary's accident didn't 'happen' to Mary, and no one else caused it either. Mary had 'attracted' the accident to herself while she, Julie, had merely been caught up in the event, her own actions simply part of a plan that was much bigger than she was. In other words, there was nothing Julie could have done to change it, even if… She tried to absorb this new information and realised that, if anything, maybe it was she, Julie, who was the victim. In the next chapter *Pathways to Possible* took the idea further. By their rules, an unfortunate event provided *a valuable opportunity for self-improvement and personal growth.*

What would Edward think of this? 'What's this American crap?' he had said last week after he'd found the book in the car. He had given her one of those hard, unnerving stares he reserved for people he deemed ignorant or slow – or, worse, people who *can't just choose one*. No, she thought, Edward wouldn't believe in improving himself or jump-starting his joy, but that was hardly a surprise. 'Negative energy?' he had said when she'd attempted to put across to him what she had read – which, granted, wasn't that much at the time. 'I think Casimir had that one sorted in 1948, didn't he? And what about lasers?' he went on. 'What do they have to say about those?' She'd had no idea what he was talking about, but he was wearing his *aha!* face, and she knew better than to contradict him. 'They don't say anything about lasers,' she had replied, although the theories behind *Pathways to Possible* were based on proper science. On the back cover they said something about achieving happiness using quantum physics. She had held the book out to him, hoping that the mention of physics would catch his interest, but Edward had burst out laughing. 'Oh, Jules,' he'd said, shaking his head pityingly as if she were a lost cause. '*If wishes were horses, beggars would ride.* You can't just *think* something into being. Everyone can't just say they believe in fairies and make it so.' The book had a word for this too, Julie remembered: *pre-judgements* – opinions that were the very opposite of science. She wondered if Edward realised how often he spoke to her with this *brook-no-arguments* tone. These exchanges left her feeling small and insignificant, with a flat, squashed feeling around the heart that she found difficult to shake off.

'Bugger!' Edward slammed his hand down on the table. 'Bastards. Fuck.'

It had been an unsettling sort of morning. First she had managed to oversleep, and then, what with finding Edward a clean shirt and feeding the cat and making sure the toast didn't burn, she hadn't even had time to brush her hair. On her first proper day of self-work, Julie thought, she had completely failed at being *entirely present in the now*. Edward had already made several phone calls. One was to his office to say he had 'a pressing family matter'. The person at the other end must have offered him more time off because he got quite firm with them. 'No, really. No, thank you,' he said, and, 'It's fine, I'll be back first thing next Monday.'

'Bastards,' Edward repeated now. 'Fucking jobsworth.'

'Is there anything I can do to help?' she asked. A bad mood was an opportunity in disguise, the chance to offer a kind word and *demonstrate supportiveness*. Edward rarely lost his temper, and only once in the time she had known him – in a rare blow-up with Mary that Julie had done her best not to overhear. Edward didn't respond. She topped up his coffee mug, visualising herself as present yet unobtrusive, like a silver service waitress in a posh restaurant. Over the years she had learned to be patient. Edward was the sort of person who either snapped out his answers or took his time. Now he had on one of his opaque expressions, thoughtful and yet infuriatingly blank. *Don't push the river*, was the book's advice on *Manifesting Intimacy*. She watched as Edward lifted his mug, stopped midway, and put it down again.

'Is it okay?' she asked him. 'The coffee?'

'It's outrageous,' he replied.

'Sorry?'

'She's been his tenant for ages,' he went on, 'reliable, pays on time, and now he wants the fucking house back by next *week*? *Is he taking the piss?*'

'Who?' She had no idea who or what he meant. 'Who wants the house back?'

'Mum's *landlord*.' He spoke impatiently, as if he had had to repeat himself. 'Or rather, his *executive secretary*. The landlord's not back yet from holiday, and *oh, no* she *couldn't possibly* give me his number, could she?' He took a gulp of his coffee. 'Bloody woman.'

'The jobsworth,' she offered.

'Exactly,' said Edward, and looked quite pleased, as if she had come up with the word on her own.

'I'm sorry,' she said. 'I didn't know.'

'Didn't know about what?'

'About your mother's property. Being rented and such…' she said.

'Does that matter, for some reason?' Edward said.

She realised he was staring at her, holding the phone in one hand. In the distance she could hear a mechanised woman's voice saying over and over again, *Please replace the receiver. Please replace the receiver* … With a twinge of guilt she remembered the exchange with Lorraine who had been speculating on how much Mary's house was worth.

'No,' she replied. 'No, of course not.'

She was disappointed, though – and a bit surprised. Having your own front gate – it was the first goal in life, wasn't it, after a relationship and children, to secure a proper roof over your head? Her parents had been paying off their mortgage for years, but at least they had taken the chance to purchase their home when it was offered to them. They had wasted no time painting their door a different colour, proud to let all the neighbours know it was their own. Maybe it wasn't that surprising, she thought, placing a teabag into her cup, that Mary felt otherwise. Edward's mother was quite slap-happy in that way, with strange beliefs about things that, in Julie's opinion, didn't last – what Mary called *experiences*, like travelling abroad. She remembered the time Mary had made them go all the way up to London for a 'show'. The fare was expensive, and it was only later that she'd realised that Mary hadn't meant *Cats* or *The Phantom of the Opera* – which Julie wouldn't have minded seeing – but some sort of art exhibition, which had turned out to be a room full of fishing nets and rude noises. Edward wasn't that impressed with it, she could tell – but afterwards, when Julie asked if they could stop off to see the Changing of the Guard, they had both laughed at her. Mary didn't approve of 'the monarchy', Edward explained, and neither did he. 'Our family have always been anti-monarchists,' he said. She found this quite shocking. Her own parents were big fans of all the Royals, especially the Queen Mother. Her gran had knitted baby booties for all the Queen's children and grandchildren – every single one. If Edward had savings and a proper career, he never talked about buying his own home, much as he never talked about getting married or having children. Unless she brought it up first, Julie thought, watching him gazing miserably at his plate.

'According to *her*,' Edward said, 'this secretary, because the legal tenant is "deceased", the landlord's charging full market rate from today until we give the house back.'

She noticed the way he said *deceased*, separating it from the other words with his beloved inverted commas, but this time like something soiled. 'That must be very upsetting,' she said. Edward gave her an odd, sidelong look. She blushed. It was one of the 'non-judgemental' phrases she'd learnt about in *Pathways to Possible*. She still felt a little uncomfortable trying them out, though the book said that this was to be expected at first.

Edward reached over and picked up the freshly ironed shirt she'd left for him, folded tidily over the back of the chair. He examined the collar for a moment and put it down again. 'My grandmother rented Danecroft Road from the first Mr Modin,' he said, 'when we all moved down from London. After my father left. Years ago now ... ' He frowned, as if having trouble remembering. 'To be fair, neither Modin ever put the rent up. Still, no excuse. We'll just have to work faster, I suppose.'

'I'm taking this week off ... ' she reminded him.

He smiled gratefully. 'Thanks, Jules. You'll be a real help.' She was gratified to see her offer not waved away. It was almost as if her positive attitude and words of support were already having an effect. 'I'm afraid we'll have to go through the whole house rather quickly,' he said. 'And with bloody Isobel in the way ... '

'I'm sure we can get it all done,' she told him. They certainly couldn't afford to get stuck with Mary's rent!

'Which reminds me, I have to give her a shout,' said Edward. 'Make sure she's there when we arrive.' He got up from the table. 'You know what she's like,' he called over his shoulder, heading off in the direction of the bedroom. *I have no idea what Isobel's like*, she wanted to say, but she was looking forward to finding out. *Loving intimacy*, she had read, involved knowing all of someone – all their secrets, all their relationships – including everything about their friends and family and the people who were important to them. As she scraped the mess of congealed scrambled eggs off Edward's plate and into the bin, she thought about all the weekends she had wasted trying to get to know Mary. The book recommended visualising the future you wanted, which was all part of *projecting a positive outcome*. Yet she could scarcely imagine the years of carefree, Mary-free weekends that she and Edward now had to look forward to. It was hard not to look backwards, to recall the weekends of endless gardening and the documentaries about wildlife. If she never saw another meerkat or giant otter, it would be too soon. And when it wasn't wildlife it was obscure films – long foreign films with subtitles and people talking on and on in rooms. And the quiz shows! Stephen Fry and his la-di-dah mates, where instead of winning a car or a holiday everyone competed to see who was the cleverest. It was worse than school. 'What's the point when there aren't any prizes?' she had remarked to Lorraine.

'Up himself,' was Lorraine's verdict. 'Thinks he's better than us.'

'You mean Stephen Fry?' she had asked.

'*No*,' said Lorraine.

Julie rinsed the plates off in the sink and stacked them on the draining board to dry and attempted to 'visualise' all the free weekends ahead, lined up like plates of perfectly iced wodges of wedding cake. They could have romantic walks on the Downs, she thought, or share an ice-cream together on the seafront without worrying about getting over to Mary's in time for dinner. Edward would have to go through the grieving process, obviously, but, with Mary gone, perhaps he would at last share with her his hopes and dreams, his plans for their future. And they could spend time with her own family, with her nephews and nieces, who were growing up so fast and said such funny things.

In the other room drawers were being opened and closed, punctuated by the odd swear word. Edward resented even having to carry a phone and she wondered if constantly forgetting where he'd left it was some type of unconscious behaviour or *acting out*, as the book put it. 'Well, I don't much fancy being on the end of a lead,' he'd laughed when they were first going out and she'd asked him why he never replied to her texts during the day. His office discouraged personal calls, he told her. There was an emergency number. Edward had presented it to her along with a key to his flat, shortly after she moved in with him. But, unable so far to conjure an actual emergency, she had never dared use it. Occasionally she managed to catch him on his mobile at lunchtime, but he was always queuing up at Prêt à Manger or about to get into the lift, so that their conversation was an exasperating series of 'Sorry, pardon?' and, 'No, say again' and, finally, 'Can't it wait until I get home?' Lorraine texted Declan all the time.

In the beginning she had been given to understand that Edward's family consisted of just him and his mother. Then on her first visit to Danecroft Road they sat in Mary's lounge drinking tea and she noticed the girl in the photos. The girl almost never looked directly into the camera but gazed a little to one side, as if shielding her eyes from the sun or looking at someone standing slightly out of the picture. She looked shy, Julie thought, and wondered why Edward had never mentioned her. One photo showed her sitting on a sloping, pebbly beach with an arm round Edward, though she looked smaller and younger. In another she sat in a rowing boat, alone save for a large black dog. There appeared to be no photos of her taken much after her teens. As the months went by and nothing was said by either Edward or Mary, Julie, feeling it was rude to pry, had settled on the obvious explanation: that the girl was a sister who had died tragically young – maybe even by falling out of the boat in the photo – so that now neither Edward nor Mary could bring themselves to speak about her.

It was Mary who finally brought her up. Edward had gone up to the DVD shop, Julie remembered, and she had watched Mary pick up a photo – a small one, in a silver frame – which showed Mary and the girl sitting together in deckchairs under the tree in the back garden. 'My daughter, Isobel,' said Mary. Julie couldn't believe it. More astonishing, far from being dead, Edward's sister was apparently alive and 'doing very well for herself', according to Mary, though she did not say where. Julie wondered if Edward's sister was in prison. If so, you could hardly blame Edward or Mary for their silence. Lorraine was always telling her son Jaydn about a distant cousin of theirs who had knocked over a petrol garage and had 'a lot of previous'. This was understood to mean that he had served time in prison and now, because of this, couldn't find a job. But if Edward's sister was in prison, Julie had wondered, what would 'doing very well for herself' mean? Was she doing a degree or getting her GCSEs from behind bars? *Wasting taxpayers' money*, her father called that sort of thing. But as usual she had been letting her imagination run away with her – Mary later revealed that Edward's sister was living in America. 'Don't Edward and Isobel ever talk, then?'

Julie blurted, the next time Mary casually dropped Isobel's name into conversation while Edward was out of the house. 'Well, they do live a *long* way away from each other ...' Mary had replied. As she said to Lorraine afterwards, what sort of answer was that? Mary might pick up one of Isobel's photos and say, almost to herself, 'She's a good daughter,' and then, after a reflective pause, 'Such a good girl,' as if she'd had to think it over for a moment but concluded that Isobel was, as she had first thought, a perfectly nice person.

For a while nothing else was said. Mary never mentioned Isobel when Edward was in the room – or even in the house. Julie had enquired about Isobel only once and got a terse reply in return. She had let it be. Once or twice a year, though, seemingly out of the blue, Edward would announce that they were skipping Mary's that weekend. After a while she had come to realise that these were weekends when his sister was visiting from America. He never offered any explanation and she never let on about knowing, although these were exactly the weekends she would have loved to be at Danecroft Road. Edward would become morose, refusing any suggestions of going out or of making the most of the time as a couple, preferring to sit obstinately with the curtains drawn shut and stare at the television like her father, until one day it finally dawned on her that he was sulking. Come the next weekend, it would be as if the clouds had parted and Edward would be in one of his jolly moods, stopping on the way over to Danecroft Road to buy flowers or one of Mary's favourite cakes – and frequently both. If anything at Danecroft Road needed painting or repairing, if the grass wanted mowing or the hedges trimming, these were the times when Edward took care of it, all smiles and compliments about the garden. Once or twice she might catch him grimacing or glancing irritably at some random, innocent-looking thing around

Mary's house – a fruit bowl, a chair, or a book. She would watch him pick the offending object up and place it fussily a few inches to the right or left, or in a drawer, as if someone had put it back in the wrong place. If they were magazines or newspapers, they went straight in the bin. Once she knew what to look for there were clues everywhere: elusive traces of the person she began to think of as her future sister-in-law. A pot of moisturiser, or a bottle of nail varnish left on the edge of the bath. One time, slung over a chair in Mary's front bedroom, there was a large scarf. The day had turned chilly, she remembered, and she and Edward had gone upstairs to close all the windows. It must have cost a bomb, Julie had thought, feeling the material, which was unimaginably soft and fine, as if knitted out of kitten's fur. She imagined Edward's sister placing it over her knees during the long transatlantic flights to and from America. And then she'd been stupid enough to remark on it in front of Edward. 'Oh, look, what's this?' she'd said in a casual voice, and lifted the scarf from the chair and held it up for Edward to see. Deep down, perhaps, she had been hoping that it might prompt him to reveal something, to share his feelings about his sister, however unpleasant or upsetting. 'Cashmere, must be nice and warm,' she said, and instantly wished she hadn't. She waited helplessly with the scarf in her hand, already knowing – somehow – that Edward was not going to answer. The room had seemed to go very quiet, and then Edward had glanced over at her thoughtfully for a moment as if he was going to say something, though she dreaded what. 'I'll see you downstairs, then,' he said, and walked straight past her and out of the door. By the next day everything felt back to normal again, and, although no unpleasantness had been exchanged, no shouting or harsh words, she still thought of it as their first fight.

They were going to be late, and Edward wasn't happy about it. Maybe if they hadn't driven back to the flat to get the paper shredder, Julie thought. Edward had insisted on bringing it with them, though it weighed a ton. 'My mother doesn't need her private papers blowing about all over the street,' he'd informed her, as if Mary could possibly object now. They drove past the marina and on to the coast road, where she decided that it was all very well the book telling you to *turn that negative energy into kinetic energy* but with Edward she was starting to feel a bit invisible. *Creating a more wholesome reality for yourself can be successfully achieved anywhere – at the supermarket, the mall, or even dropping the kids off at camp!* It was hard to imagine an ordinary person being able to master this, she thought, but she closed her eyes anyway and imagined herself standing with Edward under an apple tree. In the background she added a hill, some flowers, and nearby, a gently flowing stream, before turning to face Edward, who took her hand and looked deep into her eyes...

'*Jules!*' Edward had spoken her name rather more loudly than was called for, and she felt herself being pushed forward into her seatbelt and the car slowing down. She opened her eyes and saw they had pulled into a lay-by. 'Jules, what's *wrong*?' Edward had a look of concern on his face. The car shook and several lorries passed them, blasting their horns. One driver made a gesture through the window.

'Sorry, I was resting my eyes for a minute,' she said. 'I must have fallen asleep.'

Edward let out a breath. 'I thought you were in pain,' he said, easing the car back out into the road. 'Honestly, Jules, I don't have time for this, not today. We're cutting it fine as it is.'

Give yourself a pat on the back, the book said, *as you get better at recognising opportunities for growth*. Perhaps the exercises were best not attempted when you were sleep-deprived. A long traffic jam snaked ahead of them and Edward leant forward to twiddle at one of the knobs on the radio. 'Where the hell is the fucking traffic station?' he said, jabbing several buttons in quick succession. A loud buzzing sound filled the car.

'It's on 98.6, I think,' she told him.

'It'll be more ammunition for her,' he went on, 'us turning up late.'

'I'm sure she'll understand,' she said as Edward continued his attack on the radio. 'Anyway, she seemed really nice.'

'Did she?' said Edward sharply. 'Must be the jet-lag.'

'Not that I expected her to be *not* nice. Or unfriendly … or anything …' She hoped she hadn't said the wrong thing.

'Yep,' said Edward, smashing at the dashboard again. A blast of air-conditioning started up. Quickly she leant across and pressed the button for the correct station. She'd programmed it in herself ages ago, but Edward had never got the hang of it. He really was quite clueless about some things, she thought fondly.

'So Isobel's not married?' she asked.

'Thanks,' he said. 'Dunno. Haven't the foggiest. Why?'

'I was just wondering. You've never said much about her.'

Edward shrugged. He had opinions about weddings, Julie remembered. *Unnecessary*, he'd called them once, *an invasion of privacy*. Another time he'd called marriage *a deplorable anachronism*. She'd had to look that one up, but been none the wiser. Wasn't it possible, she'd suggested, that he'd simply never been to the right one? 'The right one what?' he'd said. 'The right wedding,' she had replied. You could make it your own, say with a ceremony in an orchard or on a beach. Edward was wary of religion and churches, so the outdoors seemed a safer suggestion. And you could make up your own vows, she told him; you were allowed to these days. When her cousin got married they read out passages from their favourite children's book. 'An even worse cliché,' Edward had said sourly.

'Did you and Isobel have a row?' she persisted now.

'Jules, what's all this about?' Briefly he turned to her. 'She's not going to be your friend,' he said, 'if that's what you're after.' He sighed. 'Look, my sister's selfish and irresponsible. She turns up if and when she feels like it, and never when you need her to. She seems nice to you, maybe, but one day you'll need something and mark my words you'll find out she doesn't give a shit about anyone except herself.'

'But—'

'But *what*, Jules?' She felt the car slow down – never a good sign.

'I don't know. I mean, do you think she's still like that?' She knew she was treading on thin ice, but she couldn't seem to stop herself. 'After all this time, I mean?'

'For fuck's sake ...' said Edward.

'Maybe she's changed,' she offered.

'People don't change, Jules.' He glanced over at her and smiled, but it barely reached the corners of his eyes. 'I'm sure you'd like to think they do, but they don't.'

That wasn't what *Pathways to Possible* said, she thought to herself. 'I expect you're right,' she told him.

They were silent for a minute or two, and then, unexpectedly, Edward spoke up again. 'We're nothing alike,' he said.

They drew up outside Danecroft Road to find Isobel sitting forlornly on the front steps, just inside the gate. Edward turned the engine off. 'I don't mean to be harsh but let's not make a big thing of all this, all right?' he said briskly.

'We have to box clever and keep her on-side. Play the long game, okay?'

'Okay.' She weighed up whether to ask Edward what all this meant. Did 'the long game' mean Isobel staying for longer?

'The sooner we get everything sorted out here, the sooner she can go back to where she came from, can't she?' He spoke in the strained, jollying-along sort of voice people used with small children. And then, more harshly, 'And after that we can draw a line under the whole damned thing.'

'I'm just trying to support you,' she said. Letting someone know you were on their side was a key part of the *Perfect People Principle* from *Pathways to Possible*. Used in the right way, people felt safe enough to open themselves up and let you in.

'Shame I'm not a bridge, or a pair of breasts,' said Edward, unclicking his seatbelt. 'But I appreciate your *support*.'

For a few seconds she stayed where she was, listening to the car's engine cool and tick over. Edward could talk in riddles and be hard to understand, but today, when she had expected them to draw closer to each other, he seemed farther away than ever. 'All right, then?' she heard him call to Isobel in a casual tone. It was obvious he had little interest in an answer. Opening her door, she got out and saw that Isobel was still standing by the gate.

'Hi,' said Isobel, and raised her hand in a funny little half-salute. Yesterday Julie had noticed how sleek and well turned-out Edward's sister looked. Her hair must be cut by an expert, she had decided on the car ride down, and had made a mental note to tell her own hairdresser not to cut so much off next time. Today, in contrast, Isobel's hair had been thrown up in a raggedy bun, with another bit of hair wound half-heartedly round it as if she'd given up partway through. Under her eyes, Julie noticed, there were little puffs, as if she hadn't slept. As she wondered if Edward's sister cared what people thought of her, Isobel yawned loudly and Julie felt she knew the answer. In a funny sort of way, Julie decided, you had to admire a woman who let herself go out looking so untidy.

'Sorry we're a bit behind,' she told Isobel. Too late, she saw Edward shoot her a reproving look.

Isobel indicated the pile of flattened cardboard boxes Edward had begun to unload from the boot. 'I was going to get some of those,' she said, 'but I wasn't sure what we had in the house...' There was a pause, and then she said, puzzlingly, 'I haven't been inside yet.'

Edward was lifting the shredder out of the boot, its power cord trailing across the wet grass. Isobel stepped forward to help, but Edward shook his head brusquely. 'I've got it,' he told her.

'Actually, I decided to stay somewhere else last night,' Isobel said, turning to Julie.

Where had Isobel stayed? Yesterday they'd dropped her off – rather unkindly, Julie felt – outside the supermarket, where it was understood she would buy some food for her tea and make her way back to Danecroft Road. Had she stayed in a hotel? There weren't any hotels in the town, as far as she knew. There were some scruffy-looking houses along the seafront with makeshift bed-and-breakfast signs hanging outside, but she couldn't see Edward's sister staying in a place like that.

Edward seemed to have no interest in any of this, ignoring Isobel's announcement and making a meal of pulling the last of the boxes from the boot with lots of unnecessary huffing and puffing. 'Right you are,' he said, addressing neither Julie nor Isobel in particular. He slammed the boot shut. 'Best get started then. We've got the undertaker's at eleven.'

At Mary's front door Julie stood to one side to let Edward and Isobel go in first. Isobel stood back, lingering on the path. Julie had the feeling she didn't want to go in. Even Edward seemed to hesitate, before putting the key in the door and decisively turning it. Inside, she felt surprised to find Mary's hallway looking as it always did, and exactly as she had left it on Sunday when she had run out of the house and into the ambulance. Possibly Edward and Isobel were thinking the same thing, because they all stood silently in the hallway for a second, as if to get their bearings. 'Come to think of it,' said Edward, turning back to Isobel, 'could you nip up to the pound shop and get some more bin bags? I don't think we'll have enough.'

She was about to remind Edward that they already had two giant rolls of bin bags in the boot – but something told her to hold her tongue.

'Sure,' said Isobel, and disappeared back out.

Should she have volunteered to go to the pound shop as well? It would have been the perfect excuse to find out where Isobel was last night. She couldn't believe Edward didn't care or wasn't curious to know. Meanwhile he had disappeared upstairs. She stood in the hallway for a minute or two, waiting for him to come back down, and when he didn't she followed him up. She found him in Mary's room, kneeling next to the bed. Next to him were two thick files of papers. On his lap was a shoebox, and as she moved closer she saw a thin brown envelope lying inside it.

'What is it?' she asked him.

Why was she whispering? It was eerie being in Mary's house with Mary not here. She kept expecting to hear her voice calling from downstairs, or to see her at the doorway demanding to know what they were doing poking about in her bedroom.

'It's her will,' replied Edward. He took a single sheet of paper out of the envelope. 'What she wanted done for when she wasn't here any more.'

Wasn't here any more? That was a long-winded way to say it, she thought, and noticed again that Edward had yet to use the word 'death' or 'died' – or even 'passed on', which in Julie's view was the proper and appropriate term.

'When we were little,' he said, 'she told us that if anything happened to her we had to come straight in here and get the envelope inside this box and take it to the solicitor.' He cleared his throat.

'You and Isobel?' she said.

'I didn't even know what a solicitor was,' he went on, 'and I used to worry about how we'd actually get there, what bus, what train – all of that.' He laughed thinly. '"The Important Box", we called it.'

How resigned and worn-down he sounded, Julie thought, as if all the fight had gone out of him. She went over to put a supportive hand on his shoulder.

'It's not much, is it?' he said, holding the piece of paper up between finger and thumb. 'Only a page.'

She shook her head. She felt terribly sorry for him, and yet at the same time she was overcome by a feeling of anticipation and pleasure that the opening of the Important Box was something he was sharing with her. She watched as Edward ran his eyes rapidly down the page, face as blank as a mask. It didn't seem fair to exclude Isobel, whom he had sent off on a needless errand. What was it like, seeing your own flesh and blood after such a gap? What if Julie hadn't seen her own sister for years? She remembered Lorraine, rosy-cheeked and laughing, wheeling a tiny Jaydn along in his pram. Years later, Lorraine barely looked like the same person. Julie recalled the way Mary's photos of Isobel

83

seemed abruptly to trail off, as if Isobel's life really had been cut short by some tragic childhood accident – or had stopped the day she went to America. Outside the airport yesterday, she had wondered what to expect. Would Edward's sister come wiggling up to the car like one of the women in that American television series, all dolled up in high heels with piles of luggage and ready to knock back cocktails at all hours? She had noticed the well-manicured nails, the watch that looked quite pricey, but otherwise Isobel had turned up looking much as she had today: friendly, normal, and, Julie felt, altogether nice. She had also noticed how Isobel seemed addicted to lip balm, taking it out nervously between sentences – sometimes even in the middle of one – to swipe it across her mouth, snapping the top back on with a small 'click', when she'd done the same thing only five minutes before. Julie had liked her immediately.

'Bloody Isobel,' said Edward, 'Where the hell is she?' He put Mary's will back into its envelope, and scooped up the two files.

'You sent her up to the shop…' she said.

'Right. Well, she should have been back by now.'

He set off, muttering to himself, and she followed. Downstairs they found Isobel in the kitchen. Her head was buried in one of the cupboards.

'What are you doing?' Edward said sharply, causing Isobel to jump and bang her head.

'Ouch, fuck!'

'What are you looking for?'

'Sticky tape.'

'*Sellotape*,' corrected Edward. 'What do you need it for?'

'To tape things up…'

'What things?' Julie wondered if Isobel and Edward were going to have a row about Sellotape.

'Uh, boxes?' offered Isobel. She gestured towards the pile in the hallway. 'I mean, Jesus, Edward. I didn't expect the Spanish—'

'*All right*, that's enough,' Edward cut in. 'We need to crack on.'

Isobel looked across at Julie and pulled a face and she felt herself going red. Then he put the envelope from the Important Box down on the kitchen counter, slapping it down firmly the way people did when they were playing Snap. 'Mum's will,' he said, nodding at it.

'Oh, right,' said Isobel. She made no move to pick it up. 'I have a copy at home.'

'She wants a humanist ceremony,' he said.

'I know,' said Isobel. 'She told me.'

There was an awkward pause in which Julie got the impression Edward wasn't at all happy about any of this. She watched brother and sister look round the room for a moment with identical expressions – as if they didn't know where to start. It was peculiar, she thought, how certain mannerisms picked people out as belonging with other people. They didn't look that much alike, Edward and Isobel, but you could spot instantly that they – and Mary, for that matter – were related. Isobel had that same mysterious aloofness – friendly on the surface but, underneath, cool, and sealed off like a Tupperware container. Except that Isobel, Julie felt, was obviously an *evolved* sort of person. Clearly she was one of those people who, whatever dreadful thing happened, or however unkindly someone spoke to her, managed to stay happy and positive. There seemed little hope of getting to know her, with Edward so keen to keep all the conversation confined to the job at hand.

'I'll start in here, I guess,' Isobel said, with a bleak little smile.

'That's fine,' said Edward. He picked up Mary's will and the two large files from the counter. 'We'll be in the front room if you need anything.'

'I don't mind helping in here if you like?' Julie offered, and got a sharp nudge from Edward in response.

'That's all right,' he said loudly, taking her arm rather forcefully under the elbow and steering her into the hallway like a criminal under arrest. 'We'll leave you to it,' he called to Isobel over his shoulder.

3

Tuesday

The Faraway Tree

It shouldn't be that complicated, Isobel decided, the fifteen-minute train journey from Martin and Sean's in the morning. As the train glided into the station she stood waiting for the doors to open, until a voice behind her hissed, 'Press the button, for fuck's sake!' Before she could respond, a hand appeared by her right ear and poked at a big blue button that she'd not noticed before. It was fat and primary-coloured like a child's toy, and as it was pushed the door slid magically open and the hand's owner elbowed past her, cursing under his breath. 'Bloody foreigners!' She followed along at a safe distance behind a clutch of other passengers and tried to remember when it was that English train doors had begun to slide, rather than swing open, and since when they had opened only on command. Probably ages ago, she thought, and yet for a brief moment today she had forgotten. 'And how's that working out for you?' an unpleasant woman at a dinner party had asked recently when Isobel had remarked, half-jokingly, that she had moved to New York to seek her fortune. Isobel had explained that, despite rampant unemployment, twenty years ago England had been a gentle sort of place, misty and grey-green and dotted with red pillar boxes. 'Now you're contradicting yourself!' the woman had declared triumphantly, and Isobel had had to agree that she had a point. 'And isn't that all a bit cliché?' the woman drawled, going on to cite riots and strikes and lack of central heating. Isobel conceded that perhaps her more romanticised notions had only taken root after she left, and that they got shredded every time she landed at Heathrow or Gatwick. And yet, the instant she landed at JFK, this reversed itself and the idea returned – of England as a land preserved in aspic.

Coming out of the station, she saw that the little café next door where she had intended to grab coffee was boarded up and covered in graffiti. She walked on, towards the fairtrade coffee shop on the high street. The woman at the party wasn't wrong, Isobel thought. Since she'd left there were new words she had to ask the meaning of, like 'chav' and 'chancer', while other words reflected an uneasy blending of – or seeping into – American culture that made her uncomfortable. There was a wrongness to this, she thought, turning on to the high street, as if she had moved to America only to return and find that it had moved over here. Did this make her a ridiculous Little Englander, or merely out of touch? On the high street she saw that more charity shops had sprung up since Christmas. '*Charity shops*?' Martin had remarked tut-tuttingly last night. 'They aren't exactly a good thing, Isobel.' She had mentioned needing to find a funeral dress. Charity shops were a measure of urban blight and decay, Martin informed her, of 'the slow death of civic life'. 'I had no idea,' she'd replied, and this revelation had left her feeling a bit bereft, as well as guilty and foolish.

Meanwhile the coffee shop was closed, though it was close to 7.45am, so she kept going. Aside from a smattering of commuters rushing by in the opposite direction, the town felt placid and defunct. At the chemist's she made a left, veering off into the twitten, a short-cut that gave on to her mother's road. This was the route she'd always liked best. It had the Enid Blyton appeal of secret passages, even if, unlike in *The Magic Faraway Tree*, you always came out at the same place.

It was a couple of minutes later that she rounded the corner on to Danecroft Road and spotted the tree. She must have passed it a million times before, but presumably never early enough in the day or at the right time of year to properly appreciate it. *Isobel, look, what a pretty little tree!* It was her mother's voice – or her memory of it – a facsimile, Isobel thought, a cheap copy conjured up from her memory. Surely she could jog the half-block to the house and tell her mother to come out and see it? There was no one else who could appreciate or understand the tree as well as her mother would – the way the light played between its leaves, how the leaves moved in the breeze and fluttered their pinkish gold undersides towards the sun, and the contrast with the gum-speckled pavement below. She should be here to witness it before the sun climbed higher and the little tree was consigned to being ordinary again. It was inconceivable that she couldn't be. Her mind played out their conversation in various sentimental versions – Isobel suggesting that the tree looked brave somehow and her mother agreeing, remarking how symmetrical its branches were and how it stood so straight, adding worriedly, 'Do you think it gets enough rainwater to drink?' A man walking past with his dog appeared to give Isobel a conspicuously wide berth and it occurred to her that she might actually have been moving her lips. Had she been standing in the middle of the road talking to a tree? As the man continued up Danecroft Road she had the urge to run after him. 'I can explain!' she would cry as he broke into a sprint. She thought of her mother and how this idea would amuse her, and how they would laugh. But Isobel could never tell her, and her mother would never know. She would never again arrive at the house to find her mother opening the front door before she had even rung the doorbell, and it was too late now, she thought, to ask how she always managed this trick. If Isobel called ahead from the station, she would be waiting on the front step, always with a dab of 'lippy', hovering with one hand on the doorpost, the other patting at her hair in that way that was both anxious and girlish. Isobel would lug her suitcase through the gate and her mother would come down the steps to help and, in recent years, to chance the brief, awkward little hug that Isobel returned just as self-consciously, before breaking off to pull her bag inside and breathe in the familiar smell of the house – hairspray, traces of mildew and lemon Pledge … 'Now, Izzy, did you manage to get any sleep on the plane?' her mother would always ask as they went into the kitchen. The kettle would already be boiling, and she would remember how much she loved it when her mother fussed – none of which, it occurred to Isobel for the first time as she stood in the middle of the empty street, she had ever really appreciated.

The house looked the same. There was no real reason, she supposed, that it shouldn't. She stood outside looking up at it for a minute or two until she started to wonder if it was possible, in some weird way, for something to look too much like itself. If the gate was firmly closed and the windows sparkled, Isobel thought, if the flowerbeds were raked and the bins lined up neatly along the side path, as they always were, the house appeared too normal and just-so, like the cleaned-up scene of a crime. It had acquired a look of hyper-reality, its presence significant and overly defined in the space that surrounded it, the way someone appeared when you were in love with them. She opened the gate and closed it carefully behind her, listening for the 'clink' of the latch falling. As she walked up the steps to the front door she found herself almost tiptoeing, aware of her movements in great detail like a bad stage actor – that her arms were hanging loosely at her sides, that her hand brushed the brambles along the path. Her attention was drawn to the front room window. The curtains were wide open and would have been all night, she realised, which seemed wrong and faintly obscene. She cupped her hands up to the glass and saw that the light in the living room reflected the palest green. The old sofa, the armchairs and the bookcases appeared as if they were floating under the sea. A drowned world, she thought, an underwater place, like one of those ghostly, submerged towns you saw on the news, abandoned and yet perfectly preserved. She found herself taking in the details of all the furniture – the sofa and the armchairs, the coffee table and the clock on the mantelpiece. Everything was where you would expect.

She left the window and walked round the side of the house, stepping round the muddy patches on the path, past the window of the pantry, a store-room now that smelt of boot polish and soft rolls of old wallpaper. It had rained during the night, and as she reached the back garden she could feel the intense green of the grass in her eyes and the ground giving slightly under her shoes and this, and the particular odour it gave up – petrichor or whatever the word was – made her think of graveyards and she stepped back quickly on to the path. 'Isobel likes a nice graveyard,' her mother used to tell people when she was little. On Sundays, which in her memory were always rainy, they would sometimes drive out into the country in their mother's tiny blue Fiat where it was customary to stop, if they came across a church, so that Isobel could be let out to explore the churchyard and ponder the dead names. Her mother stayed in the car with the radio and smoked Silk Cut cigarettes while Edward traced miniature aeroplanes, JCBs and flying police boats on the insides of the windows.

Stepping carefully across a flowerbed, she peered through the kitchen window. There was nothing to see, only the cooker and the fridge, the countertops with their lined-up jars of coffee and tea. To anyone watching, Isobel thought, she would look like a burglar. There was a static, dormant quality to the house, and to the day itself, as if they had been stopped in time. She fixed the image in her mind, of the house exactly as it was – unremarkable and ordinary – and turned back to the garden. There was her mother's stepladder, propped neatly against the wall next to the water barrel. At the far end of the garden, grass cuttings had been spread out in the sun to dry, while her mother's secateurs lay open on the path, as if she had just run inside to answer the phone.

When Edward's car drew up outside, Isobel was surprised to see two heads silhouetted through the windows. What was he doing, she thought, bringing his girlfriend – Jules or Julie or whatever her name was? It had never occurred to her that he would do such a thing, or that he wouldn't at least check with her first. What if Isobel had brought someone along for the ride? Chris, for instance? And today was a weekday – didn't Jules have a job to go to? Or was *this* her occupation, Isobel thought: trailing after Edward like a passive appendage or a pet that could not be left alone. She couldn't help being struck by the contrast with his previous girlfriend – the modelly one he went out with in college. As their mother had once remarked, Sophia was thick as two planks but at least she was decorative – and *interesting*, apparently, which as far as Isobel could recall from Edward's stories back then meant interesting in a crazy-girlfriend kind of way. Did Jules have *compensating qualities*, as her mother would have put it? They were taking their time getting out of the car, she thought irritably, after making her wait a good fifteen or twenty minutes after the time Edward had said she should be here. He'd been so snippy about it on the phone this morning. She watched his door open and his head and shoulders appear over the roof of the car. Jules appeared to stay where she was. Was she waiting for Edward to go round and open the passenger door for her? She hoped his girlfriend wasn't one of *those* types of women, slavish and adoring and totally useless in a crisis.

'All right?' called Edward neutrally.

'Hi,' she said, attempting to echo his offhand tone of voice. To anyone else they must look so normal and work-manlike, she thought, watching Edward pull a bunch of flattened boxes out of the trunk. He stacked some under his arm and placed the rest on the grass verge. They looked like workers preparing to strike a theatre set. In truth, they were burglars, here to ransack their mother's home, to pack up her whole world in rubbish bags and cardboard boxes and leave her house empty.

Julie climbed out of the car. 'Hi,' she said. The girl smiled shyly and Isobel felt a pang of remorse for her unkind thoughts. Julie, with her frightened little eyes, wouldn't want to be here either. Edward, who clearly had the whip hand in the relationship, would have bullied her into it with his terse new law-and-order voice. Most likely he didn't want to face Isobel alone, much as she had tried to bring Chris over so that she wouldn't have to face Edward – the only difference being that Edward had been successful. His girlfriend had appeared sympathetic on the drive down from the airport. She made Isobel think of Jane Eyre, 'plain and little', timid and watchful – but without Jane's underlying spirit. She hadn't had much to say, but at least she had asked Isobel how her journey was and listened, Isobel assumed, to her painful attempts at making conversation. Which was more than Edward had done. Julie had also let Isobel have the front seat, something that used to wind Edward up when they were children, arguing that their mother was giving Isobel preferential treatment, she remembered, when he knew full well that Isobel suffered from horrible car-sickness.

It was from their mother that Isobel had first heard about Julie – 'heard about' perhaps being a bit of an exaggeration. After their falling-out, her mother had been cautious, only ever referring to Edward in oblique terms, perhaps mentioning that she had had visitors or had been somewhere nice for dinner, painting a picture in the broadest, most watery brushstrokes and leaving Isobel to fill in the gaps with the obvious candidate. Recently she had been more forthcoming, if not about Edward himself then about his girlfriend, though Julie had remained nameless, a cipher. Then, when she was visiting this past Christmas, and bored with this dancing around the point, Isobel had taken a chance and asked her mother what 'she' – this girlfriend – was like.

'A bit … off-piste, I suppose, compared to the others,' her mother had answered, sounding slightly wounded. 'Quiet,' she added thoughtfully.

'You don't like her?' said Isobel. She was intrigued by this piece of information, hungry for more. 'Is she *awful*?'

'Well, I wouldn't say that,' her mother said disapprovingly. Her forehead creased in an imitation of mulling the matter over. 'I dare say she's a nice enough little thing underneath

– but I can never tell if she's enjoying herself or not,' her mother continued, in the manner of someone stumped by a puzzle. 'Sometimes I think she finds it all a bit boring here. Maybe it's not what she's used to ...'

Boring *how?* Isobel had been dying to ask. It was such a contrast from before. 'Such a striking girl! So outgoing and friendly. Talks to everyone!' was what her mother had used to say about Sophia. Edward had had problems with Sophia and used to worry – rather touchingly, Isobel always felt – about their relationship and where it was going. Sophia was definitely not a no-questions-asked, lock-and-leave sort of girlfriend. And yet years later there was always a card from her on the mantelpiece at Christmas, and Sophia and her mother kept in touch and talked on the phone. How did Jules feel about this? Isobel wondered, watching the girl creep round the car and come towards her. Jules had fallen foul of her mother's desire for people to be interesting and clever, and, if not those, entertaining – and, if not entertaining – unfortunately for Julie – attractive. Isobel knew what it was like, if only from her mother's point of view. She herself had similar unfair requirements of people and was perpetually disappointed. Obviously Edward was far less shallow. Or maybe Julie had hidden depths.

When Isobel arrived back from the pound shop she let herself in with her key and was surprised to hear the murmur of voices upstairs. *Were they kidding?* Here she was contorting herself into pretzel shapes to avoid ill feeling and all the rest of it, and there was Edward letting Julie – harmless, sure, but still a total stranger – into their mother's bedroom to paw through her private belongings. Edward was leaving her no choice, Isobel decided, throwing the garbage bags into the living room. She would have to go upstairs and say something, even if it hurt Julie's feelings, and even if it turned into a full-blown row. At the door to her mother's bedroom she was confronted by a surreal scene – Edward, silhouetted by the light from the window, was kneeling on the floor by their mother's bed, head bent and eyes downcast as if in prayer. Jules was standing over him, one hand raised over his head, as if poised in benediction. The scene had the appearance of a religious tableau, posed and unnatural – and it gave her a sense of trespass. She withdrew and crept back downstairs, grateful that neither had seen her.

By Edward's decree they were to start on the downstairs rooms first, he and Jules disappearing into the front room with the shredder and an armful of files, and shutting the door behind them. She had been wandering from the kitchen to the dining room, and back again, for some time, unable to make a decision about where or how to start. Each cupboard, each shelf or drawer, was set with its own booby trap, a snare of precious objects. Whenever she got up her courage and managed to make an actual decision – to tackle a shelf of ornaments, say, or the postcards stuck into the sides of the dining room mirror – she would make her approach only to find the object suddenly caught in the glare of some imaginary spotlight – *Exhibit A* – and feel instantly guilty. It was like being asked to go round with a Sharpie and perform triage in some mass-casualty disaster. Who would get loaded into the ambulance? And who would get the 'X' on their forehead? In the interim, as some sort of unreliable insurance, she had gone through the process of imprinting each object, each ornament and every stick of furniture, on her memory. She noted the colours, textures, patterns, the object's place in the room, and then the room that surrounded it. In this way, Isobel realised, she had been drifting endlessly between the kitchen and the dining room and back again without getting anything done. In the other room Edward and Julie were powering along – she caught glimpses of them now though the interior window, due to their efforts now almost clear of its piles of books, which they were steadily packing into boxes. The room was being dismantled with astonishing speed, whereas, as Edward had tartly observed when he'd poked his head in a few minutes ago, all Isobel had done was wash up a plate, hoover the hall, and unnecessarily tidy some coats and hats that were headed for the charity shops. For a few minutes, though, the task had let her feel better – or less worse. Or worse, Isobel thought; she couldn't decide. Straightening the collars and sleeves and organising her mother's hats, the smaller inside the larger, had lessened the heresy and put off, if only for now, the monstrous offence of chucking the entire contents of her life into the garbage. In the kitchen she picked up a coffee cup and sniffed at its rim in hopes of a trace of lipstick. She had done the same thing twenty minutes ago, she remembered. On the fridge, a shopping list was pinned under a pony-shaped magnet, items written out on the back of half an envelope in her mother's neat handwriting. *Veg, more toms? cheese? Crackers, cockles, bread.* She wanted to take the list and put it in her pocket and cherish it. That was the problem, she was beginning to realise, with lowly things – especially these – which felt both redundant and precious, like artefacts or relics, the smallest finger bones of a saint.

Out in the hallway her mother's handbag was exactly where it had been ten minutes ago, hanging by one strap off the banister like an inept suicide. Isobel remembered buying it for her a couple of Christmases ago. For the last half-hour she had been in a weird stand-off with the bag, eyeing its general situation but not daring to make the first move. No doubt this was all magical thinking, she thought, childish and silly. And yet, to touch the bag, to feel its surface smooth under her fingers, felt like caving to an unthinkable reality, a final admission of defeat. Instead she would tackle what had sounded like a terrible job when Edward had suggested it just now, but which now felt like the easier task.

Some while later she replaced the phone on the hallway table for the last time and stood up from her place on the stairs and stretched. How long had she been sitting there? Twenty minutes? An hour? She looked at her watch. Almost two hours. Barring anyone obviously marked 'plumber' or 'chiropodist', she had called every single name in their mother's address book. It hadn't been as difficult as she'd thought it would. There had been a few moments, the odd silence in which she had sensed the person at the other end trying to gather themselves and respond with the right words. But no one had dropped the phone or burst into tears. Then again, Isobel found herself thinking, they were British, with a stoicism unimaginable in the land of Oprah and confessional television. All had asked politely when 'Mary's funeral' would be – and Isobel had experienced again the utter wrongness at this word being in conjunction with their mother's name. She put the address book back in the table drawer – an utterly pointless act, she realised as she closed it – and tried to recall exactly what she had said to each person. She had wanted to project herself as supremely calm and matter-of-fact, but now worried this might have come across as clinical or callous. There was only the cloudiest memory of having the same conversation multiple times. It was like her flight over, which had also vanished, wiped from her mind as cleanly as if someone had taken an eraser to it.

'Need anything?' She had decided to pop her head round the sitting room door to see how Edward was getting on. The floor was completely covered in boxes – a shocking number of which, Isobel saw now, were already taped up and ready to go. But go where?

'Nope. We're fine in here,' said Edward.

'Okay,' she said. 'I'm going to make a start on the dining room right now. Sort it properly, I mean.' Every time she actually took hold of some object – an ornament, book, or picture, she found herself thinking, *This was Mum's favourite. Didn't she talk about it all the time?* Or, *Didn't Mum find this years ago in that flea market she raved about?* How were they supposed to throw anything away? Edward was managing, though. And going breathtakingly fast – too fast, she thought. His system seemed to comprise a cursory glance at each object, before making a snap decision and thrusting it at the hapless Julie with some barked instruction. Julie's job, as far as Isobel could tell, was to put whatever it was into the box marked either 'Charity Shop', or the one marked 'Flat' – the latter, she noticed, being small and only partly filled.

'Okay. Funeral director's soon,' said Edward. He looked tired and stressed out, Isobel thought. She needed to start pulling her weight. In the kitchen she tore one garbage bag from the roll and went back into the hallway. Gingerly she lifted the handbag from the banister and cradled its bulk for a moment, noting the worn leather, the brass catch which never quite closed properly, tarnished and familiar in a way that was specific and unique – *and surreal*, Isobel thought. *Surreal, unreal* – the words she had been searching for all morning. The bag contained much the sort of stuff she had in her own bag, the things most women carried round with them, she supposed – tissues, lipstick, hairpins, various tattered rolls of Polo mints, a dog-eared red notebook. They were nothing special. She set each thing down carefully on the stair, aware of her own air of dumb reverence and the faint whiff of her mother's perfume – freesias, and something else that was fresh and green-smelling. A memory came to her, of her mother complaining of the rheumatism that had started in one of her wrists. She had shown Isobel an area of crêpey skin on the inside of her elbow. 'It's what happens, Mum, I guess,' she'd offered, 'as we age.' In retrospect this was rather patronising. 'Not me,' Mary had replied, quick as a flash. She had taken this as an expression of her mother's exceptionalism, of what everyone must feel, coming face-to-face with ageing and death. Yet the sense of disbelief and of taking it personally had seemed stronger in their mother than in other older people she knew. And now her mother would never get old.

In the purse she found a pension card, some banknotes and change, and took them out with the feeling of observing herself. She counted them on to the stair in a deliberately dispassionate manner, like a bank cashier or someone in a TV police procedural. Seventeen pounds and fifty-two pence. She put them into a neat pile of bills, two little towers of coins alongside the lipstick and the notebook, the sundry contents of her mother's life laid out like a row of dead children, fragile and defenceless – her care coming too late, the reality seeming to descend on her. 'Block it all out,' Martin had suggested over two slices of limp toast this morning. If you didn't think about what you were doing while you were doing it, he'd said, it was like pulling off a Band-Aid: *painless*. 'You reckon?' said Sean. Was this the key to Edward's system of sorting and ruthless chucking? Not *thinking* … but *not* thinking? Whether you practised grim-faced acceptance, or meditation, or denial – the label hardly mattered – maybe the important thing was that it worked. After all, Isobel remembered, the goal was to get through and out the other side without screaming.

Making her decision, she put everything except the money back into the handbag. Then she took the bag in both hands, lifted, upended it, and tipped. She pulled the bin bag closed without looking – knotted it, knotted it again, walked it through the kitchen to the back door, and placed it outside next to the nearest bin. *Done*. Martin would be proud of her. It was easy if you didn't think about it.

Their mother's writing desk was the next obvious place. She had kept all manner of things in there, from make-up to small, broken objects that fell under the category of *might come in useful one day*. Predictably, opening the lid, Isobel saw that it was crammed with sheets of paper – exercise books, old electricity and gas bills, and, as she dug farther, more of the same, along with several US stamps that had escaped their postmark. Her mother had never owned a computer and so they still wrote by hand a couple of times a month. Any unfranked stamps were posted back to Isobel to re-use, and in her next letter Isobel would put a tiny exclamation mark next to it – their secret code for having got one over on the USA's corrupt 'powers that be'. She continued sifting through the desk's contents and found that without too much difficulty she was able to drop most of the items, if she set her mind in a very definite, away-facing direction, straight into the bin bag next to her. Wasn't it said that people's reading glasses were the most poignant, impossible thing to throw away? The desk contained so many humble, equally deserving and frequently non-functioning objects that bore significance. Her mother appeared to have kept every single electricity bill since 1981 and more notebooks than anyone could ever use.

As her fingers reached the back of the desk the last, stubborn scrim of paper broke free – a bundle of letters, half trailing and half wrapped in an electric-blue silk scarf. On the top one was her own handwriting. Well, of course, Isobel thought, Mary would have kept every single one of her daughter's letters and postcards over the years. Stopping to examine them was fraught with the sort of laborious pausing and reminiscing that would keep them all here for weeks – which, as Edward kept reminding her, they didn't actually have. If Isobel was sensible she would save herself any more grief and simply toss the lot out right now and be done with the whole ordeal. Inadvertently she must have loosened the scarf because the letters slipped out of her hands and fell on the floor. With a sigh she squatted down to pick them up and was struck by two things simultaneously. That her letters were addressed, not to her mother, but to 'Edward Vernon'. And that not a single one had been opened.

Tuesday

Painting the Town Red

Early morning was when Edward felt at his best – undisturbed and alone with his thoughts, a blessed interval of peace before the noise and aggravation of the day ahead. He sipped his coffee standing at the sink and watched Happy Meal perched unsteadily on top of the garden fence making bizarre predatory faces at a gang of twittering sparrows. Like playground bullies the birds had positioned themselves tauntingly out of reach. It would not end well, he thought. He worried about him, the animal – for a cat, especially, he wasn't too quick on the uptake, and Edward feared it was only a matter of time before he got eaten by a fox. Next-door's cat, a burly indoor-outdoor tom, had been attacked last month. They'd found its head in the fish pond. What was the alternative, though? To keep the animal locked up inside? He didn't have the heart for it. Better to let the cat take his chances, Edward thought, placing his mug in the sink as Happy Meal wobbled drunkenly farther along the fence, towards the birds, at which point he attempted a graceful feline swipe with his paw and promptly tumbled off and vanished into next door's garden. Edward sighed and looked at his watch. 6.05am. Jules must have slept through her alarm. He would give it fifteen more minutes and then take her up a cup of tea.

For a moment he continued to stare into the garden, which was, Edward supposed, more properly a yard than a garden, managing to be both short and narrow at the same time. The small patch of grass needed a trim, as did the hedge that surrounded it. These would have to wait. Today was for starting the formidable job of clearing his mother's house. When he and Jules had briefly discussed it last night, she had referred to it as 'cleaning'. 'What time should we go over to start cleaning tomorrow?' she had asked, not meaning any offence, but giving it all the same. His mother had kept a number of things over the years, but she also ran a tight ship, and the word 'cleaning', with its taint of dirt and hoarding, of jumble sales and mummified corpses discovered under piles of newspapers, had stuck in his craw.

He wondered what they would do with all her belongings. Their flat was already so congested. Maybe it was finally time, as Jules had once proposed, to turn the shed into some sort of workshop where Edward could store his own mass of papers and boxes of stuff. In the past, his response had always been to laugh, to say that this, surely, was the slippery slope to Old Geezerdom, a lair for the lonely tinkerer, the serial killer at the bottom of the garden. And so on. 'It'd be somewhere for all your books and things,' Jules had said, though, more to the point perhaps – as his girlfriend well knew – Edward relished his privacy. 'You mean somewhere to store all the bodies?' he had answered. 'I could go in a couple of times a week, I suppose, and have a quick spray round with the air freshener,' he'd added. This was a tasteless reference to a famous serial killer, and Jules had laughed. That was another great thing about his girlfriend, Edward thought – she always laughed at his jokes, even when she didn't get them.

Radio 4 was burbling quietly away. He went over and turned it off. Normally he liked having the soothing voices in the background, but today, unusually, he couldn't bear the sound of it. The news sounded trivial and meaningless. The words sounded like a foreign language. Once more he went through the mental list of all the tasks he had to take care of. His mother's doctor, Dr Marsh, had rung back late last night. She had been fond of Dr Marsh, who was genial and harum-scarum with mad-professor hair. An Oxbridge man, he was pawky in that particular way his mother appreciated and found charming. That he would devote himself to being a GP in a small seaside town, Edward thought, when he could have rooms on Harley Street and be stuffing his mouth with gold, was admirable. 'Lovely woman, your mother, delightful. Always a pleasure, never any trouble,' Dr Marsh had said. 'We'll all miss her at the surgery.' They'd talked for a little while longer. Dr Marsh had asked what Edward had been up to of late ('Not much, I'm afraid!') and Edward had duly enquired after the doctor's family. These formalities over with, there seemed little else to say. Marsh had assured him that he would drive over to the hospital first thing this morning and 'sign off on all the necessaries' so that Edward could make his arrangements. As Edward thanked him and they said goodbye, he had realised that this was probably the last time they would ever speak.

Happy Meal appeared at the window, apparently finished with his exertions and none the worse for wear. Edward unlocked the catch and the cat shimmied through and jumped on to the floor to drop something at his feet. He bent down to pick it up – a bit of tin foil – and dropped it into the jar he kept on the windowsill which held all the shiny items the animal had brought him over the years. He had never quite worked out what they were about, the cat's shiny offerings. He bent down again to tickle its ears, and it promptly started washing itself. Animals, Edward thought, were only ever themselves. They were pure in that way, innocent and without guile – yet they remained fundamentally unknowable. How on earth would he cope when the cat's time came? As it would, and in a matter of years. That was the trouble with having a pet, he thought: the built-in, guaranteed fucking heartbreak of it all. But it would bother him more *not* having one, so he made do.

He rinsed out the coffee jug and poured fresh water through the machine and recalled that last night he had dreamt about his mother. Even now, the dream still clung to him like a thin layer of film. They had been in the countryside, a barren area of rolling hills that he didn't recognise. A long, impenetrable membrane ran between them, like a border fence separating two countries. He had walked along it in the pitch darkness, feeling his way for what seemed like miles, trying to locate a space or gap where he could squeeze through. The whole time he kept calling to his mother to do the same on her side, but she couldn't seem to hear him, and as her voice got farther and farther away he became increasingly frantic. He could conceive of her death only like this, he realised, as he switched on the kettle and took Jules's yellow tea mug down from the cupboard – in complicated metaphors, faintly Freudian and contrived. Lacking any framework on which to arrange the idea, it was like trying to stitch something to the air. Once or twice, in some hypnagogic fugue state between sleep and waking or vice-versa, he would feel certain he had grasped the very kernel of the thing – only to find on closer inspection that, while his metaphor remained intact and elegant, the thing itself had slipped through the middle and vanished, like a rabbit under a handkerchief. Perhaps, for now, this wasn't all bad, Edward thought, watching the cat nudge his empty food bowl across the kitchen floor. Someone more clever would find some third way, he thought, a path to understanding that he was unable to conceive of, some place of respite where he could rest his mind and suspend both belief and disbelief and simply accept the disreality of it. Conflicting things, equally weighted and held in abeyance, while in his heart it was impossible to believe any of it.

He let himself watch the cat perform its post-prandial ablutions for a few more moments and then turned his thoughts back to the day ahead. There were some cardboard boxes, he remembered, left over from when Jules moved in, in the cupboard under the stairs. None of the other tenants used the space, and some years ago Edward had taken ownership for extra storage. How many were there? Out in the hallway he brushed off the dust and cobwebs, trying not to think of spiders, and counted seventeen in all. That would do for now. If only he could remember where they kept the string. Since Sunday his memory had become pocked with odd holes and blank spaces where certain mundane words or facts had become difficult to retrieve. Stress, worry and lack of sleep, Edward thought as he leaned the boxes inside the flat door, uncomfortably familiar from years before, when Isobel had left.

He remembered the moment he saw Isobel marching towards them outside the airport yesterday. *Incoming!* he had thought. It would take presence of mind and all his strength to deal with both his sister and all the logistics this week – not forgetting the house itself, which they would get stuck into immediately. A humanist service would have to be organised, ideally next Friday – after which, Edward supposed, the funeralgoers would expect a gathering of some sort, where each would need to be spoken with and lightly consoled. He made a mental note to ring the Brentwood Inn on the seafront. His mother liked the place and they had a room there, he seemed to recall, pleasingly old-fashioned enough for his mother's friends, with curtained French doors separating the room from the main bar area, where things could get a bit rowdy at the weekend. 'Oh, no need for all that palaver. Just scatter me over a horse field somewhere,' had always been his mother's instructions. 'Right, I will then!' he'd retort. 'I won't care, really,' she'd say in a singsong voice, 'I'll be dead!' And then they'd laugh as if it was the funniest thing in the world.

A few hours later they arrived at Danecroft Road to find Isobel lounging on the front steps. The first order of business was the 'Important Box', containing his mother's papers – including her will and the rental lease for the house. Upstairs in her bedroom, with the box actually in his hands, he realised how completely unprepared he felt for her name written neatly at the top in her handwriting, the ink ever so slightly smudged, and her signature – *Mary M. Vernon* – beneath its meagre single page of instructions. The sight caused him physical pain, as if someone were pushing a large sliver of glass through his chest. He took a moment to collect himself. 'It isn't much, is it?' he said to Jules, caught between feeling grateful that she was there and wishing that she had stayed downstairs and left him to it. Earlier, he'd thought Jules had looked a bit taken aback by the news that his mother didn't own her own home. Possibly she thought he had kept it from her. It was true that there was no 'estate' to speak of, no valuable jewellery or priceless antiques. He might have pointed out that her own parents had bought their council house – a three-up, two-down semi with cardboard walls – in a run-down area of the town thirty years ago and were still paying for it, in more ways than one. He had never been concerned about having anything beyond what he needed. He didn't need a new car every week or the latest phone. His upbringing had been memorable for *experiences*, and those could not be bought at any price. Christmases and birthdays had been suffused with magic, a quality his mother had conjured up out of thin air. On Christmas Eve they used to go out to find a tree – always real, never imitation. His mother used to lead him and Isobel on a sort of roundabout treasure hunt to find just the right one to 'rescue' and carry home in triumph. Invariably this involved a slightly stunted tree or one with a branch askew. Only many years later did he understand that more than anything else this was from necessity. How incredible, Edward thought, that he had once been young and naïve enough to be taken in by such a ruse. And yet he had, more than once, and was grateful for it. Other people were not so lucky, Edward thought, aware of Jules's eyes on him as he read through the document once more. You only had to look at Jules's nephews and nieces to see why. Her sister spent a fortune on toys and computerised gadgets every Christmas, only to see them broken, lost or rusting in the back garden by January. Whereas one Christmas his mother had given him an intricately constructed multi-storey car park. Only when he'd looked at it from underneath had he seen the outside – the colours and the writing – and realised that she had made it from cereal boxes – *cereal boxes*! Such a thing would be cringeworthy and mawkish now. People would laugh or assume it was some *Blue Peter* parody, or worse, as if you thought yourself superior in some hipsterish *make-do* way. But as Christmas presents went, Edward thought, it was still the most memorable, and the one that had brought him the most joy.

The rest of the day passed remarkably quickly, though by the end of it he felt quite knocked out from tiredness. They had used almost all the boxes, many of them marked to go back to their flat, filled with books and knick-knacks, each one wrapped carefully by Jules in layers of newspaper. Much of the front room was done, while Isobel, who had had a shaky start, seemed to have made headway in the dining room and the kitchen. Their mother's potted geraniums had been donated to Mrs John, the old girl next door, left by Isobel on her doorstep with a scribbled note. The pushy undertaker had been met with and – as he put it to Jules – successfully subdued. Tomorrow they would have to start walking boxes and bags down to the charity shops and think about moving on to the upstairs. Yet he didn't feel pleased by their progress. The speed, the Teutonic efficiency of it, bothered him. He wondered if they had made decisions he would regret. They should be treating his mother's cherished belongings with care and consideration, but here they were, acting with the heedless brutality of CIA doctors. At one point, during the afternoon, Jules had found him standing slack-jawed and knee-deep in boxes and papers, panicking quietly over a squashed-looking straw donkey his grandmother had brought back from Gibraltar in 1978. 'I can't decide what to do with it,' he'd said to Jules helplessly. He had made the fatal mistake of hesitating, of thinking too much, so that now he felt utterly paralysed by the donkey and its fate.

'You'll need some time,' Jules had said kindly.

'I suppose so,' he said, but he didn't feel at all certain. How many minutes had he already wasted pondering it? He seemed unable to bring his mind to bear on the object in any useful manner.

'The grieving process,' said Jules gently, prying the donkey out of his fingers. 'We can take it back with us and give you some time until you feel able to let go.'

It was these last words of Jules's that had snapped him out of it, caused the panic to recede and be replaced by irritation. She would keep harping on about this awful feel-bad New Age quackery, and it was beginning to get on his nerves. What ever was the matter with her? That mealy-mouthed phrase *able to let go*, for example, made him want to barf. And besides, who was Jules to say whether he should let something go or not? He was letting himself get stupidly overwrought, he'd decided. *Tired and emotional.*

'Okay, fine. Can give it a go, I suppose,' he'd told her, and seen that she looked almost touchingly pleased.

By the end of the day he had managed to load up the car boot and most of the back seat. They closed up the house for the night, and, after rejecting another of Isobel's requests for 'you guys' to 'grab a bite to eat', he and Jules squeezed into the car and left Isobel to walk to the station.

'Why does she have to talk like that?' he said to Jules as they drove away. '*Grab* this and *grab* that. Does she think she's still over there?' He was too tired for socialising, he had informed Isobel, and anyway it was almost nine o'clock and there wouldn't be anything open. *Unlike where you're from,* he almost added nastily. And what did Isobel expect them to all talk about? New York? Her glamorous career, whatever that was, and all the famous people she hobnobbed with? Not that he had ever given Isobel's life a moment's thought, he informed Jules, and he didn't intend to start now. Today, he went on, through sheer luck and happenstance, they had fallen into a rhythm of cordial co-operation at Danecroft Road. So it was best to count themselves lucky and leave it at that, and not push their luck with her. As they passed the train station it occurred to him that he barely registered Isobel as family any more, more like an interfering stranger. As children, they had battled and squabbled over everything, not least their mother's attention, Isobel being competitive and difficult, even then. Ancient history. What connection they shared consisted of blood and genetics and chemicals – chance, not choice or free will.

Impulsively he decided to turn the car on to the coast road. It was a slightly longer route back when he and Jules were both shattered and had another early start tomorrow, but there was still light in the sky, and the evening was clear and calm, and he felt like a drive along the sea. Their flat was a mess. Maybe they could stop off somewhere and get something to eat after all, he decided. It was ages since they'd had a night out.

'Jules, fancy stopping off for a drink on the way back?' A big bottle of Jack Daniel's would be ideal. 'We've earned one, I'd say. And something to eat...'

'I thought you were too tired,' said Jules. 'That's what you told Isobel...'

'Well, yes, I told *her* that, obviously,' he said, and felt pleased with the deceit.

'But won't everything be closed?' countered Jules.

He found her response rather suspect. He wouldn't put it past Isobel to use all that guff about wanting to 'grab' dinner to appear friendly and sympathetic in front of his girlfriend.

Were he and Jules supposed to feel sorry for her? He didn't buy it for a minute. *I feel, I feel...* he'd kept hearing Isobel say on the way down from London. And that ridiculous *crestfallen* expression she had put on just now when he made their excuses, which was especially unconvincing – Oscar-winning, really. His sister had definitely missed her calling as an actress. Isobel was nothing if not manipulative, he thought, and likely she had her reasons, none of them nice ones.

'I didn't mean the kebab shop,' he told Jules, 'if that's what you're thinking.' He heard himself laugh for no particular reason, perhaps to dispel the atmosphere in the car, which felt laden with something tiresome and significant. 'You all right?' he asked her.

'Yes, fine.' Jules smiled.

'Just checking,' he said. There was another silence.

'She was very good today, though,' said Jules. 'Didn't you think...?'

'Who, *Isobel*?' He could hardly believe what he was hearing. 'Hoovering for ten hours? Don't make me laugh.'

'She rang all your Mum's friends...'

'Yes, I suppose so.'

'And did almost the whole kitchen... all those *drawers*...'

'There was that,' he admitted, realising, with a twinge of annoyance, that he couldn't actually think of anything Isobel had failed to do, or done badly. In fact his sister had been conspicuously well-behaved, almost docile. A couple of times he'd even found himself being nice to her by mistake. True, she had called all his mother's friends, and come to the undertaker's with them, and picked out some clothes and things – granted, another unspeakable task – and this evening, Edward remembered, Isobel had arranged a phone call with the humanist minister, Mrs Something-hyphen-

Something. Knowing Isobel, though, all this would be the usual calm before the inevitable shitstorm.

Another silence settled over them, the atmosphere laden with that same oppressiveness he couldn't quite put his finger on. 'Anyway, never mind bloody Isobel,' he told Jules. 'I should be thanking *you*, for all *your* help.' He hoped this effusiveness didn't come across as insincere. He had not been pleasant company these last forty-eight hours. If the situation were reversed, he would have advised himself to get off his high horse and shove his head up its arse. 'Sorry,' he said, 'I've been a bit rubbish to be with, haven't I?'

'Don't be silly,' said Jules. 'I'm glad I can be there for you.'

Be there for you. There it was again. He felt another surge of antipathy and annoyance. He couldn't help it. These cringe-inducing platitudes about *feelings* and *creating your own reality* – he could scarcely keep up with it all. *On the bright side, though,* Edward thought, *if we're all so special in our very own unique, rainbow-scented way, then no one is perfect, are they?*

'You are unique, just like everyone else,' he said.

'Sorry?' said Jules.

He hadn't meant to speak aloud. 'Nothing,' he said, and hoped they could just sit quietly for a bit.

'She just seems so *nice*,' Jules was telling him as they neared home. 'I don't know. Harmless. I felt a bit sorry for her ...'

'Jules,' he said patiently, turning to her, '*please* don't keep on.' He had absolutely no interest in discussing his and Isobel's not very special relationship. Since they'd set off from Danecroft Road, Jules had been steering their conversation round in smaller and more intense circles, as if gradually drilling a hole in his brain. 'We've been over this and you'll just have to take my word for it.'

She turned away from him towards the window. 'Then we shouldn't talk about it any more,' she replied offishly.

He looked over at her, surprised. It wasn't like Jules to get huffy or upset. Had he been labouring his point too harshly? They almost never disagreed about anything. Women could be funny, Edward thought – before rewinding the conversation a few seconds and realising Jules had said *not* talk about it' Not talk? That was a gift horse, Edward decided, that he would certainly not look in the mouth. Best to perform a tactical retreat and deal with it all in the morning. As he wedged the car into the only parking space along their road, he reminded himself that it was not news that women could be fickle with their likes and dislikes. They were ruled by their emotions – and emotions, as everyone knew, clouded judgement. Even his mother was no exception. She had a weird thing about Jules, seeming to misinterpret his girlfriend's natural reticence and shyness as some sort of silent judgement. She had never said anything outright, of course, preferring to hint around it with, *Isn't she quiet?* or *Is she feeling a bit under the weather, your girlfriend?* – tactics that were especially galling to Edward because, after a haphazard parade of highly strung, neurotic, over-the-top girlfriends – plus a few years in which he had steered clear of relationships altogether – Jules was the first non-hysterical, non-high-maintenance one he had brought home in years. He really was lucky to have her.

'There's still time,' he said now, turning off the engine. He looked out of the window at their flat. The darkened windows made the place appear depressing and unwelcoming. 'The new pizza place on Venlo Square – it's open late.'

'Pizza?' said Jules. 'But we said we were going to be careful.' For a while now he and Jules had been teetering together on the edge of fatness, as if on the perilous event horizon of middle age. They had both acknowledged that if they didn't cut back they would soon pass the point of no return and he'd have *a verandah over the toyshop*, as Jules's father fondly called his own beachball-sized paunch.

'Oh, come on, let's throw caution to the winds,' he said. 'Cheese and mushroom?'

'Mushroom...?' Jules stared at him. 'But I don't like mushrooms...'

'Cheese and tomato, I mean,' he said hurriedly. Cheese and mushroom was Isobel's favourite. *Why was he thinking about what she liked?* When they were children, pizza had been a Friday-night treat, while every other Friday they had been allowed a big bar of Fruit & Nut or Dairy Milk. He used to look forward to it all week... Edward stopped the thought and unsnapped his seatbelt. It was another pointless trip down Memory Lane, and today of all days when his brain could barely keep up with where he'd put his phone, let alone the ins and outs of pizza and who liked what. He had wondered, only out of curiosity, what his sister would do for dinner – whether she would eat on her own, whether her friends would cook for her at their house. The town she was staying in had become painfully trendy in the last few years, and he decided Isobel would have plans with her posh friends to eat at one of its restaurants. That would be more up to her standards than slumming it at Five Eyes Pizza with him and Jules, Edward thought, getting out of the car. Halfway up the steps to the front door, he realised he'd forgotten all the boxes on the back seat and in the boot. 'Bugger,' he said. It would take another fifteen minutes at least to haul them all out and inside. 'I can't believe she's living it up at some restaurant,' he told Jules as he stumped back past her, 'while we're stuck here with all this.' He opened the boot and stared at the jumble of boxes and bin bags squashed inside.

'She did ask if we wanted to go out for a meal…' said Jules.

'Whatever,' he said roughly. 'You win. We're better off staying in tonight, not painting the fucking town red.'

What Would Mum Like to Wear?

For the last two hours, after Edward had instructed his sister to ring Mary's friends, Julie had heard the steady murmur of Isobel's voice out in the hallway. Now the sound of the hoover started up. 'Just seeing if it works,' said Isobel, poking her head round the door. 'I thought the charity shops might like it.' Isobel had already arranged all Mary's hats, jackets and scarves into neat rows on the coat rack, which only proved how grief affected people in different ways, Julie thought, as Edward swept another shelf of videotapes into a bin bag. Who could blame Isobel for not knowing where to start? Mary had so very many *things*. Not what you would call clutter or junk, necessarily, but so many ornaments and books, and whole cupboards full of objects. And this wasn't even counting the things you used every day but never thought about – the plates and cutlery, the cushions and curtains, the washing machine and the ironing board. The only way to approach the task, she had decided, was to focus not on how much time and effort it would take to dispose of everything, but instead on all the positive energy that would ensue once it was all done.

She watched Edward examine another shelf of mementos from Mary's travels abroad. Russian dolls and painted spoons sat next to a collection of angry-looking masks and some tatty jewellery made out of brightly coloured beads. Mary had liked to reminisce about her life, Julie remembered, which sounded comfortable and well-off – full of horses and piano lessons and ballet dancing classes. But all this, she'd been made to understand, was before Mary met and married Edward and Isobel's father. Were there any photos of him? Julie had asked Mary once. 'Long dead, I'm afraid,' Mary had replied shortly, which as usual didn't actually answer her question. And then there was Mary's own mother – Edward's and Isobel's grandmother – whose husband was also absent – or as Mary had put it, *lost at sea*. In the 1920s Mary's mother had gone round the world with her sister playing the saxophone and the trumpet in an all-women's band. She was in several of Mary's photos, dressed in old-fashioned clothing, laughing and posing on foreign-looking seafronts with men in blazers. 'What sort of band was it?' Julie had made the mistake of asking, imagining something from *Talentspotters* but with longer skirts. 'Like that lovely old film with Marilyn Monroe,' replied Mary, and then Edward had chimed in with, 'Yes! Haven't we got it on video somewhere? Let's watch it tonight!' and her heart had sunk. She had sat through it before, an incomprehensible black and white film about two men dressed up as women, and something about a train.

Everything had to be sorted into its proper pile, Edward had told them – 'Keep', 'Chuck' and 'Charity Shop'. 'It's like triage,' Isobel remarked, and Edward had laughed in that brief manner that meant something wasn't that funny. *Poor Isobel*, she thought to herself, seeing Isobel's face fall; as she knew from her own experience, it felt so much worse than Edward not laughing at all. Next to the armchair she came across Mary's pink quilted sewing box. 'What about this?'

she asked, holding it up to Edward. He had finished with the Russian mementos and African masks and was again snatching up videotapes, barely looking at the labels before discarding them.

'Just put it on the right pile,' he said without looking up.

'Don't you want to have a look at it first...?' she asked. This was a problem she had been having all morning: how did Edward expect her to know what the 'proper pile' was?

'Use your own judgement, Jules,' he said, lobbing more videotapes into the bag. 'Chuck it if you like.'

'Well, if you're sure...' Tentatively she placed the object on the 'chuck' pile. *Use your own judgement* – wasn't that what Edward had told her right before she'd texted Isobel the wrong thing about the airport? She hoped he wouldn't turn to her one day and demand to know what she'd done with his mother's sewing box.

'Look at this, Jules!' Edward had moved to one of the drawers in the sideboard and was holding up a bit of faded pink newspaper. She leaned over and squinted at it. In the middle of the page was a photo of what appeared to be a vast sand dune and an animal skull poking out from a patch of dried up bushes. 'This must be from ten years ago,' he said wistfully. 'You have to take three planes and two boats to get there. Sounds brilliant, doesn't it?'

She nodded in agreement, though it was hard to see what was so brilliant about it. It always made her a bit uneasy, how each week Edward saved the travel section of the Sunday paper until last, poring over it at the kitchen table during dinner, cutting bits out and placing them in the special manila folder next to the pile of old language tapes he kept on the shelf under the television. Julie's mother thought it was harmless – 'like stamp-collecting', she said, 'Your grandfather was the same.' Julie wasn't so sure. When

Lorraine and Declan splurged and went to Florida last year for their anniversary, Julie had mentioned it to Edward. Florida was a bit far, she told him, but Lorraine said it was a proper resort – and one of the better ones as well. You could walk from the hotel straight on to the beach, and whenever you were hungry there was a big buffet waiting for you. All this, Lorraine had told her, without the local men sticking their hand up your skirt like in France, or having to watch gap year students being sick over everything. 'They all speak English, obviously,' she had told Edward. She had thought he'd be pleased, but he had just laughed in a derisive fashion. They had exactly the same weather in bloody Spain, he said, and for half the price. 'And virtually the same people, come to think of it.'

At 10.45 sharp Edward instructed them to down-tools and marched them down to the funeral director's office on the high street. This was another job that she felt awkward being included in. There were bound to be ructions between Edward and Isobel about Mary's ceremony, and on the way down she tried to prepare herself. The undertaker showed them into a dark, stuffy office room where dusty plastic flowers seemed to loom out of every corner as the undertaker asked about Mary and what she 'would have wanted'. As his voice droned on, she saw Edward and Isobel nodding, now and then, in agreement, and found herself feeling weirdly disappointed. She wondered where Mary actually was. Was she still at the hospital? Or was she laid out underneath them somewhere, only feet away, as they sat politely discussing the music and what Mary would have liked 'in lieu of flowers'?

'Now, what about clothes?' the undertaker said, pausing for a moment at his computer keyboard. He had a slight twitch, Julie had noticed, and a very prominent Adam's apple. Under his suit he was wearing large black trainers. 'What would

Mum like to *wear*?' he said, smiling fondly at Edward and Isobel, as if he and Mary had been best friends or were closely related. It was an insensitive thing to say, she thought, seeing as Mary was not in any position to make decisions. Edward and Isobel exchanged a look, and Julie glanced over at Isobel, who smiled back briefly in a sad and tired way, with an expression that reminded Julie of Mary when she complained about people who threw litter on the railway tracks. She felt herself reddening in response. 'What does Isobel do in New York?' she had asked Mary once, when Edward was out returning some videos. 'Oh, she's over there living in the fast lane,' exclaimed Mary. 'A real career woman!' The phrase was strangely old-fashioned, Julie thought, like something her grandmother would use. 'Turn her hand to anything, as well,' Mary went on. 'Jack of all trades.' Whatever mysterious thing Edward's sister did in the fast lane, Mary implied, it was something admirable and glamorous. Isobel, apparently, was 'pally with all sorts of people'. 'Like who?' Julie had asked. 'Oh, all sorts,' said Mary, waving a hand airily. 'Diplomats, drug addicts, *military* types. *Pop stars...*' It had struck Julie then that Mary talked about Isobel as if she were a celebrity in *OK!* magazine, rather than her own daughter. Which was peculiar when you thought about it, more so when Mary was such an overly travelled sort of person who had been to the sorts of places and met the sorts of people that Julie could only hope never to. The undertaker, she realised, had cleared his throat twice in quick succession, and Julie wondered for a minute if he had spoken to her. Now he started up again, this time with a little speech about 'mortician services' and 'your plans for the casket'.

'That's all right,' Edward said, interrupting him. 'My mother asked for something very simple.' Julie saw Isobel immediately nod in agreement.

'Well, it's up to you – you're the client…' said the undertaker grudgingly. For someone who had five minutes ago referred to Mary so chummily as 'Mum', Julie thought, he could hardly complain, or be surprised by Mary's actual wishes, could he? Even Julie could understand that Mary, of all people, wouldn't have wanted one of those Irish-type wakes where they had a big drunken party and left the lid open. She had been to one of those funerals herself, for an uncle on her father's side of the family, and she remembered the day as full of punch-ups and recriminations.

'I can drop some clothes off later,' Isobel was telling the undertaker, and Julie watched her jot something down in a small, pricey-looking leather notebook.

By the end of the first day at Mary's house they'd managed to get the worst of the downstairs done, and Edward suggested they knock off for the night. Outside, they all stood awkwardly on the doorstep for a moment as Edward locked up.

'So do you guys want to grab a bite or something?' asked Isobel.

'I'm afraid not,' said Edward. 'We're both a bit shagged out. It's pretty late for round here and there won't be much open.' Somehow, thought Julie, he made this sound as if it had something to do with Isobel herself, as if she had gone round turning all the town's lights off. She wished he wouldn't be so rude to her. In the last day or so she had begun to notice how often Edward answered on her own behalf – and not just with Isobel, with whom she wouldn't have minded having a meal at all.

'Raincheck?' said Isobel, smiling directly at her. She had heard this term once or twice on American TV shows. Lorraine used it as well. She felt too silly to ask what it meant, but needn't have worried because once more Edward stepped in before she could respond.

121

'Have to see later in the week,' he said, bending down to lift a box of Mary's books. 'We're a bit pressed for time. Lift to the station, though? We'll drop you off.' He set off down the path, leaving Isobel and Julie standing there.

'I don't think you'll have room for me,' said Isobel, indicating the car, which was clearly chock-a-block with boxes and bags. 'Doesn't matter, though. I'm fine to walk.' She seemed to study Julie for a moment, and then she said, 'I thought we could have a little chat.'

The way Isobel leaned in, Julie thought, pitching her voice very low – it was as if she were being singled out – but in a good way, as if for something special. 'Now?' she asked.

'No, *silly*!' Isobel laughed – a tinkling and friendly sound – although Julie saw her glance nervously towards Edward, as if worried he might overhear. 'I just mean some time soon. You and me. A hangout or whatever.'

Julie looked round. Edward had stopped at the front gate and she could tell he was searching his jacket pockets for the car keys. 'I should probably check with Edward first,' she told Isobel apologetically. 'I mean, we might not have time ...'

'What, no time for a *chat*?' Isobel said with another little laugh. 'Come on. *Seriously*?'

'I'm sorry, I don't know ...' she said, and felt terrible having to say this. Edward was now standing next to the car, staring at her and jangling the car keys impatiently. He was putting her in such an awkward position, Julie thought. Was she, too, expected to be rude to his sister? Did Edward really think this was the best way of keeping the peace?

Isobel waited, a half-smile on her lips whose meaning Julie could not work out. 'You and me,' said Isobel. 'I guess we'll just have to *make* time, won't we?'

Julie nodded.

'Okay, that's a date. We'll do lunch or something? This week?'

'Yes,' she answered, shyly. 'We'll *do lunch*.' The words felt exciting and foreign. 'That would be really nice.'

As Edward pulled the car away she chanced a small wave at Isobel, who smiled and waved back. Surely it was only normal to want to get to know your future in-laws, she thought – even if Edward, she remembered then, had not been keen to get to know hers...

The first awkward moment had occurred when Edward went to shake hands with her father and present him with an expensive bottle of whisky. Her father had practically snatched it out of his hands, rudely looking Edward up and down. Julie's mother had rushed in to save the moment. 'Well, isn't this nice of your young man!' she had exclaimed, while they all stood there trying not to notice as her father whisked the bottle over to the glass-fronted cocktail cabinet, placed it inside and closed and locked the door with the little key he kept in his front trouser pocket. *If the floor swallows me up right now,* Julie had thought, *I wouldn't mind one bit.* After they sat down, her mother, on the alert, was all flustered smiles, popping up at the door for no reason, wiping her hands on her apron and beaming at Edward. 'Well, isn't this nice!' she kept saying, as if everyone was thinking the opposite – which Edward, Julie realised, probably was. For the next hour her father showed off the family photo albums, and then Edward stood and asked where the toilet was so that he could wash his hands.

'You might've told us he was foreign,' said her father. He sat back in his armchair.

Julie saw her mother look behind her for a moment, as if preparing to run. 'He's not that dark, though, is he, Frank?' her mother said anxiously. 'Just a touch of the tar brush.'

'*Mum!*' Julie hissed. What if Edward heard them? 'He's English, born and bred.' She had been looking forward for ages to bringing Edward home, but at that moment she felt ashamed of her family, and ashamed of herself for thinking it.

'I'm just pointing it out, luv, that's all,' said her father. 'You can't be too careful. Not these days...'

During their tea her father started on about September the 11th. 'So what do you think, Ed?'

'It's Edward, actually,' said Edward for the second time.

'So what's your opinion, then?'

'On what?' Edward looked from Julie to her father and back with a bemused expression that she didn't quite trust.

'Why they fell down,' her father replied. 'The Twin Towers.' He looked over at Julie and her mother and made a face. *We've got a right one here!* it said.

Edward took a thoughtful sip of his tea. 'Well,' he said, as Julie sensed everyone leaning forward a little on their seats, 'I should think because someone flew a plane into them.'

It was all downhill from there. The rest of the evening passed with agonising slowness. Her father continued to address Edward as Ed. 'So, Ed – if I can call you that – what does your father do?', and she watched as Edward sat straighter and straighter and responded with icy politeness.

'It really is just Edward, *if you don't mind,*' he said at last. There was another long-drawn-out interval where no one said anything.

'And what's your view on all this immigration business?' her father tried again, stabbing his spoon into his bowl of ice-cream as if trying to spear a fish. The way he smacked his lips and ate with his mouth open, Julie thought – she had never really noticed before how disgusting it looked.

After that, whenever she had suggested they visit her parents, Edward had pleaded work or tiredness, and she had gone alone. On the rare occasion that he came with her he was unfailingly, meticulously polite, which only seemed to provoke her father's rudeness and her mother's anxiety and make the whole occasion more fraught with unpleasantness.

After their first year together, Lorraine had started to pester her about marriage plans. 'What's he waiting for?' she said loudly over the sink one night. 'You're no spring chicken, you know.'

'We have been talking about living together...'

'*Living* together?' Lorraine snorted. 'Give over, that's a recipe for gin and misery right there.'

'Gin and misery!' sang Lorraine's daughter, Janelle, running round the kitchen.

'Lorraine's just concerned, pet,' said her mother, 'that you're getting crumbs from the king's table.'

Her mother meant well, but when she spoke like that Julie always felt like a bit of a failure, at least compared to Lorraine. But family was important, whatever they were like. Edward might say he wanted nothing to do with Isobel *now*, Julie thought, as Edward accelerated the car past the station, but Isobel was his only blood relative and she couldn't help feeling that in time he would change his mind. When that happened, wouldn't he be grateful that she had taken the trouble to get to know Isobel? What if they drove her back to her gay friends' place one evening? Isobel had explained where she'd spent last night and it might be nice if they could all have a meal out together. A key ingredient of being *self-evolving* was being *compassionate and receptive* towards the lifestyles of others. Although, thought Julie, if only for Edward's sake she did rather hope Isobel's friends wouldn't be like those couples you saw in Brighton, lying about on the Pavilion lawns all summer, pinching each other's nipples.

She was surprised to hear Edward suddenly suggest pizza. Hadn't he brushed Isobel off for suggesting exactly the same thing less than an hour ago? She couldn't believe it. *Use your own judgement*, Edward had been telling her all day, and for once, Julie decided now, she would do exactly that. She would *do lunch* with Isobel, and if Edward didn't like it, she decided as he continued to debate pizza toppings with himself, at least she would know she was only trying to help. Edward would thank her for it later.

4

Tuesday

Something Suitable

There must be at least twenty-five of her own letters, Isobel thought, as well as postcards and Christmas and birthday cards – all addressed to Edward at Danecroft Road, *c/o Mary M. Vernon*. After she had lost touch with Edward, Isobel couldn't be sure of his address, but she had never imagined their mother not passing her letters on to him. It would explain why, after so many years, Edward remained so stubbornly cold towards her. She examined each envelope again to make sure none had been opened. Decorated in her own hand, one featured a badly rendered Easter egg, replete with manic-looking chicks, the black felt tip forming a smooth, unbroken line over the seam between the flap and the envelope. Why would their mother keep them from Edward? It made no sense, Isobel thought, as she checked through the remainder of the pile. Unless, perhaps, she considered it from what, the last time she and Edward met, he had claimed was their mother's point of view. At the time it had not occurred to her to believe it.

127

She put the letters to one side and gathered up the rest of the contents of the desk. Within a few minutes she had managed to divide the larger piles into smaller ones. On the 'Undecided' pile was a dog-eared Italian dictionary, two pencil sharpeners, and an old grey eyeshadow scraped to the very bottom, its lid fastened with an elastic band. She thought again of Martin's advice. Presumably Martin had never had a shrink who'd advised doing the very opposite: hauling everything out into the daylight and picking through it with a fine-tooth comb. It was true, Isobel thought, seeing now that she had ended up with two different piles tagged 'Keep' and 'Save', and two identical ones labelled, 'Bin' and 'Trash', that there had, that one time, been that small spat with her mother.

In the first months after she and Edward had stopped speaking, her mother had come to New York on a visit. Isobel had booked it months before and she'd felt they were both looking forward to it. They explored Central Park, 'did' the Staten Island ferry, and strolled across the Brooklyn Bridge. One utterly clear night they had stood at the top of the Empire State Building, the wind roaring in their ears. Isobel pointed out Brooklyn and the World Trade Center and they watched the tiny Matchbox cars seething soundlessly below. And then her mother's last day had arrived so quickly, and they'd found themselves outside Grand Central Station, waiting with a small knot of other travellers for the Carey bus back to the airport. It was March. New York was cold and grey, with dirt-flecked slush clogging the gutters. They had had such a lovely time together, they agreed as they stood shivering with their coats pulled round them. All week, Isobel had promised and promised herself that she wouldn't bring up the subject of Edward. So when it did come up, barely a minute or so later, there was a horrible inevitability to it. Even as she asked her mother, oh-so-casually, how

Edward was doing – adding with a transparent 'by the way' that she had received no news from him – she had known in her bones that it was a mistake. And yet – *why?* – she had ploughed on anyway. 'After all, you were there when it happened, Mum...'

A faintly startled expression had crossed her mother's face. Then she had blinked several times rapidly in succession, as if blinking away something accidental and bothersome, a particle of dust or grit. 'It was weeks ago, Izzy,' she replied. 'I really don't remember much about it.'

'Mum, you sound like Ronald Reagan!' Isobel joked.

Had she spoken too loudly? A woman waiting nearby looked across sharply at them. Her mother must have taken this in too and reddened slightly as in some displacement gesture she reached down to touch the luggage tag on her suitcase as if to make sure that it was still there. Half a block away the bus to JFK rumbled round the corner of 41st Street and came into view. People started jostling for position, the New Yorkers among them trying to estimate precisely where on the kerb the bus would stop so that they could get on first.

'I've done my part,' said her mother suddenly. 'My conscience is clear.'

'I don't know what that *means*, Mum,' Isobel said. She genuinely wanted to understand. The bus pulled up level with them. Her mother stared at it with a fixed expression. 'I guess I just need you to admit that you heard what Edward said to me,' she went on.

This was only partly true, of course. It was only the first step in getting her mother to acknowledge that what her brother had said was not only unfair – but untrue. 'We don't want you here.' It had been his parting shot as Isobel ran from the room. 'Oh, Edward, don't...' she had overheard her mother say.

As people started to get on to the bus, she suddenly felt unsure whether she wanted her mother's answer or not. 'I'm not asking you to take sides,' Isobel said.

A flicker of what looked like anger crossed her mother's face. In its unfamiliarity it appeared transgressive – deviant and frightening. 'All I remember, Isobel,' she said, 'is *shouting*. And then *you*...' Her mother took a breath, the sound almost a sob. 'And then *you* – *flouncing* out of the room, and me worried the neighbours would hear.'

Afterwards Isobel would replay the words in her head and discover in them a haiku-like simplicity, something melodic and poetic in the phrasing of these two, devastating sentences. When she got back to the apartment she had written them down. This piece of paper was probably still floating about in her apartment somewhere, tucked into one of her notebooks:

All I remember
is
You
Flouncing out of the room.
And me
Worried the neighbours would hear.

But 'The *neighbours*?' Isobel had laughed at the time, though it was the opposite of funny. 'Are you kidding me?' Her mother had looked away. By now the last of the passengers had boarded the bus. Wordlessly she helped her mother on to it. Then, as the bus pulled away, Isobel saw that that she was crying, her face crumpled in misery behind the dirty glass in a way that seemed to both echo and deny Isobel's own feelings. She was furious at the injustice of it – though later this image would come floating back, the utter despair in her mother's face staying with her and appearing at odd times over the years.

A week or so after this, Isobel remembered, she had rung her mother up in a misguided attempt to clear the air and apologise for her behaviour. But her mother, who famously disliked 'ill feeling' and had an innate English distaste for 'dwelling on things', seemed to sense the conversation coming and immediately steered it elsewhere. The hollyhocks were coming into bud. It must be all the sun they'd been having that month. So unusual for this time of year. 'I shouldn't have been so surprised,' Isobel had told her therapist later. Although she *was* surprised, as well as disappointed and confused.

In the next months the situation only seemed to grow worse. Her mother appeared to withdraw even further in a way Isobel could not quite pin down. Asking if she had received the photos she had sent – the two of them perched laughing on the Alice in Wonderland statue in Central Park, another with their mouths full of profiteroles in the best booth at Raoul's – had elicited a short acknowledgement but not the anticipated fond recounting of her mother's memories of that day, or any others from her time there. At first Isobel had blamed technology, writing it off as the usual long-distance telephone hiccups and delays. Yet she sensed the chill lay in something beyond that. She tried sending gently humorous cards and little gifts. She made more frequent phone calls, in a bid to regain her mother's trust. Sometimes the phone just rang and rang. Her mother would say that she had been out at the shops or visiting someone, but Isobel got the distinct feeling that this wasn't true. 'It might not be the best time to come over,' her mother had said over the phone towards the end of that summer. 'Why not?' Isobel asked. They hadn't seen each other since the winter. 'If I book now I can get a cheap fare.' There was an uncomfortable silence, and then her mother offered, 'Well, they say it's going to be very cold and miserable ...' adding with an unnatural jauntiness, 'Wouldn't you rather wait for the nicer weather, Isobel?' Isobel told her therapist she was beginning to wonder whether her mother ever wanted to see her – even at Christmas. She didn't go home for Christmas that year, nor that next summer. The following year her mother was ready with another battery of excuses: they had predicted snow on the rails, and floods on the roads. And on the news, she continued, they were talking about a train strike.

'But I love snow,' Isobel said. 'And I can take the bus. A bit of snow is hardly going to affect the trains, is it?'

'You'd think so,' her mother replied thoughtfully. 'But they've been telling us it might be the *wrong* kind of snow.'

The wrong kind of snow? 'I'm sure I can figure it out,' she said.

'You could try,' said her mother. 'But they've been talking about the IRA, a terrorist attack ...'

Carefully, she tied the ribbon back up round the letters. It had taken another two years for their relationship to return to normal, for their conversations to no longer feel threaded with an undercurrent of tension. Their mother had always claimed she loved her children equally, and Isobel had always felt secure in her love. Over the years, she had even suspected that she loved her the best. Now she wondered if Mary had actually shared Edward's opinion all along, as Edward himself implied, with or without their New York spat. Had their mother told Edward about it? Had she told him, confidingly, that she had travelled thousands of miles across the ocean to see her daughter, placing herself in Isobel's care, only to have that trust betrayed? It didn't bear thinking about – and yet, finding her letters to

Edward shoved into the back of a drawer, it seemed the only explanation.

'All right in here? How's it going?' Edward had appeared at the doorway. He was smiling for once.

'Not too bad,' she told him, placing a hand over the envelopes in her lap.

'The curtains,' he said.

'Sorry?'

'We'll have to take them all down.' He gestured towards the window. 'It'll take a while to unhook them all. Fiddly job.'

'I can take care of it,' she said, 'if you like.'

'Okay.' Edward regarded the room for a moment. Whatever would their mother make of it if she were to walk in now? Isobel thought. It was hateful, all her stuff scattered about over the floor like this – the disorder, the total disrespect. 'Well,' he said, turning to go, 'I'll leave you to get on with it.'

'I keep finding things I think I should keep ...' she said.

'...but there's nowhere to put it. I know,' said Edward. He smiled ruefully. 'What about the horse brasses?' He pointed to the opposite wall. 'Charity shop, I s'pose.'

'Oh, but Mum loved those ...' This was the conversation, the to-and-fro she had been having with herself all day. There was a certain comfort in being able to have it out loud with someone.

'Yes, she did,' said Edward. He shrugged. 'Same with everything else, isn't it, though? I think she'd be pleased if we donated them. Unless you want to take them, of course ...' he added.

Isobel considered this, picturing herself at the airport with boxes and boxes of all the things her mother loved: the horse brasses, the books, all the furniture, and half the garden.

'We can't keep it all, can we?' she said. She had managed to slide the letters under the other papers littering the desk. Shouldn't she take the plunge now and ask Edward about them? He ought to know that she had not simply returned to New York and forgotten about him, even if he deserved exactly that. And yet, even if Edward had never seen her letters, why had he not tried to contact her anyway? Her own anger, if not the feeling of injustice, had waned over the course of months. On 9/11, when all the phone lines were busy, she had imagined Edward trying to get through to her – frantic, all resentment put aside. It was said in the weeks afterwards that people got in touch with those they'd wronged or fallen out with. Or so the newspapers would have it. Thinking about it now, the idea was absurd, though back then it had made complete sense. She had imagined Edward imagining her, pulverised under two hundred and ten floors of concrete. And later, strung out on regret at her memorial service, sobbing along to 'Ave Maria'.

' ...tomorrow,' he was saying, 'a few trips down to the charity shops.'

He had smiled at her a couple more times today than yesterday, Isobel thought, but she couldn't tell if there was warmth in this, or just an attempt at mollification: Edward insuring himself against further conflict. She got the impression – possibly mistaken – of being 'handled' or fended off by him, as opposed to being hated outright. Which was worse?

'I'll leave you to it, then,' he said, and disappeared back to the other room.

Their twenty-minute allocation with the undertaker was surprisingly businesslike, if deeply weird, Isobel thought, as she watched her brother deftly deflect the undertaker's amateurish sales pitch. Had this guy gone on a special course to get his insincere and somewhat sympathetic act down pat? And who had let him think it was a good idea to refer to other people's dead mothers as 'Mum'? As he blathered on obliviously about 'loved ones' and cars, and how many cars, and what *colour*, Isobel wanted to ask him to clarify who, exactly, the *loved one* was – the living, or the dead – because his sales patter didn't seem to distinguish between the two. She realised that he had just said her name – *Isobel* – and that he was aiming his words directly at her. 'And some suitable clothes?' he said, and automatically she looked down at her jeans and shoes. 'What would *Mum* like to wear?' he said, a bit more sharply this time, and she finally understood what he meant. 'I'll have a think,' she told him. What would *un*suitable entail? The mind boggled. The word carried the unmistakable whiff of euphemism, Isobel thought, as if in the past the undertaker had learned the hard lessons of relatives showing up bearing wedding dresses and rabbit costumes and sparkly low-cut mini-dresses. She made a note in her book – *Black trousers, flowery top. Shoes (?)* – and left Edward to politely decline the stretch limousine and something called 'genuine beech wood finish'.

'*Twat*,' said Edward when they got outside. 'Can you believe he was trying to wring more money out of us?' He seemed to be looking to her for an answer. 'What do you call it over there?' he said.

'Over *where*?'

'In the States.'

'Oh.' She thought for a moment. 'I don't know. Upselling?' she offered.

'*Upselling!*' said Edward, pouncing on it like a trial lawyer. She got the feeling she had incriminated herself simply by knowing the answer.

'Well, it's obviously not just there, then, is it?' she said.

'Where?'

'America.' *Jesus*, Isobel thought. 'I'm not disagreeing with you,' she explained, 'it's wrong and his attitude sucked. But you've obviously got the same shit here, no?'

'I'm sure your sister's right,' said Julie.

Isobel watched Edward's girlfriend look up at him with wide eyes. Like a baby seal begging to be clubbed, she thought. She had a feeling it was rare for Julie to disagree with Edward about anything.

'Well, *nowadays* maybe that's the case,' said Edward, completely ignoring Julie's comment, 'with the *Americanisation* of everything.' He glanced over at Isobel. 'No offence,' he said in a token kind of way.

'None taken,' she said coolly, and promised herself to definitely pin his girlfriend down for a chat, and soon. Their mother, Isobel mused, was only half right about Julie. She was a colourless little thing, it was true, and she didn't have much to say, but there was a mind of her own lurking in there somewhere, and Isobel was determined to root it out and see what the girl had to say. Edward must have discussed their family history with Julie, and let her know what an awful person his sister was – but for this reason, she decided, Julie was exactly the right person to ask about her brother's thoughts and intentions, and, in time, perhaps get some answers about their mother.

As it happened, the black trousers in question were freshly dry-cleaned and still in their plastic bag, folded over the blue slipper chair in their mother's bedroom. In the wardrobe she found her mother's favourite top, a printed chiffon 'floaty', as she called it. Was it 'suitable'? Isobel laid it flat on the bed and smoothed it out. Or was it a bit festive? Then again, it wasn't as if anyone would ever see her in it. As she folded the top and put it into a bag, another thought occurred to her: were they supposed to pick out underwear? Ever since they left the funeral director's she had found herself wondering, unwillingly, whose job it was to pull clothes on to the dead body. The image elbowed its way into her thoughts – the lolling head, the flopping rag-doll arms. It was hateful to picture her mother like that – impossible that she should be reduced to an inanimate object of revulsion and grim comedy. On another day she and her mother would have enjoyed speculating on this horror – the blueish-green skin, the herky-jerky puppet limbs, the jaw hanging open – as they sauntered along the seafront eating choc-ices, not considering that one day the horror would be them. What had it been for, Isobel wondered, all their talk about death? Possibly, unconsciously, there was some belief that it guaranteed immunity, a special vaccine to ward off death when it came looking for you. *Wrap me in a sheet and throw me on a bonfire*, had been her mother's thoughts on the subject. *Or scatter me on a field – a horse field would be lovely*. She thought longingly of the sheet at the mortuary, which appeared now in her mind as a shroud, pure and unadorned – and far more *suitable*, Isobel decided, than regular clothing which more properly belonged to a body that lived and breathed and moved though the world. But she could only imagine how a plain cotton sheet would go down with the upselling undertaker.

As the day wound down she was left with the problem of what to do with the letters. Upstairs in the front bedroom she had noticed several boxes marked 'Flat', and now she left the dining room and went out into the hallway to see where Edward and Julie were. From the living room came sounds of packaging tape being ripped off a dispenser. She played an idea out in her head. She would go upstairs and place the envelopes in one of the boxes headed back to his flat. Then they wouldn't have to get into it all this week, when there was so much else they had to deal with, but Edward would find the letters shortly after she got back to New York. He would call her, full of apologies, at which point, if only to be gracious, Isobel would offer her own. They would solve the mystery together, this puzzle of their mother's motives, for which there must be some logical explanation. It was, Isobel thought, as she went quietly up the stairs, the perfect plan.

Wednesday

Summink and Nuffink

The next morning, Edward left the women to work on in the front bedroom, and went down to the Brentwood Inn to confirm the booking and go over the vegetarian menu with the caterers. Jules's father had given them the name of one of his cronies, a second-hand furniture dealer called Des, and on the walk down the man texted to say he could get to Danecroft Road in an hour's time. Edward agreed to meet him there at 11.30am. At 12.45 the man arrived with a clipboard and a decidedly downmarket appearance. They all trailed after him through the house as he stroked his chin and hemmed and hawed at the pictures on the walls and prodded and poked at the underneaths of all the chairs. Afterwards, they stood in the dining room, where Des folded his arms and frowned.

'Can't say any of it's worth much,' he said.

Edward was astonished. There were several items in the house that could be sold on for a good price, he told Des. Des shook his head and smirked as if to say he'd heard it all before since most of his customers were wishful-thinking amateurs and Edward should not consider himself any different.

'So you're saying you'll take it all away for us for fifty quid or something, is that it?' said Edward jokingly.

The man, not sensing Edward's tone – or perhaps not caring – paused for a long moment to suck his teeth – or, as Isobel would observe later, to complete the caricature of a crook who robbed the elderly and vulnerable of their valuable antiques. 'Two-fifty,' he replied. 'Cash.'

'What?' Edward was sure he'd misheard or misunderstood. '*Two hundred and fifty pounds*?' he repeated. 'And you expect *us* to pay *you*?'

'That's right,' said the man.

It was laughable, Edward thought aggrievedly, and yet this was how they got you. Des knew that Edward needed him more than he needed Edward. Earlier he had agreed with Isobel that it would, of *course*, be preferable to dispose of their mother's furniture in a proper fashion, but that involved time, and they didn't have any. He reminded her that they had to return the keys to the landlord's office by next Monday, at the latest. There was little point faffing about with antique dealers and the like, when they'd lose what little they made paying an extra month's rent on the house.

'So this is what you do, then, is it?' he said, as Des made to leave. 'Every day, you get up and do this.'

'Come again?' Des seemed to draw himself up to his full height of five foot six and Edward imagined him starting fights in the pub, jutting out his elbows as people tried to sidle past him.

'I'm saying,' Edward explained, 'that it's a bit steep.'

'Look, mate,' said the man, 'I don't know what you're *inferring*, but there's nothing I can do with all this…' He let the sentence trail off meaningfully. Edward silently dared him to use the word 'junk'. But the man left the implication hanging there, artfully saying it, Edward realised, without saying it. 'That wardrobe upstairs,' Des continued, 'them *beds*. And *that* … that thing over there …' He gestured with a faint air of disgust at the dresser, now stripped of its plates and cups, its postcards and dishes, its containers of pegs and spare buttons. 'Full of woodworm,' he said. Edward stared. The man shrugged. 'Lot of heavy stuff to bring down them stairs, too,' he added. 'I'll have to bring the boys with me, obviously.'

'Obviously,' said Edward. 'I'm sure it's a far more complex operation than I can imagine.' It was the sort of condescending and pointless remark his boss came out with, but he felt justified and only slightly ashamed as he enunciated each word, practically spitting them out on to the man's shoes. In the end he negotiated a price that was barely acceptable. It wasn't worth getting into a bunfight over, he told Isobel and Jules afterwards, and it was worth it to get rid of the man, who was seedy and had played, dismayingly, exactly to type.

'So, that went well, then,' Edward said as they all sat down half an hour later. Isobel had finally got her way and dragged them all to a café for lunch. After their dealings with Des he hadn't had the strength to say no.

'Ugh, *horrible*,' said Isobel with a shudder. 'Grubby little man. Like some sort of … *spiv*, wasn't he? I kept expecting him to flash us the watches lining his jacket.'

'Dodgy as a DC-10,' Edward said.

Isobel laughed. 'I mean, was he *kidding?*' she continued. 'Take Mum's kitchen table and chairs …'

'I think he's going to …' He regretted giving in to the man now. And regretted agreeing to lunch as well. His sister would insist on speaking in such a loud voice: turned up like a foghorn and racketing off the walls.

'No, I mean take them as an *example*,' said Isobel. 'They're *vintage*. From the Fifties.' She took a gulp of coffee. 'Just like him!' she added, laughing at her own joke.

Vintage, Edward thought to himself, and mentally ticked the word off a decade-old list he only now realised he'd been keeping in his head. Some years back, sundry items from the charity shops had begun to appear at Danecroft Road. It was unfathomable, Edward had told his mother, why she would want to go rootling about through other people's old clothing – most likely clothes belonging to people who had died, and possibly died wearing them. Worse than jumble sales. 'Edward, it's not second-hand – it's *vintage!*' she would tell him, holding up yet another deplorable moth-eaten item for Edward to compliment her on. 'Well, it still looks like bloody old tat to me,' he'd reply, even when it didn't. His mother would just laugh. Privately he had resented this new habit, discerning in it the influence of his sister. It was much like the time he'd gone round to Danecroft Road after one of her transatlantic flying visits to find the furniture in the dining room all in the wrong place. 'I'm not sure I like the table over here like this,' he'd remarked passingly, although he had seen immediately that it was a more logical arrangement for the room, offering more space and a better view on to the garden. The following weekend he saw that his mother had quietly moved it all back again and he said nothing more.

'I mean, seriously, what the *fuck*?' Isobel said. 'You'd get a *fortune* for them in Williamsburg!'

'Well, we're not in Williamsburg,' he said. What was she on about now? Chairs? Clothes? Neither? He tried to think. All morning he had sensed part of his brain trying to wander off elsewhere. He watched Isobel tip another pot of cream into her coffee – her third, by his count. He'd been keeping tabs.

'I think I'll ask the server for another one,' she announced, as if reading Edward's mind and doing the very opposite of what was called for. *Greedy American*, he thought. He looked forward to hearing what the 'server' – a harassed-looking middle-aged *waitress* – would have to say about this. Customers, presumably, were allocated only their fair share.

'Hi,' said Isobel, when the waitress appeared. 'So sorry to be a pain,' she gushed, throwing the woman one of her high-wattage smiles, 'but could I possibly get another one of these, do you think?' She indicated the three empty containers. His sister had no shame.

'Of course, my duck,' the waitress replied, and made an odd bobbing motion and scurried off to return post haste with not one but five of the little pots, all set out on a saucer with a little paper doily underneath. 'There you are, lovey,' she told Isobel dotingly. 'And you speak up if you'd like any more.' *Or if madam would like a muzzle*, Edward thought to himself. He couldn't believe it. Did she think his sister was some unfortunate shrinking violet? Why did she have to grovel? Worst of all, why did she have to do it so blatantly?

'Me and Mum came here all the time,' said Isobel, opening two more pots in succession and tipping them quickly into her cup. 'For coffee and biscuits.' As if either he or Jules had the remotest interest in Isobel and her tiresome biscuit habits, Edward thought. 'Anyway, whatever,' Isobel continued, 'you know what I mean. In London or Brighton that stuff would fetch a bomb, wouldn't it?' Her voice was rising again and it seemed only a matter of time before she thumped the table. 'And look at Martin and Sean,' she was saying, 'they love that sort of thing.'

'I'm sure you're right,' he said quellingly. Jules was being abnormally quiet, he thought, staring rigidly down at her plate even as Isobel laid into the last of her sandwich. She was probably embarrassed. 'We could have got quite a lot of money for it in all sorts of places.'

'Yes, *exactly*!' said Isobel. She scrunched up her napkin and flung it extravagantly on to her plate. He saw a look of alarm pass over her face. 'God, I'm *so sorry*,' she said.

Jesus, Edward thought to himself, *what now?* 'What? What is it?'

'*Me*. Ranting on. I was talking too much, wasn't I?'

'Oh,' he said, surprised, and heard himself laugh. 'I suppose you were a bit.'

'Well, anyway,' she said, 'moving on, I had an idea…'

'Oh, dear. Go on, then…'

'No, seriously, it's a good one. So I was thinking, why don't we see if the charity shops want to take it?'

'You mean Mum's stuff? But we've already agreed to let Des take it away.' His sister was as impractical as ever. 'Not that it's not a *good* idea,' he added hastily. 'I just don't think they'd take larger pieces.'

'No, but they do!' Isobel insisted. 'The Sally Army has a room in the back with chests of drawers and sofas and things. I've seen it. I bet they'd be thrilled with it all.'

'Are you sure?' he asked. 'I mean, even if they have, how would we get it all down to them? Wheelbarrows?'

'Trucks.'

'You mean a lorry? Come on. I don't know about over there but here you'd need an HGV licence to rent one.'

'No, silly, *their* lorries. They send one and pick it all up for you,' said Isobel. 'Seriously.'

His sister had it all worked out, Edward thought. He felt himself caught between an automatic resistance to any of her suggestions, and a feeling that she might, for once, actually be on to something. There would be an interesting symmetry in donating their mother's furniture to the Salvation Army, as well. Years ago, after their father left, the organisation had provided the family with support. Every Christmas he put a few pounds in the tin and hoped it wouldn't go to proselytising Born Agains.

'Is that wise, Edward, to mess the man about?' Jules spoke up now. 'You don't want to upset him.'

'And?' said Isobel before he could answer. 'What does that matter?'

'I think what Jules is trying to say,' he explained, 'is that we don't need any more unnecessary aggravation.'

'I get it,' said Isobel. 'But really, what's he going to do about it?'

This was a very Isobel response, Edward thought. But on this occasion he had to concede to the logic of her argument. If the unsavoury spiv Des was doing them such an enormous favour by removing their mother's 'junk', he could hardly complain when there was less 'junk' for him and 'the boys' to cope with, could he? In fact, Edward realised, Des would be unable to say a thing about it. It was comedy gold, really. He couldn't wait to see the man's face.

'Tell you what, if you can sort it out by this afternoon we'll do it your way. How's that?'

'It's a deal!' she said. Next to him he heard Jules make a little 'hmph' noise. 'So how did you two meet?' Isobel said, turning back to Jules. Edward hoped this wasn't the beginning of a tiresome conversation about relationships.

'Edward came to my school,' said Jules. 'During Career Opportunities Week.'

'So you're ... ?' said Isobel, looking a bit lost.

'I'm a professional educator,' Jules replied.

'Wait, so you mean like a *school* teacher?'

'A teaching assistant.'

'*Exactly*,' Edward cut in, feeling obliged to clarify on Jules's behalf. They all gazed for a moment after a passing plate stacked with cakes and miniature sandwiches.

'Edward did a presentation for my class, didn't you?' said Jules. He nodded. He always felt deeply uncomfortable when couples rehashed their private lives. The story of how people met was rarely interesting.

'Wait, I'm confused. You're a teacher,' said Isobel, 'or an assistant?'

'I work with disenfranchised young people,' Jules replied primly. Edward winced. Where did she get them from, these cringeworthy and convoluted terms?

'Oh,' said Isobel. 'Right on.'

'Edward says there are a lot of them in America,' Jules continued.

'A lot of what?'

'The disadvantaged.'

Had he said that? Edward thought, starting to feel a little bit out of his depth. He probably *had* expressed a version of this to Jules, and worse – if not in the same terms. *The disadvantaged.* Why couldn't she call it what it was? And what was this, an intentional dig at Isobel? Doubtful, Edward decided. Jules wouldn't mean anything by it – *just trying to be supportive*. That was another thing, Edward thought: this continual attitude of enquiry and support was starting to feel oppressive, like suffocating to death in an overheated room.

He watched Isobel lean forward in her chair with a pained expression, perhaps, like Edward, in an effort to understand what Jules was getting at. '*Poor* people, you mean?' she said.

'Individuals with learning difficulties and suchlike,' Jules explained in a strange teacherish voice. 'That's who I help.'

'That's nice ...' Isobel said blandly.

He sighed, grateful that Jules's words hadn't prompted some outburst from his sister. Smiling faintly at the table, he decided that now would be an excellent time to turn a deaf ear and concentrate on his cheese and tomato sandwich.

'Sorry, what?' He was jolted back to the present by his own name, and something that ended with ... *and we were all very impressed*. 'What's that? Miles away, sorry.'

'I was saying that you had quite an effect on the class,' said Jules, beaming at him in an alarming way.

'Oh, I wouldn't go that far,' he said modestly. That day, he had seen something in her students of his own schoolboy self, something ineffably hopeful in the way they all sat there so wide-eyed, poor little sods. Only later, after he and Jules got chatting and went out for coffee, had he understood what nasty little shits they really were.

'And Edward's so good with children,' Jules said, glancing at him with the gormless, soppy expression newsreaders took on when they mentioned the royal family. Isobel murmured something in response – words, Edward could have sworn, which sounded a lot like, *Woof, woof, wrong tree*. What was going on? Stealthily he slid one of the little pots from Isobel's saucer and tipped it into his coffee and hoped no one would notice. Ever since he got back from the caterers he had sensed something between the women – an atmosphere or crackle that hadn't been there before. Were they making fun of him? It was bad enough that Jules was going against his explicit instructions and had seemed bent on making friends with Isobel – but had she also spent the morning telling his sister all their private business? He imagined them trading secrets and gossiping while he was out haggling over finger rolls. He felt desperately tired. Had he made a strategic mistake leaving the women alone together, or was he being paranoid?

'Sorry, pardon?' said Jules.

'I mean, is he really?' said Isobel, bright-eyed with interest. 'You know: good with children.' A loaded atmosphere had settled over the table. He was conscious of the women's eyes on him. He was too tired for this routine, this rubbish. *Too knackered, and too old.* They seemed to be speaking in their own code, steering the conversation in some wrongwards direction, into a fraught little cul-de-sac that he felt an urgent need to reverse out of. He hoped his girlfriend and his sister weren't about to gang up on him. He had his views on marriage and children, as Jules well knew. Over the years he had watched his small supply of friends dwindle, swallowed up into their marriages. When he did manage to steal half an hour with a mate at the pub, they turned up looking slightly abashed, like a dog who knew it had shat on the sofa. More than a few ordered shandy or lemonade, claiming to be in solidarity with their pregnant or breastfeeding wives. Quite often, without notifying Edward beforehand, they arrived in the company of these wives or the women would turn up later and it made him furious. Inevitably the wives hijacked the conversation, enquiring smilingly – and indiscreetly – about Edward's girlfriend, about their 'plans'. At such times it took an almost physical effort to bite his tongue, to not reply that marriage was a funeral where you sent your own flowers, and that the whole wretched construction made him think of that plane graveyard in the Mojave desert, hundreds of Boeings and Airbuses and Bombardiers, parked out in the sun, moribund and defunct. 'Not for me, to be honest,' he would say in his jolliest tone, and hope they could take the hint and leave it at that. But they never did.

He realised that Isobel had started on again about the Sally Army, while Jules, who had gone quiet again, appeared to be folding her napkin into smaller and smaller triangles. He wondered if she was angry with him about something,

147

but he couldn't imagine why. 'Well,' he told them, making to stand up, 'we should get moving.' Ostentatiously he consulted his watch. 'Jules, aren't you off to your sister's this afternoon?' he said, and got an injured look in return.

'Lorraine said she'd drop Jasmyn off at ours,' Jules replied sulkily. 'I'll take her to the playground or something.'

She should be pleased, Edward thought, not having to troop back to Danecroft Road with him and Isobel this afternoon. They were starting on his mother's bedroom – her clothes and keepsakes, the drawers full of school reports and baby teeth. It wasn't his idea of fun. Mind you, Edward thought, it was only *marginally* less fun than being marched to the local playground, and having to deal with Lorraine. Jasmyn, Jules's niece, was almost three. And there were two more as well, teenage nightmares Janelle and Jaydn, tough little nuts with adult faces who said 'summink' and 'nuffink' – the sort of children, his mother once remarked, who threw bricks at policemen.

At the counter he watched the girl take his twenty-pound note with one hand and reapply some repulsive greasy substance to her lips with the other. How dismal everything was, Edward thought suddenly, and was struck by another wave of exasperation. Why did he have to put up with such bizarre and unexpected behaviour, this week of all weeks, with Jules embarrassing him and dropping coy little hints about children? He had been utterly frank with her, right from the start. Was it something women just did, he wondered, as he accepted his change and tossed a pound coin into the tip jar for the long-suffering 'server'? Did all women – even Jules – lull you into a false sense of security about your choices before trying to change your mind? It put him in mind of the 'helpful' suggestions they offered about your jeans or the way you tucked in your shirt. The subject of children, Edward realised, as he left the café, was brought up with increasing and non-sequitorial frequency. He did his best to conceal his annoyance, patiently reiterating his stance while Jules smiled at him in an indulgent manner, as if he didn't know his own mind. Perhaps she thought some male biological alarm clock would one day go off and impel him into fatherhood. But in his mind the mess and noise, the wholesale disruption and lack of sleep, remained an unacceptable price for the dubious privilege of passing on your own genes. Partly he blamed her family. After this last Christmas at the Brewers', with the thousands of relatives, the high-pitched squeals and toys bashed repeatedly into the skirting boards, the multiple televisions blaring everywhere and the lights left blazing in every room, Edward had been forced to draw the line. He'd rather chew off his own arm than spend another Christmas locked up with them all. Every other year he managed to get out of it by using his mother as the excuse. 'Now she's older, I don't like to leave her on her own at Christmas,' he'd explained once to Jules's father. 'And she hates to travel anywhere these days,' he'd added, neatly pre-empting the offer of hospitality that never came.

This year, Edward remembered with an unpleasant jolt, would require a different excuse.

Wednesday

The Ambulance

Next to her Edward emitted another series of sighs and turned over, taking most of the duvet with him. Julie didn't mind. Watching him sleep, seeing him so vulnerable, was comforting. A damp bit of feather from the pillow clung to his forehead and she picked it off gently, so as not to wake him. The idea of disturbing him caused her brain to sputter to life again and she felt her thoughts start to scurry round like small caged animals, frantically searching and nosing into corners. Getting ready for bed last night she had stood in front of the bathroom mirror brushing her teeth when a fire engine had blasted past their flat, sirens blaring, and a terrifying question had come into her head: *Who called Mary's ambulance?* She had been lying awake for hours thinking about it. She had tried turning her mind towards more positive thoughts such as her soon-to-be friendship with Isobel and all the things they would share together. But, as before, the more she tried to not think about Mary, the more Mary occupied her mind – Mary in the garden on Sunday, her legs sticking out stiffly like the witch in *The Wizard of Oz* – the image appeared to loom larger and larger.

It had been unbearably warm and close on Sunday. After Edward went off to the pub Julie had stayed at the house to help his mother as she did her gardening. Every now and then she was asked to fetch this or that tool from the shed – a task that was impossible for Mary, she had been told, because of the spiders. At some point, after standing about in the hot garden watching Mary fiddle with bulbs and bags of earth, Julie had felt overwhelmed with tiredness. How much longer did Edward expect her to stay out here, when all she wanted was a quick lie down and to rest her eyes from the sun for fifteen minutes?

Mary must have noticed the way Julie kept inching into the shade and fanning herself with the Sunday supplement, because a short while afterwards she stood up from one of the flowerbeds and said, 'I'm perfectly able to carry on without you, you know. I really don't require being watched and monitored.' She came over towards Julie, holding her secateurs. 'I tell you what,' she said, more kindly, 'why don't you go inside in the cool, and I'll give the tulips a drop more water.'

Even as she felt relieved to get away, and have the chance for a quick lie-down in Mary's spare bedroom, Julie had felt hurt at the way Mary had dismissed her. And then, for some reason, she must have fallen asleep, because the next thing she knew the doorbell was ringing – once, or maybe twice – and then a third time. *It's got so dark*, Julie thought, groping for the bedside clock. Not finding it, she remembered that she wasn't at home, but at Mary's. *It'll be Edward forgetting his keys again*, she decided, as the bell rang twice more in succession. *Mary must be in the back garden watering her precious flowers.* Quickly she slipped into her shoes and ran downstairs. Opening the front door, she saw, not Edward, but a man in a white shirt and black trousers – some sort of uniform. For a minute she thought he was a policeman, and then she noticed the ambulance parked haphazardly in the road behind him, its lights whirling in the dusk. *Edward!* she thought, as panic took hold of her and she imagined him hit by a drunk driver, beer glasses smashed in the pub, a bomb.

'We got a call about this address, miss,' the man told her.

This address? 'I'm sorry, you must have the wrong house,' she told him. A mistake, she thought. Nothing to do with Edward at all.

A shout came from somewhere nearby, and another uniformed man appeared from the direction of the back garden. 'Round here, Mike,' he told the first man, who disappeared after him. Julie ran back through the house and out into the garden, where the men crouched with their backs to her over someone lying on the grass.

At first the two men didn't say much. In the ambulance, devices and screens beeped and thumped and she watched as they hooked Mary up to various tubes and machinery. Of course, she had rung Edward at once. 'Bugger, what is it now?' he'd said. 'I'm always telling her to be careful.' Through the noise and chatter of the pub in the background she had sensed his irritation. 'Tell her I'll be there in a minute,' he had told her, and rung off before she could explain. The ambulance men started to ask her questions about Mary's medical history and she had to tell them that Mary was not her mother but her boyfriend's, and he would be coming right behind them. 'Doesn't look too good, Rob,' she heard one remark. She asked what the matter was with Mary. The doctors would make a proper diagnosis, they told her. As the ambulance rocked and swerved she pressed herself against its side and tried to take an interest in the instructions and labels posted on its equipment. There was something very impolite about staring at someone who was unconscious, Julie thought, as awful questions battered at her. How long had she been asleep? Was Edward's mother going to die? And how long had Mary been lying there trying to call out for help, not knowing why no one came, until she finally slipped into unconsciousness, bewildered and in terrible pain?

Edward, she realised now, would have assumed it was she, Julie, who had called 999. But she'd never got the chance. It wasn't Mary, whose mobile, Julie remembered noticing during her rush through the house, was sitting on the dining room table. She tried to remember the exact details of Mary's garden, and the houses that overlooked it, but could only picture the plants that made her sneeze, the pink worms that writhed and slithered about in the earth, and the mass of leaves and trailing things that ran riot everywhere. A nosy passer-by could have glanced over the low wall, seen Mary, and called the ambulance. But wouldn't this person have stayed to help? Surely they would have knocked at the door. Somebody else, then, Julie thought, somebody who saw Mary lying outside alone and called 999, and … and then? None of it made sense. The garden was visible for several houses each side, but more widely from the backs of the houses in the next road. She thought of them now, the countless windows with their net curtains or trendy, brightly coloured blinds, each as opaque as the windows of Mary's ambulance, and each concealing a stranger.

By the time they arrived at Danecroft Road, and after a night of no sleep, she had thoroughly exhausted herself with worry. Around 10.30, Edward went off to meet with the caterers at the Brentwood Inn and she decided to take her chance with his sister. 'I can stay here and keep going if you like,' she offered, and Edward didn't object. They had all spent the first part of the morning wading through another mountain of Mary's books, but for the last half-hour she and Isobel had been sitting on the floor of Mary's spare bedroom, chatting away over coffees as if they had known each other for ever.

'God. You should have seen it,' said Isobel. She had been telling Julie all about a wedding she had been to recently. 'And get this, Jules,' she'd added, and Julie had felt a weird little thrill at hearing her own name, 'they got the whole thing sponsored by *Hello!* magazine! It was so vulgar, like some kind of reality TV show. Can you believe it?' Isobel shuddered. 'Ghastly,' she said, and paused, as if waiting for some response.

'Ghastly,' Julie agreed. She liked *Hello!* and *OK!*, and inside their pages it was a different world. To her mind the celebrities and film stars on the wedding pullout page looked elegant and tasteful, but it would look a bit rude to disagree with Isobel, she decided, when their friendship was so new. She found herself rather admiring Isobel for her opinions, which she stated confidently and knowledgeably. Maybe this was what Edward really meant when he'd talked about his sister having 'outbursts'. He had made it sound like temper tantrums or fits.

'What do you do?' she asked Isobel. 'In New York?'

'Hmm,' said Isobel, picking a book from the 'Charity Shop' pile and placing it to one side. 'I guess I'm an underachiever. You know, a late developer? A little late to the dance?'

'Oh,' she said. Isobel had given three answers in one breath – none of them very informative.

'I'm kidding,' she said. 'It's just that I've never had a regular nine-to-five job, or known what I really wanted to do. I work freelance, for the company that created the Manhattan Film Festival?'

This must be what Mary meant, Julie realised, when she talked about Isobel and all the *high-up* people she mixed with.

'You're a film director?' she asked, impressed.

'No, not quite. I wanted to be.' Isobel took a sip of her coffee, and Julie did the same. 'Used to, I mean. I tried it out, in a small way.'

'What was it like?'

'Oh, God, don't get me started!' Julie waited, and Isobel continued. 'Not as glamorous as it sounds, honestly. Lots of waiting about in the cold or the heat, and sometimes dealing with the actors – the tardiness, the massive egos, the tantrums – but mostly not. Stuff like that. You know how those people are.'

'You didn't like it?'

'Fuck, no. I wanted to hang myself! I like my filmfest work, though. Every day's different.'

Julie wondered what it was like to be Isobel, to wake up not knowing what the day held. On one hand, it would make for an interesting sort of life, but on the other it sounded nerve-racking. 'Always new films to see, cool new artists and directors,' Isobel was saying. 'I love it, actually. And being in the city ... there's always something going on.'

'What about your partner?'

'My partner?' Isobel looked confused.

'Your boyfriend ...' In the car down from London Isobel had mentioned someone called Chris. Edward had been no help when she'd asked him about it.

'Oh, right,' said Isobel. 'Sorry, you guys say "partner" now, don't you? It always makes me think of business partner. You mean Chris. We only just started dating, really.'

'Is he coming over for Mary's ...' She found herself searching for the right word. 'For the ceremony?'

'No, I don't think so,' said Isobel. 'He's got so much going on at work. Anyway, between you and me I think he'd be a bit useless.' Isobel took out her lip balm and performed a quick swipe across her mouth with it. 'Ex was the same way,' she said. 'Hopeless in a crisis.'

'X?' Isobel was so hard to keep up with.

'My ex-boyfriend,' Isobel replied. 'Fantastic at first, but we get on much better *now*.'

'You're friends with your ex-boyfriend?' Was it true? Mary had been in touch with one or two of Edward's ex-girlfriends, but Edward never spoke to them. Why would Isobel want to be friends with her ex?

'Sure we are,' said Isobel breezily. 'Actually, I'm really good friends with his new girlfriend. He and I are way better as friends. But it's always like that, isn't it?'

'What is?' asked Julie, hardly daring to ask about the girlfriend.

'Like how when you start dating it's this wonderful, kind of ... *froth*, right? It's like we were just saying about weddings and stuff.' Isobel shot her a knowing, all-girls-together sort of look but gave her no opportunity to reply. 'You know, before you get to know someone properly?' Isobel seemed to wait again, so Julie nodded and Isobel continued. 'And then one day it dissolves – *pouff!* And there's only two ways that can go, aren't there?'

'Yes?' she said, curious to know what they were.

'Heartbreak and misery!' Isobel declared with a dramatic sigh. 'Tears in the toilets and all that.'

Just when she thought she was getting the hang of things with Isobel, Julie thought, she felt completely lost.

'Heartbreak is painful,' explained Isobel, 'like pulling off a Band-Aid. But *misery* – ugh – that's more long-term, and that's the *worst*. I guess it's inevitable when you're with someone for enough time and you start to see the "real" person underneath. At which point ...' Isobel paused to place another book on the 'Keep' pile. 'At which point, you realise you're kind of *stuck* with them.'

Almost every other word, Julie noticed, Isobel said as if it were in italics. You could never be certain exactly what she meant or whether she meant it seriously, and, most tricky of all, whether you were meant to laugh or keep quiet.

'Of course they're stuck with you, too, aren't they?' Isobel laughed again. 'You're stuck with each other! But we've all been there, right?'

'Sorry?'

'Guys. Men,' said Isobel, attaching a strip of Sellotape across the top of one of the boxes they'd just filled. 'We've all been there.'

'What about Chris?' she asked. Isobel seemed much more interested in talking about her ex-boyfriend than her current one.

'Chris is great,' replied Isobel. 'Really fun, and interesting and laid-back. We have these amazing talks…'

Did she and Edward have amazing talks? Julie wondered. Did Edward find her fun and interesting and…laid-back?

'Will you get married, do you think?' she asked.

'Married?' Isobel looked perplexed.

'Yes… To Chris.'

'Oh, right.' There was a pause. 'Why?'

She was conscious again of Isobel's gaze – that bright, sharp look of curiosity. She wasn't used to people asking for her opinion as intensely as Isobel was now, and, even though it seemed obvious to her, she had to think for a moment how to explain what she meant.

'I suppose because you said you and Chris have amazing talks and everything? And that he's nicer than Ex.'

'Well, sure,' said Isobel, who then paused and seemed to ponder this for a moment. 'The thing is – and not to sound clichéd or anything – but however much I like someone – even if I love them – it's not how I'm built.' She paused again. 'I value my independence, I guess.' She sighed.

'Because you want to go out with other people?'

'Not really. Well, maybe,' said Isobel. 'Actually, no,' she added confusingly. 'I mean, I wouldn't rule it out or anything, but that's not what it's about, no.'

'But you'll get married one day, won't you? When you meet the right person?' For some reason, Julie realised, she badly wanted Isobel to say yes. She wanted Isobel to tell her that she was sure everything would change the moment she met the right person, the one she was destined to be with. She let herself imagine Isobel coming back next Christmas, unwrapping presents with Edward and Julie under the tree. Isobel would tell her that she'd been right all along, because she was in love with Chris and they were moving to England and getting married. *Why not split the cost and make it a double wedding, with you and Chris, and me and Edward?* Julie could say...

'God, no,' said Isobel.

Some years ago, when Edward had suggested Julie move in with him to save on rent, she had been surprised at how relieved she felt, as if until that moment she had been holding her breath. Living together was 'a step in the right direction', her mother had said. 'Congrats,' said Lorraine. 'Now he's got a free skivvy to do the housework.' If Edward loved her, Julie thought to herself, as Isobel got up and fetched over another armful of books, why was she still just his live-in girlfriend?

'Look, don't get me wrong. I know some married people.' Isobel put the books down on the floor. 'Some of them are even fairly happy.'

Julie had noticed the way Isobel had stared at her when she brought the subject up – with that odd birdlike manner, as if not comprehending what she meant – or as if she, Julie, were the person with peculiar ideas. It put her in mind of Edward, the day she had told him that she wouldn't mind some children of her own one day. 'Not for me, I'm afraid,' he had told her. 'Not in the plan.'

'I guess I don't plan the future in that way,' Isobel said, in an eerie echo of Edward's words. 'It's not about relationships *per se*, it's just that you never know what's going to come round the corner, do you?'

'No,' she agreed. Unfortunately, as Julie had recently learned, this was quite true.

'It's not always good, of course, what's round the next corner,' Isobel said sorrowfully. She stared for a moment at the tumble of boxes waiting for Mary's belongings and the sheets folded on the bed. 'I just can't bear the idea of closing myself off to things, to the rest of the world. And travelling is way more fun to do on your own, right? There's so much out there to see and do ...' Isobel stopped, and looked towards the window again. 'Mum taught us that,' she said.

Us. Did Isobel mean Edward? Was this what Edward was thinking, Julie wondered, when he went rifling through the travel section of the Sunday papers and cut bits out?

Isobel picked up the roll of Sellotape and finished sealing the lid on the large box containing all Mary's candlewick bedspreads. 'Look, what I'm saying is: the idea of spending the rest of my life *Sieg-Heil*-ing away to some guy and picking up his dirty socks? It just doesn't appeal to me, that's all.' They looked at each other for a moment, and then Isobel laughed. 'Something dreadful in my upbringing, I'm sure!' she said.

It was as if she were plucking Julie's own, most recent anxieties from the air and confirming all her worst fears.

'So what's your take on it?' said Isobel.

'Pardon?'

'Marriage and all that. What do you think of it all?'

It was really unsettling, she thought, how Isobel appeared to be reading her mind. Then again, wasn't this what real friends did? They developed a sixth sense about what you were thinking or feeling – or so she had heard; she had never had a proper friend, not really, let alone a best friend. If you believed in *Pathways to Possible*, though, your thoughts and emotions virtually shot out of your mind and manifested as reality.

'You and Edward,' said Isobel, applying another layer of lip balm. 'You must be super-close. It obviously works between you both.'

'We've been together eight and a half years,' she replied. 'So I suppose so.'

'Eight and a half years...' echoed Isobel. 'That's impressive.'

Was Isobel impressed? Or did she think Julie and Edward were like Isobel and her ex, their froth gone flat, but stuck with each other.

'You guys must know absolutely everything about each other by now,' Isobel went on. 'You must share all your thoughts and secrets.'

'We're very honest about things,' Julie replied. 'With our *talks*,' she added. 'You know how Edward is.' Edward was scrupulously honest. He would never lie to her.

'Mm,' said Isobel. 'Actually, I don't. Not really.'

Julie waited for some further comment or for Isobel to ask more directly what her and Edward's future plans were, as most people did, but she had fallen silent, staring down at the dog-eared copy of *Marley and Me* that Julie had just placed on the 'Charity Shop' pile.

'About that,' Isobel said now. 'About Edward...'

'Yes?'

'And my mother as well. I wanted to ask you...'

Julie realised that this was the first time this morning that Isobel had referred to Mary. She wondered if Isobel was about to confide in her, to reveal something important about Edward or their family background. 'You're the only person I can ask about it, obviously,' Isobel continued with a significant look, as if peering into Julie's soul. 'Because you're the only person who *knows*.'

Julie saw that Isobel had stopped smiling, and felt a small tremor of unease. 'Sorry?' she said.

'About my mother,' Isobel said. 'What happened on Sunday. Because I know you were here, you see.'

Isobel seemed agitated, and had started pulling at her own wrists as if trying to pull off her hands. And she was speaking more rapidly than she had before, if haltingly, in short bursts. 'You know what Edward's like,' she said. 'How he is. How he thinks. And after we're finished with the house – when this…' she indicated the mess of boxes around them '…when this is all over and he's had time to think, seeing as what happened to our mother…' Isobel looked up at her with that odd look on her face – much sharper and keener this time, like Happy Meal's when he was stalking a sparrow. *Seeing as what happened*,' Isobel said, 'what do you think he'll do?'

With a sickening lurch, Julie understood. The floor seemed to drop from under her, the feeling in her stomach like the nightmare in which she was sent barrelling over the top of a rollercoaster. *Isobel knew.* She knew everything. Julie didn't know how, but she did. She knew that she, Julie, had gone to sleep, right here in Mary's spare bedroom, while Mary died alone. Isobel also knew – because she had grown up with Edward – what he would do if he ever found out what Julie had done; how it would change how he felt about her. And she knew exactly what it would mean for their future together.

'You know my brother better than I do, don't you?' Isobel was purring in a silky, threatening voice. 'You must know what he'll do…'

Julie tried to think. How was she going to get through the next ten seconds? 'I…' She stopped.

'Regardless of what Edward decides,' Isobel said, 'you need to tell me what happened. I *need* to know. It would be best if you just tell the truth.'

'The truth?' Julie managed to bleat. If only she were as small as she felt, she thought, small enough to run away and hide under Mary's rickety floorboards. Her mind scrabbled for explanations that she could offer up to Isobel, like a victim throwing their purse at a robber. Isobel continued now in a strange, brittle voice. 'I'm sure you'd rather not talk about what happened, Julie,' she said. 'But you have to tell me. About my mother. About everything that happened. Tell me the truth.'

The words, she thought, the way Isobel kept repeating them, were terrifying. There was something else simmering underneath the voice, Julie sensed, but her thoughts were in too much turmoil to work out what it was. If she confessed, if she told Isobel the truth, there would be a rift, such a terrible, unbridgeable rift between herself and Edward. Edward was clearly capable of rifts: he had been pretending his own sister didn't exist for years. Why hadn't she listened to him? And how had she let herself think, even for one moment, that someone like Isobel would want to be friends with someone like her? She felt the tears hovering in her eyes. What could she tell Isobel that wouldn't sound as terrible as it actually was?

'I really couldn't say,' she replied in a small voice. She was surprised to hear herself speak. She hadn't meant to say her thoughts out loud. But it was too late. Isobel seemed to gape at her in disbelief, her features seeming to work or twist against something, some violent *impulse*.

'You *really couldn't say?*' Isobel repeated. The words seemed to drip slowly from her lips in great globules of disgust. '*Seriously?* I find that hard to accept.'

Julie tried to meet Isobel's gaze, the eyes that looked red and shining, and suddenly feared for her life. *Edward! Where's Edward?* she thought. *Please, oh please! Let him come back!* And then, like a miracle, from downstairs came the sound of the front door opening, and then closing, with its soft, familiar click. Isobel must have heard it too, because with it Julie saw her face smooth over, the obvious anger folded away and concealed. Isobel reached past her, snatched the copy of *Marley and Me* from off the 'Charity Shop' pile, and smacked it down on top the 'Keep' pile instead. Then, without another word she rose and walked quickly out of the room.

Julie held her breath and stayed very still, waiting to hear Isobel's voice, expecting the exclamation from Edward, and then the thunder of his feet coming up the stairs. Their voices floated up from downstairs – Isobel's bright and normal-sounding, Edward's lower and matter-of-fact. After a few minutes she realised that Isobel must not have said anything. She rang her sister.

'Look, you're just having a wobble,' said Lorraine. 'His sister's a bit off her rocker, he told you that, and now you're jumping to conclusions because of some random crazy shit she came out with. You want my opinion, it sounds like drugs,' Lorraine said. 'Which means it'll never hold up in court. Look,' she said now, 'I've got to go. I'll drop Jas off at yours in a bit, yeah? Oh, and by the way,' said Lorraine, right before the line went dead, 'don't get me wrong. I'm not saying that bitch doesn't have it in for you.'

'Budge up, Jules!' said Isobel boisterously as they all squeezed around a small table. On the walk down Isobel had appeared so abnormally cheerful, and laughed so loudly at everything Edward said, that Julie could hardly believe it was the same person who'd threatened her in the bedroom. The difference was frightening in itself. How false and affected Isobel was. She could see it now. She still felt very shaken and as they ordered their lunch, Isobel seemed to be going out of her way to make her feel even worse. If Isobel wasn't monopolising the conversation, she was ignoring or ridiculing Julie's own contributions – for instance, purposely misunderstanding her role as a teacher. Edward seemed not to notice. As Isobel boomed instructions to the waitress, Julie wondered again why she didn't just come out and say what she wanted to say. She couldn't believe Isobel hadn't already told Edward – or accused her in front of him. What did it mean? If only she'd listened to Edward's warnings about his sister being unstable and unpredictable. She was dangerous as well, judging by her behaviour this morning. Was she biding her time, waiting to get Edward alone? Julie wished she hadn't committed herself to watching Jasmyn, because she was now doomed to spend the whole afternoon wondering and worrying, tormented by all the things Isobel would tell Edward once she was out of the way. She watched Isobel wave her sandwich around, laughing unnaturally and telling Edward how they could sell Mary's furniture and make more money for themselves. *Isobel doesn't care about Mary at all*, Julie thought. A thin, rubbery piece of cheese flopped out from between the crusts of Isobel's sandwich and she waited for it to drop on to the table. The sight of it made her feel ill. Would Isobel spend the week toying with her, like a cat with a mouse? She caught Isobel studying her for a moment, head cocked to one side like a bright-eyed bird. A moment later her gaze moved on, as if not finding Julie very interesting. Everything, Julie decided, must be written down in Isobel's expensive blue leather notebook. Her phone vibrated and she saw it was Lorraine with a text. *Blackmail u??* it said. *Ha ha ha!* Julie slipped the phone back in her bag and tried to calm her breathing. Three breaths, she thought, in through the nose – out through the mouth. Was Lorraine right? Was Isobel going to *blackmail* her? But what could Julie give her? There were the diamond chip stud earrings she got for her birthday last year, and the five hundred and forty-three pounds in her savings account. But such a small sum of money wouldn't impress Isobel, would it? She had nothing Isobel would want. In fact, Julie thought, the only thing in her life that had any value was Edward.

Well, a little voice piped up in her head, *there's your answer, then.*

5

Lucky Cow

Was she stupid, Julie, *Jules*, whatever her name was? The girl couldn't even throw her a bone. Leaving the café, Isobel was determined not to give Edward's girlfriend, creeping out right behind her, the satisfaction of seeing her upset. Instead she crossed the street on the pretence of looking in a shop window and decided to ring her friend Melissa back in New York. Yes, it was true, she told Melissa, that yesterday she'd thought Jules a bit of a nonentity. And then she had started to feel a bit sorry for her and tried to make more of an effort. And then, just now, Isobel continued, she had asked about her mother and what exactly had happened and what she thought Edward was going to do – and the girl had been an utter cow about it! In the glass reflection she watched Jules watching the café door like a devoted lapdog.

'Wait, run that by me again?' said Melissa.

'I *told* you, she was with my mum in the garden on Sunday. When it happened…' Referring to 'it' as anything other than *it* or *that* or even *the thing*, Isobel had found, made her death seem to happen anew.

'Yeah, that part I get – but what Edward's going to do about what?'

Melissa could be weirdly dense, she remembered, and she rephrased. 'Well, she has to know what my brother's intentions are, right? Whether he wants to stay in contact with me after I leave? Or if it'll be, you know, back to business as usual, and us not speaking again.'

'Oh, right. That sounds like a lot for her to answer,' said Melissa.

'What? Really? I think it's pretty simple. I just thought she might have an idea what he was thinking, since they've been together for *years*!' Isobel's voice was rising and she saw Julie glance at her; she turned her back on her and cupped her hand around the phone. 'But that's not the main thing; it's what *happened* that I really need to know about...'

'Okay, hon, I hear you. So did she tell you what went on with your mom?'

'No! I'm sure it's tough for her to talk about, and I acknowledged that; I let her know that I totally get it from her point of view. But what the hell? I have a right to know, don't I? Her reaction just blew me away.' She took a breath. 'And here's the best part: *she couldn't even be bothered* to sound interested in the question! Can you believe it? She sounded utterly bored by my even asking.' It was early in New York, Isobel thought, and she was ranting on and on. But she couldn't seem to help herself. 'And the *way* she said it – *I really couldn't say* – in this snotty little voice, like I'd asked her how to get to the bus stop.'

'Uh-huh,' said Melissa. In the background she heard the faint click of computer keys.

'You're working. I should let you go.'

'Izzy, I'm listening! Keep going.'

'Look, the reason I'm pissed,' she said, trying to take a more measured tone, 'is that it cost me to even *ask*. She's the *only* person I can bloody ask, isn't she? You should have seen how desperate I was. It was so pathetic. Like I was begging permission to ask her a question about my own bloody family in our own bloody house. I was practically grovelling at her feet…'

'Listen, Izzy. I am sorry you're having to go through this, all this ….*crap*, basically.'

'Thanks,' she told Melissa, grateful for her words. 'This thing with her, it's just thrown me for a loop. I can't believe someone would be so *mean*.' It made her furious to think of the girl, grubbing about in her mother's house, poking and pawing through her private things, chucking her favourite book on the trash pile. 'I can't believe I'm saying this,' she went on, 'and I know I said before that she was a bit naff and everything, but for about half an hour back there I'd honestly started to like her. I thought she had a good heart. I thought…I don't know…that maybe I had a friend in her, you know? And now…well, God forbid she might be my sister-in-law one day – can you imagine?' Across the street she saw Edward coming out of the café. 'I'm such an *idiot*…'

They agreed to speak later and hung up. As Jules and Edward walked towards her it started to rain and she saw Jules pull out an umbrella. Edward was almost a foot taller than she was, and she struggled martyrishly to position it over his head until he made an impatient *no, you have it* gesture with his hands. Jules looked at him helplessly, before folding the umbrella back up and following him across the road.

In a perverse kind of way, Isobel decided, once they'd dispatched Julie off to some babysitting job for the afternoon and walked through the drizzle back to the house, she had enjoyed herself at lunch. The change of scene had provided a break from the day's deadening tasks, while in the café Julie's behaviour had confirmed all her recent feelings about the girl – the passive-aggressive nibbling at her salad like some especially sulky species of rodent, and the stopping every once in a while to give Edward one of those sly up-through-the-eyelashes glances Princess Diana used to affect. Did Edward not see the girl for what she was, as she hung all over him, pop-eyed with devotion? She didn't need Jules, she decided, to act as some go-between with Edward. At some point this week she would get up her courage and talk to her brother herself – about the past and their falling-out and their mother and everything else – and, if not this week, he'd read her letters soon enough and realise what a huge misunderstanding it had all been.

'D'you want to have a look through this?' Edward pushed a plastic box of clothing across the carpet towards her.

'Sure,' Isobel said. The task of going through their mother's bedroom – the drawers of underthings, the green enamel alarm clock and the half-glass of water still sitting next to her bed – had been left almost until last. Without its having been delegated specifically, Isobel had been assigned their mother's clothing. It was the first time she and Edward had spent any time alone, and they had been chatting easily enough, back and forth, if in a business-at-hand kind of way. Their mother's potted geraniums were already gone from the front garden, left with a note for Mrs John next door, leaving dark rings staining the crazy paving. At the end of the week, Isobel realised, the house they grew up in would be gone too – the beds stripped, the curtains pulled down, and the floors swept clean. Even the carpets were to be taken up, before the keys could be returned to the landlord. And then the house would be empty, as if neither she nor Edward nor their mother had ever been there.

She lifted out a sleeveless patterned sweater and ran the fabric under her fingers. Conscious of Edward's eyes on her, not wanting to appear to be wasting time, she examined the buttons as if considering whether the item was worth keeping or not. She folded it carefully into the 'Charity Shop' box. Later she would carry the box downstairs to join its counterparts, lined up along the passage like tiny coffins. Edward had been through their mother's papers and put most of them through the shredder. Among the old Christmas cards, he said, were an assortment of receipts and bills dating back to the 1970s, and a ration book from 1951. Did Isobel want any of them?

She got up and opened the heavy brown wardrobe. There were far more skirts and jeans and belts and dresses than she could remember her mother ever wearing. *My own fault*, Isobel thought, *for encouraging her to go digging about in the local thrift stores*. It was heartrending, the neatly folded jumpers and cardigans, the trousers hung carefully on their hangers. She took everything out and piled it on the bed and, catching faint whiffs of her mother's perfume, realised that she finally understood all those embarrassing scenes in films where people staggered into the bedroom closets of the recent dead to bury their noses in all their jackets and shirts and dresses.

'Chuck 'em?' said Edward, holding up a pair of sneakers. They had bought these in Eastbourne together, when their mother had started going to the gym. White, with a smart green stripe, the design had recently become cool again.

'Yep,' she told Edward. 'Chuck 'em.'

At six o'clock they finished for the day, and without much hope, promising herself it would be her last attempt, she asked Edward if he fancied grabbing a quick drink down at the Peeping Tom. In the middle of locking the door, he paused for a second as if actually considering it, and then, to her amazement, he turned and shrugged, and said simply, 'Yes, might as well. Why not?'

Yes, might as well. Why not? She couldn't believe her ears. It sounded so ordinary, Isobel thought, so casual – and yet it meant everything. 'So when I was at the pub with Edward…' she could tell Chris later, even as her next thought was, *I can't wait to tell Mum…*

'I could murder a scotch,' said Edward as they walked in. The place was quiet and dark with that friendly, familiar beer smell, Isobel realised, that pubs back in the US lacked. One or two older men were seated alone in corners, while from the kitchen came the occasional sound of pots and pans banging – but otherwise they seemed to have the place to themselves. 'Crisps?' said Edward as they approached the bar.

'Ooh, *crisps!*' she replied with a bit too much enthusiasm, 'Yes, please.'

'Crisp shortage over there, then?' said Edward quizzically.

'No, but they're not the same,' she replied. 'And for some reason they call them chips.'

'Indeed,' said Edward, looking satisfied as he asked the barman for one salt and vinegar and two packets of cheese and onion. That he remembered her favourite flavour gave Isobel a silly sort of hope. She asked if he minded sitting at the bar and Edward shrugged. She preferred the bar, Isobel explained, even in a proper restaurant, because it was more entertaining – sitting at a table, you might as well stay home.

For the first few minutes they turned to what Edward called the 'boring-but-important' stuff concerning the rest of the week – the humanist minister, who judging by her voice, Isobel informed him, sounded like a rather jolly-hockey-sticks type. Edward had confirmed the front room and catering at the Brentwood Inn after the service. Meanwhile the house would need 'a last big push' tomorrow, he said, which meant another early start in the morning.

'Doubt Mum's friends are big boozers,' he said, 'but we'll put some money behind the bar, just in case,'

'Good idea,' she agreed. How long had it been, she wondered as their drinks arrived, since they had agreed about anything? So far, they had managed to work through the week almost as one mind, settling everything – the disposing of their mother's possessions, what to keep and what to throw away, the type of service and who would preside over it – in sensible, grown-up voices, without a single point of disagreement. And yet, she thought, these were the only things they'd concerned themselves with. There had been no mention of the past, or of her or Edward's day-to-day lives. She had enquired about his job, but he'd been very vague.

She watched him take another careful sip of his scotch.

'You can always have another one,' she said. 'I don't think there's a scotch shortage here, not like with crisps in New York.' But Edward seemed not to have caught the joke, instead giving her a suspicious look, as if she were aiding and abetting a drunk driver. 'You're not driving,' she reminded him. 'You're taking the train back, right?'

'Yes, you're right,' said Edward. 'I forgot.' He smiled wearily. 'Out of the habit lately. I can't say we're out socialising that much.'

'You're allowed to take a bit of time out for yourself, though, aren't you?' she said, adding quickly: 'I mean, you both are,' in case he thought this was some elliptical and critical reference to Julie – which it was, of course. It was an added bonus that the girl was safely ensconced at home, and she could imagine Jules's ears straining to hear Edward's key in the door – a greedy bird listening for worms, beady eyes stuck to the clock.

'She's been a real help to me this week, actually,' said Edward.

Isobel considered this idea. Had Jules been 'a real help' to Edward? If so, how, exactly? Hadn't she, Isobel, been a real help as well? Didn't she deserve some credit?

'Oh, sure,' she told him. 'Though I've not gotten a chance to get her know her properly yet.' As Edward nodded vaguely, she dived in. 'I really was hoping to talk to her,' she said. 'Being that she was with Mum when it happened.'

She was painfully aware that either Julie or Edward – or both – would have been privy to their mother's last words – if there were any. But Edward was clearly reluctant to discuss any of it, not even this one basic fact.

'Right, no, yes,' said Edward, picking his drink up again.

'And you were at the hospital…' she ploughed on, as Edward shifted on his stool and gazed off uncomfortably towards the bar like a VIP cornered at a party. 'Look, I know it's not easy to talk about.'

It was ridiculous, Isobel thought, feeling obliged to strategise, to gently tack the conversation across towards their mother – the spectre at the feast! – with the air of a supplicant. Why on earth should she have to walk on eggshells, to explain herself and justify her own interest in the subject? She knew why, of course. The fear of another row, another descent into ill-feeling and never speaking again. And yet, Isobel thought, the fact remained that Edward had been there when she could not be. Edward had been present for their mother's last, precious minutes of life, as her heart ticked fainter and fainter and finally – unbelievably – stopped. He had witnessed the death of someone they both loved. Did he really have nothing to tell her about it? Edward might well feel there was little to say, or that what there was might be upsetting, but as they stared ahead at the bar and the silence deepened it felt far worse not knowing. He should just suck it up, Isobel thought, just as she would, were their positions reversed. She had a natural right to know, however meagre the information, or however ill-advised it might seem to him to convey it. 'If I could, I would have been there myself,' she said, as calmly as she could manage.

A pensive look crossed Edward's face and he cleared his throat as if about to say something. And then he picked up his glass and drained it in one gulp, as if he had thought better of it. 'I expect we'll get to it at some point,' he said, and she wondered who the 'we' meant and if it included her. *I have to say something else*, Isobel thought, no matter the risk. *I have to*. But, as Edward stared blankly, she didn't trust herself to do it.

'Same again?' she said, indicating his empty glass. Maybe more alcohol would draw him out.

'Okay. Yes. Thanks,' Edward said, brightening.

There was another lull in the conversation.

'Look ...' he said, and she waited. 'Those two over there ...'

'What?'

He nodded behind her towards the entrance, and she turned to see an older couple walking towards them. The man was nondescript, but the woman was wearing a tailored man's shirt of the sort their mother favoured and had something about her. As she came closer, Isobel saw that there was also a familiarity to the way she had arranged her hair, which was a grey-blonde, pale and fine and fluffed up delicately around her face, as if to give the illusion of volume and make the very most of it. From a distance the resemblance was striking – the shirt, the hair. 'I never realised how many women there are in this town who look just like Mum,' Edward said.

'It's true,' she told him, and, seeing his broken expression, she felt her anger towards him lift and dissipate. The couple passed them and disappeared, arm in arm, in the direction of the garden. At first glance you could easily make the mistake. In a more unhinged moment, Isobel thought, she could see herself chasing one of these tall, unsuspecting lookalikes down the high street.

'Have to get more bin bags tomorrow,' Edward said. The barman had come out from behind his counter and was making a round of the room. As he passed, he nodded across at their empty glasses. 'Same again?'

'Thanks,' Edward told him.

'I can pick some up on my way over,' she said. 'Bin bags, I mean.' They must have filled dozens today, all bulging with coats and jeans and jumpers and shirts. She pictured them rejoining some huge, eternally tumbling circle of garments that made its way round and round town via all the charity shops, recycled and purchased by women who looked like their mother, and returned at some unspecified and sorrowful date, to be taken up by someone else.

'We need to get a move on getting everything down to the charity shops tomorrow as well,' said Edward, just as she said,

'—I can't believe she's just gone.'

Her words – blurted and unconsidered – were in such contrast to Edward's immensely practical statement that she felt her face ablaze with embarrassment.

'I know,' said Edward softly, looking into his own drink with a defeated air, and she wished that one of them could say something more or better, something that might acknowledge, in some human way, that their mother was dead – and how stupid and shitty and deeply absurd this was.

'Gareth at work – his mum died a few years ago. I remember going over to his cubicle to say a few words. I thought I was being really decent and good, going in person, not tapping out a message on the computer.'

'What did you say?'

'"Sorry for your loss"?' Edward gave a hollow laugh.

'*Sorry for your loss*?' She had to admit, this did seem rather lame. 'Really? Was that it?'

'Yep. A tepid pile of old wank.'

'*Sorry for your loss*,' she repeated. 'Jesus, even the up-selling undertaker didn't use that one.'

Edward laughed.

'Okay, so you win that round,' she said. 'So what happened to her?' she said, after a pause.

'Sorry?' Over the rim of his glass, Edward regarded her warily.

'Gareth's mum?'

'Oh. Right. Alzheimer's. Well, sort of.'

'How awful …'

'Yeah, but it was worse than that. Apparently she decided to put an end to it before it got too bad.'

'Switzerland? You can't blame her for that …'

'No, of course not. But that's not what I mean. I doubt she had the ability to get herself to the airport by then anyway. Or remember where the airport was or what it does.'

'And there's the rub,' she said.

'Yes. You can promise yourself to end it when it gets bad. But the instinct is to hang on and hang on. And then one day you wake up and it's too bloody late, isn't it?' He tore open a bag of crisps and offered it to her.

'Thanks.' She took one. 'I hogged all mine.'

'I noticed,' said Edward. 'Anyway, Gareth had gone away on assignment for a couple of weeks. His mother was fine when he left, but when he got back—'

'What? Died?'

'Hold your horses, I'm getting to it...'

'Sorry.'

'So he found her when he got back.'

'Found her where? At the airport?'

'On the sofa,' said Edward. 'With a plastic bag over her head.'

'What? And she was...gone?'

'Well, yes. I would have thought so.'

'Dead?'

'Gone. Dead,' said Edward. 'Passed on,' he added, with mock-solemnity. 'Deceased...'

'Don't!' she said, trying to stop the laughter. 'It shouldn't be funny...'

'Demised,' Edward went on. 'Shuffled off her mortal coil...'

'Seriously,' she said, 'that's a God-awful way to go. I'd rather take pills, wouldn't you?'

'I'd rather not have to kill myself in the first place,' said Edward, 'if you're asking.' He appeared to study a row of bottles lined up on the bar. She wondered if their conversation was going to peter out again like the end of a volley.

'Well, I certainly hope you'll bundle me on to a plane to Switzerland when my time comes,' she told him.

'Duly noted,' said Edward, and she felt the years shrink for a moment, put in mind of their younger selves, walking along the pier feeding chips to the seagulls and snidely commenting on passers-by.

'Actually,' she said, 'did she leave a note?'

'Sorry?' That look again – wary, slightly fearful.

'Gareth's mum. Did she leave a letter or anything?'

'Oh, right. She did, depressingly enough. Apologising to Gareth, and enclosing some money for the electricity bill.'

'That's the saddest thing I ever heard ...' All the ways you could die, she thought – Alzheimer's and dementia, MS and cancer and stroke – diseases that dismantled you piece by piece and gave you a ringside seat to the whole performance. There were choices, she supposed, once you were diagnosed – the blood-filled bath, the slow strangulation in the hotel closet, the hose stuck in the car window. Or jumping off Beachy Head and having time to think about it all the way down. And then there were the 'silent killers' – the aneurysm that felled you like an axe, blown up from the inside – or the Eurostar, she thought, feeling slightly crazy. The train moved so quietly along the tracks that cows straying on to the line failed to get out of the way before being struck down. They never heard it coming. Had their mother been lucky? Had she known what was happening, the haemorrhage bursting in her brain like a blooming and bloody fast-motion flower?

'It could be worse,' she told Edward. 'You know, if you think about it.'

'Yes,' agreed Edward. 'Worse.'

'Worse than Mum, I meant,' she said.

'Yeah, I know.' A thin smile. 'Worse,' he repeated, and for the first time she noticed that he was slurring his words.

'Drink to that, then,' she said.

'Cheers.' Edward drained his glass.

For a while they watched people coming in and out of the door to the beer garden. The bar was in full swing now with an after-work crowd, while along from them three thirty-something men with suit jackets thrown over their arms ordered a round of vodka-cranberries in important voices.

For the last fifteen minutes the men had been trying to chat up a group of bored-looking women in office-appropriate skirts and tops. At weekends, Isobel thought, there would be the young families Edward had mentioned – greying fathers and harassed-looking mothers trying to keep their kids amused in the beer garden and braving the chilly sea mist that in summer never failed to descend by the late afternoon. As children, Isobel remembered, they had come to this exact pub with their mother and various boyfriends – afternoons of shandy and cheeky sips of beer, and raucous hide and seek under the tables. Did Edward remember those days? Then again, maybe now was not the time to bring up the past, Isobel thought, not any of it. They had made real progress this evening – why rock the boat?

'Got time for another one?' she asked him.

'Your shout?' said Edward. She nodded. 'In that case, yeah, sod it. You only live once.'

Thursday

Nothing to Write Home About

'Edward…I don't understand.' Her voice was vulnerable and beseeching, like that of a child. Edward was furious with himself. How could he not have known? He should never have left the hospital. He should have waited with her, instead of believing the doctors, instead of assuming the worst. After he left, she had woken up and made her way back to Danecroft Road. Where were all her things? she asked. 'I'll get them all back,' he told her, and thought of the rhyme about the ladybird, her house on fire, her children all gone. Edward was his mother's son, and he was still here, wasn't he? 'I'll get it all back,' he promised, 'there's still time…' but it was a lie. Then he remembered that it was the bank holiday. The black bags he'd put out earlier for the bin men – they would still be there. He left her and went to the front door, but the bags were gone. At least there were the things they'd donated. He would return to each one and make his case. They were charity shops, after all. They would understand. And if not he would offer to buy it all back. He set off, but halfway along Cairncross Road the air grew stiff and syrupy and he found himself having to reach down with his hands and physically pull his legs along, until what felt like centuries later he reached the high street, only to find the shops closed, the windows dark. *Closed for the bank holiday.* He would have to go back and tell her what happened. He wondered how his mother would feel about being dead. Or rather, about Edward thinking she was dead. Now that he'd decided to tell the truth his legs seemed to move more easily and he started to jog. He found he could run, and he ran faster and faster, amazed by the speed of it, his body feeling light as air yet moving with purpose, his limbs part of a well-oiled machine. Then, as he sprinted effortlessly through the twitten, he happened to glance down and saw that his legs had disappeared, and he woke, gasping for breath, as his own bedroom took shape around him, the thin, watery light filtering through the curtains and the dreadful, flat realisation of her death washed through him all over again.

He sat up abruptly and too late felt his brain slide and crash into the side of his skull like a lump of hot mercury. He lowered himself back down and put his hand to his forehead in a fruitless attempt to steady the movement. Last night a drink with Isobel had seemed like the least-bad option, the alternative being to return to the flat and risk crossing paths with either Jules's niece or, worse, her sister, who tended to linger when she came to collect any of her kids. He tried to bring up the details but could only remember eating crisps and Isobel trying to tip the barman. The alcohol must have greased the wheels because he seemed to recall them slipping into an easy banter – like an echo of the short, not unhappy interlude between Isobel coming out of hospital and the day, just over two years later, when they had stopped speaking.

At first even their mother had written it off as typical high-strung Isobel and nothing to worry about. Then her mood swings had segued into bizarre delusions and hallucinations, and her behaviour had become more difficult to explain away. Remarkably, Edward remembered, it was Isobel herself, caught in the midst of it, who had seemed to recognise the severity of her situation and taken herself to see the doctor. Edward had broken the news to their mother and offered to take Isobel there – insisted, really, for their mother's sake. She would worry so much more if she actually set eyes on the place. As it turned out, the hospital was situated in a quiet residential street. He was struck by how normal it looked, even on the inside, white and bright, with high ceilings. Outside were gardens and winding gravel pathways. It wasn't half as bad as he thought it would be, Edward had decided, as he sat waiting for Isobel on a nearby empty bed, though he noticed the metal strips nailed to all the window frames. Then the nurse drew back the curtain and he saw Isobel seated on the narrow hospital bed with her hands in her lap, docile and sad-eyed. The nurse informed them it was time to say goodbye and he went over and sat next to her. 'It could be worse,' Isobel said, before he could think of what to say. 'This is the least bad option.'

A-levels were abandoned, the idea of Oxbridge thrown over, and after six weeks and a course of medication his sister

– to everyone's surprise – came out of the hospital and found a job waitressing at a hotel. Their mother was still concerned, so during his first year at Imperial most weekends he found himself catching the train down from London to check up on both of them. He would arrive on a Saturday morning and he and Isobel would spend a pleasant afternoon together. Afterwards, depending on Isobel's work schedule, they would go to see their mother. At first his sister had appeared fragile and quiet. He tried not to pry or burden her with questions, but spent a good deal of his time wondering whether to mention the hospital – or whether it was better not to. He felt guilty about leaving her there and was grateful when Isobel didn't bring it up either. In time she was more forthcoming, more like her old self, and feeling relieved, he let her lead the conversation. It was better anyway, their mother had advised, to let Isobel talk. Although she was concerned that it was all a bit of an inconvenience for Edward – wasn't it? Trekking down from London every week, neglecting his friends and his studies? Not such an ordeal, Edward assured her, and realised that this was true. He looked forward to his visits with Isobel, to their long, meandering talks, the random subjects which were neither past nor future, but rather some odd passer-by or a film they had been to see or the contents of the various shop windows as they wandered aimlessly round town. As the months went by Isobel seemed to grow less watchful and more confident and he began to feel that the hospital had ultimately been a good idea, that it hadn't been a mistake to leave her there. His sister still came out with the odd far-fetched story – one tall tale involved her serving drinks to a famous film director and his producer and then the hotel's manager letting her off her shift to attend a film première.

Next to him the radio started up with its reassuring Radio 4 voices, and gingerly he reached over and pressed the 'off' button. He lay back down and tried to remember when it was that Isobel had developed her obsession with New York. Of course, Edward remembered, he knew exactly when it was. They'd been to a matinee showing of a Woody Allen film and as they left the cinema his sister had been unusually animated and had announced, with her customary impracticality, that she was *going to save up and move to New York*! 'Yes, but what would you do there?' he'd asked. 'You'd need work papers.' Even before her 'episode', it was so like his sister to have these outlandish ideas, verging on the incoherent, and think they could actually be carried out. 'Well, obviously,' Isobel had said impatiently as if Edward had brought up a somewhat irrelevant point. 'but what's that got to do with the price of carrots?' He couldn't believe what he was hearing. 'You mean you're going to just pack up and leave? Just like that? Isobel, you've never even been to New York.' He had decided to humour her, to adopt a less oppositional stance. 'What if you don't like it?' 'But I will like it, Edward,' she had replied, and grinned as if this were the most obvious thing in the world.

From the kitchen, he heard the banging of cupboards and plates – surprisingly loud for Jules, Edward thought, who was generally considerate when he needed a lie-in; maybe it was just the effects of his hangover. Somehow he would have to get himself out of bed and into the kitchen with some sort of decorum. Carefully he shifted his hips and tried to get into a sitting position. Both his head and knees throbbed in response. *Getting old*, Edward thought, as in ultra-slow-motion he brought his feet on to the floor and felt a searing pain in the sole of his right foot. '*Fuck!*' He looked down and saw what looked like part of a doll's head with a piece of glittery wire or thread wound around it. Something about the moulded plastic hair looked familiar

– probably it belonged to Jules's niece – he was too bloody aggravated to work it out – plus he now had to worry about the cat swallowing some other missing part of the thing. Jules wasn't usually this careless. He bent down and another sickening wallop vibrated through his head. Had his hangovers always been this bad? he wondered, managing to stand up. The light in the room was leaden and low-wattage and hurt his eyes. Outside, a low canopy of heavy clouds raced over the anonymous houses, the grimy windows with their scragged-back net curtains and wilting pot plants. His mind drifted forward to the next weekend at Danecroft Road. If it didn't rain there would be raking to do and grass to be composted, Edward thought, before catching himself, as he had numerous times since Sunday.

He found Jules in the kitchen dressed in neat-looking jeans and a freshly ironed T-shirt, her hair brushed and tied back. Not like himself, Edward thought enviously, lurching in, zombie-like, in his raggedy pyjama bottoms and – he realised, looking down – last night's shirt. She had her back to him as he approached, a small saucepan in her hand, poised midway between the sink and the cooker, seemingly transfixed by something at the window. 'Morning,' he said a second time, and she turned, looking startled, and he had a fleeting sense of intruding, of interrupting some private reverie.

'Oh,' she said, as if not expecting to see him there. 'Edward...'

'Yarp,' he said, and with great care lowered himself down to the table.

'Coffee?' suggested Jules. 'What about some eggs?' As she placed his coffee cup down on the table the sound seemed to shatter the air around him and reverberate like a sonic boom. Was it the effect of his hangover, Edward wondered blearily, or had Jules put his cup down rather sharply?

'No, that's all right,' he replied. 'Thanks, though.' The smell of eggs – the sight of them – even the *thought* of them, Edward thought, sliding and wobbling across the frying pan like massive islands of phlegm – was enough to make him heave. His sister hated eggs, he remembered, and anything that tasted *eggy*. 'Maybe some toast?' he suggested.

'I've got some in the toaster,' said Jules.

'Can you remind me to pick up my suit from the dry-cleaners later?' He had had the foresight – God knows how – to drop his suit off on Tuesday, in preparation for tomorrow. He lifted the cup to his lips and took a small, experimental sip. Scalding hot, exactly how he liked it.

On the table, under the *FT*, was something that looked like a tabloid. 'They delivered the wrong paper again,' he told Jules, sliding it out.

'Didn't you phone them about it?' said Jules over her shoulder.

Tabloids really were a guilty pleasure, which would explain why he kept forgetting to complain about it. SICKO SLAVE CAKE RITUAL, blared the front page. The print made his eyes hurt and his stomach lurch, and reluctantly he pushed the paper away again. He had little appetite for its outrage today. Breakfast was a placid time – an idea Jules found funny for some reason, though never during the *morning grump* itself, as they had named it – and they laughed about that too. They had a good life, Edward thought, he and Jules. There was something to be said for it, the comforting rhythms and rituals of domestic life, for clean sheets and a full belly.

He watched as Jules moved from the sink to the cooker and back again. Funny, Edward thought: though he couldn't quite put his finger on it, there was something different about her this morning. Had she done her hair in a new way? He couldn't tell. Maybe she had PMT or whatever it was. Then again, what with the week they were having he could hardly blame Jules if she was behaving more like Edward usually did at this hour. *And yet*, Edward thought, that wasn't quite it either, was it? He watched as Jules lifted two pallid-looking slices of bread out of the toaster, apparently forgetting that he preferred his toast almost burnt. There was, Edward remembered, the possibly glaring fact that he had come home rather late last night – and possibly a bit the worse for wear. But when had Jules been one to disapprove or to police his actions? Women really were a puzzle. The last thing he remembered was Isobel getting off the train, two stops before his, and telling him to put his ticket in his wallet. How had he made his way from there to here? From the station to the flat? Had he walked? Or got a taxi? A hazy memory floated into his head of the roundabout flashing past, and a taxi driver helping him up the front steps to the flat.

'Must've got in a bit late,' he said by way of apology. 'I hope I didn't wake you up.'

'I was asleep,' replied Jules. There was a pause. 'Your drink with your sister, how was it?' she said. Was he imagining it, Edward thought, or was there a weird, gleaming edge to this question?

'Oh, it was all right, I suppose,' he said. Better to wait and see where the conversation was going, before committing to any sort of… *strategy*. Amateurs made that mistake all the time, rushing in with explanations. Besides, having a drink with his sister hardly merited an excuse, did it? 'Shouldn't have had that third one, though,' he added with a laugh, and the effort sent a new pain through his head.

'Mm,' said Jules, continuing to bang plates together in the sink. He was beginning to feel like a stand-up comedian, trapped in a pub basement with a bad audience, laughing at his own jokes. As Jules performed another excessively lengthy and head-piercing manoeuvre, Edward resigned himself to the prospect of not being able to have his hangover in peace.

'She spoke to that minister woman,' he said. 'The humanist.'

'Who, your sister?' said Jules, over her shoulder, with a breezy air that felt to Edward slightly put-on. Another non-BAFTA-winning pretence at nonchalance, he thought to himself.

'Yes, right after lunch yesterday, when we got back to the house. She wanted to know a bit more about Mum's life.' He paused. No response. 'Isobel gave her some notes, apparently,' he added, as if delivering the punchline. 'Can you imagine what she said!' It was another failed injection of levity into an uphill, multi-layered conversation, a potential assault course he could do without negotiating his way through this morning.

'No,' said Jules, 'what did she say?'

'Well, I don't know,' he said, confused. 'That's the point.' He was starting to feel very much on the back foot, as his boss might put it, although he couldn't for the life of him work out why – and why, for that matter, he felt the need to defend himself. Jules made a huffy 'mmff' noise. He wondered if he'd broken something or been sick on the carpet and forgotten about it. He couldn't have been that rat-arsed, surely.

'You just discussed all the arrangements and things with her, then?' said Jules.

'With Isobel? Yep, we got it all sorted pretty quickly.'

There was another odd little silence, and then Jules said, 'So what did you talk about the rest of the time?'

He was unsure how to answer this. In part because he could barely remember what he and Isobel had talked about, but mainly because this was an unusual line of questioning from Jules. It verged on an actual 'tactic', Edward decided, more like the kettling-type questioning he'd expect from a TV litigator – or Jules's sister Lorraine.

'Nothing much really,' he said. 'I feel a bit sorry for her, to be honest.' This was nonsense, of course. One of the tricks to mollifying women and their concerns, Edward had learned, was to express pity for someone rather than let them think you'd had a jolly nice time *with* that person, and *without* them. Not that he and Isobel had had some mad night out, or not that he could recall. They'd had a few drinks. And he'd only agreed to *them* through a sense of *realpolitik* – to avoid Lorraine – so it was a perfectly logical decision – if one that he couldn't very well share with Jules.

'Do you? Why?' Jules turned to look at him now, face-on.

'Do I why what?' he asked, befuddled. His girlfriend really was being very strange and difficult. He felt himself being inextricably and unexpectedly drawn into some tedious couples rigmarole.

'Why do you feel sorry for her? For your sister?'

'Oh,' he said, and found himself considering the idea. 'I don't know, really. I think... perhaps I've been a bit hard on her. You know, leaving her on her own at Mum's house the first night and everything.'

'Mm,' said Jules. 'By the way,' she added, 'you never told me you'd been to America.' There was an unfamiliar pitch to her voice, bordering on shrill, the tension singing right underneath like a violin string pulled taut and ready to snap.

'Sorry?' He laughed. 'Ages ago, yes. I spent barely a few days there. I'm sure I told you.'

'No,' replied Jules, briskly drying her hands on a dish towel. 'You never mentioned it.'

What's brought all this on? Edward thought. Jules was right, of course: he had never mentioned the visit – a sin of omission, rather than an all-out lie. She had never asked, and he had never felt like bringing it up, part and parcel as it was with the spectre of Isobel.

'Why do you ask?' he said. He was careful to keep his own voice modulated, confined to some neutral conversational register. 'Was it something Isobel said …?' He took a stealthy gulp of his coffee and wondered what was coming next.

'I don't remember,' said Jules, vaguely.

Obviously it was bloody Isobel! His sister was the only person who could have told her.

'I see,' he said. He let the words drop and allowed the silence to gather. He caught Jules glancing quickly down and sensed that he had gained the upper hand. It would be bloody Isobel, he thought, making trouble, and for a brief moment he forgot his earlier words, the pity and feeling sorry for her, and felt instead the familiar annoyance flaring up behind his eyes, his head seeming to throb with a lumpy purple shape the size of a potato. Why did Isobel have to dredge up the past, and with Jules, of all people? Had the women compared notes or passed some judgement on him? He thought of Isobel, constantly writing things down in that stupid notebook she carried everywhere. At lunch yesterday he had considered the idea and written it off to paranoia, to feeling tired and stressed out.

He looked at Jules's pensive, slightly anxious expression and decided that this wasn't worth puzzling over. She had virtually accused him of hiding something from her, but it wasn't true. His visit to New York didn't seem real – not then, and certainly not now, years later, when it had so little relevance to his present life. He had been so young then. Young and naïve and the world still full of possibilities.

'To be honest, it was so long ago I'd almost forgotten about it myself,' he said, truthfully.

'What was it like?' She put the dishtowel on the counter and sat down opposite him. Her face was expectant, like a child waiting for a bedtime story. He stirred his coffee and for the first time in a long time pondered the answer.

'It's hard to remember now,' he told her. 'I suppose everything was exactly how you'd imagine it.'

'Yes...?'

It wasn't enough, Edward knew. Worse, he sounded like a moron. And yet, he was speaking the truth, and this was his first impression of the place. 'Skyscrapers...' he offered inanely. 'You know, like in films...'

'Films...' Jules echoed. That's torn it, Edward thought. Why had he gone and brought bloody Hollywood into the discussion? He'd made it sound far too glamorous and interesting. He'd made it sound exactly how it was.

As a young man he had been curious about America and hadn't known what to expect – the Wild West, or the Midwestern plains with its suburban families, and everywhere the advert smiles as white as picket fences. On the bus from the airport his sister had been full of it, and Edward was irked to be relegated to the status of a tourist. Then the bus let them off, outside Grand Central Station, and this was all forgotten. He stood in the street with his head tipped backwards, unable to help himself, trying to take in the sheer density of the city, the meaning of the cathedral-height buildings and the canyon-sided streets stretching as far as the eye could see like a lesson in perspective. 'It's definitely not London,' he told Isobel. 'You can say that again,' she replied, grinning. Sprawling, unmanageable London, Edward thought, with its endless grey, drizzled-on swathes of terraced houses and low-level buildings. He put up with it for uni, but, given a choice, who would choose to live in such a place? Isobel let them inside her flat and he couldn't believe how tiny it was. When you opened the front door it immediately bumped into the one leading to the bathroom. To their right was a miniature kitchen. 'Come and check this out,' said Isobel. He followed her back to the kitchen where she turned on all the taps and they both stared at the steaming water rushing into the sink. 'Look – heat and hot water included!' she said. They went back into the teeny-tiny hallway where Isobel cracked open the door to the wardrobe-sized bathroom and flicked on the light. He peered inside and glimpsed insects, sent scattering at the corners of his vision. 'Oh, yeah, roaches,' declared Isobel, waving a dismissive hand. And then, seeing his aghast expression, 'Not a big deal, is it?' The other thing that was not a big deal, Edward found out that night, was the pub-cum-club located right underneath them. There was no sign to indicate that it was there – but, 'That's the point,' said Isobel. 'This flat – it's like living in "The Tell-Tale Heart",' Edward had observed, rather brilliantly, and Isobel had looked hurt.

They spent their days wandering the city, much as they had in England on those Saturday afternoons, and, since the nightclub under Isobel's apartment kept them awake, half the night as well. He met her friends, of which she seemed to have an extraordinary number and variety. They were nice enough, interesting too. If his sister had gone searching for the Land of Misfit Toys, Edward remembered thinking, she had found it. Near the end of his stay, he had admitted to Isobel that she was right: if you lived in New York you could walk out of wherever you lived, any time of the day or night, and have a one-in-three chance of something interesting or improbable happening. More remarkably, Edward had noticed, this happened whether or not you sought it out, spoke to anyone, spent any money, or made any effort whatsoever beyond minding your own business and simply walking along the road. The city was compact and intense, humming with activity and interest, with subways and buses and shops that never closed. You might not want a Mars bar at 3am, but the option of acquiring one was there. He saw too that his sister appeared more stable – that, in spite of the tiny apartment and the cockroaches, and the dead-end sort of job in a trendy cinema selling cappuccinos, Isobel was happy.

'So what are your plans for the future?' he'd asked her one evening as they sat in Tompkins Square Park.

'Proper chocolate,' she had sighed. 'It's the one thing you can't get here.' The giant bar of Fruit & Nut that he'd brought from England was already half gone. The park was full of tramps but they weren't dangerous, Isobel had assured him. And almost no one got mugged in Central Park any more, she'd added. 'One day you'll be able to walk through Central Park at night-time,' she predicted.

He'd had to laugh at that one. 'I mean your plans for work,' he said. 'For your career.'

'Plans?' Isobel had echoed. 'Hmm. Something in films, I guess. Not sure what yet.' She broke off another square of chocolate. 'I don't fancy acting,' she added. On the contrary, Edward thought, he could see his sister as an actress, sweeping through restaurants in a ballgown, dashing off autographs for dazzled admirers.

'So you won't stay at the cinema?'

'No fear! It's so boring. Maybe production? I have an interview next week.'

'Oh, who with?' He was unsure what 'production' involved. The phrase 'productive cough' was all that came to mind.

'Some company that's starting a film festival in the city.'

'Is that the one with Robert de Niro?' Hadn't he read something about this in the Sunday papers?

'No,' said Isobel, 'a different one.'

'Well, that sounds interesting,' he said, and hoped he didn't sound patronising or disapproving.

'Yeah,' Isobel continued. 'So I'll probably do that for a while, and then I'll see.' For Isobel, Edward thought, whose New York self appeared less brittle and more confident, it was like merely deciding which profession would be the lucky recipient of her presence, which thing she would alight upon, like a child selecting a fairy cake in a shop window. New York had done wonders for her. Perhaps the city had even saved her.

'Edward?' Jules was speaking to him.

'Sorry?' he said. She was scrutinising him intently. Were they about to have an argument, he wondered, or was Jules simply curious? His head throbbed and at that moment he realised that he couldn't tell what she was thinking. 'Sorry, what were you saying?' he said.

'No, *you* were saying,' she said. '*You* were saying, Edward. About New York. You said it's like in films.' The city had looked exactly like the one in the Woody Allen film, he thought. It was just as incredible as Isobel had said it would be. Had he just told Jules this? He couldn't remember. All of a sudden he felt overcome by tiredness.

'Yes,' he agreed. 'Just what you'd expect. It was nothing to write home about.'

Wednesday

The Apex Predator

It wasn't as if she was prying, thought Julie, or deliberately going through Edward's personal things. The truth was, she'd found the letters quite by accident. That afternoon Lorraine was late dropping off Jasmyn, and then the rain started pelting down and they ended up staying indoors. Jasmyn seemed happy enough, arranging her toys and dolls on the bedroom floor, directing them in various dramas, so Julie decided to catch up with some housework. Several times she found herself in the middle of sweeping up slivers of vegetable peelings behind the bin, or on her knees on a folded towel about to clean the inside of the oven, only to hear the child calling to the cat, and once more she'd have to immediately stop what she was doing and go in to check the girl was okay. You heard about it all the time, cats smothering babies and young children, and when Jasmyn was at the flat Happy Meal – who slunk about as if up to something or at least planning it – made her feel very on edge. She took the duster from the hook behind the kitchen door and ran it over all the surfaces in the lounge. She couldn't help remembering how different the cat had been the night she'd found him – a weak, shivering ball of wet fur cowering under a car. Somehow she had managed to lure him out and carry him indoors, where she'd found an old comb, laid out newspapers on the kitchen floor, and got down on her knees to tease out the animal's matted, blood-encrusted fur. It had taken some time and she'd received several scratches for her trouble – all of it, really, for Edward's sake, knowing he was fond of animals. And because she couldn't bring herself to pretend she'd never seen the cat because that would be an untruth. In time it had fallen to Julie to feed him and top up his water bowl, but, despite her efforts, Happy Meal had never taken to her. When they settled themselves in front of the telly in the evenings it was Edward whose lap he curled up on. After Edward left for the early train in the mornings, Happy Meal would slope off outside after a patch of sunshine to stretch out in. Arriving home after school, she might catch his shadow looming briefly between the window and the curtains, but he rarely came out to greet her. When Edward walked in each night he called out to the cat before he'd even taken off his tie or asked Julie how her day was. And then Happy Meal would come creeping out from under or behind something, running at a surprising speed for an animal of its size and bulk, lumbering round the corner almost on two legs.

When Jasmyn was round, it was Happy Meal's habit to heave himself up on to the television and remain there until her niece had left. How he was capable of jumping up that high was beyond her. He would switch his tail and eye the child in a way that looked calculating and evil. Once or twice she had mentioned this behaviour to Edward. His reaction – aside from implying that children who were bitten or attacked by animals were asking for it – was to laugh. '*Pounce*?' he said. 'Like some sort of *apex predator*?' Happy Meal was overweight, she replied, but didn't that make him even more dangerous, more easily able to sit on a small child and suffocate it?

A shrill cry came from the bedroom and she dropped the cushion in her hand and rushed into the bedroom to find Jasmyn staring up at her as if threatening to burst into tears. There was no sign of Happy Meal. 'What is it, Jas?' she said. 'What happened?'

'Na,' said Jasmyn.

Much as she loved her niece, Julie thought, a whole afternoon of it, the endless questions and sudden tears over nothing, did tend to get on her nerves. What did the child want? And what was Julie expected to do about it? 'It's always something, Jas, isn't it?' Jasmyn was like the television, she thought, the way you could leave her in a room and she would carry on talking anyway. Yet with the child in the flat Julie felt constantly on tenterhooks, fearful of things being knocked over or into or that surfaces were being covered in invisible sticky fingerprints.

Jasmyn wandered off, and when Julie went out into the hallway she found her niece drawing spidery felt-tip flowers on the sides of Mary's cardboard boxes. After their long days at Danecroft Road she and Edward had been too tired to do anything except lug the boxes in from the car, stack them against the wall, and fall exhausted into bed. She gazed at the growing pile in dismay. To get to the front door you now had to squeeze yourself through an ever narrower pathway. What was it Isobel said earlier about couples and their 'baggage'? Maybe she would make a start on going through Mary's boxes. Better to focus on what you could control, as her book advised, than on these upsetting thoughts of Isobel and what she was saying or not saying. She regretted it now, of course, suggesting to Edward that he keep so many of Mary's belongings. It was too much for their little flat. And she couldn't see Edward going through them on his own. Likely as not, she thought, a few months from now he'd have forgotten what was even in them.

In her head she started to plan out her strategy. Books could be added to Edward's collection in the bedroom and the lounge, while she could put the photos and other genuine keepsakes into flat plastic containers and slide them under the bed. Unfortunately, this meant going out and buying containers in the first place, and that would mean getting Jasmyn organised and dressed and into the car, and then dragging her round Home 'n' Wear for three hours. She remembered a box Edward had taken straight into the bedroom, placing it up on a high shelf, where it now stuck out untidily. It was, Julie thought, going into the kitchen and unhooking the step-stool from behind the door, almost as if he didn't trust her not to interfere with it in some manner. She had told Edward to take his time, because it was important to let him know she was there for him and that she respected his feelings. But with Mary's possessions clogging up their home it was almost as if Mary were still here. And what about Edward? How was he expected to move on when he was surrounded by all his mother's stuff every day? Wonky knick-knacks and grubby old items that were of no use to anyone could be quietly disposed of, and Edward would be none the wiser. In the long run, he would thank her for it. Taking care of it herself, Julie decided, would be a positive step to *jump-start the grief process*, the sooner for Edward to go through all the stages and *achieve closure*. Once that was done, they would both be able to move forward again as *equal stakeholders* in their relationship.

It would be different if they had the room – a larger home, with a garage and extra bedrooms for family when they came to stay. 'Couldn't we manage it?' she had asked Edward three years ago. 'It's possible,' he'd replied doubtfully, 'with both our wages. But it would completely wipe out my savings. We'd have nothing left after we'd paid the mortgage every month.' Only now, Julie realised, here in the flat without Edward for the first time in days, could she admit to herself the terrible disappointment, the awful let-down of learning that Mary's house didn't in fact belong to Mary at all. Yet *Pathways to Possible* was full of

197

people who had *manifested the soul journey experience on the material plain* and as a result received bigger houses – in one case, a whole palace in California. In the bedroom she set the step-stool down and took a moment to close her eyes and visualise a real home, a proper grown-up dwelling with two storeys and a patio and a kitchen island, instead of neighbours yammering in the entranceway and slamming the front door at all hours. Did she dare *open the cosmic window* wide enough to include a nursery? Too late: she had already pictured a room painted in cheerful colours – in pink or blue, depending.

The box was wedged in very tightly, right under the ceiling where another patch of damp had recently appeared, spreading out from the corner towards the main light in the centre of the room. Trying not to think about being electrocuted, she climbed on to the step stool and stood on tiptoes and managed to insert her fingers under the box, which she could tell wasn't so much heavy as unwieldy. As she eased the box off the shelf the stool tipped and wobbled for a moment, and in the nick of time she managed to put her arm out to steady herself and felt the box came loose and slip out of her hands. She watched helplessly as it hit the floor, narrowly missing Jasmyn, who was standing right underneath. 'Fuck. Cow,' said Jasmyn tearfully, as the box's contents spilled out over the carpet, pointing to the doorway where Happy Meal's tail was just disappearing. 'Fuck. *Cat*,' said Julie under her breath – it would be the bloody cat, she thought, trying to kill them both. 'Let's get this all tidied away nicely, shall we?' she told Jasmyn, hoping they could turn this latest mishap into a funny game before the tears started again. 'Want to give Auntie a hand?' she asked, propping the stool carefully against the bed and kneeling down to gather the box's scattered contents. Jasmyn stared back at her for a moment and burst into tears. 'Oh, please, Jas, don't cry. Come and help Auntie,' she said coaxingly.

Six or seven ratty lengths of tinsel trailed out across the floor, and once she turned the box the right way up she was surprised to see what looked like balled-up old newspapers but were in fact little parcels. 'What does Uncle Edward want with all this old stuff?' she asked Jasmyn. One by one, with Jasmyn looking on in rapt silence, she unwrapped each package to find Christmas tree ornaments, scratched and worn, some fairy-lights wound around a twisted and yellowing section of *The Independent*, and, hanging half in and half out of a jumble of pink tissue paper, a cheap-looking one-armed plastic doll or angel. 'Is that it?' she said to Jasmyn. 'All that fuss over some rotten old Christmas decorations? What's so special about it, eh? Just a lot of old rubbish, isn't it, Jas?' Jasmyn, who had stopped crying, reached out towards the doll. 'You don't want that, Jasmyn. Dirty. *Dirty* old thing. *Germs.*' The girl started to cry, a soft whimpering sound. Julie ignored her and continued to sort through the last few layers of old newspapers and paper bells and half-unglued paper chains. Once this was finished, she thought, there would be one less thing to worry about.

At the very bottom of the box was what appeared to be a bundle of envelopes tied up in blue ribbon. She picked them out and thought how typical it was that Mary would keep her correspondence in a box of old Christmas decorations. She turned the package over and felt the crackle of the paper in her hands. What were they? Love letters? Like everything else of Mary's, they were probably not worth bothering about, Julie thought, as she found herself, almost without meaning to, easing the knot loose. There was no harm in just looking, was there? Mary could hardly ask for them back, she thought, as the ribbon fell away and she saw that the letters were not Mary's at all.

For a long time she sat at the kitchen table with the letters in front of her, pot of tea cooling as Jasmyn chattered away to her toys. Lorraine would be here any minute to collect her daughter, and Edward should be home within the hour. Yet she was in a quandary, and had been for the last hour, caught between putting the letters back where she had found them and the desire to have the tiniest peep inside before Edward got home. Was it prying, she thought, if you found something in your own home? She had immediately consulted *Pathways to Possible*, which said, as she'd known it would, that *secrets between stakeholders* were unhealthy, a bad omen for the future. 'Care of Mary M. Vernon', the envelopes said, but above that: 'Edward Vernon', written in hectic, forward-sloping handwriting. It was surprising that the letters had even arrived at Danecroft Road in the first place. The script was almost indecipherable, looped and crossed inconsistently – the 'e's, especially, written one way and sometimes another, for no discernible reason. So it was no surprise to Julie that, on the top left-hand corner of each envelope, the sender's name, once she made it out, was 'Isobel L. Vernon'. She held the top envelope up to the kitchen light again and squinted and tried turning it this way and that. It was no good. The words inside might as well be Jasmyn's squiggly, haphazard flowers. Under the table Jasmyn clutched at her knees and let out a high-pitched whine. Julie ignored her. *Where was Lorraine?*

'I'm in a rush so I won't stop…' said Lorraine forty-five minutes later, stamping her cigarette out on the doorstep. 'Can't you bring her out here? I'm parked on a yellow line.'

'I found some letters,' she said, 'of Edward's,' at which point Lorraine pushed in past her, traffic warden forgotten.

'Why haven't you opened them?' her sister said. She was holding them up to the window and then the lamp, just as Julie had done.

'It doesn't seem right. They're not mine.'

'They're in your house!' Lorraine looked round the kitchen as if expecting someone to pop out from inside one of the cupboards. 'Where is he, anyway?'

'Edward? He should be back soon. About the letters, though … is it okay if I think about it for a bit?'

'Suit yourself,' said Lorraine coldly, turning away and picking up her car keys. 'You asked me what I thought and I've told you.'

Life was so simple for Lorraine, Julie thought, as she watched her sister bundle Jasmyn into a miniature cagoule. Everything was either black or white, wrong or right, with nothing in between. Her mobile lit up with a text message and without thinking she picked it up to look.

'*Is that him*?' hissed Lorraine, quick as a flash.

'Yes,' she replied. 'He says he's stopping off for a quick drink on the way back.'

'What? Are you joking? He's going to the pub?' said Lorraine, as if Edward had announced he was flying to the moon. '*Who with*?'

Have to stop off at the pub w/sister to discuss arrangements, etc. Back soon, the message said.

'Her,' she admitted miserably. 'His sister.' Even saying her name felt frightening, as if Isobel might suddenly appear in the middle of the kitchen with a bang and a puff of black smoke. After everything he'd said about Isobel, it seemed very peculiar to be going to the pub with her. An uneasy shiver went through her bones. Was this Isobel's chance to say something? 'He says they have to discuss Mary's arrangements.'

'Well, he would say that, wouldn't he?' said Lorraine. '*Himself* uses that trick all the time.'

'Who, Declan? What sort of trick?'

Somehow she knew what her sister would say before she even said it. 'Having an alibi,' said Lorraine, flipping open her lighter and lighting her cigarette. She wished her sister wouldn't insist on smoking in their flat. She knew how much Edward hated it, and it put Julie in a very awkward position. 'Out with some tart,' Lorraine went on, 'I fucking know he is.'

'Declan?'

'Yeah, who else?' Lorraine exhaled in a big cloud of smoke. 'There's always one of his bastard mates who swears up and down they were down the pub together or in the arcades or whatever.'

What was Lorraine implying? That Edward was like Declan? But even Declan wasn't like Declan, at least not the Declan Lorraine claimed he was. He was a good husband to Lorraine and a good father to their kids. When did Lorraine think he had the time?

'They're just discussing the arrangements and things,' she said. What bothered her was that Edward kept saying that being anything more than 'cordial' to Isobel would be 'appeasement'. Isobel was obviously dying to get her claws into him for one of her 'chats', so she could tell him how dreadful his girl-friend was. 'I know he wouldn't lie to me,' she told Lorraine. 'I'm just worried about her and what she's saying.'

'Yeah, well, I don't blame you,' said Lorraine, clacking her car keys impatiently against the kitchen counter. She took another long puff of her cigarette and blew the smoke out towards the ceiling. 'I thought he hated her.'

'I know. I don't know what to think either. I'm sure he has a good reason and that she's who he's with. Not someone else, I mean,' she added quickly.

'So you're saying she bullied him into it, this sister of his who he claims he hates so much?' said Lorraine, chucking her cigarette end in the sink. 'That she forced him down the pub against his will?' She laughed. 'Christ, you're so naïve.'

I almost wish Edward was down the pub with 'some tart', Julie thought to herself. *With anyone, in fact, rather than Isobel.*

She had been pleased at first, finding all the ingredients for a green bean and aubergine bake just sitting there in the vegetable basket, so that she could save herself a trip to the supermarket in the rain. But that was hours ago, and for the last two she had been keeping all the pots on a low simmer and hoping her sauces wouldn't dry out. Finally, with still no sign of Edward, she turned them all off. In the other room she heard Big Ben chime the ten o'clock news on the TV. It wasn't like Edward to leave her hanging like this. Had Isobel put her oar in after all? Then again, to be fair, Edward hadn't said exactly how late he was going to be, had he? Still. What if he'd been in an accident? An hour later, unable to stand it any more, she decided to text him. She typed out a very short message: *Everything all right? Just checking.* And then, in an afterthought: *Hope you're having a nice time!* Thirty-five anxious minutes later a strange and almost incoherent message lit up on her phone. *On teh next traim,* it said. *Bacon son.* What did it mean? Edward was always so strict about grammar and spelling, it literally didn't make any sense. Her mind couldn't help going back to another comment of Lorraine's, that even if you were married – and *definitely if you weren't* – sooner or later *men take advantage.* 'Look at *himself,* taking the piss,' Lorraine had remarked. 'Imagine how much more of a prat he'd be if we *weren't* married!' As Julie transferred the cold and stodgy remains of their dinner into Tupperware containers, this idea struck her as having a chilling sort of logic. 'The bad news is they're not like us,' Lorraine had said, 'but the good news is, they're all the fucking same.' She got undressed and brushed her teeth and decided to read *Pathways to Possible* in bed until Edward got home. She must have fallen straight to sleep because the next thing she knew she woke up to Edward sprawled out next to her, half-undressed, socks still on, reeking of alcohol. She switched off the bedside lamp and lay in the dark thinking. Was her sister right? *Would* Edward behave like this if they were married? As if in response he let out a loud snore and turned towards her. His arm landed heavily on her chest. If they were husband and wife, she thought, trying to remove the arm without waking him, would he have stayed out until all hours? Or would he have come home to her at a proper time? Or perhaps not gone out with Isobel in the first place? She was very used to Edward working late up in London. She understood he was under a lot of pressure at work and he always kept her informed. But death and heartache were meant to bring you closer together, not make one of you ignore the other and disregard their feelings.

Wide awake, she eased herself out of bed, put on her slippers, and went along to the kitchen. She would sit quietly and practise *deep calming breaths* with a cup of herbal tea. Edward had spent the evening getting drunk with Isobel, she thought, taking a sachet of Evening Soothing from the tea caddy – in other words, he had gone off on a pub crawl with someone he claimed to dislike and had been very harsh in telling Julie to keep away from. She turned this over in her mind as she put on the kettle, and then she went to the cutlery drawer and selected a sharp knife.

'Screw her, just open them,' Lorraine had suggested earlier. 'That precious book of yours,' she went on, 'if it worked

204

we'd all be bleeding rich, wouldn't we?' Julie had said nothing. 'And you'd be married!' Lorraine added unnecessarily. *And you'd be divorced,* Julie had thought, *if Declan got a wish,* and had been surprised to hear herself having such a negative and unkind thought.

'What if Edward finds out?' she'd said.

'Are you joking?' said Lorraine. 'Everyone knows how it's done.'

As it happened Julie knew nothing of the sort, and so her sister had explained it to her step by step. 'Privacy? What's that when it's at home?' sneered Lorraine, cigarette dangling, ash falling on to the table. 'Fuck her, that hoity-toity cow.'

Alive to the perils of actually trying to be pleasant to Isobel, Julie had found herself half nodding in agreement. Maybe the universe had delivered the letters to her for a reason.

Unfortunately, every time the electric kettle boiled it efficiently switched itself off, so she had to resort to keeping a saucepan of water on the boil instead. Even using the smallest and sharpest knife in the drawer, she discovered, the operation was much more fiddly than Lorraine had made out. What didn't help was that on the back of most of the envelopes Isobel had stamped or sketched some infantile image of an elephant or a dinosaur or some other animal. If she managed to steam one open and translate its contents, she also had to take into account the time involved to align the image perfectly when it came to glueing the envelope back up again. Filled with anxiety, terrified of hearing Edward's footsteps out in the passage, she couldn't decide what to do. What if he woke up and wandered into the kitchen for a glass of water or a snack? Alcohol had her father waking at all hours, blundering into the furniture downstairs and leaving the fridge door open. Then she remembered the dinner she had prepared earlier, dried up and ruined in the fridge, and it gave her the push she needed.

A number of the envelopes turned out to contain cards, as opposed to proper letters. There seemed to be nothing notable about any of them unless you counted the disturbing 'artwork' by Isobel which, Julie thought, judging the peculiar scratchy ink drawings, would not even pass at GCSE. *Less works of art than a cry for help*, Mary had remarked when they went to see an exhibition by a local art group, and for once she and Edward's mother had been in agreement. Her teacher's eye couldn't help noticing the exclamation marks Isobel sprinkled everywhere, the clumsy-looking capital letters. *Happy EASTER! Thinking of you*, shouted one card, illustrated with what looked like a beady-eyed rat proffering an acorn. Yet another of Isobel's efforts, raggedy and home-made, had shreds of red and green tissue stuck all over it, underneath which you could just make out, *Hope you have a SUPER-DUPER Happy Christmas! With lots of SNOW!!!* There followed more hand-drawn stars, with practically every other word underlined in green glittery pen. It was the sort of thing, Julie thought, that people in mental homes did, when they weren't weaving baskets.

Trying to assemble the letters into any rough chronological order was impossible. She spent some time puzzling over the postmarks, for instance, 04.21.98 and 09.13.01, before realising that Americans must write the date in the wrong order. Generally, the postmarks were illegible, while, inside, Isobel almost never bothered to include the date. Among the loops and whirls of Isobel's wayward scrawl, she was, though, able to discern some source of ill feeling with Edward, if not precisely what it was about. There was news about Isobel's life and what she was doing – a job at a film company, an apartment in a better area, travel to this or that far-flung place with names Julie had barely heard of. When she read each letter a second time, she noticed an odd tendency for an item of good news to be immediately followed by some other, less good news. The 'amazing view' in a new apartment seemed less impressive when balanced against an 'insanely loud' neighbour. It was true, Julie thought, what Edward said – that Isobel was ungrateful and never satisfied with what she had. *So how have you been?* Isobel wrote, and, *Would really love to hear all your news!* At the bottom of the page, Isobel always signed off with the same suggestion: *Let's try to have a talk* or *Is there a good time to chat?*

That again, thought Julie with a shiver.

When she next happened to glance at the clock, she was surprised to see that it was almost 5am. The alarm would go off in an hour. She took the saucepan off the boil and went over to the sink to tip it out, and to locate a tube of glue in the 'everything' drawer, and noticed a letter she had earlier placed to one side. There was a particularly tricky (and hideous) drawing on the back that she knew would be difficult to match up again. Now, taking the knife, she managed to get the flap open without tearing it, and carefully unfolded the single sheet of paper inside, only to find the usual rubbish – parties, friends, jobs. News about nothing, Julie thought bitterly, holding it under the light just to make sure. The airmail paper was very thin and so generally Isobel only wrote only on one side. But for some reason, on the other side of this letter, she saw now, Isobel had written something else. She turned it over.

P.S. About your decision, about moving to New York – I think it's great, I really do! I knew you would love it. And, as you say, this way it'll give you the best of both worlds! Izzy xx

Was Isobel mad? She couldn't believe what she was seeing. Why would Edward want to live in New York? He couldn't stand the States, everyone knew that. And he would have said something to Julie, wouldn't he? Or to Mary? On the other hand, she thought, why would Mary have shared this with Julie even if it were true? Mary had hated her. She might even have told her nothing out of spite. She examined the envelope again. The postmark was a black smudge. She turned the paper back over. Undated – of course it was. *Bloody Isobel.* When had she written it? Ten years ago? Last year? *Last week?* There was no way of knowing. She thought of Isobel's smug smile this afternoon as she and Edward had walked off together. She read the words again and felt gripped with panic. *And, as you say, this way it'll give you the best of both worlds!* What did it mean, 'the best of both worlds'? And what about their future together, hers and Edward's? Their life was in one world only, and that world was *here*, not in America. The idea – clearly – was that Edward would be going over there on his own. Was this 'decision' one he had made, and agreed to? Wasn't he happy with her?

And yet, the letters had never reached him. They were unopened, hidden away in Mary's Christmas box. Maybe Isobel had imagined it or made it up, and Edward knew nothing about it. But why? And then why would she write it all down and send it to him? None of it made sense. If only she knew whether Isobel had written it – and Edward had agreed to it – during the last eight years and ten months. She read the words one more time and tried to decipher their meaning, to find some other, more positive interpretation, as opposed to the unfamiliar worrying past and the terrifying Edwardless future that Isobel's words implied.

There was one small – or not so small – thing, she remembered, that she had to be thankful for – and that, strangely, was Mary. Because it was obviously Mary who had chosen not to give the letters to Edward. And this must be why, Julie realised now, Mary had hidden the letters away in an old box of Christmas decorations – so that Edward would never find them. Mary hadn't opened them either. Possibly she had intended to hand them over one day in the future. Either way, Edward's mother deserved a positive thought in return, and, even though she had passed on and it wouldn't do her much good, Julie sent out a *prayer of thankfulness* from her *Quantum Being* and hoped that it would get to Mary somehow. Carefully gluing up the flaps of the envelopes, she thought back to one other letter, equally mysterious and unexplained. It had contained just two lines on a single sheet of tissue-thin airmail paper: *If we could have a talk, just five minutes, if only for Mum's sake… I know she would want us to.* For Mary's sake! For Mary, she thought, who had intercepted Isobel's letters in the first place. Despite her anxiety, despite everything, Julie wanted to burst out laughing at the irony of it. Isobel was dangerous, but her words only proved how deluded she was, willing to use even her own mother to get what she wanted. *Selfish*, just like Edward said. As she gathered the letters back into a neat pile and knotted the ribbon, she noticed that her hands were trembling.

6

Thursday

Bloody Mary

As Isobel entered the shop, the assistant looked up and smiled. 'Are you all right?' she said, her pencil hovering, poised above a sheet of sticky labels on the counter in front of her.

Isobel put a hand to her face. Was there was a smudge on her nose? Did she look weird or ill? No, that wasn't it. It was simply the English way of doing commerce, and another custom, Isobel thought, another cultural difference that she had apparently lost touch with.

'I'm fine, thank you,' she said. 'Just having a browse.' She feigned interest in a basket where scarves and hats lay tangled together in depressing acrylic-looking fabrics, and the woman returned to her labels.

'I'm here if you need anything,' she called from behind her counter.

'Great, thanks!' Isobel said. She had blue eyes of an almost Mediterranean intensity and would be about her mother's age, possibly older. Although her mother wouldn't be seen dead in that high-necked Edwardian blouse, Isobel thought, before remembering the 'floaty' which, as Edward had made clear to the Upselling Funeral Director, their mother would not be seen dead in either. She wandered over to a rack of clothes and slowly passed her fingers through the hangers, surreptitiously keeping one eye on the woman, who had abandoned her sticky labels after all and was folding a shelf of scarves. Isobel noted the Victorian tortoiseshell hair comb, the long black velvet skirt and the chic ankle boots in navy suede.

'We've been seeing you here all week, haven't we, darling?' the woman went on. 'You've been so generous with all the lovely things you've let us have.'

'Actually I'm here to find a dress...' she said, and it occurred to her that her mother's taste was at last being given the seal of approval.

'A *dress!*' The woman looked thrilled. 'I'll tell you what, darling...' And then confidingly, *sotto voce*, 'We just got in some utterly exquisite pieces, given to us yesterday, from a lovely old duck, God rest her soul...' Clearly she would never regard herself as an old duck, Isobel thought, lovely or otherwise. 'Come and have a look,' she whispered, as if inviting Isobel to inspect some stolen jewels in the back room – and for a horrible black comedy moment she wondered if she was going be shown a selection of her mother's own dresses. The woman indicated a small rack standing behind the counter. Six or seven dresses hung from the rail – all perfectly unfamiliar, Isobel noted with relief. At this point feeling slightly obligated, she went over and picked out a hanger at random.

'Oh, yes, that one's absolutely stunning!' the woman said approvingly. '*Vintage* – but you would have spotted that, wouldn't you? 1950s. You'll look like Audrey Hepburn!'

'Do you think so?' It was unbecoming, Isobel thought, to be fishing for compliments from a stranger, but today was not the day to say no to an offer of blatant flattery.

'Yes, but I didn't ask you what it was for. Is it for a party?'

'It's for a funeral,' Isobel said. 'My mother's. It's tomorrow.'

'*Oh*!' It was the woman's turn to put a mortified hand to her face. Isobel felt terrible. She hadn't intended to say anything, and probably shouldn't have. The words had tumbled right out of her mouth. 'Oh. Oh, darling. I'm so *dreadfully* sorry! Oh, goodness…there I was going on and on; I don't know what to say…'

'No, please,' Isobel said, 'it's my fault…I dropped you in it…' She felt sorry – and yet, she realised, selfishly she felt better for having said it out loud.

'I should have known, with your donating so many lovely things all week…' They went on like this for several more rounds, two women falling over themselves to apologise. It was so English, Isobel thought. Meanwhile someone more real seemed to have popped her head out from behind the façade, from behind the flirtatious rococo Edwardian froth and sophistication. 'It's an appalling loss when it's your mum,' the sales assistant said, staring into Isobel's eyes with a look of deep concern, and she had the sense of not having fully grasped the truth of this yet herself. 'Well, look, my darling, the changing room's all ready for you, just over here. I'm here if you need me, okay?'

As the woman gestured towards a curtained cubicle behind the counter Isobel had to fight the urge to cry, to pour out the whole week, about her mother and her brother and the spiteful Julie and the funeral and all the rotten rest of it, to this lovely woman with her ocean-coloured eyes. A broad tinkle of bells above the door announced another customer. 'Great, thanks,' Isobel said, and fled into the changing room.

For all the times she and her mother had scoured the charity shops, Isobel thought as she stepped into the dress, and for all their minute investigations into death it had never occurred to her until this week that it might be dead people's clothes they had cooed and exclaimed over, brought in by the grieving relatives of the town's 'old ducks'. In the mirror she fixed her gaze on the dress itself, a knee-length black crêpe sheath with a small belt that fastened simply, Prada-like, with a minimalist silver clasp. She recalled the unsettling run-in she had had with her own reflection on the way over, when a haggard-looking woman had stared furiously at her from behind a shop window; startled, Isobel had actually turned to see who this frumpy, glaring fright could be and what her problem was. The dress fitted perfectly; the seams, the material, were pristine. Someone must have treasured and cared for it for many years. 'Oh, Izzy, well done, what a find!' her mother would say. *Would have said,* Isobel thought – or rather, *won't.* 'And it's the first one you picked out!' her mother continued, oblivious to her situation, to the reason her daughter was buying such a dress in the first place. She checked in the mirror one more time, ignoring her own face, which seemed to float moonlike above the rest of her, pallid and abstract.

Outside, the high street was seething with people, presumably trying to beat the 'periods of patchy rain and drizzle' that were forecast for later in the afternoon. Since last night, when Edward had put the idea into her head, she had seen at least three women who from a distance, for a hopeful, misguided second, looked exactly like their mother. Invariably, each time she caught sight of one of these doppelgängers the thought 'just in case' would pop up in her mind and she would feel compelled to march rapidly after them, overtake, and then glance back just to make sure. *Madness*, Isobel thought, as she rapidly assessed the features of the latest one – make-up too garish, features all wrong – who was soon meandering a good distance behind. There were the disconcerting mental reminders that sprung up, Whack-a-Mole-like, each time she came across a forgotten keepsake in one of their mother's drawers or overheard a funny conversation on the train over – reminders to tell her mother about it when they next spoke. *Perfectly normal thoughts*, Isobel told herself, turning off the high street towards the seafront.

It was Edward who had suggested lunch today – a quick pub lunch, he'd announced, where they could sit down (as of this morning, the charity shops had taken all the chairs) and go over tomorrow's plan – the service at eleven, the gathering of friends afterwards at the Brentwood Inn. Following on the heels of their successful outing to the pub, the invitation felt like another development, another promising sign of a future relationship. The humanist minister had sounded excellent on the phone, she had informed Edward last night, a no-nonsense sort with exactly the right amount of sympathy. She had expected a terse response, along the lines of its being the woman's job – but Edward had looked pleased. 'Oh, good, well done,' he had said. Later, getting off the train on her way home, she had felt optimistic, almost happy – if maybe a wee bit tipsy. But then, this morning, she had woken up feeling less certain. Shouldn't their hours together have given her some grasp of who her brother was, who he had become since they last met? What did he do? Where did he work? What did he do in his spare time? How did he feel about such-and-such aspect of his life? Somehow she had managed to come out of the pub no wiser than when she went in. There had been more urgent matters to discuss, of course. And if Edward had said nothing specific about their staying in touch after tomorrow, not everyone felt the need to spell things out, did they? Feelings could be implicit and understood. You didn't have to trumpet them from the rooftops or push yourself on people like in the US. Edward's obvious evasiveness about their mother was kind of weird, but, considering how well they were getting on, being a family again would make sense to Edward as well, wouldn't it? As for the past and its unpleasantness, Isobel thought, maybe that should wait. The way things were going there would be plenty of time for this discussion when Edward was ready, and they were both less stressed, and at the very latest as soon as he found her letters.

Edward and Julie were already there, sitting together at a small table, Edward with his head bent over the menu, Julie ignoring the coffee cup in front of her and staring across the room towards the window. As Isobel approached, Edward looked up and nodded towards the carrier bag in her hand. 'You found something, then?' he said.

'I think so,' she replied. 'Do you want to see?'

'If you must,' Edward said, with a mock ho-hum air.

She took out the dress and held it up. 'Not bad, right?'

'It looks new,' Edward said approvingly. 'You'll look quite respectable.'

'*For a change*, you mean?'

Edward laughed and she watched Julie give one of her tight non-smiles – more of a grimace than anything, as if she'd just sat down on a pin. 'It's vintage,' Isobel said, as she watched the girl's eyes slide over the dress. *What was her problem?* Bloody Jules – didn't she have some kittens to drown? She pictured the dumpy little figure, crouched at the edge of the River Ouse like a gargoyle, features softening with pleasure as she took the sack with its helpless wriggling lumps and plunged it firmly under the water. 'And it fits perfectly,' she said, to rub it in.

'They do a decent ploughman's,' Edward said, closing the menu and glancing, Isobel thought, fleetingly but longingly at the bar.

'Why don't you let me get all this?' she offered. 'How about a Bloody Mary?'

Edward, who all morning had been looking very much the worse for wear, appeared to hesitate. 'Erm, Jules?' he said. 'Drink?'

'Just water, thank you, Edward,' answered Jules primly.

'Yes, me too,' he said. 'Water's fine.'

'What, no Bloody Mary?' she said. 'Are you *sure*? I'm just saying, it wasn't me chugging coffee and complaining about my hangover all morning, was it?' She had felt quite pleased with herself since, last night, conscious of their early start, she had interspersed her own alcohol intake with plain soda. Edward must have downed four at least. This morning she had heard him opening and closing the empty medicine cabinet at Danecroft Road and cursing, finally asking Jules to nip up to the shop and get some painkillers.

'Oh, sod it, why not?' he said. 'Jules, what do you say? Drink? Might as well, eh? We deserve one.'

'Just water for me, thank you,' Jules repeated doggedly. *Whatever*, Isobel thought, *hateful little goody-goody.*

'Right. Just *water* for Jules, then,' said Edward.

Jules's hand came to rest on his. 'Do you think that's wise, Edward, having more alcohol?' she said, and Isobel had an almost uncontrollable urge to snatch up a nearby plate and bring it down on Julie's fingers. 'It's only two o'clock...'

'Mm,' said Edward thoughtfully, and shifted his hand a few inches to the right – consciously or unconsciously, Isobel couldn't tell – out from under Julie's. Isobel sat back down again. Were they going to keep on like this?

'Right, so what shall we have? The ploughman's?' Edward said, addressing Isobel.

'Sounds perfect,' she replied. How ordinary they must appear, she thought, the three of them, like a group of jolly friends meeting for a post-hangover brunch. All week she had been operating on autopilot, a wind-up toy fuelled by a maniacal and unthinking sense of purpose. By taking one resolute step after the other she had succeeded in thinking forward, but not too far – and, with limited success, not backwards. 'Like pulling a plaster off,' Martin had reminded her on her way out this morning, and she thought of the long days they'd spent prising the books off their shelves, and the dishes from their cupboards, and the photos from their frames, with the cold efficiency of art thieves or executioners. This morning an echo had appeared. Pausing briefly in the hallway, listening to Edward moving about upstairs, she had realised that the smallest action – a box slid across the floor, the pop and snap of the tape dispenser – now made itself known throughout the house. The air, too, was different, and had lost its familiar smells, its special quality of home. This was almost the last time, Isobel thought, that she would hear the house's creaking floorboards, the wind whistling through its windows or the particular rattle of the letterbox.

'Order whatever you fancy,' she told Edward. 'My treat.'

'Thanks, Izz. The ploughman's and a Coke,' he replied with slightly unnatural brightness. He turned to Jules, who was wearing her sour lemon face. 'And a sandwich or something for you?' he asked her. 'What do you want?' *Good question*, Isobel thought.

'The green salad, thank you,' said Jules, and pushed the menu away like a porn mag. Isobel saw Edward shoot her a look, intense and hot like a tiny thunderbolt. Had Jules caught it? She couldn't be sure. It was momentary, something only a film camera would catch – and even then only in close-up. But Isobel had caught it, and, to someone who had seen it before, the look was chilling and unmistakable.

At the bar she waited for their order and found herself once more perusing the various creative and far-fetched explanations for the undelivered letters stuffed into the back of their mother's desk. She had concocted several theories, but had been unable to come up with a single one that didn't involve their mother deliberately keeping the letters from Edward. But why? Why would she have done such a thing? The bartender put the drinks down and said that the waitress would bring their food over, and she paid, careful not to tip or say anything cringeworthy or American. Turning to take their drinks back to the table, she saw that Edward and Julie were in what appeared to be an intense conversation. He was leaning in to say something, to make a particular point, perhaps, while Julie was sitting back with her arms crossed tightly over her chest. Were they arguing *again*? Isobel thought. Did they argue a lot? This certainly wasn't the impression Julie had given her yesterday morning in the bedroom – but then Julie, she remembered, had proved tricksy and unreliable. What she wouldn't give to know what it was all about, Isobel thought as she threaded her way slowly back though the untidy clutter of tables and chairs towards them. It struck her that the scene was reminiscent of the incident with the umbrella – except this time their positions were reversed: Julie looked pissed-off, while Edward appeared anxious to explain himself.

I Know the Feeling

What is she cross about now? Edward thought. He couldn't believe how difficult Julie was being. On the walk back to Danecroft Road he and Isobel had paused briefly to watch a seagull. The bird was engaged in a furious battle with a hamburger wrapper, unperturbed by the amused passers-by. Isobel had asked him a question about how birds stayed aloft and he had made the comparison with man-made flight – with a helicopter, say, or an Airbus. Or the poor old defunct Harrier, Edward added, which was his favourite plane and could take off or land on a tennis court. *And was tragically sold off to the Septics for parts and badly redesigned,* he tactfully didn't add. Isobel had listened intently to his explanation, to the difference between ailerons and elevons, the nuanced interconnections of pitch, roll and yaw, until finally the seagull readied its wings and with a triumphant shriek made off with its fast-food bounty. Only then did he notice that Jules was already some distance ahead of them. Even from here, Edward thought, he could tell she wasn't happy, holding herself stiffly with her arms wrapped tightly round her body. Her posture implied that he and Isobel were meant to look sharp and catch up, when in fact it was Jules who had rudely removed herself from the conversation and marched ahead. She had been strange all morning, interrogating him about the past, and during lunch behaving like a spoilt teenager, obtuse about what to order, refusing to join in the conversation – she'd even tried to make him feel guilty about having a drink! When at last he was forced to pick her up on it and ask what was wrong, a sullen, 'Nothing,' was all he'd got in response.

219

What made it all the more galling, Edward decided, as he and Isobel walked on towards her, was that after last night's misunderstanding about dinner (he had noticed the food in the plastic containers in the fridge this morning) he had been doing his best to cheer her up. And yet this morning, for example, when he'd suggested a proper lunch with Isobel – exactly the sort of thing Jules had been pestering him about, *ad nauseam*, all bloody week – her response had been lukewarm. And then, 'What do you say, Jules?' he'd suggested when they arrived at the pub. 'Fancy sitting at the bar for a change?' He had been conscious of trying to jolly her along, and of how much he sounded like his mother, who was all for having adventures and trying new things, however small or minor-seeming.

'Won't it be full of drunk people?' Jules had answered, her mouth set in a little moue of distaste.

'Not likely on a Thursday afternoon, is it?' he told her. In his university days, tables had been the territory of old fogeys and visiting parents. On the rare occasions they ventured out, he could not recall himself and Jules ever seating themselves at the bar. An odd panic seemed to rise in his chest, a sudden desperation to not find himself marooned at one of the depressing little tables. 'Come on, Jules,' he said coaxingly. 'Why not?'

'I don't know …' said Jules, who had come to a stop in the doorway and was staring down at the beer-stained carpet. And they had found themselves taking one of the sticky, teak-effect tables instead.

'Are you going to say anything tomorrow?' Isobel asked, as up ahead Jules gazed sullenly at a lamp post. Why were he and Isobel expected to rush to catch up? Why should he be made to feel in the wrong? It was infuriating.

'At the service?' he replied. 'I expect so. Not sure what, though.' For days he had been composing a eulogy, but he couldn't seem to hit the right tone – whatever that was, Edward thought to himself. 'You?'

'I've been typing something out on my computer,' Isobel said. 'A speech. Well, not a speech – that's a bit grand, isn't it? Don't worry, I'll make it short. I'll try not to go on.'

'We can only hope,' he told her, and she laughed. He felt uncomfortably aware of Jules, standing stiffly on guard, watching their progress as if scrutinising his every footstep. He deliberately slowed his pace.

'The thing is,' Isobel continued, 'every time I go back and look at what I've written, it's as if someone crept in and tampered with it when I wasn't looking.'

'I know the feeling,' he said, and thought ruefully of his own attempts, jotted down and endlessly crossed out at the kitchen table each morning on the back of the unread copy of *The Guardian*, while his coffee cooled and his breakfast went uneaten. The nights felt very long, and when he couldn't sleep he found himself mulling over and editing various paragraphs in his head – a mistake, of course: the results veered wildly between the maudlin and the coldly matter-of-fact, depending on how close he was to sleeping. 'I wouldn't worry,' he told Isobel. 'I'm sure no one expects it to sound as if you're addressing the UN.'

'We can only hope,' she said.

In front of them a large moth-eaten black Labrador trotted across the pavement. On the other end of the lead was a red-faced man in a blue blazer with the look of a retired colonel. 'What have I told you, Stanley?' he told the dog, huffing wheezily as it plopped itself down in a small patch of sunlight.

'Hey, wait,' said Isobel, stopping abruptly. 'Shall we stop and say hello?'

On the other side of the road Jules regarded them steadily, arms folded, shoulders hunched.

'Excuse me,' Edward asked the man. 'Is it all right if we stroke him?' Whatever emotional blackmail Jules had in mind, he thought, he wasn't falling for it.

'Go on, then,' the man told them. And to the dog, 'There, Stanley, more admirers for you.'

Isobel squatted down and to Edward's embarrassment cupped the dog's entire face in her hands and planted a loud kiss on the dome of its head. 'Velvet...' she murmured. The dog appeared to grin at her.

'Isobel, *please*...' Edward mimed a gesture of apology to the old boy. Why did his sister have to take such liberties, lunging at the animal like that? 'I'm sure the dog doesn't want you slobbering all over him.'

'She's not doing any harm,' said the colonel. 'He loves the attention. *Don't you, Stanley*?' The dog's tail rotated and thumped slowly on the pavement.

'I expect he's just after the sunlight,' observed Edward.

'I wish I had a dog...' said Isobel wistfully. *I wouldn't mind one either*, Edward thought to himself, as several heavy warning drops of rain landed on the pavement. Jules was nervous of dogs and Happy Meal was their compromise, though apparently what Jules really wanted was a baby. A child was a poor substitute for a dog, though, Edward thought, especially a Labrador. Labradors were perpetually cheerful, happy about everything, whatever the weather. As Isobel launched into an obscure exchange about animal psychology, he bent down to pat it. With his bright chocolate eyes, Stanley reminded him of Otter, the dog they had had when they were little. Their mother had brought her home, a stray she'd found rifling through the bins behind the Co-op. Likely she was the runt of the litter, their mother explained, much smaller and weaker than her siblings. He had buried his face in the dog's, barely able to believe she was theirs to keep, her muzzle as soft and fragrant as a raspberry.

The rain turned into a fine drizzle and, as the colonel tugged at the dog's lead and they moved off, Edward let his hand brush the animal's back for a moment. Was it possible, he wondered, for its fur to feel sad? The touch of it filled him with an intense melancholy, as if the dog shared his own mood – or more probably, Edward reasoned, was a repository for his own sadness. The animal would have its little life, with concerns and sorrows of its own. He looked back and watched it scrabble at the pavement, attempting to dig its claws into the concrete in a useless gesture of refusal. 'Oh, do *please* come on, Stanley!' repeated the colonel. 'Let's leave the nice people alone.' The whole encounter seemed to move in surreal detail – the dog, the man, Isobel beside him, Jules standing guard by her lamp-post – the whole landscape of the street, the mundane aspect of pedestrians and parked cars and shop windows, floating past like strange, two-dimensional fish. The dog complied with a grudging step, its tail still wagging slowly, gazing back at Edward with a world-weary expression. *I feel for you, mate*, Edward thought. *I really do.*

'Poor old bugger,' he said.

'Which one?' said Isobel. 'Gum?'

'What?' He saw that she was holding out a packet of chewing gum. 'Oh. Right, thanks.' He took the packet from her, extracted the little oblong from its foil pod, and handed it back. 'Both, I suppose.' As they stood waiting for the lights to change, Isobel informed him that allegedly if you were run over at a zebra crossing you got a free funeral. 'Not that I'd advise testing it out,' she said, as the little green man lit up. 'Speaking of – what do you think, do we thank everyone for coming tomorrow? Or does that sound a bit flippant, like it's a concert or something? Totally the wrong thing to say, right?' They had reached Jules and her lamp post.

'*There you are,*' she said huffily.

'Here we are,' agreed Edward, and made a note not to let Jules wind him up.

'You'll have to give your hands a wash when we get back,' said Jules. 'Mangy thing, it probably had fleas.'

'Wilco. And if I forget I expect you'll remind me, won't you?' Pointless to retaliate, Edward thought. Taking the bait would only ratchet up the situation – which was *what*, he wondered irritably, aside from a mystery known only to Jules? He hoped Isobel wasn't listening to it all, this ... *performance*. What must she think? He and Jules were behaving like one of those wretched couples who took pot-shots at each other in public, forcing everyone to look away politely and pretend it wasn't happening. As Jules walked ahead of them once more, he watched Isobel jog to catch up with her. His sister was making an effort, Edward thought, and that was more than he could say for Jules.

Thursday

The Seagull

'I said pack it in! *Not you, Jaydn!*'

Julie waited, aware of the clock and listening for Edward to come out of the shower. Lorraine had a knack for ringing at inconvenient times and then breaking off without warning to talk to other people. '*You need to relax!*' she snapped when Julie tried to explain how confusing this was. She heard a shout – a swear word, and then something like '*I hate you!*' And then a clatter of furniture and the noise of a door slamming. Lorraine came back on the line sounding out of breath. 'I can't bloody control her any more,' she sighed. 'Anyway, what was I saying?'

'About her, Isobel …' she replied.

'Right, so like I keep telling you, she'll be back in the States in a couple of days, so what's your problem?' She heard a drawer being opened and closed, followed by the click of Lorraine's cigarette lighter. 'You're not wrong, though,' Lorraine continued, inhaling deeply. 'She's definitely trying to turn him against you.'

Julie had said no such thing – or not in so many words, and certainly not since they'd been on the phone. Obviously she'd seen with her own eyes how deranged and peculiar Isobel was. But after talking to Edward this morning, and completing a very detailed affirmation exercise, she had decided that worrying about Isobel was pointless. In fact, it was exactly the sort of negative focus that *Pathways to Possible* warned you not to *give power* to. Of course, Julie realised, her mistake had been announcing this to Lorraine just now, since for the last ten minutes she had talked about nothing else. As Lorraine talked on, she remembered the other problem that she had promised herself not to focus on or share with her sister – the queasy, uneasy feeling in the pit of her stomach which felt impossible to put into words: the feeling that Edward was being different – not only with her, but with Isobel, and in completely opposite ways.

'I opened the letters,' she said, interrupting Lorraine mid-sentence.

'*What?*' her sister replied after an off-putting pause. '*Edward's* letters? *You opened his personal letters?*'

Wasn't Lorraine the one who had argued the letters were not Edward's but Julie's own? Last night, they were 'the letters' or 'that cow's letters' – meaning Mary's or Isobel's, either one. This morning, somehow, they had turned into 'Edward's personal letters'.

'*And*?' said Lorraine impatiently – and, seeing there was no other choice, Julie felt obliged to tell her the whole story. Edward hadn't been at all defensive when she'd asked him about New York, she explained at the end. He obviously wasn't trying to hide anything. 'And really,' Julie went on, recalling Edward's genuinely puzzled expression and casual tone and relieved to be making the situation clear to Lorraine, 'his visit was so long ago that I honestly think he'd forgotten about it. I think it's just … some stupid old letter of Isobel's, and me jumping to conclusions again – like you always say.' On the other end of the line, her sister was silent. 'Lorraine? Are you still there … ?'

'Yeah,' Lorraine answered flatly. 'I'm here.'

Julie persevered. 'He said it wasn't anything, really …' How had Edward put it? 'He said it was *nothing to write home about*.'

At this point Lorraine let out a sharp snort of laughter. 'Are you having a laugh?' she said. 'He would say that, wouldn't he? I mean, what's he going to do, admit that he's been dying to piss off to the States and that it's all planned out and now's his bloody chance? Do me a favour.'

Julie had felt so panicky this morning, so unsure about confronting Edward and how he might respond – but his reaction had put her mind at rest. Now she felt herself getting confused again, her insides preparing to turn somersaults.

'What did the postmark say?' Lorraine demanded,

She had let herself be put on the spot again, like a witness on *Judge Judy*. 'I don't know …' she said. 'I couldn't tell. I suppose I just *assumed* it was from before, from before I met him.'

'That's the trouble when you assume ...' Lorraine began. No, that was the trouble with Lorraine, thought Julie, who petrified you with ideas you'd never let yourself take seriously. Was Isobel out to get her? How stupid she'd been, Julie realised, to think that Isobel, for her own unfathomable reasons, or because she was the sort of person who enjoyed holding things over people's heads, would keep Julie's secret about her mother.

'Edward's very strict about honesty—'

'Is he?' Lorraine interrupted.

'Is he what?'

'*Honest*. How do you know he's telling the truth? Did you ask him directly if he was moving over there, and when? Or did you just witter on about whether he'd been there on bloody holiday?' Lorraine sounded furious.

'But I couldn't ask him that, could I?' Julie reminded her. 'Because then he'd know I opened his personal letters ...' She felt sick and close to tears. 'He said it was nothing to—'

'Yeah, yeah, *nothing to write home about* – what*ever*,' said Lorraine. 'God, you're naïve sometimes. I said all along you have to keep an eye on them or they take advantage. Didn't I? Well? Haven't I said that, like, *a million times?*'

'Yes,' she agreed. 'Yes, you have.'

Was Edward keeping things from her? She tried to think but couldn't get her mind to focus. Yet again, within minutes of talking to Lorraine, she had gone from blessed relief to crippling anxiety.

Edward finished his shower, gulped down his third black coffee, and was dressed and ready in record time. As they walked to the car he was unusually cheerful and talkative, suggesting they take Isobel out for a meal – what he called 'a nice pub lunch'. 'Today's the last chance we'll have. She's flying back the day after tomorrow, remember?'

How could I forget, Julie thought, attempting to stretch her mouth into a smile. 'That sounds nice,' she told him.

'Cool,' Edward said in a bored voice, pulling rather abruptly out of their parking spot. *Cool? Where did that word come from?* But she knew where.

By lunchtime, trapped in the pub, she realised that she wasn't imagining it at all. Edward *was* different. He smiled more when Isobel was about; he appeared happier and more relaxed. He listened to her outrageous opinions and laughed at her inappropriate jokes, and questioned her intently as if he was interested in her strange likes and dislikes.

'So,' said Isobel, appearing back at the table with their drinks and throwing Julie one of her artificial, patronising smiles. 'Was it love at first sight?'

'Sorry?' said Edward.

'With you two,' said Isobel. 'I mean, who asked who out?'

She wondered whether Isobel, creeping up on them, had overheard their tense exchange and Edward's cross words. What had they talked about for all those hours last night, joking and sharing confidences, while Julie – the *muggins* – had sat at home watching the dinner burn? Did they wish she hadn't come with them for lunch?

'It was a mutual decision,' said Edward before she could answer. *He's doing it again*, she thought, *not letting me speak*. Maybe he was ashamed of her, she thought, remembering the mortuary, and the way Edward had snatched his hand from hers as Isobel approached. Because that was how they made her feel, Julie realised: like the gooseberry or the third wheel, excluded and overlooked.

'"Mutual decision"?' Isobel laughed and bared her teeth, which were very white, Julie thought now, too white really. 'Jeez, that sounds so … *legal* and official.'

Turning to Edward, Julie tried to compose her expression into a hint or request, to let him know that she could answer for herself – but Edward already had his back to her. 'Didn't we discuss all that, Izzy?' he laughed. 'Or did you have too much to drink?' So it was true, Julie thought, Edward had shared details of their private relationship with Isobel.

'Ha, I *so* wasn't drunk,' said Isobel, not answering the question and nudging Edward, hard, in the ribs with her elbow. Julie held her breath. Edward wouldn't take kindly to that sort of treatment – he couldn't abide people who were boisterous and took liberties. But Edward merely sighed in a resigned sort of way. Isobel continued to yap on. She couldn't believe it. Was it true? Were men really that silly and gullible? *Most men would go for a rip in a fur coat*, Lorraine had observed once, retelling a favourite story about popping into Declan's office party one Christmas to find 'some minger fawning all over him'. There had been a terrible row about it in the minicab home, but, 'to really take the piss', at work the next day this same woman had gone up to Declan and told him that it was *really lovely* to meet his wife and what a *shame* it was that Lorraine was so insecure because she could be *quite pretty if she lost the weight*. 'Bitch,' Lorraine had said, 'I'll cut her fucking face up.'

Julie watched Isobel lean towards Edward and point at the cheese on his plate. 'Are you going to eat that?' she said.

'All yours,' he replied, and forked it over without even asking Julie if she might like some. She couldn't help noticing that Isobel's nails were no longer perfect but bitten down to the quick, the glossy red varnish almost completely chipped off – but not quite – which had the peculiar effect, Julie decided, of making her look rather common.

'Yes, but who made the first move?' Isobel insisted. 'Who actually asked who out?'

'Hmm,' said Edward, frowning. Couldn't he see that Isobel was just trying to humiliate her? 'Well, let me think,' he went on, as if the day they met – which was burned into her own memory – wasn't worth remembering. 'I was probably making a phone call in the corridor, something like that…and then maybe Jules came out of the classroom and we got chatting, and went for a coffee.'

'Cool,' smirked Isobel, who appeared to have got what she wanted, poking indifferently at the donated cheese. Julie wanted to stick a fork in her hand. She let them get on with it, nursing her tepid cup of coffee while Edward and Isobel passed their private jokes across the table like condiments. First it was politics and films, then boats and aeroplanes. 'Far safer to have the seats facing backwards, of course.' 'Sure, but super-bad from a PR perspective, right?' 'Precisely.' *I might as well be back with Mary at Danecroft Road*, Julie thought bitterly. She couldn't stand it, Isobel's constant patter of unfunny observations, the way she flicked her eyes at Edward. *All the better to eat you with, my dear*, said Isobel's smile, while Edward, already on his second Bloody Mary, went, 'Come off it, Izz!' to everything Isobel said. You'd think they'd behave with a bit more decorum, she thought, considering their mother had just passed and was barely cold. There were weird catchphrases she had never heard Edward use before – not even with Mary – as if he and Isobel were speaking another language or using secret code words. 'Always look on the bright side of life!' he told Isobel at one point in a funny, sing-song voice – actually *sang it*, Julie realised. Considering the negative remarks he made about *Pathways to Possible*, this advice was very hurtful. As another raucous burst of laughter went up, she wondered if Isobel's face ever got tired.

Edward went to the men's room and she walked out into the chilly sunshine, grateful for some fresh air. Across the road, past the beach with its grey pebbles and crushed plastic bottles, the sea looked brown and unfriendly. She had never felt comfortable with large expanses of water. As a child she always feared that the waves would surge forward and swallow her up. The sun emerged from between the clouds, lighting the surface with a dull, silvery shine and making her think of the foil insides of cigarette packets.

On the way back to Danecroft Road they passed a seagull, at which point either Edward or Isobel might have made some comment about the bird – by then she couldn't say she was listening any more – but it must have been a full minute later when she stopped and turned and saw that the two of them were a long way behind her, still standing in the same place. The sun was out here and there, but a cold, squally breeze had blown up, threatening rain, and she drew her coat around her. Why was Isobel so interested in a stupid bird? And Edward, Julie thought, wasting time after chivvying them out of the house so early this morning, all action stations at Danecroft Road for their 'last big push'. The seagull let out a shriek. *Birds*, she thought with a shudder – *nasty things, noisy and scavenging*. Animals weren't people – although Edward behaved as though they were, perpetually soppy over the ungrateful cat which felt free to display its scorn and disregard for Julie every chance it got. Not that Edward noticed, much as he had never seemed to notice the way Mary looked down on her – or the way Isobel did, for that matter. She saw Isobel turn to Edward, her dark hair blowing round her face, and point up towards the sky. Edward said something and spread his arms wide like a child pretending to be an aeroplane, and Isobel nodded vigorously. It was obvious that this was all for show. She very much doubted that Isobel had any genuine interest in the bird or what Edward was saying. Everyone knew how talented he was with science and mechanical things, with planes and trains and what went on with their innards, and this would be simply another attempt by Isobel to take advantage – calculating, flattering, pretending to admire Edward's superior knowledge, as a way to get her claws in. Even if she chose to believe what Edward said this morning, if he really did have no intention of joining his sister in New York, it didn't mean Isobel wasn't trying to get him there. *Bloody Isobel.* Isobel, who thought she was being clever and funny when she was just making an exhibition of herself, who had outbursts, who was selfish and unreliable and fell out with her family and who had now turned on Julie. Everything Edward had warned her about had come true.

Edward and Isobel were walking on again, strolling towards her in an infuriatingly leisurely way. Then Isobel stopped to pat a dog. Edward waited patiently at her side. Why was he letting her hold them up like this? Why was he letting her get away with it? It was another few minutes before they finally crossed the road towards her. 'Totally the wrong thing to say, right?' she heard Isobel say as they reached her. What were they talking about? Were they talking about her? Then, not two minutes later, they fell behind again. Were they doing it on purpose? It was raining more steadily now and she picked up her pace.

'Hey, Julie, wait up!' Turning, she was dismayed to see Isobel trotting up behind her, holding out a small silver object. 'Can you take a picture of us?' she said. 'Me and Edward, I mean,' she added unnecessarily. Julie took the object and saw that it was a pocket-sized camera, surprisingly out-of-date and cheap-looking. She wondered why Isobel didn't just use her mobile like anyone else. But then, Julie realised, that was Isobel through and through, wasn't it? Trying to be different for the sake of it. Anything to be the centre of attention.

'Nice camera!' said Edward, puffing up alongside them. 'I should start using a proper one again.'

'I thought we could get a picture,' said Isobel. 'What do you think? Shall we?'

'Have I got a choice?' said Edward with mock annoyance. Isobel pulled at his coat so that they were both standing directly in front of the antiques shop, whose window was full of battered old furniture and which was, Julie remembered, one of Mary's old haunts.

'Make sure you get the sign in the frame, okay, Jules?' Isobel instructed bossily.

Peering into the viewfinder, Julie located Isobel standing in the very middle of the picture looking very pleased with herself. One hand was on Edward's shoulder, the other posed on her hip. *Fine Antiques, Bric-a-Brac – Ring bell for entry*, said the large sign over her head.

'Hold up a mo, Jules,' Isobel said as she was about to push the button, 'I'll tell you when.' She watched her fiddle with her hair. Isobel's own mother had hidden her daughter's letters from Edward because Mary *understood* what sort of person she really was, Julie thought. It all made sense. Mary must have known Isobel wanted to spirit her son away from her, to America, and – quite rightly, in her opinion – she had put a stop to it. Was Isobel now threatening to do the same to her, and giving her no choice by holding Mary's accident over her head like an axe? Up until now it had been a mystery why she hadn't gone straight to Edward and told him everything, but as she watched Isobel through the viewfinder, preening and posing, the answer came to her: *Isobel was waiting to worm her way into Edward's good books first*. There was no other explanation. That way, Julie thought, when Isobel delivered the news, his sister could be there waiting for him, like a shark with its mouth open. She waited as Isobel and

Edward swapped places, Isobel briefly moving in and out of the frame as she instructed Edward where and how to stand. They already looked thick as thieves. When would Isobel make her move? After the funeral? *At* the funeral...? Julie shuddered, imagining the burly policemen, handcuffs at the ready, bursting into Mary's ceremony, marching up the aisle to find Julie and arrest her. After all, Isobel obviously had a taste for the dramatic.

All day Julie had been struggling with the decision of whether or not to hand over the letters to Edward. By rights they were his property. And she wanted badly to see his reaction: what would he think of Mary keeping them a secret? Would this make him feel differently about her? And what about Isobel – knowing his sister had spent years trying to get in touch with him, how would he feel about her? As Isobel fiddled about and put her hair up and took it down again and undid a button on her coat and applied more lip balm while Edward playfully rolled his eyes.

'Come on, Jules, hurry up and take the bloody picture, for God's sake,' Edward called out. 'We have to get back.'

She couldn't bear the idea of Isobel's letters in their flat. Like Mary's boxes, it would be like having Isobel herself there – except worse, Julie realised, because *Isobel* was worse.

'I'm ready for my close-up!' Isobel chirruped. '*Cheese!*'

Pathways to Possible said there was no such thing as accidents. Mary had hidden the letters for a reason. Now Mary was gone, and – not an accident – the letters had found their way into Julie's hands. Which meant that it was up to her to preserve Mary's wishes – which wouldn't be hard because, it struck her for the first time, she and Mary were in agreement. Their intentions were *perfectly aligned*.

Carefully she aimed the camera ever so slightly above and to the right of Isobel's head and pressed her finger down on the little button. Deep inside the camera a mechanism whirred and something made a sharp click. 'All done!' she said, handing the camera to Isobel, who gave her a suspicious look and took it without saying anything. There was nothing she could do to stop Isobel and her big mouth, Julie realised, but she could make sure Edward never, ever saw her letters. And, when Isobel got back to New York and developed her precious photo, she would find no Edward – no 'us' – just a nice picture of a brick wall. And if that wasn't *visualising your intentions*, Julie decided as they turned on to Danecroft Road, she didn't know what was.

7

Bambi and Red Jelly

There was no need for the umbrella Martin loaned her that morning. The day dawned with a holiday feel, viciously sunny with bouncy, fluffy clouds and the lightest of breezes. In Martin and Sean's local high street, people were out early to make the most of the spring weather. Older people stood gossiping outside the supermarket, while the cafés pulsed with fashionably dressed mothers sipping lattes and ignoring their children. As they drove across the Downs, a kite jigged and dipped over the sea and the radio predicted warmer temperatures. *It's all wrong*, Isobel thought: the blue skies, the jolly radio announcer, the wildflowers lining the road as if waiting for a parade to come by, their colourful heads bobbing along to an invisible brass band. Years ago, she and Edward had gone to see *Harold and Maude* at the cinema. They had agreed afterwards that the effect of the rain and black umbrellas was not so much zanily upended but ruined by the cheery, saccharine Maude showing up with her bright

236

yellow one. She stared out of the window and dared a posse of wide-eyed woodland Disney creatures to leap out and burst into song. *Bambi*, Isobel thought. Their mother let them watch *Psycho*, but never *Bambi*, because Bambi's mother was killed by a hunter. To this day she had never seen it.

This morning it had taken a few moments to remember. She had woken early with a feeling of something 'off', like her period coming on or the arrival of a long-dreaded social obligation. And then the black dress came into focus, folded over the back of the chair. *Today*, Isobel had thought, *it's today*. Although the idea didn't feel any more likely, she realised, or less ludicrous, than yesterday. The whole week had felt partitioned off, as if she were observing it impassively through the eyes of an impostor who had gone through the motions on her behalf, mouthing the correct things – as presumably, she thought, they would again today. As they reached the last stretch of cliff road, she checked her pocket for the piece of folded paper that held her speech.

They were descending the hill into town, genteel semis and modest cars parked in tidy driveways giving way to shops and shoppers. Oblivious, Isobel thought, all of them. They drove on through the town centre and up a steep hill where they were greeted by an industrial-looking sign: *Crematorium – Parking*. Edward slowed the car and turned them into a smooth tarmac roadway. As they rounded the corner, Isobel saw a squat concrete building, topped by a thick chimneystack. It looked like a bunker.

'Are you sure this is the right place?' she asked Edward.

'Yep, certain,' he said. 'We're much too early.' He pulled into a parking space and turned off the ignition. No one made a move to get out. Edward was immaculate-looking in a black suit, but her dress was scratchy and uncomfortable and she tugged at the hem. The silence in the car felt unbearable.

'Maybe we should go inside?' she suggested. 'Just check everything out?'

'Okay,' said Edward with a sigh. 'Might as well, I suppose.'

'Weird, right?' she murmured as they approached the ornate and overly wide set of double doors at the front of the building. MAIN ENTRANCE was posted in red all caps above them. 'A McCrematorium,' she joked. 'Or maybe they wanted a cathedral and ran out of money halfway through.' Edward shot her a wry sort of look. Of course, Isobel thought, the doors would have been constructed to accommodate not so much the living, but the dead arriving in coffins. The lobby was empty and at Edward's suggestion they went in search of the chapel.

'Chapel? Do they call it that? I wonder what they call it?' she went on. There would be some secular term, unpoetic but straightforward. Edward shrugged. She was being annoying, and as they followed the corridor round she willed herself to shut up.

There was no signpost or nameplate to indicate the chapel, just a plain piece of A4 paper stuck to another set of large double doors. *Mary Vernon. 1100hrs–1130hrs.* It felt like a jolt and they all stared at it for a moment. Isobel stepped forward.

'What are you doing?' said Edward.

'It's crooked,' she said, going to pick off the Sellotape and reposition it.

'Isobel, please – don't touch things ...' he said in a pained voice.

There were other funerals today, Isobel realised, noting the precise and meagre amount of time allocated for their own goodbyes. She hated knowing this, in the same way that she hated knowing that nearby, on the other side of some other teak-effect panelled MDF door, was a printer spewing out people's names, one after the other. Someone's job each morning would involve printing and stacking the names in chronological order, perhaps for convenience's sake next to the coffee machine and not far from the tape dispenser. All through the day this person would have to put down what they were doing, come out into the corridor, put the new one up, rip the old one down and chuck it in the bin.

It was twenty to eleven and the chapel was empty. Perhaps there had been a cancellation. Inside they found themselves in what to Isobel resembled a warehouse-sized, 1980s-era vegetarian restaurant – all pale wood and stripped pine benches. *An IKEA chapel*, she thought, but kept this to herself. Without the swooning Marys and bleeding Jesuses the place lacked *gravitas*, but what had she expected? They had grown up going to a Roman Catholic school a short journey away, mainly to avoid the local one where on your first day, or so they had heard, the older kids shoved your head down the toilet and flushed. The downside was having to make an appearance at the parish church each and every Sunday or risk the priest telling on you and you getting expelled. The Church's *biggest* mistake, said their mother, had been getting rid of the Latin mass. Solemn, incomprehensible Latin had lent meaning and mystery that the 1970s guitars and folk masses could never hope to, she said. Sensibly they had kept the heavy robes and the billowing incense, though, and the drawn-out cannibal palaver with the Communion bread, with the little handbell that was rung at random moments by the frightened-looking altar boy. 'Quick,' their mother would hiss as Communion finished and the priest sat dozing on his 'throne', 'before the bell wakes him up!' There was an art to it. You had to sit in a pew far enough forward for the priest to get a good look at you, but far enough back to make your stealthy escape.

She watched Edward, staring down the aisle with a determined expression, as if trying not to move the muscles of his face. Following his gaze, she saw a high table or dais – the un-altar, she supposed – where the sun, still coursing disrespectfully through the high aluminium-framed windows, glinted on a huge, golden cross.

'That's coming down right now,' she said, and started up the aisle towards it.

'No,' said Edward. 'Isobel, don't!'

She turned round. 'But we told them it's a humanist ceremony...!'

'I know,' he sighed, 'I know, but it could be wired up to a security system.'

This seemed rather elaborate, Isobel thought, and unlikely. And even more reason to yank the ugly thing off its security wires, to set the alarm bells ringing as she marched back down the aisle with the cross in protest, like a reverse Joan of Arc. Why have such a humongous thing on display, she asked Edward, when the crematorium had gone so above and beyond to make the place as cold and uninspiring as possible? 'They can't have it both ways. Plus it's the worst logo ever,' she said, gesturing towards the crucifix. 'You know, if you think about it...' Okay, their mother had wanted a humanist ceremony, which was as it should be, but the whole set-up was a joke – from the tactless, belching smokestack planted front and centre, to their mother's name laser-printed on cheap office paper and stuck half-heartedly to a door. And the ridiculous 'altar', she said, which had the appearance of a home bar in a suburban mansion and lacked only a few ugly barstools.

'Look, Izzy, I agree with you, but just calm down,' said Edward. 'We'll find someone here to sort it out. We've got time.'

'You're quite right, Edward,' said Julie. So far today, Isobel realised, though she remained pressed to Edward's side like a barnacle, Jules and her priggish teaching-assistant voice had seemed to fade back into the scenery.

A whoosh of stale air blew over them as the doors behind them opened. They all turned to see someone who could only be the hyphenate-surnamed humanist minister. '*Incoming...*' Isobel whispered.

'The Vernons, I presume!' Mrs Finsbury-Turle strode towards them with an outstretched hand.

'That's us,' Isobel replied, and felt the need to stand up straight.

'You're all good and early, I must say!' Mrs Finsbury-Turle declared – a bit ambiguously, Isobel thought – seizing Isobel's hand in a hearty, bone-cracking grip. After what seemed like an awfully long time she released it. 'Superb to make your acquaintance *in persona*,' she said.

It was both gratifying and disappointing, Isobel thought, when people turned up looking just how you pictured them. In Mrs Finsbury-Turle's case she did indeed look exactly like Mrs Tufty the Safety First Squirrel – that was, if Mrs Tufty had been a keen hockey player. She was perfect. With her bulk firmly buttoned into a tweedy jacket and skirt, accessorised with sturdy lace-up shoes, Mrs Finsbury-Turle was exactly the reassuring presence Isobel had hoped for.

'How do you do,' said Edward stiffly as her enormous paw clamped down on his. Isobel waited for him to flinch, but his expression remained fixed in a polite and approximate-looking smile as he turned smoothly towards Julie, who appeared to shrink back in fear, and said, 'This is Jules.'

'Nice to meet you,' said Jules in a small voice. Mrs Finsbury-Turle seemed to register the grudging wet-fish squeeze and looked briefly from Julie to Edward, and then back again, as if trying to work out what their relationship was.

'Right, then,' said Mrs Finsbury-Turle, 'first things first. I noticed that some of your guests are arriving in the lobby. Let's gather them up and bring them in. The service will start in – ' she consulted her wrist ' – approximately ten minutes.' Such matter-of-factness, Isobel thought admiringly. 'The hearse will arrive soon,' she continued, 'and everyone should be seated as the coffin is brought in.' *Hearse. Coffin.* The words sounded almost harmless, Isobel thought, coming from Mrs Finsbury-Turle's mouth. Was there in fact a car, she wondered suddenly, or a stately hearse of some sort? It was Edward who had dealt with all that while Isobel was busy agonising over the word 'suitable'. She pictured their mother's coffin gliding up outside in Cinderella's carriage as Mrs Finsbury-Turle forged ahead, a general, readying her troops for battle. Even Edward had begun nodding his head obediently. They must look like spaniels, she thought, taking instruction from Barbara Woodhouse, the formidable TV dog trainer.

'I expect you'd both like to say a few words?' said Mrs Finsbury-Turle.

'I'll speak briefly,' said Edward. 'Isobel? You said you had something prepared?'

Would you call it 'prepared', Isobel wondered, the document she had been labouring over since Monday? Late last night she had added the finishing touches and printed it out in Martin and Sean's home office on a sheet of A4 – the non-eulogy, like the non-chapel, and the non-altar.

'I guess so,' she said.

'Marvellous!' Mrs Finsbury-Turle brought her hands together. 'I shall start the ceremony and introduce you both, and afterwards close out the proceedings with a few words about your mother.' She made the whole ordeal sound like the Oscars, Isobel thought, patting nervously at her pocket. The paper seemed to crackle and shrink with inadequacy.

As her mother's friends began to filter in, Isobel realised that if anyone touched her, if they spoke kindly or placed a hand on hers, for even a moment, she might break. She repositioned herself across the aisle from Edward and Julie, and several non-pews away from anyone else. Her old schoolfriend Francesca came over. 'You sure you want to sit here all on your tod, Izzy?'

'Thanks, Francesca,' she said. 'I'm good.'

There was a beat as Francesca narrowed her eyes. 'Okay.' She smiled. 'Have it your way. I'm here if you need me.'

There was some muted kerfuffle at the back of the room and Isobel turned to see the doors being propped open. Others were also turning in their seats, discreetly but expectantly, as if the bride was about to come down the aisle – which in a way, Isobel thought, she was. Then the coffin emerged through the doorway, carried by six strangers in black suits, and she had to catch her breath and turn back to face the front. Had Edward been asked to be one of the pallbearers? She couldn't remember. Perhaps he'd refused – or declined, as he might put it. *I won't be carrying the coffin, thanks.* Across from her, Edward faced front, his hands folded in his lap. Mrs Finsbury-Turle had ordered the cross removed at his request, and he appeared to be staring at the empty space where it had once stood. Did Edward believe in God, or religion? She realised that she had no idea any more. For herself there had been a window of chance, a fleeting hope. At school they had sung about Him each morning, and how he created 'all creatures great and small'. However good you were, they were told, without a soul the Gates of Heaven were closed to you. She had decided to ask the two priests – the school priest, and the one from their parish church – whether their dog, Otter, would go to heaven. After all, both claimed to have God's ear and that God spoke through them. And yet…they gave conflicting answers.

The coffin drew level. As it continued smoothly past her, she had to stop herself from stretching out her fingers to touch it. The image of her mother's library card floated into her mind, bobbing gently and insinuatingly, like a piece of debris coughed up from a flood. She had returned it to the library yesterday afternoon, prompting an awkward conversation with the hapless woman on the desk, but it was easier than tossing the card in the bin. Just this morning, in another sticking-plaster moment, she had taken the enormous step of removing their mother's number from her phone. Afterwards she had waited, expecting an onslaught of reality, 'closure' – something. There had been only a sense of profound wrongdoing, as if playing a joke that wasn't funny and would have to be paid for later.

The men lowered the coffin on to a metal bier, a tense moment during which Isobel felt she couldn't be the only one willing them not to drop it – like that scene in *Brazil*, she thought, where the body falls out in a tumble of bones and red jelly. Earlier, under Mrs Finsbury-Turle's direction, she had gently chivvied people out of the lobby area towards the chapel when she saw a large black car pull up outside. Instinctively she had looked over at Edward, a few feet away, and seen the grimace of anguish in his face. And then, bizarrely, it was gone, replaced by the expression he had been wearing all morning, the supremely neutral and tolerant look of someone hosting a slightly tedious cocktail hour. *Self-control*, she recalled from somewhere, was known as *the emblem of survivors*. Across the aisle she watched Edward sit marmoreal and straight-backed as a soldier, his face a mask. She tried to decide which was more unsettling: this official Edward, or the glimpse of the one underneath.

Rocks and Stones and Trees

'For those of us who do not believe in a supernatural being...' Mrs Finsbury-Turle began pointedly, inspecting the room over her glasses. He had watched her march to the podium and take her place in a rustle of paper and it was an introduction his mother would have loved. *My mother*, Edward thought, staring at the coffin, *unable to love anything or anyone ever again and presently nailed – in all likelihood glue-gunned – into a box*. No longer a 'she', she was at most an 'it', reduced to something less human than mineral, unresponsive and cold. Countless times since Sunday he had found himself thinking how she *would have* or *wouldn't have* liked or wanted this or that, and felt angry for succumbing to the tautology. What would Mrs Finsbury–Turle think, Edward wondered, if she could see under the expression of mild appreciation plastered to his face and know how much he longed for the mindless, dim-witted comfort of religion, for the ritual of prayer? Like his mother he had never been able to give himself over to religious faith, let alone believe in a supernatural being. But that hadn't stopped him from wishing he felt differently – this week, anyway.

'Death is a part of life,' Mrs Finsbury-Turle went on, pausing once more to sweep her eyes across them all. He wondered how she would describe the handful of people assembled in front of her. 'Congregation' had dodgy religious overtones, while 'audience' smacked of the music hall. She cleared her throat with what Edward thought was a surprisingly decorous little cough, like a fat man light on his feet. 'Death,' she said, cocking her head. 'What is death?' *You might well ask*, he thought, though of course she wasn't asking – not really. It was the third such pause in as many minutes, and it was clear to him that she was inserting them for dramatic effect. Maybe 'audience' was the right word, after all. 'Death is a natural process whereby our bodies are returned to the elements,' she continued brightly, 'to the state from whence we came.' She was beginning to depress him, her words bringing to mind the priests who glossed over the reality of death, whose 'dust to dust' might as well be fairy dust. How fucking disappointing, Edward thought, to hear the humanists mimic the Catholics and frame death as a mere detail, a vaguely irrelevant pit stop en route to something more – he searched for the right word – 'authentic'. And yet, what had he expected? A poem from his school days seemed to mirror Mrs Finsbury-Turle's attitude, a version of eternal life that only an environmentalist could take comfort in. Wordsworth? Keats? He searched his memory. Isobel might know. Somewhere between the 'pathetic fallacy' and the 'negative capability' had lurked the poet's dead girlfriend – which was no cause for sadness, the poem explained, since Lucy was now 'rolled round … with rocks, and stones, and trees'. 'Inspiring' and 'comforting', his teacher had called it. Edward thought it sounded like a fucking nightmare. 'God bless us, God spare us, that's all, amen,' their mother used to say when she tucked them in at night. 'In the name of the Father, the Son, and the Holy Ghost, that's it, that's all, that's your lot, amen!' He had never thought of it as having much to do with God, or thought properly about the words, or what they might signify save for a rhyme that bound them together, a nightly ritual and invocation that meant nothing more than their mother keeping them safe. 'Because we are *here* today not to mourn, but to *celebrate* the life of Mary Vernon,' Mrs Finsbury-Turle continued. *Speak for yourself*, Edward thought, and glanced across at Isobel. What did his sister make of it all, sitting there with her hands in her lap? 'Are we not being returned to the place from whence we came?' asked Mrs Finsbury-Turle again, surveying the room for dissent. *And where's that, then?* Edward wanted to ask. It was exactly the same stench of denial that he found so distasteful about religion. Except that, somehow, this dogged, *dogmatic* emphasis on 'celebrating' death was worse, the parental because-I-said-so of religion tarted up as enlightened acceptance – minus a supernatural being to call on when things went pear-shaped or you wanted a new bike. Last summer, Edward remembered, he had wrenched his knee so badly that he had lain in bed whimpering until finally, at 4am, he'd hobbled into the kitchen and taken some of the cat's pain medicine. If at any point he had prayed to God – and naturally he hadn't – would it have made any difference? *Would it now?* Edward thought, as he listened to Mrs Finsbury-Turle, the coffin floating in his peripheral vision. Like a capricious and mercurial dictator there was no rhyme or reason to what 'God' did or what *He* chose, save that his creations were too lowly to understand *His will* when prayers went unanswered, when children died, and when – despite *His* alleged omniscience – God was occupied elsewhere, doling out disease and disaster. The most fun part of this game – *God's Plan* – being that you never really knew when it was your turn or the turn of someone you loved. God enjoyed keeping you in the dark. 'See you later,'

Edward had called out to his mother less than six days ago, and strolled blithely off to the pub.

Had some duty slipped his mind? Mrs Finsbury-Turle had fallen silent. He looked up, hoping that he hadn't forgotten something. He had said his piece a few minutes earlier and had no wish to say more. He saw a movement, a shifting of the shapes and colours from the pew to his right – Isobel. Of course. He'd forgotten she was going to speak. He watched as she walked up to the front, holding herself rather self-consciously upright like a drunk driver treading the centre line in the road. As she stepped up to the podium he found himself hoping she wouldn't start crying or say anything embarrassing.

Even from here he could see the paper shaking in Isobel's hands. She looked very young and unsure, though her voice was level. At certain intervals her shoulders heaved slightly and he wondered if she had scored her breaths in advance. Was his sister worried about fluffing her lines? He held his breath, relieved when she spoke about their mother's love of dancing and horses and her encouragement of her children to do what made them happy. He had said little himself – possibly *too* little, he thought. Isobel was sprinkling in some humour, a couple of harmless little quips, so that the people around him laughed in the gentle and restrained way appropriate to the occasion. Isobel's little speech wasn't as bad as he thought it would be and he made a mental note to tell her so afterwards, if not in those exact terms.

His sister finished and stepped down, and there was an odd extended silence, as if everyone was suppressing the instinct to clap. Given all the guff they'd heard from Mrs Finsbury-Turle about the jolly Celebration of Life, Edward thought to himself, what was her policy on applause?

'Goodness, I don't know that I have been left anything to

say!' exclaimed Mrs Finsbury-Turle with a rather corporate-looking smile that must have been practised in front of the mirror. Edward had one just like it and had trained his social persona to take part in any conversation, a listening smile glued to his face, leaving his private self undisturbed, like a submarine resting on the sea floor, free to quietly observe or contemplate his next drink. Social engineering: he had it down pat. Unfortunately there wasn't much call for this special skill in Edward's deskbound department – for persuasion and winning the hearts and minds of the enemy – except during gruesome 'team-building' events. And on days like this, he thought sorrowfully.

'Mary's life was one rich in experience ...' Mrs Finsbury-Turle chuntered along, as predictably as an old jalopy. As she returned to her theme of everlasting life in rocks and stones and trees, he felt his gaze drawn inexorably back to the area behind her where his mother's coffin, severe and unequivocal – and surely far too small – had been set down atop a folding metal bier with zigzag legs. Relieved of its weight, the men had straightened their jackets and walked away with the air of skiving off for a well-earned smoke.

At the mortuary, Edward remembered, Isobel had ventured into the room where their mother lay. Had this made her death easier for his sister to accept, or more difficult? There was no way of knowing. He might have asked her the other night, he supposed, and discussed a few other things besides. But the pub hadn't felt like the time or the place. *Maybe it's for the best*, Edward thought, and heard in the phrase the echo of their mother's voice.

As Edward had known she would, Mrs Finsbury-Turle arrived at the mandatory bit about the dead living on in your memory. 'Indeed,' she said, pausing for effect, 'Mary will live on. In your hearts and memories,' she continued, her voice rising like the last verse of a hymn or a rousing political speech at a rally, 'she will live on.' *Don't make me laugh*, Edward thought resentfully. Could he ring his mother up for a chat tomorrow, then, if she lived on? Thoughts and feelings were information, and no less meaningful for that, but they did not constitute a flesh-and-blood person. They were not real. Memories were electrical activity, chemicals caught between your temporal lobe and your occipital fissure like blurred photocopies slipped between the pages of a book. Your brain displayed them after the fact, and it replayed them like an old film – and, like a film, Edward thought, they faded more each time, no more real than the actors were real, actors who did not 'live on' any more than Marilyn Monroe in *Some Like It Hot* lived on years after she was dead and buried. There was no Ghost in the Machine. When your heart stopped, so did you, and your flesh rotted and fell away. *Ah, but what of the soul*, religious types demanded, *how do you explain that?* It was pointless arguing with them, of course, the nutters who cornered you with stories of past lives and out-of-body experiences and faces seen in clouds. He thought of the famous London surgeon who had placed a large written note on top of a cabinet in the operating room. So far not a single patient out of all those who claimed to have risen out of their bodies and floated up to the ceiling had been able to tell him what the note said.

Apparently, there were other lessons to consider: ' ... the movements of a dance. / A lifetime is like a flash of lightning in the sky,' Mrs Finsbury-Turle was intoning. 'Rushing by, like a torrent down a steep mountain.' *Tempus fugit*, Edward thought; she wasn't wrong. And yet, he found the rhyme itself distasteful and intellectually insulting, like a mass-produced bereavement card. A much better rhyme was the one their grandmother had taught them, and for a moment he wished he had the pluck to walk up and recite it on the podium. Isobel would, Edward thought, if anyone were mad enough to put the idea into her head. As children they had badgered their grandmother to recite it over and over again:

Once upon a time
When a bird shit lime
And a monkey chewed tobacca
An old woman ran
With her finger up her bum
Crying oh my what's the matter.

Just reciting it now in his head, he experienced a brief but satisfying sense of mischief. Where on earth had his grandmother learnt it? She had grown up in the East End of London and as a young woman in the 1920s had made her living criss-crossing the globe with a 'fast' and bawdy globetrotting crowd of musicians. As an older person, she'd been undiminished, an enthusiastic smoker who made risqué jokes and had a laugh like plates breaking.

'And so, to everything there is a season. A time to be born, and a time to die,' said Mrs Finsbury-Turle – another tiresome allusion to their mother being 'returned to the elements', Edward thought, glancing at his watch, factually true yet moot and meaningless, basic chemistry and physics. She reminded him of the New Age sorts who developed a sudden yen for physics, banging on about the First Law of Thermodynamics and how energy cannot be destroyed, only transformed. If that shameful book of Jules's was to be believed, Edward thought, some of these people actually *were* physicists, if generally and reassuringly American and thus able to be written off entirely. He had read an article in the paper recently about so-called 'resurrection' in which the author described some quantum process of mind, brain, or information that was separate from the body and outlived it. In some warped, ignorant interpretation of cause and effect, quantum physics had become the new Bible, accessible to anyone, bent to suit any argument. New Age ignoramuses hijacked real scientific ideas like 'quantum entanglement', and hitched them to spiritual claptrap about everyone being connected to everyone else. Surely there was a difference, Edward thought, between fuzzy logic and woolly thinking?

He wondered what each of his mother's friends was thinking. When he'd stood up to speak, carefully phrasing the 'thank you for coming' part Isobel was so concerned about, they would have made sure to pay attention – or at least appear to. He had the urge to peer round and scrutinise each face. If, now, he could catch them unawares or read their thoughts, what would he find? Boredom? Indifference? Fear...? Were they as appalled by the ceremony as Edward was? Or were they unmoved, thinking about their dinner or what they'd watch on the telly tonight? For most, funerals would be arriving with increasing frequency, many – though not all – being older people. How did it feel to witness your contemporaries, the people you had been young with – and against the odds, possibly still thought of as young – keel over one after the other another like dominoes? Did you get used to it? The scientist Max Planck said that science progressed one funeral at a time. Life, apparently, was no different, and once the process got started there was no denying it was your turn next. His day would come, he supposed, and there was no predicting when. He thought of Gareth, whose mother's death had been brutal and ugly. The last time they'd met up he had felt slightly in awe, amazed to find his friend intact and functioning, like someone who had walked away from a plane crash or emerged, decades later, from an arduous trek through a jungle. They were brothers in arms now, Edward supposed. Death had put Gareth on the other side of an invisible wall, and now Edward had joined him there. Was it fair to compare his mother to Gareth's? Pulling up weeds one minute, pushing them up the next – his mother's end had been instantaneous and merciful – or so he hoped. He had not broached the question with Jules. If there had been anything significant to report, Edward thought, Jules would have informed him. As for Isobel, she had questions, but that was just Isobel, wasn't it? She could never leave well enough alone. What did his sister make of this new-fangled, giddy-up notion of *celebrating a life*, with its implicit denial of sorrow and grief? Nowadays even hospices advertised themselves, with unintended irony, as *places for living*, their vast conglomerate owners issuing greasy all-colour brochures oozing with New Age smarm and quackery. After all, without the comforting claptrap of religion, the bells and wafting incense, what else remained? How even more ironic, Edward thought, that it had taken a humanist to make him appreciate the Catholic Church. He looked at his watch. No hymns, no psalms, and no lecture from a finger-wagging priest; it was undoubtedly what their mother *would have wanted*. And yet, Edward thought, the last twenty-four and a half minutes had left him with a weird taste in the mouth – ripped off, condescended to, cheated by the paltry, scripted send-off. A dark blue curtain began to sweep closed across the coffin – moved not by God or some 'higher power', but by the unseen hand of a funeral lackey or push of a button. He wondered if this was intentional, the resemblance to the final curtain at a theatre. Certainly their mother would not be jogging out to take a bow. He felt himself counting the seconds down. *That's it, then*, he thought as the two halves met, and from somewhere outside came the massive cry of a seagull. The sound was startling, the only noise he'd heard from outside since they had all taken their seats. He glanced apprehensively at Jules – someone who was prone to such things might regard this as a *sign* of something – but was relieved to see that she had her eyes closed.

Once off the podium and down among the proles, Mrs Finsbury-Turle appeared somewhat reduced. He watched her waddle over to an acne-scarred funeral attendant, loitering by the door in an ill-fitting suit. With her wide girth and sturdy hips she resembled one of Thelwell's ponies, he thought, or a doughty lady hiker striding across the Brecon Beacons to put the wind up various infantrymen-in-training. She had done what she could today, he supposed, given the secular limitations. With dull surprise he noticed that the attendant was looking over at him, clearly expecting Edward to stand first. The next stage of the day awaited, Edward thought as he stood and made his way to the end of the pew – the mourners congealing in the Garden of Remembrance, the exchanged banalities and endless goodbyes. His mother's friends would look to him for comforting platitudes or force him to endure theirs. 'Everyone to exit this way please, sir,' said the attendant in a low-ish voice, left hand upturned in some discreet professional reminder. *Your time is up*, it said, *please shift yourself now, and preferably through the poky-looking side door, rather than the overly grand entrance you came in by*. This hurry-up attitude, Edward thought, as they all filed out obediently, only added to the cut-price factory air, the dismaying brevity of it all. He shouldn't begrudge the man trying to keep the conveyor belt moving, even if he begrudged the commercial, Americanised world that made it necessary. No doubt in America such people would expect a tip. *Dying is a business*, Edward thought bitterly, and another party of funeral-goers would be waiting to celebrate. 'Thanks again,' he told the spotty attendant as he passed. 'Sorry for your loss, sir,' the attendant said, smiling.

Our Little Secret

Julie watched Isobel over the rim of her wine glass. If Edward's sister wanted to create a rift or any unpleasantness, she thought, Mary's funeral reception was her last chance. She wouldn't put it past Isobel to say something nasty and scarper back to America like a child knocking on the door and running away. At the crematorium Isobel had waited until everyone sat down, and then she had got up and moved to sit on her own, apparently too high and mighty to sit with Julie and Edward. This hadn't stopped her from marching up to the front halfway through to hog the spotlight, though. They had sat there on the hard benches for a good five minutes before Isobel finished speaking. And then Julie must have nodded off for a few seconds, because suddenly Mary's coffin was being shunted away behind the curtain and it was such a relief to finally stand back up again and have it all done with.

When they had first arrived at the Brentwood Inn, Isobel had darted about talking to this one and that one. Julie had watched her weaving in and out of the clusters of little tables, bobbing up and down – a bit too energetically, in her opinion – until, like a clockwork toy, she had appeared to gradually run down. For the last half-hour Julie had watched her trail sullenly after Edward who, unlike Isobel, Julie thought, taking a small sip of wine, was being the picture of politeness.

Ever since they arrived – which only *felt* like hours ago, she reminded herself, glancing at her wristwatch and realising that it was barely one and a half – he had been making slow circuits of the room to exchange a few words with each of Mary's friends. Julie had stood at his side supportively, listening as he made conversation, and, when he spotted someone standing on their own, waiting patiently as he took them over to one of the tables where groups of Mary's friends sat drinking tea and murmuring among themselves. *A shock, such a shock* – the words had seemed to ripple around the room. And then she had begun to feel awfully tired and her feet had begun to ache and she had been grateful when Edward suggested that she have a sit-down.

A few feet away, Isobel was yanking at her dress and staring at a selection of vegetable samosas and mini cheese and onion pies set out on the buffet table. Then she gazed distractedly out of the window towards the sea and walked across to one of the blue glass bottles that sat on each table and helped herself to a glass of water, taking it over to the fireplace and plonking herself down on one of the green velvet armchairs. As she took off a shoe and started rubbing at her toes, Julie looked away. Edward was so much more refined than his sister, she thought, like one of those important politicians you saw getting off planes on the news. She watched him shake hands with an elderly man and place a steadying hand on the back of the distressed-looking wife. The couple looked up at him gratefully.

A pile of leaflets were stacked under a nearby chair and, curious, she reached over and took one from the top. *The Brentwood Inn*, the leaflet said, *features tasteful antiques and stunning interiors, a modern menu of tasty bites, and picturesque views on to the nearby sea, providing the perfect landscape photo opportunity every bride and groom could wish for.* It really was a shame, Julie thought, to waste such a room on a funeral. Guiltily she wondered whether the inn did proper food or if it was all strictly meat-free. 'A *house rabbit*?' said a posh, aghast-sounding woman's voice somewhere behind her. 'When they had *a dog*?' Her father had very definite opinions on vegetarians, Julie thought, while her mother would expect a proper sit-down meal, with lamb or beef and all the trimmings and *petits fours* and *hors-d'oeuvres* passed round beforehand. 'Yes,' replied another female voice. 'It ate them both, of course.' 'Well, *really...*' tut-tutted the first voice. 'I mean, how stupid can you get?' She glanced round and saw two middle-aged women holding wine glasses, and standing not far from them a large man wearing a blue and yellow patterned jumper who looked vaguely familiar. Julie got the feeling he was trying to join their conversation – and that they were doing their best to ignore him. She turned back to her leaflet. Several members of staff had been popping in and out with trays and glasses. Would it be inappropriate to ask one of them about wedding catering? It wasn't as if she had anything else to do, Julie thought, except watch Isobel fidget endlessly and take her shoes on and off in public. They didn't mention prices in the leaflet, but the room hire and the buffet must have been quite pricey, not to mention the £700 Edward and Isobel had put behind the bar. When the time came, she thought, the inn would consider them good customers and they could ask for a discount.

'Whoops, sorry, room for a little one?'

She turned to see the man in the patterned jumper looming over her.

'Very more-ish, these pasties, aren't they?' he said.

'Yes, they're very nice,' she replied, and shifted her chair a few inches away from the buffet table, and him.

'Nice do, isn't it?' the man persisted, ignoring her hint and landing heavily on the chair next to hers. 'Phil,' he said, without offering a hand – both being occupied, as he fussily sorted his food into separate piles with an almost feminine care and concentration and breathed heavily through his mouth. His plate was filled to its rim. Where was Edward, Julie thought, when she needed him? She didn't feel at all comfortable striking up conversations with Mary's friends – especially one whose clothing and manner were so very inappropriate for the occasion. *Was* this person one of Mary's friends? Or was he some hanger-on who'd wandered in from the public bar? Lorraine was quite right, Julie thought, when she said that people took advantage if you let them.

'We've been away,' he told her, 'holidaying at our home. Our *second* home. In Spain. Myself and my lady wife. We flew back late last night and of course I checked in with my executive secretary, Briony, and she was the one who gave me the news…' He broke off to pick at something in his teeth. 'She says, "I'm afraid poor Mrs Vernon had a very unlucky fall on Sunday." And I *said* to her, "But why didn't you bloody tell me this *before*, Briony?" I check in with her every day when we're at our second home,' he added, 'so there's no excuse.' A strong odour of onions emanated from him. At the same time, Julie realised, feeling rather bilious, she could hear all the food roiling in his mouth. Would it be rude to excuse herself and run to the ladies? 'So Briony says,' Phil continued before she could make her excuses, '"But I didn't want to bother you!" *Didn't want to bother me!* I ask you …' He shook his head and let out a big sigh and in the nick of time Julie managed to breathe out through her mouth. He paused, as if expecting her to nod in agreement.

'Maybe she was being considerate,' she said, startled to hear herself speak up so sharply. Like Mary, this Phil person

258

appeared fond of long, complicated stories, but in all other ways, Julie thought, she couldn't see Mary being pally with him at all. In *fact*, she decided now, since finding the letters, and then this morning, watching Mary's coffin vanish behind the curtain, she had begun to feel rather sorry for her. She and Mary had not been the best of friends, but Mary hadn't deserved a daughter like Isobel. And she certainly didn't deserve a friend like Phil, who was far too cheerful for such an occasion and was more concerned with mopping up yoghurt dip with the end of a baguette.

'I daresay Briony *was* being "considerate" – as you put it,' Phil replied testily, fixing her with sharp look, 'but, as she well knows, Mrs Vernon's been a good tenant, and a hundred and forty per cent loyal. She's lived in that house longer than you've been alive, I daresay,' he added, eyeing her up and down in a very unfriendly fashion.

She couldn't believe it. 'You're Mr Modin, Mary's *land-lord*?' she said. No wonder Edward and Isobel were avoiding their corner of the room.

'For my sins!' Phil Modin replied.

All the panic clearing out Mary's house and giving the keys back, and yet Phil Modin had the cheek to turn up at her funeral? And not even the difficult part of the proceedings with the coffin and the speeches, but the part with the free drinks and all the food. She found herself disliking him even more, on Mary's behalf.

'Danecroft Road was my father's before me. He rented the house to Mrs Vernon's mother ...' he continued. He stopped to insert the nail of his little finger into the space between his two bottom teeth, extracting a morsel of something spongy and yellow. He glanced once at it, and flicked it on to the carpet. 'Another looker, Mary's mother,' he said, as if it was understood that Mary herself was good-looking – which she had been, Julie supposed, in a tall, slim, blue-eyed sort of way. 'Went all round the world,' said Phil Modin. 'Ahead of her time in those days. For a woman, I mean.'

As his bottom lip curled she tried not to look at the viscous dribble of white liquid emerging from the corner of his mouth. He had been leaning closer and closer towards her, and now she felt a piece of something – spit or food – land on her face. She could feel it sitting there, she was sure, at the inside corner of her eye. She longed to wipe it off.

'Mary told me all about her mother,' she said. 'And she was very talented.'

'None of that Women's Lib back then,' said Phil Modin with a lewd wink. If she was being honest, Julie wasn't too sure about feminists either. With their loud, strident views on everything, women like that made her feel a bit embarrassed.

'So,' he went on, 'you're a close personal friend of the family, are you – er … ?'

'Julie,' she offered, trying to see past him and wishing she could get away. He seemed to fill the whole space between her and the rest of the room. 'Edward is my fiancé,' she said.

Phil Modin's hand stopped midway between the plate and his mouth. '*Is he*?' She saw him look her up and down again with a professional and ultimately disappointed air that made her think of the junk man appraising Mary's furniture.

'Actually,' she told him, 'we're not engaged quite yet. But we're as good as.' She resented this person – and Edward as well, she realised – for making her admit to this humiliation.

'I see,' said Phil Modin, who clearly didn't see at all.

'There's been so much to think about, we haven't had time to set a date,' she said, trying to inject a bit of a warning 'edge' into her voice, the way Lorraine did. It wouldn't hurt, she decided, to let Mr Modin know about all the upset and inconvenience he had caused herself and Edward this week. 'And with Mary's passing, and clearing the whole house out this week...'

'*Clearing the house?*' Phil Modin put down the piece of bread he was holding. '*Already?*'

'Well, yes...' she began, confused by his surprise.

'Well, I'm very sorry to hear that Edward's been so *hasty* about it,' he replied, making a vile tut-tutting sound with his tongue. 'I was going to ask him what his plans are for the old place. It could do with a coat of paint, I'll give you that, but apparently I'm too late.'

As Phil Modin explained, there had been 'a terrible mis-understanding' about Mary's house. 'I have an extensive portfolio of properties in the area, you see. And I have my rules for tenants. You know what it's like these days.' He lowered his voice. 'Muslims and gypsies. Benefit scroungers and such. Terrorists, I dare say, some of them...' He lifted his bottom off the seat and pushed up with his hips in a suggestive manner – but he was only reaching into his back pocket for his wallet, from which he took a small card. 'My business card,' he said importantly, placing it in her hand as if allowing her to hold something valuable.

'Thank you,' she replied. 'Very nice,' she added, unsure what she was supposed to say.

'Julia, was it?' He peered closely at her as if expecting to find her name written across her forehead.

'Julie.'

'Right, well, do convey my profound condolences to Edward. And my deepest apologies for any misunder-standings,' he said, looking genuinely sorry. He glanced nervously over at Edward, who was occupied in ferrying a rather large, elderly party towards the settee. 'He's got his hands full today, I can see, so I shan't disturb him, but tell him to reach out to my seccie when he can.'

'Thank you,' she said. 'I will. That's very kind of you.'

Phil Modin stood up. 'And give my best to Isobel, will you?' he said. 'That poor girl. Must be very difficult for her after everything she's been through.' With some effort he got himself up and ambled off in the direction of the main bar, leaving his empty plate and an assortment of crumbs under his chair, and at last Julie was able to wipe the fleck of spit off her cheek. She examined his business card, which was on nice paper, very thick, with raised blue lettering. As she put it in the front pocket of her purse, she wondered if it would have looked rude to ask how much Mary's rent was.

Mary's debating group were among the first to leave, and as the room emptied Julie felt a strange shift in the atmosphere, like a birthday party when one person gets up to go and everyone races for the door. Edward had completed another round of the room and returned to the settee to squat down next to the stout, red-cheeked woman he'd seated earlier. To Julie's dismay, he now beckoned her over.

'Jules, you remember Mrs John from next door?' he said and patted the settee in the small space next to the woman.

'Pleased to meet you,' she said, reluctantly squeezing in next to Mrs John. The immediate and unpleasant sensation of heat given off by Mrs John's plump body made her feel dizzy and sick.

'Mrs John was in Mum's line-dancing group,' said Edward.

'You're the girlfriend?' observed Mrs John accusingly.

'Yes…' she replied, and looked questioningly at Edward, who appeared not to notice and continued with his introductions.

'Mrs John was just telling me she's off to Crowborough tomorrow, aren't you, Mrs John?' It occurred to Julie that Mrs John might not be all there.

'To stay with my son and daughter-in-law,' Mrs John agreed wheezily, puffing out her large chest. 'A son always misses his mother, doesn't he?' She clapped a hand to her mouth. 'Pardon me, Edward, there I go, putting my foot in it...'

'No harm done, Mrs John,' said Edward smartly, and Julie saw the older woman blush. If she weren't so fat, Julie thought, she'd probably jump up and bob back down again in a little curtsy. 'May I leave you in Jules's hands for a moment?' Edward said, standing up. 'I promised Mr Tomlinson I'd speak to him about parking...'

'Oh, don't let *me* keep you, duck.' She reached a plump hand up to pat at Edward's wrist. Julie couldn't help noticing that her other hand was clasped tightly round a packet of cigarettes.

'Get you another drink on the way back?' offered Edward.

'Two's enough for me these days, I should think!' said Mrs John. 'Thank you anyway, duck.'

'Jules?' said Edward, pausing. 'Anything for you?'

Yes, Julie thought to herself, *a bit of consideration, instead of being lumped with yet another of your mother's friends.* 'No, thank you,' she told him. 'I'm fine.'

'To think, I've known her for over thirty years. *Thirty years*! It's the end of an era...' As Mrs John dabbed at her dry eyes, Julie wondered if she and Phil Modin were related.

'It was a shock,' Julie repeated, as soothingly as she could manage. When was Edward coming back? How long she was expected to sit here listening to this person recite her boring stories over and over again? And *where* was bloody Isobel? Wasn't this her job, talking to her mother's friends? Briefly she scanned the room and spotted Isobel fiddling with her hair and talking to her friend Francesca and her mother, the three of them huddled round a table in the corner.

'She's been doing so well, hasn't she?' Mrs John remarked, following her gaze. Another one overly concerned about Isobel, Julie thought crossly. 'She left me Mary's geraniums with a lovely handwritten note. Though I suppose now I'll have to water them...'

On the other side of the room, a waiter brought Edward a drink on a small silver tray. She watched him nod thanks, and the waiter glided off back towards the bar. Mrs John plucked a mini packet of tissues out of her handbag and ripped the top open with a thick, nicotine-stained thumbnail. 'I still can't help feeling... I still can't help feeling that I let Mary down.'

'It was a shock,' Julie repeated, suppressing a yawn. How inconsiderate people were, inflicting themselves on you when it was quite obvious you had no interest in hearing about either them or their private lives.

'*I let her down*,' the woman was insisting in a thick cigarette slur, her bosom heaving. 'Let them all down.' Mrs John, Julie thought tiredly, was one of those people whose sentences went on and on until they ran out of breath, that being some time after you had lost the thread of whatever it was they were trying to tell you. She saw that Isobel was on her feet again, talking to one of the staff, directing them towards the piano with a fresh tray of teacups and saucers. 'I saw her, you know,' Mrs John said. 'From upstairs...'

'Pardon? Saw who?' Julie asked warily.

'*Mary*,' said Mrs John impatiently. The whole room seemed to dip sideways and Julie's stomach took a sickening lurch. 'The day she passed. Laid out on the back path, wasn't she? Terrible business. Gives me a turn just thinking about it...'

Mrs John's jowls trembled and she fanned at her face. Julie willed herself to breathe, to breathe away the anxiety gathering in the pit of her stomach, getting ready to swallow her up. Where were Edward and Isobel? Luckily they were out of earshot, each talking to different people on the opposite side of the room.

'You saw *Mary*?' she said. 'On Sunday?' She felt half deaf from the blood pulsing in her head, amazed that Mrs John couldn't hear it too.

'Well, you and Edward were elsewhere at the time, weren't you?' the old lady said defensively.

'Yes,' Julie agreed, pushing the word out. '*Yes*. We were … *unfortunately*.' It wasn't a lie, she thought, not really.

'Oh, and she did *struggle* …' Mrs John went on in a tone of relish. 'For such a long time …' An obscene and faintly comical image came to Julie of Mary trying, and failing over and over again, to right herself, like a tortoise or an insect rolled over on to its back. She remembered the way she had slept on upstairs, while the sun dipped down under the horizon and the garden grew darker and darker, and she began to feel very ill – literally sick from it. There was nothing she could do. She couldn't run out to the ladies' and risk leaving Mrs John alone. Not now – not even for a moment. Mrs John wanted to talk, and if Edward or Isobel – or anyone else – walked past, Julie felt certain Mrs John would start telling them her story instead. It was pure luck – not luck, fate, Julie realised – that it was she, Julie, who had been placed in Mrs John's pathway first. All she could do now was to stay put and let her keep talking. This was her mother's technique with her father, she remembered, to let him talk on, and flush out the truth that way. She breathed slowly – in, and then out – and then tilted her head sympathetically to one side and said, 'It must have given you such a turn, Mrs John …'

'It was so sudden,' Mrs John was saying, 'so *unexpected*.' She had been speaking for some time and was, Julie thought, possibly a bit drunk. If she had questions for Mary's neighbour, she was mindful of *Pathways to Possible*'s instruction – *don't push the river* – and was keeping this at the very front of her mind.

'It *was* sudden,' she echoed. 'And unexpected.'

'Yes, it *was*,' agreed Mrs John enthusiastically. '*So* unexpected. Although, you know,' she added, her eyes darting around her for a moment as if checking for eavesdroppers, 'Mary was always much too *thin*, don't you think?' Julie nodded in agreement. 'No,' said Mrs John with a quick shake of the head, 'it wouldn't surprise me *in the least* if the weight had something to do with it. That's what I think.'

Isobel was standing only a little way away from them, and far closer than she had been when Julie had last checked, like one of those terrifying statues on *Doctor Who*. Edward, who had been seeing out yet another group, was standing in the doorway looking around to see who was left. There wasn't much time.

'So what did you do?' she asked Mrs John. This was the question she had been waiting to ask.

'*Do*?' repeated Mrs John. She was one of those people who answered you by repeating the last word you said. '*What did I do?* I rang 999, didn't I?'

'You called the *ambulance*?'

'I can't be expected to get down all those stairs without my carer, can I?' said Mrs John, clearly mistaking Julie's astonishment for blame.

'No…no, of *course* you couldn't,' Julie assured her.

'Oh, and she's such a useless lump of a girl, my carer. Supposed to be getting me my weekly shopping at Morrison's, but down the front in them arcades with her fancy man instead, I don't doubt...'

Edward had stopped to speak to a man holding a tray of empty glasses. *Manifest your own reality*, Julie thought desperately, attempting to project billowing pink clouds of self-affirmation and positive thoughts.

'I did try to have a word with her,' said Mrs John, nodding towards Isobel who had drifted off once more and was mooning about next to the piano, gawping at the sea.

'With Isobel?' Her stomach plummeted again. 'When did you speak to her? What did she say?'

'At the crematorium, after the service. But she was a bit preoccupied. Busy with people. Understandable today, I suppose,' Mrs John added, somehow managing to imply that it wasn't. 'I'm not one to pester, am I?'

'You didn't actually speak to Isobel?' said Julie. 'What about Edward? Did you speak to him?'

Mrs John reddened and looked guilty. 'I meant to,' she admitted. 'But I just don't know what to do for the best.' Her thick fingers fluttered up to her face for a moment. Julie thought of the terrifying moths that used to fling themselves at the windows at Danecroft Road. Mary had called them *beautiful creatures*. 'On the way here I had a bit of a think, and wondered if it might cause more upset, them hearing about it, like *that*, you know... and Isobel being so delicate and everything...' *Ridiculous*, Julie thought, the way everyone kow-towed to Isobel and her pretend feelings.

'Yes, Mrs John, I know exactly what you mean,' she said. She couldn't believe it. *Isobel knew nothing*! It all made sense – why hadn't she understood it before? No wonder Isobel had said nothing to Edward. Even if she suspected about Julie's negligence – and at this point Julie doubted it – there was no evidence, no proof. Lorraine had been right all along.

'Between you and me,' Mrs John was continuing, 'it's all been weighing on my mind at a time when I really must have my rest.' She placed a hand on Julie's arm. 'What do *you* think I should do?' she said.

'Me?' she answered. 'What do I think?'

'Well, yes, duck. You know the family. And you seem like an understanding girl...' Mary's neighbour was gazing trustingly at her, as if awaiting instructions, and several things seemed to come to Julie in a little rush, like shiny pennies dropping all at the same time. First, that the old lady felt ashamed and guilty for not going down to help Mary. Second, that she didn't want anyone to know – but, like a lot of people, wanted to get it off her chest and needed someone to tell. The third thing, Julie realised, as the pieces all clicked into place in her head, was that this someone was her, *Julie*. It was yet another sign from the universe, she thought gratefully, another sign manifested and dropped right into her lap – *her* lap and no one else's – and at Mary's funeral of all places! And that had to mean something.

'I think you did the right thing,' she told Mrs John calmly, in a decisive, reassuring voice. 'I think sometimes it's just better not to know, isn't it?'

For a second or two Mrs John simply stared at her, and then she snatched Julie's hand in both of hers. '*Thank you*, duck, for saying that,' she said. 'Thank you, you're ever so kind.' The old woman looked quite tearful and overcome, and for some reason this made Julie dislike her even more. 'Shall we say that it's our little secret? For Edward and Isobel's sake...?'

'Yes, of *course*,' Julie said. 'We'll keep it between you and me.' For the last two or three minutes she had been trying to imbue all her words with a definite 'intention', and she could hardly believe how well it was working.

Mrs John released her hand and peered furtively round the room – for Isobel or Edward, perhaps, who both seemed to be inching steadily in the direction of the bar. '*Well*,' she said, with a stale out-whoosh of nicotine breath. 'After all that I think I'll treat myself to a taxi. I'm feeling quite tired.'

'Treat yourself,' Julie agreed. 'Why not?'

Mrs John gathered up her handbag, and with a wary eye on Edward and Isobel Julie made to stand up and hoped Mrs John would do the same.

'You're such an understanding girl,' said Mrs John again, giving the room another once-over. 'I wonder if I could ask you one more little favour?' Julie nodded. 'Say goodbye to Isobel and Edward for me? I doubt I'll be seeing them again, now I'm off to live with my son. Goodbyes are so awkward, aren't they?' Mrs John laughed quickly. 'I can see they're busy and I'm not one to pester.'

'I'll let them know,' Julie smiled.

There was much huffing and puffing and shifty looks round from Mrs John as Julie helped her up. Once on her feet, though, she was surprisingly agile, heading straight through the middle of the room, neatly sidestepping Edward with a short little wave, while Isobel looked up briefly and gave them both one of her false smiles but made no move to come over. The steep steps down on to the pavement seemed to be no problem either, Mrs John managing them easily with one hand on the handrail while the other gestured vigorously at a loitering taxi. She reached the pavement three full steps ahead of Julie.

'What a nice young woman you are, after all,' she remarked as Julie helped settle her inside and closed the door. Julie smiled, reminding herself that Mary was gone and would never again be able to badmouth her to her landlord or the neighbours or anyone else. Mrs John stuck her head through the taxi's window. 'Our little secret...?'

'Mum's the word,' Julie replied, and then, realising what she'd said, had to resist the urge to giggle.

8

Other People's Misery

Outside the chapel doors a general shifting of feet and susurrus of voices could be heard as the next funeral guests waited to be let in. Several times there was the soft 'click' of the door being opened, and hurriedly closed again, in the deliberate and futile way of someone trying not to make any noise. Isobel turned her attention back to the front, where the coffin sat like a theatre prop or cardboard cut-out, faintly improbable – or as if it was not meant to look real in the first place. How was it even possible, Isobel thought, that their mother's body lay inside, dressed up to the nines in her 'suitable' best, as they all sat listening to Mrs Finsbury-Turle. The humanist minister seemed to want it both ways, informing them all that death was final – and yet not. That they were all sad that Mary was gone – and yet not.

From somewhere nearby a faint mechanical whirring stated up and a curtain began to close across the coffin. As the two halves drew together, the high, wheeling shriek of a

271

seagull sounded from outside, the noise arriving with such bizarre and preternatural timing that Isobel wondered if she had imagined it. Around her faces hovered blankly, staring straight ahead. Then Edward stood up and Roxy Music's 'More Than This' filled the chapel and the moment was gone. They had had a brief discussion about music on Wednesday night, Isobel remembered. 'Won't it be kind of cheesy?' Isobel had said. 'Sod all that,' Edward had answered. 'Mum liked it.' And he was right, Isobel thought, and she was glad now that they had included it. As she made her way to the end of the pew and they all filed out, she noted the look of ill-concealed surprise on some of the faces – already taken aback by the lack of hymns, and presumably even more offended by the song's subversive atheist message.

Outside, people stood blinking in the sunshine and turned to their neighbours with questions about taxis and car keys. 'Well,' said Edward, looking around, 'that's that, then.'

'I guess so,' Isobel said, trying to avert her gaze from the chimneystack looming over his right shoulder. 'What did you think?'

'I thought she did a good job. Mum would have liked it,' he said. 'What did *you* think?'

All day, Isobel realised, she had been expecting something to *happen* – a portent or *sign* or Shakespearean clap of thunder, a stab of lightning from the clear blue sky or a murder of Hitchcock crows descending on to a telephone wire – some acknowledgement of the day's terrible significance. Considering they had spent the last thirty minutes in a room designed for maximum non-denominational dinge, Isobel thought, some incense and a bit of extended palaver wouldn't have gone amiss: a bit of pomp and ceremony and *in nomine* whatsit.

'Yes,' she told Edward. 'I thought it went well.'

Mrs John from next door hobbled over to speak to them in her chesty whisper. 'I got the geraniums, duck,' she said, clutching at Isobel's elbow, 'but I've been meaning to have a little word…' Isobel smiled politely. She was never sure about Mrs John, who had been in their mother's line-dancing group but was also, she remembered, part of a clique of women who had excluded her from various social outings. 'Mum, they're just jealous!' Isobel had told her at the time. It was so obvious, the sort of thing you'd expect more from teenage girls at school. Hadn't her mother made the same point to Isobel when she'd had trouble with bullies at school? 'I'm sure you're right,' her mother said, but she sounded unconvinced, and Isobel could tell she was more hurt than she was willing to let on.

'Yes, I'm sorry about that,' she told Mrs John. 'I should have knocked on the door with them and said hello properly.' Was it disloyal to have handed over their mother's beloved geraniums to the dubious neighbour? What else could they have done? Edward had no room in his flat, and Isobel could hardly put them in her suitcase and ferry them back to New York. As she began to formulate something bland to say, they were interrupted by a man from their mother's Italian class with a series of questions about the Brentwood Inn and how to get there. What was the fastest route, he wanted to know, and what sort of parking was there? And was it Pay and Display or would he get a parking ticket? 'I'm really sorry,' Isobel told him. 'I actually don't drive, but we can ask my friend Francesca if you like?' Then someone else came over asking about a lift and she was able to excuse herself to go and find Francesca, leaving Mrs John standing there with her mouth half open.

Isobel found her friend in conversation with two elderly women, sisters from her mother's salsa group.

'Mary was a marvellous dancer,' said the shorter one, turning to Isobel. 'The best in the class, I do think. Wasn't she, Barbara?' The day's 'was'es and 'were's, Isobel thought, the bizarre-sounding past-tense sentences, were making her head hurt.

'We wanted to know about donating to the animal sanctuary,' said the one who was not called Barbara but whose actual name Isobel couldn't recall.

The charity was their mother's request 'in lieu of flowers' and meant going online, so she found herself trying to explain the internet to the women until the second sister, Barbara, said gently, 'We are *on* the internet, dear. We just need the URL.'

'Well, yes...' the other one laughed. *Reenie*, Isobel remembered, that was her name. Her mother had been very fond of Reenie. 'If you could just write it down for us,' Reenie continued. 'Or put in here.' She produced a gleaming new iPhone from her bag and Isobel keyed in the address of the charity.

'I hope I've put it in properly,' she said. 'I seem to be all fingers and thumbs today.'

She handed the phone back to Reenie. Everything was happening from a long way off – except for Mrs John, Isobel thought, who appeared to have caught up with them and was hovering once more at her elbow. 'If I could have a quiet word...' she was saying.

'I'm so sorry, Mrs John, I'm a bit caught up just now. Do you think we can speak later?'

'Well, I don't want to be a pest...'

'No, you're not,' Isobel lied. 'Not at all. But we're seeing you at the inn, aren't we...?' The old lady nodded doubtfully and Isobel wondered if perhaps she had been planning to skip the inn and go straight home. 'I'll find you later on, then,' Isobel told her. There would be plenty of time for Mrs John to sprinkle them with hypocritical platitudes, she thought, peering hintingly around and over her head. Edward and Julie had made good progress, extricating themselves from the group, and were now only a few feet from the car. Edward looked over and spotted her, giving the brief upward jerk of his head that meant *get a move on*, and she started making her way towards the car.

Mrs John somehow contrived to arrive at the inn before them. 'Mrs John, have you met Mr Tomlinson?' said Edward, as she made another lunge in their direction. As Edward expertly diverted his mother's neighbour towards the Pay and Display man, Isobel couldn't help noting once more the smooth sheen of diplomacy with which her brother seemed to have coated himself today. As the man homed in on Mrs John, Edward turned and raised an eyebrow at her. Together they watched Mrs John disappear up the steps and into the inn amid a volley of observations about traffic wardens.

'You all right? Need anything from the bar?' said Edward. He had come over to where she had perched herself on the piano stool for a moment and cracked open the window.

'I'm good, thanks,' she told him. 'Just taking in the sea air.' On the drive over she had been thinking about what would happen after today, when there was no one watching and no more duties to perform. Did you sit and wait for the other shoe to drop, Isobel wondered, like the day after the wedding? Did things get better – or did they get worse? And, if so, how much worse? Both had been hinted at this week, in emails from well-meaning friends, though presumably it all depended on how well you were doing right now, and whether you were coping or being a total mess. She noticed that Edward, who was now distinctly hovering, had picked a plate off a nearby chair and was gazing around uncertainly for a moment as if deciding where to put it.

'Here, give it to me.' She took the plate from him and placed it on the sideboard. 'We can start a pile,' she said.

'Yes,' he said, looking relieved and slightly befuddled. Three or four people had ventured over to the buffet table and were picking at it with a faintly abashed air. A huddle of elderly ladies, including Barbara and Reenie, perhaps better used to such things, Isobel thought, had filled their plates and seated themselves by the fireplace. They could be overheard discussing what to drink and whether they should be 'tippling' at all at such an early hour, with it being barely past lunchtime.

'Mum would have hated this, wouldn't she?' Isobel remarked, as the itinerant plate was spotted on the sideboard and scooped up by a keen-eyed waiter.

'What makes you think that?' Edward looked genuinely curious.

'I don't know,' she said. 'I guess because it's a big group of people and being stuck in a room with them? All this fuss?' Their mother had had little patience for large gatherings. All that standing about, she used to complain, all that waiting for people to unwrap their presents and having to talk to people you didn't give a hoot about.

Edward smiled. 'She would have loved it,' he said, 'if it was for her.'

He's right, Isobel thought, stunned by the simplicity and truth of this statement, and a moment later by the realisation that she herself had missed it. Which begged the question: what else had she missed?

'I should get on,' Edward said. She wished he would sit down so they could explore the subject further: the ins and outs of their mother's social habits, her surprising likes and dislikes. But Edward, a better host than Isobel, was looking distractedly around the room again, for lone guests and discarded plates. She wondered whether he had ever thrown their mother a party. Was that how her brother knew that their mother would love one of her own? And why, oh *why* had Isobel never thought to throw her one?

'This sounds bad,' Edward said, turning back to her, 'but to be honest I'd be happy if we could wind this all up fairly soon.'

'Me too,' she agreed. Underneath the genial exterior her brother looked tired – shattered, really. 'I could go and start a discussion with someone about life after death if you like,' she offered. 'That'll chase them all off.'

'Rather you than me,' Edward said. 'Mum's debating group are here somewhere, so be careful you don't start it with them.' She watched him head off towards the bar, manoeuvring expertly through small clusters of admirers as an ambient hum of approval fanned out behind him. This adept diplomat's air, Isobel thought, this pressing the flesh and greeting their mother's friends, was another side to Edward that she had never seen. He reminded her of a giant husky that lived in her neighbourhood and glided along the street each morning, calm and composed, while all the smaller dogs yapped in his wake. In contrast to her own speech at the IKEA crematorium, which felt mealy-mouthed and overly rehearsed, Edward's had come across as simple and heartfelt.

Francesca and her mother appeared in the doorway and waved, and Isobel went over to find them talking animatedly in low voices. As Francesca's mother would have it, Francesca complained, waving her hands around, death was like going on a nice long holiday that you never wanted to come back from – and conveniently never did.

At this Francesca's mother looked daggers at her daughter, declaring that Francesca *knew very well* what she meant. The body was simply a container for the soul, she said, *for what really matters*. 'I hope you know that, Isobel,' the older woman added kindly. 'Your minister put it so much more eloquently than I could, I'll say that for her.'

Francesca raised an eyebrow, which Isobel ignored, replying meaninglessly, 'Yes, I thought so too.' When you died, Mrs Castelli went on, the container was cast off like an old husk while the 'real' you – some hitherto invisible bit that counted – continued on to reunite with all the people who had gone before you. No wonder she liked Mrs Hyphen-whatsername, Isobel thought, smiling politely.

'*All* your ancestors, Mum?' Francesca cut in archly. 'Like catching a train to a family reunion, or like the boost phase of a rocket with your *soul* as the payload?'

Her mother frowned. Francesca worked in the City as a quant analyst, but never let anyone forget that she was a physicist who'd be better suited to pure research. They had been friends since they were eleven, and Isobel had often wondered why she and Edward had never got together. Then again, Isobel thought, looking over and seeing Jules still sitting in the same chair with the same pinched expression on her face, Francesca was really not Edward's type.

'You'd think it was *her* mother who died,' she whispered quickly to Francesca, who without her being obvious or looking directly at Julie knew exactly who Isobel was talking about and laughed.

'Ah, you laugh now,' Francesca's mother said, 'but it's what I believe, and when you're my age you'll wish you did too.'

In twos and threes the mourners had gradually melted away and now the room was empty and Isobel wondered what they would do with themselves for the rest of the afternoon. It was the one question she and Edward hadn't discussed or planned ahead of time, and Isobel realised that she'd expected everything to last longer than it did. Three o'clock. The day seemed to have been happening for ages, and yet time had hardly moved. With the last of their mother's friends seen out and loaded into taxis, the rest of the day seemed to stretch out, parched and empty. She found Edward sitting at the bar.

'So what's the plan?' she asked.

'Sorry, what?' he said.

'The plan,' she repeated. 'For this afternoon. This evening or whatever.'

'Oh, right. Well, Jules is taking the car and going over to her sister's.' The bartender placed what looked like a double scotch down on the bar. Edward picked it up and gulped half of it down. 'And I'm going to stay here and get pissed, to be honest,' he said. From the other room there was the sound of plates being scraped into bin bags.

'Okay, well, I'm happy to stick around for a bit,' she told him.

Edward dipped his head and took a thoughtful sip of his drink. The question seemed to dangle there between them.

'I can make sure you get on the train later,' she offered. 'And that you don't fall over or get lost or anything,' Her own voice seemed to echo in her ears and round the bar, tinny and desperate. *That was a joke*, she wanted to add, *a reference to Wednesday night?*

'That's okay,' Edward replied, glancing at his watch. 'I've got some mates calling by in a bit. Ta, though,' he added. Martin and Sean were working late in London, she remembered, and they had said their goodbyes this morning. Tomorrow she had to leave early for the airport. 'Don't worry about me,' continued Edward unexpectedly. 'I've booked into a Travelodge tonight, and I've got to be at the house first thing.'

'That's right,' she said, remembering. 'Shit. I'm sorry.' She had forgotten about Des. The Sally Army had brought round a big truck and taken almost all the furniture, but seedy Des was coming round tomorrow for the last of it. She had offered to change her flight, but Edward had said there was no point and he would be perfectly fine to supervise the operation alone. She didn't envy him watching the last of it go, Isobel thought, the beds and wardrobes and carpets, all the things that had so far prevented the house from feeling quite as sad and empty as it was.

'It'll be fine,' Edward assured her. 'I'm going to sit on the floor with a big bottle of scotch.'

'Scotch,' she repeated stupidly. 'Good idea.' It was no wonder she couldn't shake the feeling of being a nuisance.

Over Edward's right shoulder Jules appeared, walking quickly towards them from the direction of the ladies' loos and looking inordinately pleased with herself, as if buoyed up by some unexpected happy event. *Other people's misery*, Isobel decided. 'I thought it all went very nicely, Edward,' said Jules, smiling. Somehow this remark managed to imply that Jules and Edward had just pulled off a complicated but wildly successful cocktail party, which Isobel had had nothing to do with – *and indeed*, Isobel noted, Jules barely looked in her direction.

'As well as could be expected, I suppose,' Edward replied.

'Anyone want anything?' Isobel said.

'No, thank you, Isobel, thank you, no,' said Jules priggishly. 'I have to drive.' *I've had enough of you too*, Isobel thought, and aimed her best lacerating smile at the girl. To her surprise Jules didn't look down or away, as she usually did, but met Isobel's gaze with a flat, unnerving directness that she couldn't quite interpret. 'I expect Isobel wants to get back to her friends' place,' said Jules, her smile an uncanny reflection of Isobel's own a few seconds before. 'I'd give you a lift,' she said, still smiling, 'but I have to be at my sister's.'

What's your game? Isobel thought. Cold-blooded and black-hearted, Jules resembled a snake that had swallowed something much larger than itself.

'Yes...' said Edward absently. 'Sorry, Izz, we're keeping you.'

To think, Isobel thought, that she had once written Jules off as mousy and insipid. Watching as Jules linked her arm through Edward's, she sensed an artful insouciance that was far more disconcerting than the simpering manner Isobel had complained about earlier in the week. She tried to think of something clever to say, some witty comeback or subtle put-down that Jules would get but Edward wouldn't – but nothing came to mind.

'Thanks, but I don't need a lift,' she told Jules. 'Anyway, the train's quicker.' It was ridiculous feeling obliged to plot and scheme, she thought, when any normal family would be expecting to spend the rest of the day together.

'Are you sure, Isobel? I can drop you off at the station,' said Jules, smiling sweetly.

Or was it a snarl? Isobel wondered. Was the girl laughing at her? She imagined herself going back to Martin and Sean's, being stuck in their bare, minimalist house for the evening with only their collection of bleak volcanic landscapes for company.

'Christ, was I drifting off?' Edward seemed to sputter back to life like the dormouse from *Alice's Adventures in Wonderland*, looking from one to the other of them with an old-mannish expression of befuddlement, like a preview of his geriatric self. He released a brief but benevolent smile in Jules's direction, like Jesus bestowing a favour. Jules's hard little eyes seemed to drill into Isobel's own as one proprietorial little hand drifted towards Edward and came to rest, wife-like, on his – the one that was glued to his glass, Isobel noted, as if Julie were attempting to gently restrain him.

'So you're off tomorrow, Izzy,' Edward said. 'I expect you'll be glad to get back to New York, won't you?'

'I guess,' she said. This time tomorrow she would be halfway across the Atlantic, but suddenly she wasn't so sure how she felt about it. 'I'm not in any hurry just now, though,' she added.

'Your flight's booked, isn't it?' countered Jules, narrowing her eyes at her.

'Sure it is,' she responded lightly. 'Though I don't exactly have anything planned for the rest of today.' She forced out a brittle little laugh, hoping Edward would at last take the hint and say that *of course* Isobel must stay for a bit and have another drink, etcetera, etcetera. But Edward's gaze had moved back towards the main room, where the waiters had collected the last of the glasses and plates and stripped off the tablecloths.

'Edward, your friends will be here soon,' said Jules, brushing some non-existent lint off his jacket. *Are you his new mum?* Isobel thought, watching Edward pick up his glass with a weird forensic delicacy. It occurred to her for the first time that her brother might be a bit drunk. 'Edward needs some time to himself,' Jules went on, in the manner of someone issuing a PR statement on behalf of a cheating celebrity.

'Right,' Isobel replied. Jules appeared to stare hard at her for a couple of seconds, and then Isobel picked up her bag and her coat from the empty barstool, and turned towards Edward. 'I guess I'll be off, then,' she said.

'Okay, I'll give you a shout tomorrow or something.' Was Edward slurring slightly? 'Oh, and you should take that back with you,' he added, nodding towards the scarf round her neck. It was their mother's, and she had knotted it over her jacket today in tribute. She was pleased that he'd noticed. 'Mum won't have any use for it now,' he added gloomily.

'She certainly won't...' murmured Jules under her breath.

Fuck It and Drive On

Once the sofa was loaded into Des's van, the men went to work on all the carpets, ripping them up and leaving only tufts of grey rubber stuck to the floorboards. Naturally, the van had pulled up over an hour late. For a while Edward had stood watching in some imaginary supervisory role – first in the hall, and then, as it was made clear he was getting underfoot, from out on the front path. He had a prime view of the dressing table as it was removed from the front bedroom and carried unceremoniously down the stairs. The piece had been their mother's, and then Isobel's, and eventually Edward's. In a late-1970s arty-crafty phase their mother had stencilled on to it silhouettes of dancing animals – rabbits and mice, and geese in nursery colours, pinks and blues. Their outlines were familiar and comforting, though none of this would signify for Des's men, Edward thought, as it was heaved down the stairs and dragged with much effing and blinding along the short hallway, its legs scraping across the wallpaper like a protestor resisting arrest. During the logistically complicated negotiation through the front door, one of the legs finally snapped off, and the men abandoned any pretence of delicacy and simply rolled the dresser down the garden steps and threw it into the back of the van, dusting off their hands afterwards and giving each other American 'high fives'. At which point Edward decided to sit the rest of it out and took himself into the empty sitting room and sat on the bare floor and leant against the wall. From here he had a view into the hall, close enough to keep an eye on the proceedings but farther from the complaining voices and splintering wood. With some difficulty he unstoppered the cork from the bottle of scotch that he'd had the presence of mind to leave at Danecroft Road earlier in the week for just this occasion. He was grateful now for Isobel's suggestion to call up the Sally Army. A small brigade of women had rushed round almost as soon as Isobel rang them, delirious with thanks for the odd collection of bookcases, all aflutter over the chipped nesting tables and mismatched chairs. They were volunteers – middle-aged or getting on, unpaid do-gooders – and in this way, Edward thought, taking a first swig of scotch, the polar opposite of Des.

As Isobel had predicted, the man had made no comment on the missing furniture or the unexpected sparseness of the house. He had marched inspectorishly through the rooms with a chewed pencil tucked behind his ear and then stood squinting at his clipboard, as if weighing up whether to report Edward for some illegality. There was a brief remark about 'shifting all this' not taking as long as the estimate, and a small sigh – Des being a man of principle, it seemed to say, and far too professional to mention Edward's deception. Clever of him really, Edward thought, allowing himself another sip from the bottle – far more effective and maddening than saying anything outright. The man's silence had the effect that was, Edward felt sure, intended, which was to make him feel guilty and uncomfortable. 'Best you don't think about going off nowhere while the job's in progress,' Des had warned, as if Edward might be required for further questioning. *Would you like to confiscate my passport while you're at it?* Edward had thought to himself, half amused, half angry, but mainly, desperately wishing the whole ordeal could be over. *Seedy little man.* If only Isobel were here, he thought, to witness the performance. He had taken refuge in an extreme politeness – standard practice when dealing with the 'difficult' people more commonly known as tossers. 'I have no intention of leaving,' he had replied in his iciest tone – which was true, of course: he felt a solemn and masochistic duty to remain *in situ*, and witness the whole wretched scene play out like the Stations of the Cross. In the early hours of the morning, Edward remembered, in the taxi from the inn to the Travelodge, he had managed to convince himself there would be some satisfaction and completion in the process. This marvellous idea had persisted, even when he woke this morning and remembered what had to be done and decided to walk the short distance from the Travelodge to the house; it had lasted until, putting his key in the lock for the very last time, startled by the odd echoes as he closed the door behind him, he'd realised his mistake. His optimism had been deluded and momentary, fuelled by alcohol and lack of sleep. He had walked upstairs to stand pointlessly at the doorway to his mother's room, her bed stripped and bare. The window, divested of its curtains, stared back blankly at him, while the wardrobe door hung open as if to demonstrate how to perform a thorough and comprehensive burglary. As he stepped in to close it, the sudden wiry jangle of empty hangers had made his heart jolt.

He picked up the bottle for another gulp and thought better of it, replacing the cork firmly and, after a moment, stowing the bottle in his overnight bag and closing the zip. Voices were coming from the dining room behind him. 'So there I was, porking like I'm being electrocuted,' one was saying. 'Late night, was it?' said the second voice. 'Yeah,' came the reply. 'Nice, it was. *Lovely*. But I did me sodding hip in, didn't I?' A heavy dragging sound vibrated through the floor. 'And lifting all this bloody old tat doesn't help, does it?' the voice went on, and Edward imagined the man's lip curling in disgust. He was sitting right under the interior window, below the men's line of sight. They wouldn't realise he could hear every word. Or maybe they did know, Edward thought, and didn't care. A loud 'bump' shook the wall behind him. 'Waste of time,' remarked the second voice, breathing heavily. 'What does Des want with all this rubbish anyway? Going straight to the fucking dump.' 'You can say that again,' agreed the first voice. 'Straight to the fucking dump,' repeated the second voice, followed by loud guffaws from both. There were three of them in all, Edward remembered, though from the commotion they were making it might as well be twice that. Were their homes paeans to postmodernist architecture? Were their dining rooms sparse expanses dotted with uncomfortable furniture that nobody ever sat on? Edward doubted it, and wouldn't mind storming in there right now to demand an answer. *Fuck it*, he thought. *Fuck it and drive on*. The phrase made him feel better – or maybe less worse, being one of Gareth's – and Gareth had got through, hadn't he?

Was everything really going to the local dump? He craned his neck up towards the front windows, where he could just make out Des's van, and Des himself, lounging in the driving seat shouting noiselessly into his mobile.

He would not give the bastard the satisfaction of asking, he decided, of letting him inform him smirkingly of the truth. But how could he have been so naïve? Of course his mother's belongings were not off to a new home, any more than the family pet was ever *off to live on a farm*. The men, indicated by a series of crashing noises, were continuing their rampage upstairs, and a few minutes later the edge of his mother's twin bed came floating into view through the doorway. The sight was surreal in its truest sense, the bed seeming almost to glide across the space, untethered and stately, like a plucky fishing boat making its way to Dunkirk – or, Edward thought, more like the *Titanic*. There was a 'pop-*pop*, pop-*pop*' sound, and he saw that a third man was coming down behind the first two and pulling the stair rods up one by one, as if picking up litter in the wake of a procession. *Am I drunk enough yet?* Edward wondered. Waking up in a strange bed this morning, he had felt acutely sober, sensing only the edges of a hangover, as if the alcohol had already left him. He had remembered his friends, who yesterday had left their wives at home for once and doled out the best comfort men knew, which was alcohol and plenty of it. A miracle, Edward remembered thinking as they all staggered out of the inn last night. A revelation, the way the drink had seen off all his bitter thoughts – his mother, the funeral, Des the dreaded furniture man looming like an enormous shadow over the next day. If these realities hadn't disappeared, Edward realised, they had become glossed over with a sort of genial and good-natured *acceptance*, so that by the time his friends had found him a taxi and bundled him into it, and the emptying Friday night streets were speeding past the window in an agreeable blur, Edward found himself feeling quite sanguine and philosophical about the world, and the prospect, in a few hours' time, of having the house at Danecroft Road all finished with. As he passed out on the bed, Edward could faintly recall congratulating himself for being so enlightened.

There was an odd vibration under the floorboards and he realised it was his phone, probably Jules calling to see how everything went and what time he'd be home. 'Nearly finished here,' he told her.

'Are you at the house?'

He froze. Not Jules. His mother's voice.

'Hello?' the voice repeated. 'Edward?'

'Oh, Izzy, it's you. Sorry, the phone cut out for a sec,' he fibbed. 'Yes, I'm still here.'

The really disturbing thing, Edward thought, was that he had not been in the least surprised to hear his mother's voice – shocked, yes, but not surprised. After all this, he thought, her existence must still be the default position in his mind, as was the idea that she might ring him up – impossibly, as he sat on the floor of her rapidly emptying house. After letting himself in this morning he had mentally cursed his sister. *Rat up a drainpipe*, had been his exact thought, knowing that, even as he paced the rooms waiting for Des and his cohorts, Isobel was – typically – off to the airport.

'I'm sorry,' she said now. 'It must be a bit weird being there today?'

'At the house? It is a bit surreal,' he admitted.

'I feel bad. I should have been there to help, changed my flight to tomorrow ...'

'It's fine,' he assured her. 'Anyway, they're going pretty fast. They've nearly finished.' Des's voice was emanating from the front garden, barking at his men to get a move on. 'Are you at the airport, then?'

'Just got here,' Isobel said. He waited for her to say more. 'So what did you do after I left yesterday?'

'Nothing much,' he said. He'd had a few by then. Isobel's leaving was all a bit of a blur. 'Some mates came by. I went back to the Travelodge afterwards.' Isobel said nothing, and he got a sense of his sister trying to work out what to say. 'Have you checked in yet?' he asked her.

'The lines are too long right now. I'll wait until it dies down. Anyway, look,' she continued, 'about Mum – and the hospital and everything...'

'Yes...?' He felt his stomach dip and wondered what was coming, and how much to tell her.

'I'm really glad you were there for her, right at the end,' she said.

'Yes. Yes, of course,' he said irrelevantly. There was a tragic poignancy to his sister thanking him, giving him credit that he didn't deserve.

'There never seemed to be a good time this week to get into it, I guess,' Isobel went on. 'But I know it must have been awful for you—'

'Maybe we can discuss it,' he offered, cutting her off, 'once you're back and settled?' Did Isobel expect to launch into some discussion about their mother now, on the phone? 'Anyway there's not much to tell, to be honest,' he continued, aware that this was both true and false – not a lie, but arguably a *white* lie – and certainly a case of being *economical with the truth.*

'Yes, no, you're right,' Isobel said, 'You can tell me another time.' He sensed a certain relief in her voice. *That makes two of us,* he thought. His sister wanted details, to know what had happened. She had no idea that she was also inviting him to admit to his own cowardice, how he had *fled the scene.* But that was the truth, Edward realised, and maybe it needed to be told.

'Isobel, about that, I should have told you—' he began, as a tannoyed voice spoke over him.

'Flight announcement,' said Isobel once the voice stopped, 'bing-bonging someone. Look, I should go and check in, but let's chat after I get back to New York?'

Off the hook, Edward thought – *for now*, and realised that his hand was sweating holding the phone. On the other end there was a background hum – sounds of anticipation, a shifting of feet and people readying themselves to board their flights, of airports and stations, of possibility, Edward thought, and the promise of new things. 'Have a safe flight,' he said.

'I wanted to say...' said Isobel.

'Yes?'

'Yesterday, when I got back to Martin and Sean's, I was doing some thinking...' He was struck by her phrasing: *doing some thinking*. There was an aloneness to it, Edward thought, the words bringing with them the image of an empty house, the light fading and the grey evening drawing in, and his sister sitting there on her own. He had a memory of Isobel hunched over the dining room table, crying over her maths homework. *Doing some thinking*. What about? Was she going to worm it out of him after all?

'You still there?' she said.

'Yes. You said you were thinking...' His sister's friends had been working late yesterday, Edward thought, and wondered how he knew this before remembering that she'd mentioned it the day before. Yesterday it must have slipped his mind. He waited. His sister, of all people, would be no different from anyone else in being compelled to fill a silence.

'You were saying?' he said at last.

'I was thinking about Mum,' Isobel said. 'She never got old, did she?'

'No,' he said. 'No, she didn't.'

He was struck by how immediately and emphatically he was able to answer her. He knew exactly what Isobel meant and felt no need to explain or clarify, or ask whether this was a blessing or a curse – or state what it actually was, which was both. Jules's grandmother, he remembered, was a decade or so older than their mother and already had that smell about her, decaying collagen or whatever it was. The Japanese had a word for it: *kareishuu*. He had read an article about it in *Science Weekly* where the writer hypothesised that the singular odour of old age was a survival mechanism to help others of your species, warning them away from peril or death. *Peril or death?* Where did that leave you as you grew older? What were you supposed to do when your very skin started to signal its cell decay and your impending demise to all and sundry? And there it was again, Edward thought: the thing in another form, the idea of death as catching...

'It could be worse,' he reminded Isobel.

'Worse. Exactly,' Isobel said, and he had the feeling of being spared, as if a threat had retreated and slunk back into the trees. He could let the conversation drift on for a bit longer. 'You're always welcome here, you know,' Isobel continued.

'Where?' he asked, and for some reason had a mad movie image of himself running from the house and jumping on to a train, shirt-tails flying, to arrive at the airport just as the gate was closing.

'New York,' Isobel replied, 'if you fancy a break or something. Any time, really. For as long as you want. I mean it. There's a pull-out sofa and you can have a key.' She laughed. 'Don't worry, it's a bit nicer than my old place,' she added. 'You can come and go as you like.'

This was, Edward realised, the first time either of them had made reference to his time there. He was about to reply when there was a sharp rapping noise and he looked up to see Des's face pressed, ghoul-like, to the window.

'Shit, Des wants me to sign his bloody clipboard again,' he told her.

'Ugh, Seedy Des!' said Isobel. 'I forgot about him.'

'I have to go, I'm afraid. He's staring at me,' he said, as Des's fingers mimed the sign people made in restaurants when they wanted the bill. At Isobel's request they exchanged email addresses and agreed to speak after she got back. 'Have a good flight,' he told her. 'Count the seat-backs to the exits fore and aft.'

'Ha, wilco,' said Isobel. 'Hope it goes all right at the house. I really am sorry I'm not there to help ... '

'I'm happy to take care of it,' he told her, and as they rang off he wondered whether he meant it. In the empty room he felt the sudden absence of her voice as a tangible thing – and then Des knocked on the window again and he went outside to sign off on all the forms. As he watched the van disappear up towards the main road he thought of his mother's ambulance less than a week before. Back inside, he closed the front door behind him and listened to the sound as it ricocheted around the upstairs rooms, bouncing round aimlessly as if searching for something before racketing back downstairs. He leaned back against the door for a moment to get his bearings. No wonder people believed in haunted houses – and now this hateful idea had attached itself to the place he had always thought of as his home.

In the living room he collected his overnight bag. He paused again to listen. A radio chattered next door, while outside there was a momentary snatch of conversation from passers-by and up on the main road a bus braked – sounds normally only heard when the sea mist rolled in, Edward thought, or when it snowed. The house felt sealed off from the outside world, as if in a quarantine zone, the air seeming to vibrate with a barely discernible and high-pitched whine, like electricity running through wires or the silence that descended after a bomb went off. He picked up his bag and checked again that the bottle was inside. There was no need to go home immediately – or rather, Edward thought, back to the flat. He didn't feel like talking, not even to Jules, although he had promised to ring her. He would do it now and get it over with. She answered after one ring, which made him wonder if she had been waiting, sentry-like, by the phone.

'Just finishing up here ... ' he informed her.

'Is everything okay? You got to the Travelodge safely last night?'

'Everything's fine. It all went smoothly.'

'What time will you be home?'

There was a pause. *Something's up*, Edward thought, and felt a twinge of resentment at having to ponder this or account for his movements. 'Later on. Not too late. Maybe—'

'I was hoping we could talk,' Jules interrupted. She had done this at the funeral, Edward remembered, when he was speaking with Isobel. At the time he'd let it pass. And he knew what *talk* meant, which was another treacherous New Age interrogation. What was the point of baring your soul and dwelling on things? Of probing and prodding and prying? It was an affront to his privacy, to his right to be left alone.

'Jules, everything's fine,' he told her, relenting. 'I'll be home in a bit, all right?'

'I'll have dinner ready,' Jules answered.

'Great,' he told her. 'See you later on.'

Outside, he closed and locked the front door of Danecroft Road and stood on the pathway for a moment looking up at the house. Logically, the house and its surroundings should appear the same as it always did, he thought. And his mother might be only thirty feet from where he stood now, busying

293

herself in the kitchen, putting the shopping away or heating milk for her coffee. It was feasible, he decided, noting the bare windows, that she had taken the curtains down for a wash, as she often did in the spring, and that today was an ordinary Saturday with Edward off to the supermarket or to pick up a takeaway, pulling the door shut behind him as he had thousands of times before, and would again, knowing that if he forgot to bring his keys there would be someone to let him back in – *except you'd have to be a moron*, Edward thought, *to believe all that now*. The house had acquired a derelict air, charged with the promise of neglect, as if something ineffably sad and forlorn had seeped into the brickwork. A bin bag lay across one of the flower beds, innards spilling out from a gash in one side. He went over to pick it up and saw poking out of the torn plastic the green and white checked tablecloth from the dining room, crumpled up and half covered in dust and some last poor bits of his mother's clothing, items they had decided were too woebegone even for the charity shops. *This is how it ends*, Edward thought – dignity gone, the precious things you'd loved and cared for deemed worthless, left mouldering in charity shops or chucked on to the local dump, your whole life stuffed into plastic bags for the dustmen to cart off, for neighbours to gawp at, and wild animals to paw through. He bent down and carefully, as best he could, pushed the bag's contents back in and retied the knot. The foxes would be back tonight; the dustmen wouldn't be back until Tuesday. But there was nothing to be done. He noticed a clump of geraniums and without thinking went over and snapped off one or two of the dead flower heads. A bird flapped on the fence, startling him, and he stopped and looked down at the rotting brown petals in his hands. What was the point of it all now? Edward thought, as a memory came to him, of the hospital and its empty night-time corridors. *I will never come back*, he thought. *I will never drive down this road, or come and look at the house for old times' sake.* As a thin rain started up, he threw the flowers into the hedge and turned and walked down the steps through the front gate, and closed it behind him.

Over the Moon

'If you ask me, it sounds like what I went through with Janelle,' Lorraine had said. Julie hadn't actually asked Lorraine what she thought but had simply mentioned in passing how very tired she had been feeling. After their week at Danecroft Road and the unpleasantness with Isobel, it was no wonder that she felt a bit under the weather. That was all it was. 'I can't talk now,' Lorraine had said before ringing off, 'but come over tomorrow and we'll have a cuppa and discuss your options.' There was nothing to talk about, Julie had thought, as reluctantly she'd agreed to drive over to Lorraine's house the next day, as soon as she could get away from Mary's funeral.

The moment her sister opened the door, Julie could tell she was in one of her moods.

'I've got everything ready ...' she said mysteriously, and Julie was surprised to find herself being led straight past the kitchen, where they usually sat and drank their coffee, and up the stairs, where Lorraine flung open the door to the bathroom and said, '*Ta da!*' On the top of the toilet, Julie saw, was a small box. Her sister was always threatening to turn blonde, and for a moment she assumed Lorraine wanted help dyeing her hair. And then she caught sight of the label: 'Pregnancy Sure'. '*Just to be sure!*' Lorraine chirruped, mimicking the woman in the advert.

'You're expecting?' Julie said. Her sister had been trying to get pregnant again since having Jasmyn, but hadn't had any luck. She blamed Declan and it was the cause of many rows between them.

'What? Not me!' said Lorraine. 'You won't catch me making that mistake again.'

'What are you *doing* in there? Let me in!' As the doorknob rattled violently again, Julie tried to focus.

'Just a tick!' she said, trying not to drop the test into the water. She'd never weed on a stick before and imagined it must be how an Olympic diver felt, teetering on the edge of the diving board, hoping not to miss the tiny blue square of swimming pool far below. Then again, she thought, as a weak dribble of urine leaked on to her fingers, an Olympic diver wouldn't have Lorraine shouting at them.

'I said now, not bloody tomorrow!' Lorraine yelled through the door. Using only one hand, Julie managed to reach over and open the door a crack. Lorraine forced it open the rest of the way, banging Julie's knee in the process.

'Sorry, it was a bit fiddly,' she explained, placing the stick on the top of the toilet and with the other hand pulling her knickers back up. 'It says we have to wait for fifteen minutes.'

'Yeah, I know how it works,' said Lorraine, leaning on the doorpost and flicking her lighter open. For the next ten minutes, while Julie balanced awkwardly on the edge of the toilet seat, her sister related Declan's latest misdoings. *Lucky I'm not pregnant*, she thought to herself as the room filled with smoke, *or I'd be poisoning it before it's even born.* She let the words wash over her – how Lorraine had caught *himself* giving a lift to a neighbour down the road and what a liar the woman was and how everyone knew it. For once, Julie realised, she was feeling quite relaxed. In fact she had been feeling much better ever since this afternoon, after watching Isobel skulk out of the inn with her tail between her legs. The relief, after talking to Mrs John and seeing her taxi drive away, had been like waking up in the middle of a nightmare to daylight and the ordinary sound of cars going past in the road outside, and knowing – being completely sure – that the monster chasing you was a flimsy bit of nothing that you'd conjured up all by yourself. *Silly*, she thought, *all that worry for nothing.* Tonight she would sleep better than she had all week. 'Tried to make out like he felt sorry for her,' Lorraine was saying. 'With bags of shopping and four brats hanging off her tits, and I'm like, "Yeah? And how do you think she got all those kids in the first place, then?"' A great gust of smoke blew into her face and Julie fanned it away, prompting an immediate, 'My bad! Mustn't smoke round you when you're in the family way. Anyway, like I was saying, six kids and not a man in sight, I mean, how many dads have they got? That's what I'd like to know. I'm not an idiot, am I?' Without waiting for an answer, Lorraine chucked her fag-end into the sink and said, 'Time's up,' reaching past Julie and snatching the stick off the toilet. She frowned and turned it upside down, and peered and frowned at it a second time. *Oh, well*, Julie thought, because against all the odds, though she had so often imagined what it would be like, there had been the tiniest of hopes, a wish really, for a little plus sign to materialise magically in the window. But it was impossible, Julie thought, and she would have to accept it.

'Here,' said Lorraine flatly. She held the stick out to Julie. There was no baby, Julie thought, that was obvious, and yet for some reason her sister was going to rub her nose in it.

Obediently she took the stick and saw floating in the little window a pale blue plus sign.

'But I can't be...' she said. There would only have been a few times in the last couple of months, just one or two opportunities – but, even so, they were taking the proper precautions.

Her sister shrugged, looking away and making an odd sideways twist of her mouth that Julie had never seen before – a wincing shape, as if she had just tasted something bitter or unpleasant. Julie gave the stick a little shake, certain she must be seeing things. The plus sign stayed where it was. 'I should ring Edward,' she said, as at that moment Lorraine snatched the stick out of her hand and tapped it – hard – on the edge of the sink as if – Julie thought – she was after a different result. For years her sister had hectored her about selfish women with dried-up ovaries who *left it too late*, but as she watched Lorraine toss the stick into the wastepaper bin Julie registered with dull surprise that for once she didn't actually care what her sister thought. Not today. The only thing that mattered today, Julie thought, was their baby – hers and Edward's – and the happy outcome she'd wished and wished for, and had finally been granted.

'I'll just give Edward a quick ring,' she said, making to stand up and fetch her mobile.

'What, *now*?' Lorraine looked astonished.

'Yes...' said Julie. 'Why not?'

'You don't want to do anything hasty, do you?' said Lorraine.

Was her sister right? Okay, maybe it wasn't the best time to tell Edward, Julie thought, after he'd just cremated his mother – though if anything the news should cheer him up, shouldn't it? A new life, a *baby*! What could be better than that? An image came into her mind of being interviewed on television while Edward stood supportively at her side, grinning into the camera like a footballer. *We're over the moon,* he'd say, *over the moon!*

Lorraine was still in the doorway, blocking her way. 'Are you going to keep it, then?' she said.

Julie couldn't believe what she was hearing. 'Of *course* I'm going to keep it. Wouldn't you?' Lorraine regarded her coldly for several seconds as if weighing up how to respond, and Julie realised that she had spoken without thinking. 'Lorraine, I'm so sorry, I didn't mean—'

'*He's against children,*' said Lorraine. 'He's told you that. He's told you over and over again, but you never listen, do you?'

'Edward's not *against* children. That's silly …' she replied. 'It's just that he wanted to wait for a bit.'

'A little gift from the universe?' Lorraine laughed nastily. 'Is that what you'll tell him?'

Perhaps I will, Julie thought to herself. Even Edward would have to admit that the baby was a miracle, proof of an outcome that she had worked so hard to *visualise and manifest,* and which had fallen – like so many other things that day – right into her lap. On the other hand, Julie thought, you could never predict how people might react to good news. Much as grief caused people to laugh at funerals, the shock could stir them up in unexpected ways. And Edward hated surprises – or so he said. But babies didn't count, did they? As their mother had pointed out, men didn't always know what they wanted. And, now that there *was* a child, she felt sure Edward would be as overjoyed as she was.

'I'd be careful if I were you,' Lorraine went on. 'You're not married. What if he runs off to America or something?'

Julie said nothing. A realisation had come to her, taking shape in her mind as if it had been there all along: that

Lorraine took pleasure in making her feel self-conscious about all her decisions and that it had been this way for her whole life. How long had the thought been hiding there? Another certainty seemed to wedge itself firmly into her mind, clicking into place like one of Jasmyn's Lego bricks: Lorraine was exactly like their father, always ready with the bucket of cold water.

'I need a coffee,' Julie told her, standing and taking a step towards the doorway. 'And then I'm going to ring Edward.' Lorraine looked taken aback and for a moment Julie saw herself as she must appear to Lorraine, standing there, hands on hips, a bit stroppy-looking, Julie thought, not unlike Isobel – or Lorraine herself. Would her pupils be better behaved, she wondered as Lorraine moved aside, if she took to posing menacingly in the classroom doorway like a middle-aged seductress? She imagined their terrified little faces and for the second time that day had to stifle a laugh. *What was happening to her?*

'You're being weird,' Lorraine called out as Julie went down the stairs. 'That'll be the hormones.'

'We'll have a cuppa,' Lorraine had said, following Julie into the kitchen, 'and discuss your options,' but so far she had not managed to get a word in edgeways. And she had still not had a chance to ring Edward, Julie thought, glancing at the clock on the microwave. Six o'clock. By this time Edward's friends would have arrived at the inn and it would be impossible to talk to him with all the noise, and so, as Lorraine yammered on about morning-after pills and emergency contraception, Julie decided to save her good news until tomorrow ... after Edward had got the last of Mary's junk cleared out at Danecroft Road and she could cook him a nice dinner and they could celebrate with no interruptions. 'Mind you, that'll all swell up as well,' Lorraine said, jerking a thumb at Julie's thighs. 'So you'll have to really watch him, make sure he's not up to anything. You know what they're like...'

'Mmm,' she replied vaguely as the front door slammed and Declan came striding into the kitchen.

'All right, then, Julie? How's you?'

Like almost everyone else, Julie got on well with Declan and would never understand why Lorraine went on at him so much. She watched as he set his toolbox on the floor and leant in to give Lorraine a peck on the cheek.

'I just cleaned that floor,' announced Lorraine.

'Come on, give us a kiss!' said Declan, lunging playfully.

'Get off me, you're filthy' Lorraine said, moving her face away. Declan was in carpets, Julie remembered, which meant that he could wash his hands all he liked but they'd still look encrusted with grime. Their father used to have the same problem. *Sign of an honest day's work. A real man's job.*

'What's for tea, then, ladies?' Declan pulled out a chair and Julie decided that first thing tomorrow she would get down to the shops and buy some ingredients to make Edward a really nice dinner, even if it was fattening, since it wasn't as if they'd been keeping to their diet anyway, and this was a special occasion. A new life was going to start, and with it their real life together, hers and Edward's – *at last*. She would make a special dish for dessert, strawberries or raspberries – or something continental, Julie thought, a compote or a soufflé – or the syllabub from that cookery programme they watched last night. What *was* a syllabub, exactly? Eggs and...*bubbles*? She tried to think. By the time they'd introduced the contestants and told all their life stories and got to the actual cookery part she'd been half-asleep. *A baby!* How could she concentrate on anything else? She wanted to jump for joy. There was wine to think about as well, she thought, trying to shut out Lorraine's voice, complaining to Declan about Jaydn and the girl he was going out with. Edward was so particular about wine. If she joined him in a small glass to celebrate, it couldn't hurt the baby this early on, could it? She noticed Lorraine frowning at her again. She would propose a toast and then spring the good news on him right after the first glass, Julie decided. Or maybe the second. Just to be on the safe side.

'By the way, Julie's pregnant,' Lorraine said abruptly.

'*Lorraine* …' Why did her sister have to broadcast her private news to all and sundry?

'Ah, congratulations to you both,' smiled Declan. 'Boy or girl, do you know yet?'

'Not really, no. I only just found out myself,' she replied, and decided right then that she would decline to know the sex because it was bad luck.

'Is that right?' said Declan, giving Lorraine a look. 'Bit of a sad day as well, I hear. I was very sorry to hear about Edward's ma.'

'It was a shock,' Julie replied. 'Very sudden…'

'It'll break you in half, so it will, losing your mum…' Declan appeared to gaze off into empty air. Julie smiled politely. *You didn't have Mary for a mother*, she thought.

'Oh, don't start,' said Lorraine. Naturally, it was very sad for Declan, Julie thought, but Lorraine had a point. When someone's time came, you had to accept it with a positive outlook, didn't you? Declan's own mother had suffered from emphysema and lung cancer and had passed on rather suddenly two months ago after she went to light the gas cooker to heat up some soup and forgot to take her oxygen tank off. Declan had made a real drama out of it, apparently, drinking too much and scarcely eating for weeks. At the time Julie had felt quite sorry for him – but since then, with the help of *Pathways to Possible*, she had learned quite a bit more about illnesses and suchlike and what caused them, and cancer was a sure sign of *manifesting negativity*.

'Classy lady, Mary,' said Declan, coming out of his trance. He and Mary had met one Boxing Day afternoon, Julie remembered, when Lorraine, Declan and the kids had come round to the flat for a visit. Lorraine had had her head buried in her phone, Edward had shut himself in the bedroom with a book, and Mary and Declan had sat in the corner laughing and joking, talking for hours about horses and Ireland, ignoring everyone else while Jasmyn cried non-stop, Jaydn and Janelle ran about shrieking and trying to break things, and Julie was left to scurry after them prising various objects out of their hands – which was yet another thing, Julie realised, that, with Mary gone and their own child to think about, she would no longer be expected to put up with.

'I should get back,' she told Lorraine. 'I'm going to make something special for Edward's tea tomorrow.'

'Ah, that's fucking lovely, isn't it?' said Declan, turning to Lorraine. 'Making a proper effort for your man.' Lorraine ignored him. *Why did they get married in the first place?* Julie thought to herself, before remembering that Lorraine had been pregnant. Had they ever been happy, though? In so many ways she was very lucky to have Edward as her partner in life. 'It leaves a hole in your heart, losing your mam…' Declan said.

'Oh, give it a fucking rest,' said Lorraine. 'And mind your language now she's got a bun in the oven.'

'What, can it hear me, then?' said Declan, comically tilting his head down towards Julie's stomach and holding up a hand up to his ear.

Lorraine stood up. 'I'm going to see my sister out,' she told him, 'and by the time I get back I want that filthy thing moved off my floor.' Declan reached down, lifted the toolbox, and put it back down exactly two inches from where it was before. Julie tried not to laugh.

Lorraine saw her out rather begrudgingly and said, 'Good luck,' as if Julie was off to fight a war in foreign parts. Halfway down the path, her sister called out, 'He'll *have* to bloody marry you now!' and slammed the door shut and disappeared inside like a figure on a cuckoo clock. Was she right? Would Edward finally pop the question now? Julie wondered. Walking up the aisle in a pregnancy outfit was all right for the celebrities in *Hello!* magazine, but her father would go spare.

Her mobile buzzed and she saw Edward's name on a text message. *Probably wants me to collect him from the inn,* Julie thought. She hadn't liked the idea of him staying at a cheap Travelodge tonight, and had said to ring if he changed his mind. Did she have time to drive back to fetch him *and* get to the supermarket to buy something nice for dinner? It was already seven o'clock, though. There wouldn't be time for anything elaborate, but Morrison's was open late on Fridays and she would pop in there on the way over. Yet another good sign, she thought, Edward realising that he was better off at home with Julie, than out carousing with his mates all night. And she could share their good news now, rather than tomorrow. She clicked on his message. *Pls dont forget 2 feed teh cat,* it said. *See u 2moro.*

9

The Plan Proper

She certainly won't... Had Isobel imagined it? The experience was like watching an extra from a 1920s silent film walk off the screen and start speaking. She had preferred Julie in quiet mode. As she set off from the inn, the words were still ringing in her ears and she pondered this parting comment and Jules's new butter-wouldn't-melt demeanour. *She certainly won't...* From anyone else this would be quite witty, Isobel decided, an admirable bit of British *sang-froid* or black humour – but Jules wouldn't even know how to spell *sang-froid*, let alone appreciate its nuances.

Had she underestimated Julie all along? On Monday, when they first met, Jules had seemed like a scrap of nothing, a cowed creature peering out from behind the bars of its cage – a fearful, shrinking presence, certainly not bright or clever. Now, for the first time, she appeared like an actual *something* – but what kind of something? As she continued along the seafront, past the families out walking, Isobel recalled the way Jules had virtually 'apparated' at the bar, as if out of nowhere, and pasted herself to Edward. It was such an overt display of ... of what? *Victory? Control?* Isobel tried to think. Somehow this did not seem like the same neediness she'd witnessed before, and she tried to pin down what it was, the emotion that she'd seen written on Jules's face, which in her memory seemed to glow with evil. It was, Isobel fancied, almost as if, instead of looking to Edward for reassurance, the girl was nurturing or protecting something within herself, enjoying some secret that belonged, not to them both, but to her and her alone. Was she overthinking it? Probably. Despite all its unpleasantness, thought Isobel, the experience had proved vindicating. That Jules felt free to make such a hateful and inappropriate joke about their mother would be proof to Edward of who his girlfriend really was. Then again, men could be remarkably obtuse at times, and Edward had been pretty far gone by the looks of it, on his third drink at least – had he even noticed? Regardless, the gloating and vindictive Jules had finally outed itself – and in time, Isobel decided, Edward would see it too. She had wasted enough energy thinking about the girl, and she refused to waste any more. The most important thing was that she and Edward had made a good start, she felt that quite definitely.

As she continued along the coast road in the general direction of the station, pondering the words 'cow-eyed' and 'cowed', she realised that there was little point rushing back to the empty house, and on impulse she decided to take the longer route, a last lap around the old town before leaving. There was a surreal feeling to her own actions, Isobel thought, the sheer ordinariness of them. She turned into one of the tiny side streets that wound its way up into the main part of the town, and walked past the higgledy-piggledy houses in sugar-mouse pinks and yellows. Outside the post office a long queue wound its way down the steps and spilled out on to the pavement, and as she passed she heard someone tut-tutting about the wait and the weather, which was – she overheard another remark – going to take 'a bit of a turn'.

Should she make a detour, away from the station, and take a last look at the house? As she crossed over Tyrell Avenue, a gusty squall of horizontal rain blew in from the direction of the sea and she turned up her collar and buttoned her coat. A definite squelch of wet had crept into her left shoe, and she felt almost relieved about this, since it seemed reason enough not to make her way up to Danecroft Road. As she rounded the corner on to the high street she saw something up ahead, outside the charity shop where she had purchased the dress – an object like a shopping basket balanced on spindly legs, standing out on the pavement. The rain had begun to pelt down hard but for some reason no one had thought to bring it in, and as she drew closer Isobel saw that tied to the basket was a sign. *Two 4 50p!!!* someone had scrawled in astounded marker pen on to what looked like a torn-off section of corrugated cardboard. The letters, blurred and elongated from the rain, trickled down into the basket where large blue stains blossomed on to the forlorn pile of familiar cushions that sat inside. She walked quickly on. What had she expected? She reached the main road, eager now to get away, to get to the station and be on the train and let the town fall away behind her.

At the station the rain stopped as suddenly as it had begun. She watched the conductor emerge from his office to meander up and down the platform, hands behind his back, nodding politely to people as if he were the Duke of Edinburgh. A man and a woman with two very blond children approached him, shaking out their umbrellas, and for a moment the group stood squinting up at the sky together. The train arrived and she found a seat on the sea side, next to the window. 'You grab hold of life!' her mother used to say, and she had liked this image of herself – but was it true? Networking aside, when she'd arrived in New York she had been charmed by Americans' apparent willingness to support friends in their careers, to push them along. 'They're so optimistic,' she had told her mother early on. 'Everything is possible.' And this was so *not* like in England, she had thought, where the desire for something better or more, or just different, was looked at askance. Lately this had begun to feel to her like pressure, or a burden. To live in New York had been her ambition, and once that had been achieved there hadn't seemed to be a whole lot more to be done. While she genuinely liked her job, people seemed to expect her to chase after something else still, asking about her 'five-year plan' and what was next.

She heard more than felt it as the train pulled out of the station, picking up speed with a thin electric whine, skimming along the rails as if too high-tech to actually touch them. The friendly clickety-clack sound of the wheels on the tracks was long gone, as was the exciting, off-we-go noise of the doors slamming shut one by one up and down the train the moment the conductor blew his whistle. She had appreciated these things, Isobel thought – these *differences* – but not half so much as now that they had disappeared. No doubt the conductor would soon be made obsolete and the windows would be hermetically sealed like the ones in office buildings.

She watched the backs of the houses thin out and vanish, and a yellow-green expanse of marshland came back into view, with the sea in the background. Was this what it was like to get old? Isobel wondered, tottering along perpetually dismayed and flummoxed by all the new-fangled things like some addled old duck? Her mother had escaped all that, hadn't she? Would she have welcomed turning seventy-five this year? Or eighty? It wasn't likely. Mary had valued her independence, even taking into account the current, dismaying alternative. The train turned inland to run parallel with the river. A huge flank of the South Downs passed by in a wall of chalk and green, overlaid with the scattered dots of sheep, and in its shadow the smooth hum of the rails seemed to recede for a moment. The flash of distant villages, their church steeples tiny across the fields, was unchanged from what she remembered as a child. It was treacherous, moping about in the past, Isobel thought, like venturing out on to a frozen pond and hearing the ice creak underneath. Instead she studied the poster un-peeling above the seat opposite. *Assaulting the staff of SouthEast Railways is a Crime!* it said helpfully, accompanied by a silhouette of a policeman and a stumbling man in handcuffs. For the first few years her mother used to catch the train to the airport when Isobel flew back. It had been a complicated experience for both of them – the game little jokes, her mother coming over all Mrs Miniver and trying not to cry. By tacit agreement they had stopped the practice, and last Christmas they had said goodbye at the station. A second image came to her – just as vivid – of her mother waving from the front door of Danecroft Road. Which was true? What she did recall – with horrible clarity – was the discussion they had one morning about pink toilet paper, a perceived lapse in her mother's taste – in retrospect an endearing eccentricity – that now revealed itself – surprise! – as Isobel's own pettiness and snobbery. How rich and high-handed, she thought, dropping in – and out again – last Christmas like some prodigal daughter and rampaging arbiter of taste to pick fault with the very person whose sacrifices had made all her own worldliness and would-be sophistication possible in the first place. It was yet another source of tension made utterly trivial by death, Isobel realised, as well as something she had always despised in other people. Her ex-boyfriend was a case in point, having grown up in Staten Island next to a landfill and whose blue-collar parents had gone into debt to provide a blue-chip education at Brown and Yale. On Isobel's first and only visit to their house she had listened aghast as he hectored them with a withering running commentary about their lousy taste in furniture, in TV programmes, and at what hour they ate dinner. 'Oh, we never eat before 9pm in the city ...' he had told them carelessly, although this wasn't true at all. Worse, though she said nothing, there was an uneasy sense, some notion floating about the room, that this was all Isobel's fault, his snooty, snotty British girlfriend who thought she was better than everyone else – this accusation emerging in an argument several months later when they broke up, in weird echoes of her fight with Edward ...

Edward had written as soon as he got back to England. Next year he would be finished at university, and there were various job interviews in the pipeline, he told her. If he was selected for the one he wanted, in the division he had put in for, it could mean being posted abroad. But this would be a few years down the line, he wrote, and to be honest he wasn't sure he was cut out for it – so he had been thinking about moving sooner – under his own steam – to New York – which he had really enjoyed, and would be happy to do anything – work in a bar or a shop, or 'even sweep the streets!'. Isobel wrote back and said she was all for it. For six months they traded letters back and forth, planning to hatch The Plan

Proper – as it was known – at Christmas, when she would be back home.

What had their mother thought about The Plan Proper? One of her children had moved an ocean away, the other was about to follow – and yet Isobel could not recall having a single conversation with her about it.

She had replayed it in her head so often: how she had got in from the airport two days before Christmas and popped her head into the dining room for a moment to say hello to Edward, who was flopped on his beanbag next to a stack of textbooks.

'Hiya,' she said. 'It's me!'

'Hi,' he said, but didn't look up to greet her.

'I'm just going to dump my suitcase upstairs,' she said, 'and I'll be right back.'

Edward's next words were unexpected, uttered fast, as if he wanted to get them out before he changed his mind. 'By the way,' he said, without taking his eyes off his book, 'I've decided not to move over there.'

'To New York?' She set her bag down in the hallway and sat on the edge of an armchair by the door. Across the room their mother was finishing off some sewing. In the kitchen the kettle was on, and they were all planning to go out for an early lunch.

'Got a good job offer for after uni,' Edward continued, 'and there'll be a good pension eventually.'

They had cost him a lot, these words, she could tell, so much so that it seemed insensitive to press him, to ask why he was abandoning The Plan Proper. But 'a *pension*?' she wanted to gasp, Lady Bracknell-like. It was madness, some misguided notion of security, a caving in to convention that Edward would come to regret. 'That's a good idea, actually,' she said instead – with a little too much speed, perhaps, and

311

too much sincerity, as if frantically painting over her dismay with a bright, glossy optimism. Which of course she was. Perfect tact should be invisible. You weren't meant to see the join. Edward said nothing. 'It's cool, really,' she continued, chattering into the silence. 'You'll have the best of both worlds because you can still come and visit. For vacations and things!'

There was a long pause, and then Edward said, 'Why don't you move back here, then?'

Had she seen it coming? Not for a moment.

'Sorry?'

'If it's all, you know, so *cool* and everything, why don't you move back?'

She had the sense of having walked into a clever snare or trap. Was she not being gracious enough, accepting Edward's decision without asking why? And, having been so generous, why was he trying to change her mind as well? Perhaps she had gone too far the other way, she thought, pointing out the myriad advantages of staying with too much enthusiasm, as if telling someone in a wheelchair how lucky they were not having to walk everywhere.

'I guess I like living over there,' she replied evenly, and hoped that this wouldn't imply some comparison with 'there' and 'here'.

'Do you?' replied Edward. There it was again, the sardonic, mocking quality to his voice. 'I don't know why. You're always freezing cold, and you never have the rent.'

This wasn't true. Edward knew that. He had seen with his own eyes where she lived. And yet – he had stated this idea with such bland authority that she began to feel slightly unhinged. She looked over at their mother, who was looking down at her sewing and appeared not to have heard. Edward had seen her crummy bedsit here in the UK, hadn't he? To obtain even a teaspoon of hot water in the bath had involved switching on the immersion heater for two hours while you fed frightening quantities of fifty-pence pieces into the meter and watched the dial spin round until you gave in and switched it off again. One of the first things she had written home about had been American central heating. Edward had been to her New York apartment – which was tiny, yes, and noisy – and had experienced for himself the miracle of the *hot water included* clause.

'And you've never done a day's work in your life,' Edward went on.

Was he accusing her of being *lazy?* Her new job required her to be at her desk from 8am until 6pm, and frequently later. Edward knew about this as well. Just last week she had had a card from him congratulating her, saying that it was a real step up from working at the cinema. And, if she wasn't exactly rolling in money, for the first time in her life she could see a film or have dinner out once a week and not fret about making the rent at the end of the month. And to get all *that*, Isobel remembered, she had waitressed at the crappy hotel in England for a year.

'I waitressed here...' she said. 'You know I did. Christmases, New Year, everything...'

'That's right, so you did,' said Edward. He looked across at her for the first time. '*And I bet that was hard,*' he sneered.

She didn't know what to say. She felt herself pitched headlong into a tunnel of disreality where up had been declared down, and black was white. If there was anything she could say, the words wouldn't come, and again she looked over at their mother. Edward was making her confused, Isobel wanted to say, making her new life – the one that she had worked so hard for and was proud of – sound like a lie.

'It...' she bleated uselessly.

'You know what, Isobel? You strike me as the kind of person,' Edward continued, as if they had just met, 'who would rather be *cold* and live in *discomfort* than do a job you hate.'

Across the room Isobel saw that her mother's sewing was trembling in her hands. She found herself standing up, as if in prelude to taking an actual stand, but Edward hadn't finished. 'And you're selfish, Isobel,' he went on. 'In fact, you're the most selfish person I've ever met.' Stupidly, she burst into tears. Edward gave her a cold, considering look. 'And Mum thinks so too, though she'll never say,' he added. '*Which is why we don't want you here.*' It was his parting shot. As she ran out of the room, she heard their mother at last speak up.

'Edward ...' she said, 'Edward, don't ...'

It was as if her brother had let the cat out of the bag, Isobel thought, uttering something that, though unspeakable, was nevertheless true. In the years since, the scene had acquired an overblown and almost farcical sheen, and yet she often wondered if, given a second chance, she would handle it any differently. What could she have said or done that would have guaranteed a better outcome? When she came back downstairs later Edward had already left for London. 'He has his exams,' explained their mother. Nothing else was said. Nowadays, friends who had known her only in New York were surprised when they found out she had a sibling. If pushed, she explained that she rarely spoke about her brother because he didn't speak to her. 'Well, you must have done *something*!' said more than one, only half-jokingly, curious to know what it was. 'I don't know,' she told them, and it was still true.

Around her, newspapers were being folded and phones put back in bags. As the train pulled into her station, a man stood on the platform waving at someone inside and Isobel tried to separate the two seemingly parallel memories of the very last moment that she and her mother had seen each other. It disturbed her that she couldn't remember where she had last seen her alive. There were her last minutes with her mother, Isobel realised, which she failed to recall; and her mother's last minutes, for which she had failed to be there. She got up from her seat and stepped down onto the platform. Around her a crowd of people surged in both directions and she had a sense of being outside herself, a solitary figure, watching the past racing into the distance and helpless to stop it.

Saturday

A Massive Night Out

For some while Edward had been pacing round in the dark and the rain trying to clear his head. Finally he admitted defeat and made for the Burgess Arms on the seafront. *Dead for a Saturday*, Edward thought as he pushed open the heavy door and walked in. At one end of the bar a couple of older men sat by themselves staring into space, while the only other customers were a group of giggling women who by all appearances, Edward reckoned, had already polished off several bottles of chardonnay. He chose a stool at the farthest point from all of them, hung his soaking jacket over the back, and decided to treat himself to a Talisker 18.

That afternoon he had left Danecroft Road and had a spartan lunch at the Voyager Café on Mansfield Street. The place was new – a trendy spot selling fairtrade artisanal coffee in an atmosphere of smug PC-ness. He had found himself lingering, watching people order a latte or a 'solo con panna' and various tourists stopping in to ask for directions from the surly young barista with his waxed moustache and long, bushy beard. Watching the tourists come and go, Edward had entertained himself by trying to work out where they were from. When he got bored with that he'd paid his bill and gone for a meander along the empty seafront before catching the train back to the flat.

As he entered the kitchen he had made a point of sniffing the air appreciatively. Jules was cooking with garlic, which Edward loved but knew she wasn't keen on. Pots were going on the cooker, bubbling and steaming.

'Gordon Bennett, is this all for me?' he'd said, going over to give her a peck on the cheek. 'What ever am I going to do to deserve it?' It hadn't been a bad afternoon, he supposed, but now he found himself trying to drum up some jollity he didn't feel. Jules had her sleeves pushed up and was rolling out pastry on the counter. Chopped vegetables were set out in neat rows.

'I thought we'd have something special,' she said, setting the rolling pin down.

'Bit dark in here, isn't it?' he said, flicking on the main light switch.

'I thought it was nice,' said Jules, 'with the candles – didn't you think...?' she asked, uncertainly. Only then did he take in the table and its alarming array of glasses and cutlery. Three pink-coloured tea-lights glowed in a saucer in the centre. The comfort of food and routine after a week when both his parent and his childhood home had – rather suddenly – been relegated to the past; wasn't this, Edward thought, exactly what he needed?

'Ah,' he said, 'right you are. Sorry about that.'

316

He switched the light off again and the room returned to depressing, funereal dimness.

'I wanted us to have a proper sit-down dinner. It's a special day,' Jules went on.

Women had a thing about candles, he remembered, as if by straining your eyes to see what was on your plate you attained the dizzy heights of 'romance'.

'Looks fantastic,' he told her, lifting the lid of the nearest saucepan and peering in. 'Smells delicious.' He wondered if he should go and change his clothes. Under her apron, he had noticed, Jules had on the long, flowery dress she wore to family weddings and christenings. He took off his jacket and pulled out a chair from under the table. He felt weary, much too knackered to stand on ceremony. By habit they ate their dinner balanced on their laps in front of the television, and on the train back he had been looking forward to it, this passive sitting in front of whatever cretinous programme was on, not having to think about anything or make conversation. He saw Jules smile nervously at him and he hoped she hadn't caught the thought. 'Looks delicious!' he repeated, noticing that a weird, stilted formality had crept into their exchange. He had been taciturn and unreasonable with her on the phone earlier, and now, seeing all her preparations – the candles, the table carefully set – he felt ashamed. He went over and gave her another peck on the cheek.

'How did it all go today …? she said, putting her head on his chest. They stood for a moment in a tense little embrace.

'As well as could be expected.' He sighed. 'You know.'

'How are you feeling?'

He pulled gently away and saw that she was smiling ominously up at him in that particular way she had recently. Apparently Jules was still dead set on making their relationship into a project, and not a very fun one. He wasn't in the mood to 'share'. Then again, he had behaved like a shit earlier on, so it wouldn't hurt to throw her a bone.

'I think I underestimated how difficult it would be,' he told her.

'How difficult?'

'How challenging. All Mum's stuff. Seeing it all go like that.' He rubbed his eyes and got up to fetch the box of aspirin from the cupboard over the fridge.

'A loss,' said Jules, understandingly. 'I bought some wine to have with dinner,' she said. 'Shall we have a glass now?'

'Best idea I've heard all day,' he told her, glad for an excuse to escape more scrutiny. How strange, he thought, chasing down the pills with a glass of water, that, having had an actual feeling revealed to her, Jules hadn't run it down like a dog with a ferret. Not that he was complaining. But her reaction was interesting and not typical. He opened the fridge and saw two bottles of pinot noir – Old World, not New World, he noted with satisfaction, inspecting the labels just to make sure. He had managed to disabuse Jules of the 'room temperature for red wine' fallacy as well as weaning her off chardonnay. Both bottles were open and perfectly chilled. He took a couple of glasses from the cupboard and reminded himself how lucky he was to have a girlfriend like Jules who never disagreed for the sake of it or asked for anything for herself, but in all situations considered them both. He thought of the hours she had put in at the house all week, and how willingly and uncomplainingly. And then he realised he'd forgotten to drop the key off at the landlord's office.

'Sod it. Forgot to drop the key off at Modin's.'

'I could drop it off after school on Monday if you like?'

'Oh, yes.' He laughed. 'I forgot, Modin's your new best friend.'

He had been unimpressed when Jules had informed him yesterday about the alleged 'misunderstanding' with the landlord. At the time he had been occupied seeing out the last of his mother's guests, and was irked by Jules's timing. The abrupt manner in which they had had to clear the house was made instantly worse by knowing how unnecessary it all was. If Jules was willing to deal with the man, that suited Edward fine. He had had enough of it – the house, Mrs Hyphen-Whatsit and her happy-clappy circle-of-life bollocks, the fucking furniture man and his band of pot-bellied, middle-aged delinquents.

'I'll leave the key on the hall table,' he said. *Fuck it and drive on*, he thought, and, pouring himself a full glass of wine, he surreptitiously gulped it down, and topped it up again before filling one for Jules. Secret drinking. He was behaving like an alcoholic housewife – but who could blame him for needing a drink after the week he'd had? He took Jules's glass over and placed it on the counter, where she was glueing sad little curlicues of pastry on to the top of a large pie. He went to sit down at the table and heard Jules clear her throat, a polite-sounding 'ahem'. For a minute he thought she had seen him topping his glass up on the sly, and he turned, ready to make a joke of it. She was smiling at him, though, and had picked up her own glass, raising it with a little tilt towards him.

Jules wasn't one to propose toasts, Edward thought, to put herself under the spotlight in that way, even when it was only the two of them. The gesture appeared alien, and a bit awkward, and this touched him, the fact that she was making the effort for him in this way.

'To—'

'To Mum,' he said. There was the tiniest pause, little more than a zeptosecond, in which the thought came to him that

Jules might have been about to say something different. And then she came over and clinked her glass against his.

'To Mary...' she said, and he was aware of her eyes searching out his. *Jesus Christ, not you as well*, he thought. He couldn't help it – this eye-contact tyranny, it stuck in his craw, this mania among even casual acquaintances, the dogged insistence on looking intensely, one-by-one, into the eyes of every single person in the group, when a simple 'cheers' or 'bottoms up' was sufficient. It would be that idiotic book she carried about everywhere, Edward decided, relentless with its *positive thoughts* and exhortations to psychoanalyse every bloody thing. Her eyes were still on him and he took a dainty sip from his glass. She was like a teenager looking at pornography, he thought, creeping about with it behind his back. Not that it stopped him stumbling over the damned thing everywhere. A week or so ago he had found it concealed – planted? – under the passenger seat of the car. He had left it there, amused a few days afterwards to find it mysteriously gone again. Where was it now, *Options for Opportunity* or whatever it was? Could he locate and dispose of the thing without Jules knowing? She'd only buy another one, he thought, gloomily.

She had raised her glass again.

'And to us. And our future,' she added – rather tactlessly, Edward thought, considering. Weren't they drinking to his dead, futureless mother? *Future, rhymes with furniture*, he thought, remembering the undignified departure of his mother's furniture from Danecroft Road. Five days? Or was it four? Three-quarters of a century, a life described through belongings, and it had taken them less than five days to take the house apart and dispose of it. Giving him a blank look, Jules clinked her glass to his for a second time. All this unnecessary palaver, he thought, this toasting to this and that sodding thing, made him think, unpleasantly, of weddings.

As Jules returned to the oven and bent down to open the door, he felt the heat radiating out and with it the odour of scalding metal. A feeling of resentment settled over him. The kitchen was already suffocatingly hot. He loosened his collar and moved his chair closer to the open window and topped up his glass again. These unwelcome memories, the table and the dresser being thrown into the back of Des's van, were exactly the sort of pointless emotional trivia Jules wanted him to 'share' with her. And yet, when he had virtually offered to share just now, she had ignored him and started on about wine instead. There was something fishy about this, Edward thought, something in Jules's behaviour this evening that was off in some way, and were he not about to pass out from exhaustion he might have had the energy to work out what it was. But the idea floated away and he didn't have the strength to argue when Jules brought out the second bottle and over-poured his glass. He drank it down, grateful for the special warmth of the alcohol as it flowed into the centre of his body and down into each of his aching limbs.

Once they sat down he made sure to compliment Jules on each dish. And there were an awful lot of them, Edward realised, as the conversation moved on to Jules's sister and Declan, and her going back to work on Monday, and the need to mend the ceiling in the front room. The contents of his day, and Danecroft Road, were not mentioned again. He was happy to sit back and let Jules chatter on. When pudding arrived Jules produced some sort of fruit-topped pastry concoction covered with custard and ice cream. 'À *la mode*,' she informed him, and he felt obscurely irritated by this.

'Mmm, delicious,' he said, hoping his acting skills were up to par. The truth was that he'd lost his appetite. The main course had felt like eating polystyrene, and now, lifting his spoon to his mouth, the ice cream felt gummy and eggy. He imagined it leaving a thick, viscous film on his tongue. The meal was dragging on. Meanwhile, an unfamiliar pulse of anxiety seemed to have fallen into lockstep alongside him. Jules was standing over the table, waitress-like in some oppressively patient way, and he was surprised to see a bottle of champagne poised questioningly over his glass.

'What?' he asked, wondering where it had come from. He'd already drunk far too much.

'I hid it at the back of the fridge,' she said, smiling. 'As a surprise!'

Surprise? *Bizarre* was more like it. The whole day was becoming increasingly surreal, like some kind of experimental theatre where people moved chairs across the stage and spoke nonsense. What was she thinking? One day after his mother's funeral, Jules was popping champagne corks and grinning like an idiot. What ever was the matter with her?

Of course, it was then that Jules had told him the answer, at which point the evening had taken a sharp turn for the even worse.

He motioned to the barman for another drink. Another scotch. No water this time. He'd regret it in the morning. How he wished he had a cigarette! He'd never smoked, but there was still something ineffably cool about smoking, the ritual of it – tapping the packet on the bar, languidly snapping the lighter open, the first puff, deeply inhaled, and the smoke curling lazily up towards the ceiling. On nights like this, the old adverts suggested, a cigarette was a friend – a silent friend who would turn on you eventually and kill you, perhaps, but good company while it lasted. *Bloody Jules*. Wasn't she on the pill? Hadn't they agreed? Lorraine must have put her up to it with some misguided aim of forcing a marriage proposal, the oldest trick in the book – 'a cunt's trick', *Viz* comic would call it, which was a shameful thing to say but about the size of it if Lorraine was involved. *I must be getting stale*, Edward thought, draining his glass, *if I'm no longer able to see others clearly, or see through to their selfish motives and petty wants.*

Was he was jumping to conclusions? It was possible Jules was genuinely mistaken. In which case they'd find out soon enough that it was a false alarm – a *phantom pregnancy* – in other words, women who *thought* themselves into pregnancy with wishful thinking. He couldn't even remember the last time they'd had sex. Across the bar a shriek of laughter went up from the women – the dregs from some hen party, the barman explained disapprovingly, jerking his head in their direction as he ran a grimy dishcloth over a lipstick-stained glass. Nearing fifty, most of them, Edward reckoned, desperate and perimenopausal in preposterous high heels. It was his firm belief that women who believed high heels made them sexually enticing should at least learn to walk in them properly or understand that the whole exercise defeated the object. The skeletal one in the sequined skirt had tottered up to him earlier and ordered him to buy her a drink. *Christ, it's like tart mart in here*, he'd thought. Except that he must have said it out loud, because the woman's mouth opened and then closed again, and then she ricocheted away from him like a shiny silver ballbearing in a pinball machine. 'Sorry!' he called after her, 'Sorry, I don't take orders.' And he was sorry, Edward thought, because although she was wearing a wedding ring she had emanated loneliness and had delivered her request with an expression of hope, yet without hope.

At least the women were having fun – when had *Edward* last had fun? Or even been out with a group of mates on a

Saturday night? A *massive night out*, they used to call it. As another ear-splitting peal of laughter went up at the end of the bar he found himself thinking about his girlfriend from university. *Sophia* was one of those names, wasn't it? A bit wild and posh, promising trouble and plenty of it. Back then he had been too young and naïve to know any better. And what an unmitigated fucking disaster that had been. He liked to congratulate himself that Jules was the result, finally, of learning his lesson with such women. When they had had coffee that first time, and Jules had stared up at him with those Bambi eyes, the comparison had been obvious. How economical Jules was in her movements, Edward had thought, how unostentatiously she picked up her cup or took off her coat – with the minimum of fuss. After a string of Sophia facsimiles – temperamental, unstable, and completely unsuitable – Jules was refreshing, different in her way. True, Edward thought, their relationship had never possessed the heady, adrenaline-pumping intensity of his previous ones, but on the plus side he no longer had to deal with dramas and upsets. He and Jules had, he supposed, trying to catch the barman's eye again, what was termed a *mature* relationship: a sign of having moved into adulthood, when you grew up and took on responsibilities – and, if you lost other things, some element of excitement and unpredictability, well, it was understood that you gained a life that from a long-term perspective was more valuable and meaningful. Wasn't that how it went?

Without Edward realising, the pub had emptied. The women and the two men at the end of the bar had all gone, leaving one old-timer slumped over his half-pint in the corner. As the barman called out last orders, Edward wondered where his drink had gone. *Silly old bugger*, he thought, *necked it myself*. He gestured across the empty bar for another. 'Same again?' he said. The barman looked over distrustfully. 'I'm not driving, if that's what you're concerned about,' Edward told him, making sure to enunciate each word and not slur his speech. He watched the barman trying to size him up – a tall, near-middle-aged male customer, a bit the worse for wear, in an untucked, day-old shirt and suit trousers. He had been downing scotch for hours. How many had he had? Three? Four? He'd lost count. The barman would know and would be calculating the risk/benefit of one more, whether the drink would cause his customer to take his leave peacefully, or whether it would have him toppling off his stool, refusing to leave, or starting a fight.

'Dead in here tonight, isn't it?' Edward remarked conversationally. The man's cautious expression appeared to soften, ever so slightly. 'It's all this rain, I expect,' he continued. 'Coming down like stair rods when I came in.'

'Is always the bloody rain,' the man replied. He had an accent, Edward realised, and it came out as 'bler-dy'. 'Is always the rain here …' he added sadly.

'Bit rotten for you, I imagine,' he said. 'Stuck here with no customers.'

'It is not the best night,' agreed the man, brightening.

'You can say that again,' agreed Edward.

Having agreed on the appalling state of the weather, they smiled at each other and shook their heads. The barman poured him another drink. People just wanted to be acknowledged, Edward thought, to feel heard and understood – and, within reason, to be known. It was pathetically simple.

'This one is on me, sir,' the barman announced with a courtly air. 'And then, you understand me, I am closed for the night.' He raised the palms of his hands in apology.

'Not to worry,' Edward replied. 'I'll be off home after this one.' He wondered where the man was from. The accent was French, but not from France. He didn't have the relaxed, easy way about him that he had noticed in people from West Africa. Algeria or Morocco, maybe? Noting the man's wedding ring, the large circles under his eyes, he imagined the unhappy wife waiting at home, and the mewling child, its mouth splayed open like a baby bird's, and all the nights lying awake fretting about how to feed it. It took some pluck, Edward thought, to leave your own country, to throw the dice, and he remembered Isobel's invitation on the phone that morning. Emptying his glass, he settled the bill and left the barman a hefty American-style tip.

He must have stumbled out of the wrong exit, because he found himself on the main seafront road. Whipped with rain earlier, the road was slick and shiny-black with a fresh rained-on tarmac smell. He decided to cross over and have a look at the beach. Why not? He could leave his clothes in a pile at the water's edge, Reggie Perrin-like, and disappear forever. Negotiating the traffic was more tricky than it looked, however, and as he reached the centre line he tripped. Cursing, he looked to see what it was, but there was nothing and he realised that he must have fallen over his own feet. A large black people-carrier swerved past and hooted at him. He raised his middle finger at it. 'Fuck you too!' he shouted, and in an afterthought, '*Cunts.*' A man's voice jeered at him from the window and shouted back something that Edward couldn't hear. Briefly, there was the sound of laughing, before the noise was carried away by the wind, a falling Doppler effect, distant and lonely, and he saw himself as the car's passengers might: a lone middle-aged man stumbling about in the road. 'Don't go there!' he told himself in an exaggerated American accent, wobbling slightly as he neared the opposite kerb. He steered first his right and then his left foot cleanly up on to it, surprised not to feel the ground rushing up to meet him. 'Bully for you,' he said, 'silly old git.' Doggishly he sniffed at the air. He wouldn't mind a dog, but Jules didn't like them. He smelt fast-food wrappers, vinegar and chips, salt and seaweed – and somewhere, improbably, hair gel. He spied a nearby bench and went over and sat down. Instantly the damp from the wooden slats crept up into the seat of his trousers. 'Who gives a toss?' he told it, and tried to focus on the beach in front of him. The pebbles were dirty and oily under the street-lights. He would keep himself awake by counting them, Edward decided, and managed eleven before they blurred into one, stretching away and vanishing over a slope to the sea's invisible edge. Only the faintest whoosh and clatter of tiny stones at the water's edge told him that the sea was there. He felt his head dropping on to his chest. In the distance was a faint slip-slapping noise of waves against the pier, the ruined structure rising darkly against the sky. He lifted his head and craned it backwards. The moon was out, running its arc across the sky. To his eyes it appeared to hesitate, to let itself dangle teasingly for a moment as if offering something. Cold air brushed his face and he turned it from side to side, relishing how alive it made him feel. If he looked out towards the horizon, there might be ships – ships, tankers, tugboats – he'd always liked them. He leant forward into the darkness and saw that someone had rubbed out the line where sea and sky met, and he waited, trying to accustom his eyes to the inky, fathomless mass. For a moment this made him feel dizzy, as if spun out on the end of something. And then gradually the blackness coalesced into patches of lighter dots, and then these gained brightness and structure and meaning, and he was able to make out the constellations. Just visible were the winking navigation lights of a plane, a night flight, burning at altitude, heading for cities unknown. He watched it for several minutes, the port-side lights and the anti-collision beacon blinking on the tail. The sight filled him with a yearning that he couldn't name – a place or an emotion – like a dream you woke up from and couldn't quite grasp before it sped away, though it was there, and you knew it was there, even while it remained just out of reach. 'Just something,' he told the plane, and the stars began to recede from him in a great, dizzying rush. 'Something,' he repeated, as a familiar phrase seemed to float up and form itself from under the invisible sea in watery, dark blue letters. *Never turn down the chance to travel.* His mother's advice. You had to laugh at that.

He decided to get up and walk round the bench a few times. He kept one hand on the bench to steady himself, and after a few circuits his mind felt clearer, his thoughts less confused. *Never turn down the chance to travel.* A long time ago he had believed this advice. Had his mother believed it? His sister had taken the words at face value and disappeared off to America, and, while their mother had been fearful for Isobel's welfare, she had had total faith in her as well. Then Edward had decided to join her. All their letters back and forth – no emails back then, everything written by hand. But then, in the interval between making his plan with Isobel and carrying the plan out, he had become privy to a new knowledge. This knowledge would have been available to him for some while, he supposed, if he had been paying attention – but he hadn't – or perhaps he had chosen not to – and so for a long time it had remained unknown to him, a probability wave or wave function uncollapsed, unlooked at, and also – it had to be said – perfectly concealed by his mother until he stumbled across it by accident. And at that point, of course, it was too late.

He had come down from university to Danecroft Road for the weekend and was in his bedroom trying to map out an idea for his thesis. His mother was in the hallway downstairs, talking to her cousin on the phone, an event to which he wouldn't normally have paid much attention, the conversation being typically the same thing: the weather and the cousin's ageing dog, the women's childhood recollections of the Forties – bomb sites, rationing, bucket-and-spade days out to Southend, and then – God help him – on to the Fifties – getting all dolled up to go dancing at the Palais, working at the Essex Pony Club in Epping Forest, how happy they were then if only they'd known it, and how they never knew they had it so good. Etcetera. *The old days*. The whole thing bored him stiff. That day, though, crossing the landing from the bedroom to the bathroom, he noticed that his mother's voice sounded more subdued than usual. And then he heard his own name and stopped for a moment at the top of the stairs to listen.

'I know you have to lose them eventually, it's the order of things,' his mother was saying, 'but now Edward wants to go over there as well. ...' He felt his ears redden. There was a brief silence while presumably the cousin spoke, and he peered round the corner. His mother was in her usual spot, a few stairs up from the bottom, the only place really where you could sit in the tiny hallway. He could still bring the scene to mind, the first tendrils of grey hair visible over the collar of her blouse, her free hand and the patterns it made in the air as it hovered uncertainly over the message pad – covered with birds, horses, interlocking boxes.

'Yes, of course it's a long way,' she said. 'Don't you think I know that?' Their mother almost never lost her composure, but he could hear the tension in her throat. Her shoulders heaved for a moment, with a sigh or a sob, he wasn't sure.

'I'm sorry, May,' she said. 'I didn't mean to be sharp or take it out on you. It's just so difficult to contemplate...'

It frightened him, that voice, full of grown-up things he couldn't name. And it made him think of Sophia, with whom he had recently split up, and brought an ache to his heart.

'I shouldn't feel like this, I know. After all, your children are only on loan to you,' his mother was saying. It was a phrase he had heard her use before. There was a pause. 'Oh, no, May, I'll not try to stop him, no. It's not how I brought them up,' she said, firmly. 'I could never live with myself if I did.'

Edward slunk back to his room and remembered how blithely he'd announced his plans, and gone on and on about them *ad nauseam*. He recalled how eagerly his mother had greeted news of the plan, agreeing what an experience and what an adventure it would be to move to America! How could he have been so dense, so selfish? He sat down on the bed and tried to think it through, his options and choices. If he hadn't eavesdropped, if he'd gone through with his plans and followed Isobel to New York, what then? He would have been none the wiser. But he was wiser, and, now that he was, it was impossible to un-know this knowledge or take it back.

Once he knew how his mother really felt, the wonder was that she had managed to disguise her true feelings. He never told her what he'd overheard. He simply mentioned, the next day, that he'd reconsidered the idea and that an opportunity in London had beckoned and he planned to make the most of it. Meanwhile each new letter from Isobel had brought more good news, and their mother often remarked that his sister seemed finally to be coming into her own and flourishing. As Christmas approached he started to dread the letters, which were full of news about her new life – her stupid American friends and her 'cool apartment' – almost as if she knew he had reconsidered and was trying to taunt him. He would have a quiet word with her when she got back, he decided, and perhaps be able change her mind about living there, get her to come home too. This, Edward told himself, would be for their mother's sake.

But, when the day came, all his plans for what to say and how to say it went straight out of the window. Now, circling his bench in the dark, it was hard to remember the exact sequence of events and what happened. He did recall one idea he had come up with, which was to offer to help Isobel find a job back here, in London or nearby. Even among graduates, though, unemployment was high, and Isobel had squandered her place at university. And then in she had pranced with her smart new suitcase, and he had hated her with a fury he scarcely understood, and the calm, persuasive conversation that he had planned was forgotten. He remembered her patronising largesse when he informed her of his decision – her face, and the look of pity that she didn't quite manage to conceal. Afterwards, after he'd had his say, he had been pleased by her look of pain and bewilderment. Probably he said a few things he didn't mean – untrue things that would have hurt. *That's just Isobel*, he had told himself as she ran out of the room, *hysterical and over-reacting*. This past week at Danecroft Road he had been surprised to see a far more calm and grown-up version of his sister. If she ever thought about that day, she had made no mention of it this week and didn't seem to bear any grudge – but then his sister always was unburdened by the concerns that occupied his own thoughts. Isobel's eyes were always fixed on the horizon ahead; her glittering future in New York, fully realised, would have overwritten the past and blotted it out.

He felt the sharp, warning cold on his face. In the distance he could make out the line of the horizon and the cresting tops of the waves illuminated under the moon. Due west was Canada. Roughly ten degrees farther south was New York, where Isobel's plane would already have landed, a piddling distance compared with those of deep space. He tried to make out the wink of Sirius on the horizon. He had read that the most recently discovered and far-flung galaxy was a whopping thirty billion light years away, whereas a mere sixty-three light years from where he stood was an electric-blue planet that rained liquid glass sideways. Given the limitations of speed, it would be impossible to reach in multiple human lifetimes. Crossing the Atlantic westwards took barely seven hours, Edward thought, but it might as well be a hundred thousand light years, the time it took to cross the Milky Way. 'Not asking for the moon!' he shouted at a nearby seagull. New York was hardly outer space, was it? As Isobel often pointed out, it was hardly even part of America. Manhattan – the *grid of moneymaking* – might be seething with flash gits, with strivers and chancers and blatant self-promoters, but in every other way it was a separate country, a city unto itself like a vast ocean liner moored off the Eastern Seaboard, with all the ugly American bits relegated to the other side of the river. America lacked any sense of the social contract or civic duty, this was undeniable, but if this made it a selfish country it also provided a land of second chances where, if you wanted it badly enough, anything was possible. What did his own country have to offer any more? England had fought it out with a free-market wasteland of chain pubs and minimum-wage sandwich empires, and lost, leaving only the low skies and grey-faced people cowering under windy bus stops. *Brideshead Revisited* had given way to *Muslim Drag Queens* – who wouldn't want to get out? Americans had their eye on the main chance. Why shouldn't he? There were *no second acts in American life*, but if your first act was in Britain, in the land of not getting your hopes up too much, what did he have to lose? You only had to look at what the place had done for Isobel. His sister had lived brightly and boldly. She had cut the tow and struck out on her own and practically reinvented herself. She had found her home. Was there any reason he couldn't secure a secondment in the US, if he requested one? Even if he had to accept a lower pay grade for a while? Or would he dare abandon Legoland, abandon his diminishing public pension, and make the jump into the private sector? According to his old uni friend Tom Edgehill, there were private companies crying out for people like him, and they paid many times what he was getting now. Tom had gone into business for himself some years ago, founding a Virginia-based private security firm with huge contracts from the US government. Opportunities – you had to grab hold of them or regret it forever.

There was Jules to deal with, he remembered, sitting back down on the bench, who was full of plans he had never consented to. But didn't he deserve a plan of his own? A 'plan proper'? If the child *was* real, and *if* it was his – and for millennia what man hadn't asked himself *that* question? – it meant that Jules had set out deliberately to deceive him. How could he trust her after that? Terrifying, Edward thought, how you could never truly know or trust someone. Besides, if there was a child – and, yes, if it was his – plenty of people worked away from home nowadays. It wasn't as if they lived in Soviet Russia. Gareth had been posted to Beirut for four years while his wife had chosen to remain here in her lucrative marketing job. He or his family flew back and forth once a quarter and meanwhile he chatted to his daughter every night on Skype. Albatrosses managed it for six months at a time – why couldn't he and Jules? He would ring Tom

Edgehill right now, Edward decided, reaching into his jacket for his phone. Blurry figures danced on the screen, missed calls from Jules, and he noticed, with some surprise, that it was after midnight. First thing on Monday, then. After that, with a bit of luck he'd be winging his way to America. 'Well out of it,' he muttered to himself, going to stand up and finding it a bit more of an effort than he had anticipated, and sitting back down again with what would, if he were sober, have been a painful thump. What if it all went wrong? The stars seemed to twinkle warningly at him, cold and unfriendly. But wasn't it better to try, to have a go, than to not try, and regret every second of your life that you hadn't? Even if it all went tits-up. *Especially* if it went tits-up, he thought, gleefully – because it would be an *experience*. His mind felt amazingly sharp and clear, as if he were being given a glimpse of all possibilities, an infinite multiverse of futures, laid out by some invisible hand – and as if they were all there for the taking. He could look at each one and decide which to choose, whether to give it the emperor's thumbs-up or thumbs-down. A Plan Proper. *What an adventure!* Because this time, Edward promised himself, he would take his mother's words at face value.

Saturday/Sunday

Toxic Individuals

It was horrible, arguing. To think how relieved she'd been after Mrs John's revelations, so happy with the news of the baby, and yet, when Julie heard Edward's key in the door, somehow all her positive thoughts evaporated. Deep down, had she known what would happen?

Edward seemed in a cheerful mood – all smiles and compliments on her cooking. But for some reason – she couldn't quite put her finger on why – she found herself not trusting his manner, as if there were something false and put-on about it. As she watched him lift the lid of a saucepan, a thought made its way into her mind: that Edward was delivering a performance, as if still hosting Mary's funeral. She felt her stomach begin to tie itself into smaller and smaller knots, as if her entrails were being put through the spin cycle of the washing machine. He had been so abrupt with her on the phone earlier, and as she shopped and peeled and cooked she'd had to be very firm with herself not to ring him back to talk it all over. Edward had said he needed time to himself, Julie remembered as she chopped the carrots, and perhaps this was a sign of the grieving process about to begin. There was much to be thankful for, after all, she thought, as he came in and gave her a kiss on the cheek. His mother's accident was not Julie's fault, and the proof was right there growing in her belly. Tonight's evening meal would mark their first weekend without Mary. As for their child, Mary wouldn't be able to interfere in his or her life either. She was gone, and life would go on without her, more happily than before.

After the early success of the sweet 'n' sour vegetable cassoulet, followed by the champagne, Edward seemed to withdraw into himself. The dessert hadn't turned out quite as well as she'd hoped, and now she felt obliged to keep the conversation flowing. Career Opportunities Week was coming up at school, she told him, along with the long summer holidays – what if they planned a few weekends with her parents in July or August? 'Mmm,' said Edward, digging down into his dessert. There was a lot of shifting about of the custard, Julie thought, but no actual eating. 'We'll have to see.'

'It'll be nice for us,' she said. 'You can get to know them a bit.'

Edward looked up, almost as if he hadn't heard what she said. 'My mum and dad,' she repeated. 'I thought we could choose a few weekends in August to stay with them. We never have, have we...?'

Edward seemed to scrutinise her for a moment. 'I suppose not,' he replied, moving a spoonful of ice cream from one side of his dish to the other. Was it really that bad?

'And Jaydn and my nieces...' she went on. 'We could plan a day out with them...'

'Do we have to discuss all this now?' said Edward abruptly.

'No, of course not. I was just thinking, since we don't see that much of my family...'

'Weren't you at your sister's only yesterday?' He was staring right at her, as if accusing her of something.

'I meant us. Both of us together. Just for a change,' she explained.

'*Just for a change*?' Edward put down his spoon. 'Why don't you just say it?'

'Pardon?'

'Say it, Jules. Get it over with. And then let's be done with it.'

What was he talking about? She felt conscious of their face-to-face position across the table, as if on two sides of a tremendous drop – *a rift*, she thought suddenly. She had cooked him a lovely gourmet meal and he was picking a fight with her.

'You never got on with my mum. *Fine*,' Edward went on. 'And your parents don't like me either. So why don't we leave it at that, eh?'

After all these years, thought Julie, this was the final confirmation of his mother's dislike. She didn't know how to respond. 'I'm sorry,' she said. 'I thought it might be nice to get away somewhere else for a bit,' she offered, hoping to steer them on to a more positive topic.

'Such as?'

'I don't mind, Edward. Wherever you think, really.' She still felt stung by the remark about Mary. 'Where would you like to go?'

Edward seemed to brighten. He stared thoughtfully into his coffee cup for a moment. 'Africa could be interesting ...' he said at last.

Africa? Was he making a joke? She thought of the horrible newspaper article he'd shown her at Mary's house – the mountains of sand and animal skulls. She'd been thinking of a mini-break, at most a weekend to Spain or Majorca – not going on some safari and sleeping in a mud hut with tigers howling at you half the night.

'Or maybe that island off Yemen – what was it again?'

'I don't remember,' she said.

'*Socotra!* That's the one. Remember? Amazing place ... the flora and fauna, totally unspoilt,' he continued, almost as if he were talking to himself. Like the gypsy on the pier who read tea leaves and went into fits, thought Julie, wondering then how Edward's future would look, and whether she was in it. Was it the alcohol talking? They had both had a glass and a half at least. Or was it just part of the grieving process? She would have to look it up later on in *Pathways to Possible*. She settled her face into a receptive expression and waited. 'No flights from the UK, of course. And it'd be pretty hair-raising in Sanaa right now,' Edward was saying. 'But we'd be in and out in a jiffy, and then it's only two or three days by cargo ship.' He was staring into space, his dessert forgotten.

'What about Florida?' she offered hopefully. 'Lorraine and Declan were there last year.' Edward frowned. 'And Janelle swam with the dolphins,' she added. She wasn't partial to dolphins herself, but Edward was, and at least Florida was clean and had the proper amenities.

'Well, she shouldn't have,' Edward replied tetchily. 'They're wild animals. People should leave them alone.'

She couldn't say anything right. And then she found herself thinking of Isobel, and Isobel's handwriting, the impulsive loops and swirls.

'You're not wrong, though,' Edward said, as if reading her thoughts. He paused, considering something. Julie fancied she could see the wheels turning in his head.

'Florida, you mean?' she said, finally.

'Hmm, not really ...'

'New York ... ?' she said, without meaning to.

'I didn't say that, did I?' Edward replied, reminding her of Lorraine's belief that, if men answered a question with another question, it was a sure sign of them hiding something from you. She watched him prod suspiciously at something on his plate.

'Well, if you'd rather go off somewhere without me ...' she began, before she could stop herself.

'What?' Edward looked up sharply. 'Jules, what's brought this on?'

'You're not going over there to see Isobel, then?' she said, hating herself for sounding like her sister.

'For fuck's sake ...'

Men did this to you, Lorraine said. They turned you mental and made you into a nag. It was *their* fault.

They stared at each other across the table for a moment.

'Maybe I will go and see her,' said Edward. '*And*?'

She couldn't believe her ears – he even sounded like Isobel! 'You, or us?' she asked him.

'Me or us what ... ?'

338

'Would it be us going over there together?' she said. 'Or would you go on your own?'

Edward pushed his plate away. She wondered if the custard had a skin on it. 'We went over all this, Jules,' he said. 'The other day.'

'But you never told me you'd even been there!' she cried, overcome with frustration. 'And then you said you did, but you forgot. And *now* ...' She was whining like Janelle or Jasmyn, but she couldn't seem to stop. 'And *now* ...' Hot tears were springing up in her eyes.

'Christ, leave it alone ...'

'I don't know what you want any more ...' she wailed.

'Honestly?' said Edward. 'To eat in peace.'

'But ...'

'But *what?*' he said. 'For God's sake, spit it out, whatever it is, and let's be fucking done with it.'

Miserably she stared back at him and wondered how the evening had managed to go so wrong.

'I think I missed a pill,' she said.

'What?'

'I took a test yesterday.'

'What test?'

'A pregnancy test.' The room seemed very still. Edward's expression was unreadable. She searched her mind for the right words.

'Is this some sort of joke?' he said.

'It was positive,' she said. 'We're pregnant.'

There was another silence.

'*You, or us?*' said Edward finally, and with great precision placed his spoon and fork next to each other on the plate and stood up. For a moment, despite everything, she thought he was going to come round to her side of the table – to kiss her, to tell her how happy he was. He plucked up his jacket from the back of the chair without looking at her. 'No, sorry,' he said. 'Sod this,' and then he turned and walked towards the door.

'Your jacket's still damp, you'll catch cold ...' she said as the door closed behind him. A second or two later she heard the front door shut, and then the quiet click of the latch opening, and closing, on the gate.

After a few minutes she got up from the table and started to clear away their plates. She felt an urgent need to occupy her hands, to fend off the crushed, deflated feeling in her heart. She washed the plates and scrubbed the saucepans. Then she put the baking pan in to soak and wiped down all the surfaces. As she worked she felt herself growing calmer and attempted to piece together what had just happened, and why. She made a cup of tea, took it over to the table and sat down to think. Where had she gone wrong? How could it be that she had successfully projected her desires out into the universe, and yet sat here now among the evening's wreckage, all alone? The tea towel was still in her hand, she noticed, and she thought of her mother and father arguing. '*Why?*' her mother used to cry. '*Why*, Frank?' Did it matter, knowing why? Did it help? Afterwards it was always the same – her mother hunched over the kitchen table, sobbing; her father strolling down the front path whistling, banging the gate behind him.

Once she'd got herself tidied up and washed her face in cold water, she called Edward on his mobile. There was no answer. She remembered how angry he had looked. They always took precautions, but even the box said it wasn't a hundred per cent reliable, didn't it? A few weeks ago she'd forgotten to take that one pill, and then the next day she'd been lax about the extra one. Career Opportunities Week was hanging over her and she'd been on edge and forgetful.

After a few more attempts to reach Edward, she rang off without leaving a message and prepared for bed. She lay awake, listening to the occasional shouts of Saturday night revellers and the footsteps of passers-by going up and down the road, certain that at any minute she would hear Edward's key in the flat door. And yet she must eventually have fallen asleep, because when she next looked at the clock it was seven-thirty and there was a strong smell of burnt coffee emanating from the hallway. She got up and padded along to the kitchen. Edward would be sitting at the table with the Sunday papers, she thought, the cat on his lap. He would smile at her and say he was sorry.

The kitchen was empty. The coffee machine was still on, and the jug had overflowed and coffee was baking into the hotplate. She switched it off and emptied the pot, and put it in to soak with some bicarbonate of soda. They spent most Sunday mornings in the kitchen, whether their own or Mary's – a lovely, peaceful time, Julie remembered, with toast and jam and the papers spread out on the table. Out in the hallway she found the newspapers still lying on the mat, and a terrible thought occurred to her: could Edward have come back simply to pack a bag and leave again? He could be halfway to Africa by now, she thought – or America. She almost ran into the bedroom to check, but his suitcase was still under the bed. Where did he keep his passport? She realised that she had no idea. She returned to the living room and picked a stray cushion off the floor, and held it to her face for a moment. He must have spent the night on the settee again. She arranged the cushion diamond-wise to match its counterparts and tried to imagine spending her future alone – and now, she thought, alone and pregnant.

Sunday was the worst day to feel at a loose end. She had already changed the bed sheets, scrubbed down all the woodwork, and twice gone through the whole flat with the hoover. What she wouldn't do, Julie decided, was ring Lorraine. Her sister would be only too pleased to have one of her *I told you so* conversations and Julie would get off the phone feeling more heartsick than before. There was her grandmother, she supposed, but she would go on and on about *the Lord*. *It's a test of your faith*, her grandmother liked to say about all manner of things, *an obstacle on God's path to righteousness*. She couldn't stomach all that today. On the other hand, perhaps this upset with Edward *was* only a test, an obstacle that the universe had put in her way like the lurking psychopaths in Jaydn's videogames. Maybe it was there so that Julie could overcome it and reach the next level – the better life that awaited. The perfect life she deserved. Taking a chair from the kitchen, she went out to the airing cupboard and took *Pathways to Possible* down from under the towels folded on the top shelf. She settled herself on an armchair and turned to the chapter called *Healing Relationships*. Understandably she had devoted most of any spare time this week to *Jump-start Your Grieving Process* – but there was their baby to consider now, not just Edward, and a baby exposed to arguments and ill-feeling in the womb would be especially vulnerable when he or she was an adult to *fear of love* and *inauthentic emotions. How to be CEO of your own relationship*, said the first page. *Learn to assess relationship capacity, release negative assumptions, and achieve loving oneness and healing wealth on your spiritual path*. After last night's disastrous meal, thought Julie, even her self-affirmations had begun to feel like criticisms in disguise. *I create my own reality. My negative thoughts attract negative outcomes.* And so they had, Julie thought. *My positive thoughts manifest positive reality. Accidents are intentions manifested as reality.* The list of her own

342

inadequacies seemed to get longer and longer. On Friday, after all, she had let herself get too caught up in Lorraine's predictions of doom and gloom. So was it any surprise that doom and gloom was exactly what she'd got? She decided to skip forward over the part which promised to help her embrace her authentic self, generate wealth, and release inner trauma using breathwork and quantum physics, and read on to *Removing Energy Blocks to Wealth: Productive Joyfulness and Self-Time*. She seemed to recall a useful bit of advice there somewhere. *As your intuitive wisdom lets you free yourself from toxic individuals,* she read, *say 'No way!' to their self-manifested misery and acknowledge your need for self-care. Give yourself a big pat on the back. You are now on your own Pathway to Possible and ready to realise life more fully!*

Happy Meal brushed up against her ankles and absentmindedly she bent down to stroke him. The cat let out a loud hissing sound. 'Fine,' she told him. 'You can wait for your breakfast. See if I care.' The cat fixed its large yellow eyes on her. She turned back to her book as Happy Meal, unexpectedly, jumped up next to her. They regarded each other for several seconds. 'Do you miss him?' she said, and he nuzzled her hand. It was important to have an accepting and open mind, the book went on, but allowing another's negative energy or *path of impossibility* to influence your own was *an important life lesson in giving away your power. Always ask yourself: is there a message for me in this outcome? What is my life lesson?* What was the life lesson in the upset with Edward? Was there one? *Pathways to Possible* had opened up a new world of opportunity, Julie thought, and she wanted so much to share it with Edward. And yet Edward wanted nothing to do with it. She got up and went to try his mobile again, and as his phone rang and rang and went to voicemail again, she found herself thinking absently, *He'll have gone over to Mary's to cut the grass.* And then she saw Mary's key, sitting next to the phone where Edward had left it last night, and she remembered that there was no Mary. It was just the three of them now – and, if you didn't count toxic individuals, thought Julie, placing her hand on her belly, only two.

II

Home

10

This Misery Can't Last

'This can't last,' Celia Johnson was saying. 'This misery can't last. I must remember that and try to control myself.' *But it can last,* Isobel thought, switching off the office TV – *and I can't.*

After the funeral, she had come home to a package from her friend Melissa containing a collection of pamphlets on death and bereavement. They had weirdly pressurising titles, like *Acceptance* and *Moving On*. You had to *connect* with your sadness, they said, and *move beyond it*. The message was woven into everything, an underlying yet insistent emphasis on 'closure': *acknowledge your loss*...and then...shut the hell up about it. She had thrown the pamphlets into a drawer, where they now sat, mostly unread. That first week the emailed sympathy and offers of dinners or drinks had come flooding in and had sort of bounced off her, and left her feeling vaguely bemused. *What are we doing here?* she would think ungratefully, finding herself with friends in

347

coffee shops in the middle of the afternoon, casting about for something to say. It couldn't be easy, she supposed, but she was practically able to *hear* the painful grinding of gears in her friends' brains as they tried to think of the right words. Could you make a joke? Or were jokes inappropriate and insensitive? Was it okay to talk about your own mother and that fight you had with her on the phone last night and how fucking annoying she was?

This fraught atmosphere had reminded her of the immediate aftermath of 9/11. The papers had announced that humour would never be the same, that irony was dead, and for exactly one week afterwards it was true. Briefly it became bad taste to laugh, and laughing had actually sounded *wrong*, Isobel remembered, deviant and alien. The city had tiptoed about delicately. 'I'm fine, actually,' she had informed her friends. Busy, twitchy and cruising along on caffeine and lack of appetite, it had felt true at the time. Lurking in the background was the haziest sense of waiting for the other shoe to drop, until, about three weeks in, it occurred to her that it might never happen at all. There was nothing unspeakable about to be left on the doorstep, Isobel had decided, no lump of coal at the bottom of the stocking. She had *acknowledged her pain* and everything was going to be okay.

And then, one morning, out of nowhere there it was, like a punch in the gut, and she found herself in the office bathroom shoving wads of toilet paper into her mouth. By then, of course, it was a bit late to start crying about it all. *I'm a late developer*, she recalled telling horrible Jules. *A bit late to the party.* While she'd sat in coffee shops and made dumb jokes and changed the subject, her story had gradually slipped off the front page and been relegated to page nine. Most friends had stopped 'checking in' about her mother, losing interest and drifting off like guests at a party. 'People have their own lives,' Melissa said. What was that supposed to mean? At the time, Isobel had looked at her in faint disbelief, but she could see now that any mention of her mother's death – or her life – had the power to scatter friends and conversations alike. So few of her friends had actually met her mother, Isobel realised, that going on and on about her felt pointless and self-indulgent. She couldn't help imagining how tedious it must feel, like being made to sit through someone's old photo albums.

Here at work, Isobel had been utterly professional, even though, when the monstrous feeling sneaked up and leapt on her, not being pushed under by it took all her strength. Physically it felt like trying to swallow a hole. Sleep, not drugs or alcohol, was her refuge, the only thing that helped. She took her pills at night and knew that her mind and all her thoughts would soon go limp and the world slip gently sideways. In the morning the alarm clock would go off and the thoughts would return, skittering towards her across the bed like gigantic spiders. She ignored them, hauling herself out of bed and into the shower. The only thing that got her up and out, and from one minute to the next during the day, was knowing that in twelve hours she could pull the duvet over her head and not surface for twelve more.

Not only her appetite but her attention was shot. And music – she couldn't listen to music any more. And she had developed a complicated relationship with other things as well – various, seemingly random things. The line of a building, the smell of the grass as she crossed Madison Park, or the way the light fell on the sidewalk. They were nothing she could predict, but for the same reason she couldn't avoid them either. She would be in a restaurant, and bend to pick up her napkin and be immediately distracted by the floor, its patterning, the overlapping zigzag of grey and white tiles, which made her think of the path that ran round the side of Danecroft Road. Out walking, she would pass some lovely old antique in a shop window and think, *Mum would love that*, even as she looked more closely and saw that her mother wouldn't like it at all, at which point the next thought – *Mum wouldn't have liked that much* – would *already* have dropped into her mind. She couldn't seem to escape. Places and objects and smells which might have the power to call her away from grief sent her reeling back, like a tic or a compulsion over which she had no control, slogging through the endless days, heartbroken by everything. It was, thought Isobel, kind of pathetic.

At least she had plenty of time alone, to deal with it. Chris was no longer around. When she had got back from England last May, he had appeared at her apartment door with deli flowers. He had made her tea and given her a back massage. 'I feel really badly about not being there for you,' he had said, drawing Isobel into a prolonged hug. 'But I'm here now and I'm not going anywhere,' he'd added soothingly, and she might have felt soothed, but it had sounded like a threat. Having Chris around all the time had made every-thing worse: the smelly socks and the TV blaring, the way he dumped his dirty crockery next to the sink when he stayed over, expecting her to wash it and put it away. A sour note had crept into their relationship that couldn't be ignored and she had ended it cleanly and quickly. Given enough time, she'd tried to explain, people's real selves bled through, like blood under a carpet, and, depending on who you really were, that could be good or bad – but generally the latter. Chris had blinked at her. 'You know what your problem is?' he said. 'Aside from being bat-shit crazy? You want to leave the door open. You always run away.' She couldn't commit, Chris went on – actually used the phrase, she told Melissa afterwards.

'Look, it's not you,' Isobel said, answering cliché with cliché. 'I mean, it's not me either, obviously.' A misjudged attempt at humour. *Ha ha.* Chris had studied her for a moment in that steady way of his, more accusing for its calmness, and then he had walked through the front door and down the stairs. 'It's not as if I'm cheating on you!' she had called after him.

At first when she got back Edward had replied to her emails, albeit briefly, explaining that he was busy with work. *Glad you got back okay. Did you have a good flight? Speak soon. E*, his first one said in May, arriving almost immediately after she sent hers. She had read and re-read it a dozen times, noting the 'speak soon', the inconceivably friendly and informal-seeming 'E', and the question, with its implied desire for a reply. The words had filled her with a pathetic sort of optimism and she'd promptly sent back her Skype, her work landline, her WhatsApp and Signal, and a reminder of her US cellphone number, along with the times she was generally around to chat. Christmas was months away, but she was hoping he might invite her before ticket prices went up. Was it too much? Weeks passed and there was no response. She decided to send up a flare – a casual, one-paragraph email asking Edward what he'd been up to. *Just checking in!* she'd typed, making sure to sign off with a non-pressurising, *No need to reply if you're busy!* Ten days later Edward's reply popped up in her inbox: *All well here. Sorry, been busy with a few things. Hope you're all right. E.* The message was so utterly uninformative that she re-read it several times, wondering if it was code for something. What was he busy with? Didn't Edward work in an office of some description? 'Energy consultant', she'd heard him tell someone at their mother's funeral. Or was it something to do with taxes...? It was shameful that she couldn't remember or hadn't properly asked. Edward's job and how he spent each day was yet another corner unexplored, another part of his life that she was completely in the dark about. There was so much about her brother that she hadn't even begun to get to know – facts like what his flat was like or his plans for the future, questions she should have pressed him on and snatched up the answers to when she had the chance. Since May she had accumulated so many of them that she had taken to jotting them down in a special notebook and had compiled a comprehensive list for when they next met up. But when would that be? Now it was August and weeks, months had passed. Lately Edward's messages had been the electronic equivalent of answering in monosyllables. Maybe too much time had gone by, the years separating them so completely that she was now no more than a stranger to him, like a distant, half-remembered cousin. Possibly Edward had considered their time together pragmatically and made a decision to get along with her only as long as it took to get the job done. And *how* they had done it, Isobel remembered, falling on the house with the relentless insect efficiency of locusts, stripping it bare in less than five days. Trying to picture that week felt impossible, or like watching a film starring herself as a small marauding stranger in the grip of some unconscious panic. Now, every hour of every day, motley items – clothing, knick-knacks, childhood souvenirs – rolled through her head like conveyor belt prizes on *The Generation Game*. She found herself struggling to keep up, to remember what they were and where they had gone. Her mother's set of antique matrioska dolls, for instance, which as children they had spent hours taking apart and putting together again, careful not to lose the tiniest one, which was no bigger than a pomegranate seed. Where were they? Did Edward have them? Or were they rotting in a landfill somewhere, tossed out by mistake? *Why* hadn't she brought more things back to New York? Frequently, hovering on the edge of sleep, she reimagined the week's events like a film in reverse – their mother's coffin emerging unscathed from the flames, she and Edward collecting all the boxes from the charity shops, unpacking and putting everything back where it belonged. And always, in the last frame, was her mother in the garden, rising up triumphant, Lazarus-like, from a pillow of grass cuttings to live out her life a second time, if disconcertingly backwards.

Leaving the office for the subway, Isobel stopped dead outside a tourist-clogged cupcake shop and decided to walk back to the apartment instead. It had started to feel less and less like home. She was hanging on to it by the skin of her teeth anyway: each January when her lease was up she took the 6 Train down to Canal Street, making the grim pilgrimage to the building management's office to beg them not to put the rent up – or not by much. Next year's hike could leave her out on the street. A rift formed in the steady flow of pedestrians as they divided themselves around her. A woman in a pink T-shirt elbowed roughly past. 'Stop in the middle of the street, why doncha?' she muttered. 'Fucking tourists.' Rude, Isobel thought, but not wrong. She scarcely felt part of the city any more, which to her mind had become less like the old New York she had fallen in love with, and more like any other big city with its generic people and the big-box generic stores that catered to them. More like *America*, Isobel thought, joining the crowd making its way slowly along West 4th Street. She hadn't moved here for *America*; twenty years ago she had landed at JFK in search of Alvie Singer's *Manhattan*, a city 'in black and white', mythic and romantic, and had found all her favourite films rolled into one – *Batman*, *The Wizard of Oz*, *Blade Runner*, the city packed to the gills with people who did fascinating, improbable things and had intriguing back stories, while all the great film soundtracks you'd ever heard seemed to play in your head as the steam wafted up dramatically on to the streets because – as someone informed her early on – New York was so very close to hell. The devil wouldn't live here any more, Isobel thought, skirting another backpack-wearing tourist knot, even if the ones who could afford the city now were his crowd – the financiers, lawyers and more financiers who had presided over the loss of all the things that made New York itself. Their efforts made the city feel sullied: clean and dirty in all the wrong ways. More and more of the local shops, the 'Mom and Pop' stores, were closing. More and more, anything that was small or different or independent was being shut down, knocked flat and replaced by faceless residential high-rises that 'boast world-class fitness facilities', with a Whole Foods on the ground floor and two identical 'handmade coffee' shops round the corner. She reached Hudson Street and passed two of her old favourites, the Chocolate Bar Café, and, a few doors down, House of Cards. Both stores were shuttered and dark. On one grimy window someone had pasted a flyer: *Save Vanishing NYC.* She wasn't the only one, then, Isobel thought. The city was dissolving around them, becoming absorbed into the rest of America with its malls and chain stores and fearful obese people locking themselves in gated communities. On the corner of 11th Street, where the local hospital used to be, a construction site with a wraparound hoarding announced: *A significant new addition to the neighborhood. Charming town homes, surprising and delighting at every turn.* On 9/11, she remembered, this was where doctors and nurses had waited patiently for hours on the sidewalk, stretchers and gurneys at the ready, for victims who never arrived. A bemusing number of these new buildings were given 'fancy' yet unfortunate names – The Belmarsh, The Broadmoor, a famous British prison and a mental institution for career psychopaths respectively. *You need never leave*, the billboards promised, as if whispering into the ears of the elderly or the infirm. Yet what was the point of living in New York if you never ventured out on to its streets?

Recently she had found herself rooting out and discarding all the Americanisms in her speech – at first unconsciously, then consciously – in some reverse process to when she first arrived. She had thought it would feel good, like divesting yourself of failing stocks or a long scarf on a warm day. But it had left her feeling slightly out of step and apart – and in American eyes rather pretentious. New York might be teeming with bright, intelligent people, almost none of whom 'clung to their guns and religion', but the more clever people were, Isobel thought, the more politically correct they became. The most innocuous words and concepts were off-limits. And yet for some reason – she couldn't seem to help herself – she felt compelled to challenge people and put their backs up over it. Even Melissa started to make excuses not to see her, or at least that was what it seemed like. Of course they lived in different worlds. Melissa, the notorious planner and organiser who had set out to locate a husband and approached the task like a general in a military campaign, and Isobel, for whom a relationship had never made the long list of things to be done before you died. For a while Melissa had been a sort of human lightning rod for assorted internet weirdos, which at least had been entertaining. But then this summer her friend had met her *soulmate* at a wine-tasting in Chelsea Market, and since then it had all gone a bit Lifestyle Television.

As she crossed Sixth Avenue a warm rain started coming down and she felt it trickling uncomfortably under her collar. In the window of a nearby nail salon perfectly coiffed women lounged with their smartphones in puffy leather chairs having their toenails painted by kneeling underlings. That she hated nail salons and being openly gossiped about in a foreign language by virtual slaves, Isobel thought, was not the point. There was something wonderful about living in a place where, on a whim, you could slip out of your apartment in the middle of the night and get your nails done, or rent a car or buy some M&Ms or see a movie. She had never been up the Statue of Liberty – most New Yorkers hadn't – but the option was there, and that was what counted. She walked on towards Sixth, enjoying the hooting taxis and the bustle, the unending movement of people hurrying through the streets. She loved everything about the city, Isobel decided, that passed for ordinary and mundane – striding through the subway station at Union Square, for instance, where the sheer mass of humanity, the colliding cacophony of commuters and performers and musicians, was exhilarating and made you feel lucky to live here. And tonight: seeing the buildings against the night sky, when the glorious Gershwin Rhapsody almost seemed to rise up from under the sidewalks and bring the old feeling back with it, and for a tiny moment the city felt like your own again.

That was the problem with New York. Like a dysfunctional relationship, every time you thought you were done with it, something pulled you back. Some days her surroundings felt so familiar that she barely registered them. If the city had a soundtrack today, it was the muzak you heard in an elevator. But if she had followed the Yellow Brick Road and found her Oz, she had – if only very recently – begun to entertain the idea of clicking her heels and going home again. Still, she thought, it was only an idea.

She took her time walking across the West Village, only to turn on to Fifth and see on the church clock that it was barely after ten. She turned south, making a left on to West 9th Street. In the window of one particular house, she remembered, you occasionally caught sight of a large parrot. Where could she live if she didn't live in New York? It was a question she and her friends used to ask themselves back in the '90s, but had never for a moment taken seriously. It was more an entertaining parlour game, an exercise in smug self-congratulation where the participants acknowledged that they lived in 'the greatest city in the world', while generously conceding that there might – conceivably – be somewhere else vaguely 'interesting' to live. Fast-forward a bunch of years and most had found their answer back where they came from, in Brooklyn or Jersey or the suburbs of Westchester, in the miracle of washer-dryers and kitchen islands the size of a Manhattan bathroom. It wasn't Isobel's idea of fun. Her own return, she supposed, would involve London – drab, expensive, unwieldy London, spread out over intimidating distances like LA or Mexico City. Not that long ago, on a trip back, a friend had taken her for a hair-raising ride on his red Ducati, up to Parliament Hill. 'What *is* that?' she'd said, noticing a weird grouping of skyscrapers on the horizon. 'Er, Canary Wharf,' he had replied. 'Oh,' she'd said, embarrassed. 'Right. That's the one.' The experience had brought home to her how long she had been away.

Outside the parrot house she paused and saw that the shades were drawn. She walked on. There was the countryside, she supposed, upstate, Martha's Vineyard, the North Fork, Maine – all beautiful in their own way. But what could she do in these places? In countless movies, people fled the city for better lives in the country only to find themselves punished, menaced in the bathroom mirror by wraiths and axe-murderers. By the end credits they had always moved back to the city again, opening a nice bookshop somewhere urban but picturesque, like TriBeCa. Such plans required an awful lot of money, though. And then, Isobel thought, she couldn't be sure that the minute she left she wouldn't start pining for the city again. It had taken a couple of years, when she first arrived, to build proper friendships, to get her head round all the little cultural differences that provided social lubrication, that were understood implicitly by anyone who was actually born here. If the past really was a foreign country, she thought, what if you no longer spoke the language or got the cultural references? At this point, they – Isobel, her friends, the city – had a shared history lasting almost twenty years.

She continued along Ninth to University Place, and meandered up towards Union Square. A sense of her own identity infused almost every corner of the city, its buildings and streets and architecture. Almost every corner of every block came with a tag tied to it – a scribbled memory of a first date, a break-up, an office job, or an apartment where she had lived or loved or fought. Back story. If she left, this history would be erased – or as good as.

Ten past ten. She decided to circle the dog-run a few times. If she left to make her life elsewhere, Isobel thought – back to England, for example, which likely had changed far more than she realised on her brief visits, it would mean starting over again with nothing, in a place where your past was merely a collection of boring stories and no one shared or cared about the experiences that had formed you. Except for those of her early life, Isobel remembered, shared with friends like Francesca. And Edward, of course. *We don't want you here*, he had said. Was it true? Since their mother died, the words, spoken so long ago, had been eating away at her. Had their mother not wanted Isobel at Danecroft Road? Or in England? Was this why she had hidden her letters from Edward? They used to write to each other every week, and at the end of her visits, when she left for the airport, her mother used to cry. Once, as Isobel walked away towards the departure gate, her mother had run back to her and embraced Isobel in a hard, desperate little hug. And Mary had appeared genuinely hurt and upset by their rift. *We don't want you here.* Was it a lie? But then what would make Edward say such a thing? Round and round it all went in her head, a chorus of doubt and unanswered questions, until her head hurt, until she came back, finally, to the one thing that she did know for sure: that her brother was the loyal one, the child who was there at the end, making his vigil at their mother's bedside while his selfish sister was living it up in New York.

Twelve minutes past ten. She could hardly believe how the time was crawling. She found an empty bench near the entrance to the dog-run and sat down to watch the parade of owners and their pets passing in and out of the gate. She'd love to go inside, but it wasn't done – it would seem as suspect as loitering in a playground without the excuse of a child. If she went back now, what would people think? Would her friends see failure, and Isobel returning home with her tail between her legs? There, her life here would look to people as her UK life once did to people here – as a gap in time, an unbridgeable space separating her and everyone else. Her past here wouldn't sound real or genuine. Being *there*, with no one who had witnessed her years *here*, these last twenty years would start to fade, becoming so unreal that in time it would be as if she had never been here in the first place, until, Isobel thought, she would dream of returning.

Ten-thirty. Sweaty and irritable from the heat, she decided to call it a night. She made her way up to Gramercy Park, leafy and tranquil in the dim light spilling from the surrounding buildings, a mishmash of Regency, modern and neo-Gothic, and along the eastern end where the gaslights flickered on the sidewalk. When five minutes later she let herself into the apartment, the silence was oppressive. She turned on the TV, only to flinch as she hit the adverts. A man was standing in front of an SUV, shouting directly into the camera. In England adverts were crafted as little stories. Here, like immigration officials at JFK, people yelled in your face. There's something wrong with this country, Isobel decided, feeling as if she'd spent the last twenty years working diligently on a huge jigsaw puzzle only to find that the last piece was missing. *Strangers*, she thought, *I'm living among strangers, aliens gorging themselves on buckets of chicken*. Perhaps she needed to be with her own people, ones who didn't alternately ignore and psychoanalyse you, but made you a cup of tea. Or was this a futile idea, as fanciful as the Faraway Tree where the hole at the top, which led to different worlds, revolved away from you and you lost your chance and your way back? Was she homesick, Isobel thought, or timesick?

August

Spilt Milk

After lunch Edward helped Julie's mother clear away the plates. Jules stayed in the sitting room with Lorraine discussing Jules's swollen ankles while their father dozed in front of a home improvement programme. As they rinsed the plates and put them into the dishwasher, as usual Mrs Brewer was doing her best to make the conversation go smoothly, and as usual this was having precisely the opposite effect.

'I expect you're all settled in at the new house...' she said.

'More or less,' Edward replied. He had been thinking about cleaning out the dilapidated shed at the bottom of the garden. Would it be admitting defeat? As a child the shed had been a hideout he had associated with good things: with solitude and having time to himself – its plethora of rusty tools, its creosote smell, the place where his mother had hidden the blue Chopper he got for his tenth birthday. There were some repairs to be done, if he ever found the time, but it might be worth it to have a place of his own to tinker about in.

'We'd love to come over one day and see you...' Jules's mother added.

'We're a bit disorganised, I'm afraid, Mrs Brewer,' he replied. 'Still living out of boxes.'

'Hazel...'

'Sorry. *Hazel*.'

'I meant just to help you unpack a bit,' she said, smiling anxiously.

'Yes, of course,' he replied. 'It's awfully kind of you, really.' He wondered whether to feel grateful. Unlike the rest of the Brewers, Jules's mother – *Hazel* – seemed to have genuinely warmed to him. No doubt she was thankful herself, Edward thought, relieved that he was 'doing the decent thing' – and, like the rest of them, keen to make sure he continued doing so. When he and Jules had given them the news, Mr Brewer had offered only guarded congratulations. He was an unpleasant man, Edward thought, a bully – fully retired from work and yet overt in his efforts to sit idly by while his wife shopped and cooked and did all the cleaning up afterwards. When Mr Brewer finished eating, Edward had noticed, he got up from the table without waiting for anyone else to finish. 'Excuse me,' he'd say stiffly, leaving his dirty plate and going to sit in his favourite armchair.

'To be honest, Mrs Brewer,' Edward said, fishing another greasy fork out of the sink, 'sorry, *Hazel*... what with one thing and another we've both been rather overwhelmed.'

'Well, yes. Yes, you would be,' said Mrs Brewer thoughtfully.

It was fascinating, Edward reflected, how Jules's mother managed to thread meaning over and under words that were on the surface quite ordinary. In that way she reminded him of his own mother. He watched her rearrange the plates in the machine for a second time, and then a third, trying different angles, placing various objects on top of or under other objects. Were all mothers like that? He pondered this and found himself dodging a memory that had been plaguing him recently. It concerned a quarrel he and his mother had had about Isobel, not long after their falling out. He had been home from uni for the weekend and had come downstairs on Sunday morning to find his mother in a frenzy of tidying and cleaning. 'What time is your train back to London?' she had asked airily, but he had smelt a rat. *Isobel*. Clearly his mother was preparing for one of his sister's flying visits. He'd already noted the hairdresser's appointment up on the wall calendar. 'I'm not in any rush,' he told her. There was an awkward pause. 'Up to you, Edward,' she said. 'I've got a few bits and bobs to do today.' He had called her bluff, and she had called his. At least, Edward thought, closing the dishwasher, that was how he had seen it at the time. Then, just after lunch, his mother had answered the phone and had a brief conversation, talking the whole while in such a low voice that he'd felt all his suspicions confirmed. Worse, he had thought he heard his name mentioned, and when his mother rang off he had told her exactly what he thought. His life was none of Isobel's business, he told her, as fury rose uncontrollably in his throat like vomit. What had he said next? The words were lost, had vanished as soon as they left his mouth. But the force of them remained, immense and powerful, as if it could pull down the ceiling and shatter the windows. There had been something hideously comic or slapstick in the way that his mother literally staggered backwards, like someone in a pantomime, flailing blindly for the doorknob behind her as if she were fearful of turning her back on him. He was instantly sorry, and, though he could not recall his words, had the desperate desire to un-say them. And then she must have got the door open, because he'd found himself rushing over to the window and watching helplessly as she picked her way across the back garden where some terrible *coup de vieux* seemed to have transformed her gait and posture into that of an old woman. It was this that had shocked him the most, Edward remembered, as if his anger had its own power, far more than he possessed himself.

Over the years he had wondered if his mother had ever told Isobel about this shameful scene. More recently he had begun to wonder whether the event could have had some unforeseen effect. Could the rise in blood pressure have weakened the blood vessels in her brain and caused them to rupture? He was fairly certain that this was not what the doctors would say, but he couldn't seem to rid himself of the idea, which made no sense but came at him again and again as if trying to batter down his reason. His mother used to speak about keeping the peace and not 'creating ill-feeling' with people who were unkind or unpleasant – for instance Mrs John her next-door neighbour, who was apparently to be neither ignored nor confronted. Edward understood all this now. You did whatever it took, to get through the day and survive. Was it worth it, he thought, in the long run? There was no knowing until it was too late.

He pulled the plug out of the sink and gave its slimy sides a quick swab with the dishcloth. In the other room Jules's mother was asking who wanted tea or coffee. Soon enough, Edward realised, Christmas would arrive – was already looming, in fact, though it was only August. One shop in town was already advertising late shopping nights. He used to look forward to it, the whole run-up to Christmas, but he was dreading it this year. He turned his mind to the task at hand, to the dishwasher with its intricate controls and moving parts, reminded of the formidable problem of Jules having twice mentioned their getting one themselves. It was up to Edward, she said, but it would make life easier, and, after all, they had the space. That was moot, he had pointed out, because they didn't have the money. Besides, what was the point when you had to rinse everything before you put it in? Such a purchase was a waste when it was just the two of them, he had told her unthinkingly. '*Three*,' Jules had corrected, and burst into tears. In the New Year, Edward thought, this would be true, and he could hardly believe the monstrous items that he was required to think about as a result. Dishwashers and nappies, furniture covers and fire-safe blankets, indoor swing-sets and childproof kitchens. And milk pumps! God help him, he had no need to know what those were. What other horrors lay in wait? Luckily he had not yet been herded into the Breathing 'n' Birthing class or whatever it was Jules attended every week. Nor had he been instructed to look up the whole gory process on the internet. But it was only a matter of time. Was he expected to be in the hospital room during the event itself? Nothing had been said and Edward hoped that if he was, somehow, browbeaten into it, this would not involve standing at the *business end*. Last week he had managed to sneak half an hour in the pub and been treated to the overhearing of two men discussing their wives' pregnancies. 'Not to be crude or nothing,' said one, 'but it was like watching someone shit all over the kitchen of your favourite restaurant.' 'Well, this is it...' remarked his friend philosophically. 'That's why they have to get the extra stitch afterwards,' the first one retorted. 'That's what mine had.' The men had chortled uneasily to themselves. Was it true? Edward thought, as Mrs Brewer came back in and opened the dishwasher. Even if it was, there were some things a man was not meant to know about. He dropped an errant fork into the little plastic basket and watched Jules's mother swoop down and pick it back out again.

'Tines down,' she said, turning it the other way up. She smiled. 'Not to worry, Edward. Lorraine does it all the time.'

An excellent incentive not to, then, he thought to himself.

'I expect it's been quite a change for you the past few months, hasn't it?' said Mrs Brewer as she measured out and poured some thick, noxious-looking liquid into a hidden compartment in the door.

'I suppose it has, yes,' he replied.

'Difficult...' she said, gently closing the dishwasher door and wiping her hands on her apron. When he thought of Jules's mother, Edward thought, she was always here, in the kitchen, wiping her hands on her apron, frequently in retreat from some unkind remark or other of her husband's or Lorraine's.

'It's been an adjustment for both of us,' he told her, keen to deflect an overly personal discussion, but not wanting to hurt her feelings.

'You've got a bit more space for yourselves now, with the house. Another bedroom.' And then, as if realising this sounded insensitive, she said, 'Sorry, I didn't mean...'

'Not at all,' Edward said quickly. 'Completely fine.'

'I was thinking of the nursery,' she explained. 'It'll be nice for you, won't it? For all of you, I mean.'

From anyone else he would mark this down as a reproach, Edward thought, picturing the still-empty room, the would-be nursery with its blank, curtainless window overlooking the dreary back garden. The walls of the room had a bare look, painted in a stark white. You could still smell the new paint, though he kept the door closed and never went in. Any day now, he was sure, Jules expected the room to become magically wallpapered with pink and/or blue kittens and rabbits. Coming from Mrs Brewer, though, it was perhaps an acknowledgement of the unique predicament Edward had found himself in, and he was grateful for it.

'Yes, the extra room will certainly help,' he agreed. 'Can I help you with the coffee?'

'That's all right, Edward, you go in and relax. I'll be there in a minute.' She smiled, but he thought she looked relieved to be done with the conversation.

In the living room Lorraine seemed to be reading aloud to Jules from some sort of thriller. 'In actual fact, Edward,' Lorraine informed him tartly when he commented, 'it's about post-partum depression. Which I myself had very seriously when I was expecting Jaydn. I could've died.' *If only*, Edward thought, watching her fat fingers pluck another baby magazine from the ominous pile of them sprouting on the coffee table. Next to that, he noticed, was a copy of something called *Bride Beautiful*, other editions of which had likewise been ever so artfully and conspicuously placed at strategic intervals throughout the house. Naturally he had steered well clear of them. In fact, whenever he was at the Brewers' house he made a point of using *Bride Beautiful* as a place mat for his coffee cup. The sight of the brown ring spreading over the face of the drugged-looking woman in the cover photo gave him a childish satisfaction he felt only slightly ashamed of – and only then when he was sober, which on Sunday afternoons cooped up with the Brewers while they rattled a stick at the bars of his cage was not that often. If only a passing gale would come and whip all the magazines up into the air, Edward thought, the pages whirling faster and faster until they stuck to him and he suffocated, like the man in that film – what was it called? He searched his memory. *Brazil*, that was it. Directed by one of the Pythons. He had seen it years ago with Isobel.

'Where's Declan got to this evening?' Jules's father asked Lorraine.

Edward himself had a pretty good idea where Declan was, but he didn't say anything. Some years ago he had seen Declan's van parked outside Burger Tree, and Declan looking extremely pally with a woman Edward recognised from the post office. Declan, likely on the lookout for the traffic warden, had happened to glance up right as Edward drove past and they had locked eyes for a moment. So personally gratifying had it been to learn that Lorraine's efforts to drive away her husband – her inept surveillance and constant hectoring – had finally borne fruit that Edward had never referred to this event with Declan or anyone else. *Good for you, mate*, he thought to himself each time Declan turned up, all smiles, three hours late for Sunday lunch. Pressurised into making regular appearances at the Brewers', Edward's response was to take his entertainment where he found it. And if this involved baiting an embittered, frizzy-haired harridan who laughed with her teeth clamped together and used words like 'liaise', Edward had decided, so be it.

'Yes, where *is* Declan today?' he said solicitously, smiling at Mr Brewer. 'Does he work on Sundays as well, then?' This was one of his favourite ploys, to gently roll a grenade through the doorway, or to plant and detonate awkward questions he already knew the answer to.

'Pardon?' said Lorraine. *You heard*, he thought thuggishly.

'Declan,' he repeated, knitting his brow in an expression of familial concern. 'We were all wondering where he is. Weren't we?' he added, looking genially round the room as if to gather support. No one spoke.

'I expect he's on the way,' offered Jules gamely. There was a Pinteresque pause. He sensed everyone holding their breath as Lorraine stalled for time, placing her coffee cup on the table with slow and uncharacteristic delicacy. Edward waited; he would not be the first to blink.

'In actual fact Declan's not coming on account of his dad being very poorly,' Lorraine said. 'Why are you so concerned?'

Edward watched her narrow her eyes at him like a mugger sizing up his mark. He wanted to laugh. 'No reason,' he replied mildly, helping himself to another After Eight. Lorraine shot him an expletive-deleted look. *Howzat!* Edward thought, as with great nonchalance he slid the chocolate out of its slim, shiny jacket and popped it into his mouth. There was another unpleasant silence in which he had the strange feeling of being on a stage, the entire audience looking on in appalled fascination. In the corner, Jules's grandmother let out a low fart. 'Right then, anyone for a Bailey's?' said Mr Brewer. How he fucking *loathed* them all, Edward thought, coarse and potato-faced and devoid of basic manners. Even their house offended him – the air thick, reeking of old sandwiches lodged down the backs of sofas and things bought on the knock. 'White Lions', pronounced a plaque outside, nailed above the garage door, while balanced on the small gateposts not ten feet away were a pair of the fearsome animals themselves, white plaster casts purchased from the garden centre. Edward had vivid fantasies of driving round and knocking them off in the middle of the night. Being forced to spend more time at 'White Lions', he had found out a few things about the family as well, concerning various married cousins. He considered these as Mr Brewer reverently fetched the Bailey's bottle from the drinks cupboard and held it out to the room with a proud flourish.

'Bailey's, fantastic!' said Edward, rudely holding out his coffee mug in the direction of the approaching bottle. He didn't care how it looked. Long ago he had noted Lorraine's and Mr Brewer's identical puglike noses, the receding chins and the lack of a top lip that the *New Scientist* advised was positively correlated with foetal alcohol syndrome. Did their small-minded, clannish sensibility stem from a high-inbreeding coefficient and lack of gene-shuffling? Or were they, Edward thought, Mrs Brewer excepted, simply complete and utter cunts? Lorraine and Mr Brewer might not-so-secretly look down on him for being less white than they were, but there was something to be said for hybrid vigour. Still, it could be tricky to distinguish between nature and nurture, and for the sake of their impending offspring he would remember to keep his fingers crossed for the latter.

Frustratingly, the Bailey's bottle appeared to be frozen in mid-air. Mr Brewer was looking questioningly across the room at Jules. The air seemed to crackle with cross-currents. Had Edward had a few too many again? No doubt he would find out first thing tomorrow when he was greeted with a thumping headache and another fruitless set-to with Jules. He aimed a sober, magnanimous smile towards Mrs Brewer – whose antennae were always finely tuned to trouble – and in response she leant towards him with the plate of Viennese whirls.

'Another biscuit, Edward?'

'One was just right, thank you.' He happened to be very fond of Viennese whirls, but he was painfully aware of his waistline, expanding in some possible act of *solidarność* with Jules's and her pregnancy. 'A drop of Bailey's would be fantastic, though, Mrs Brewer,' he added.

'Hazel,' said Mrs Brewer.

'*Hazel*,' he said. 'Of course.'

Mr Brewer gave his wife a look, before tipping a begrudging measure of the liquid into Edward's mug.

'I was just saying to Jules,' Lorraine said into the strained silence, 'how lucky it was that I happened to drive past and see that *For Sale* sign when I did. Right, Dad?'

'Never been one to turn up an opportunity, our Lorri,' said Mr Brewer approvingly. Lorraine smirked.

What *was* the opportunity for *our Lorri*, Edward wanted to ask, as the apt phrase 'nasty, brutish and short' floated to him out of the ether. Did none of them feel the need to point out that they had had this ridiculous conversation at least ten times before? Lorraine never missed an opportunity to crow about 'finding' Edward and Jules 'a new home'. The purchase had opened up a new front in the war, although, understanding that this was less about Lorraine's massive self-regard than about trying to antagonise him, he tried to ignore her and was mostly successful. He saw Lorraine exchange an unreadable look with Jules. There was an unsettling shrewdness to Jules's sister, a vindictive and unnatural aspect, Edward thought, watching as she snapped her lighter at the cigarette dangling from her lips: she was in a perpetual state of self-congratulation and assessment, weighing up the most hurtful thing to say – and then promptly saying it. The only snag with this idea was that it credited Lorraine with a bit more intelligence and cunning than he'd like. Safer to settle for good old Occam's razor: Lorraine was her father's daughter, intrinsically self-occupied and oblivious. Which brought him back to the most obvious and pressing question: *what was Jules's excuse?* Jules seemed utterly in thrall to her sister lately. He had pondered the question at some length and was yet to find a palatable answer. As his friend Gareth had remarked when he found out that his stepsister was posting her knickers to convicts, some things could be written off to hormones – and some could not.

Edward had not been in favour of the move – for many reasons, aside from the glaringly obvious one that nobody – except Mrs Brewer – seemed to appreciate nor care about. His official objection – the party line – had been that with a baby coming they were hardly in a position to buy a house. 'But where are we going to put him or her?' Jules had said. Fearing another conversation about baby names, Edward had acknowledged that they had barely enough room to swing Happy Meal, but they simply didn't have that sort of money. Then, more and more, he had found himself unable to avoid the Brewers' house on Sunday afternoons, where silent television-watching had been replaced by pointed comments about the *once-in-a-lifetime opportunity* – the *bargain* of a house that *for some reason* Edward kept stubbornly turning down. The subject was brought up in as many ways as possible – a classic interrogation technique, Edward thought, though knowing this didn't really help. Sure enough he soon felt so isolated and worn down that gritting his teeth and saying what the Brewers wanted to hear was less painful than continuing to say no. They had moved in a month ago.

'So what *are* your plans, then, Ed?' said Mr Brewer.

'We've got a lot on our plate at the moment. I'm sure you understand,' Edward replied evenly.

'I expect they'd rather wait for the cooler weather, don't you, Frank?' interjected Mrs Brewer. The deft averter of disaster, she had developed the convenient habit of leaping to Edward's rescue and he was happy to let her get on with it. If, on the surface, this reminded Edward of the way Jules insisted on 'handling' him lately, as if he were a pressure-release IED wired to go off the second you took your foot off it, on Mrs Brewer's part he was fairly sure that this was a courtesy provided less for Edward's sake than to spare her daughter's pride.

Officially he and Jules had done the paperwork in late May. After Jules had told her father the news, Mr Brewer, clearly less than pleased, had asked Edward, in front of the whole family, if they would 'do the deed' before his daughter was 'too far along'. Edward, still in shock at the unexpected pregnancy, had assented, and the following week he had been frog-marched down to the register office by Lorraine and Jules, with their mother anxiously bringing up the rear. But at the time he had also been firmly given to understand by Jules's father, who hadn't come with them, that 'at the end of the day, a proper ceremony is in order'. Like any debt, Edward had decided mutinously, this could be put off until later.

'Next June, we thought,' said Jules. 'And the reception at the Brentwood Inn.' *News to me*, thought Edward, before remembering that he'd informed Jules during one of their arguments that he wanted nothing to do with planning the thing.

'Eh?' In the corner, Jules's grandmother spoke up. 'Will it be pop dancing, then?'

'Course it will, Gran,' said Lorraine. 'Are you joking? It's perfect for a celebration, that place!' *Twisting the knife*. Was it malice aforethought? Edward wondered, or was Lorraine really that dense? In other words, was she incomprehensibly cruel or incomprehensibly tactless? He felt engulfed by a wave of tiredness.

'Not in a church, mind you,' Jules's grandmother was saying in a scandalised tone. 'Not in your state. You'll burst into flames, so you will.' Jules's grandmother had converted to Catholicism, apparently, after her husband ran off with someone else, and she had the fury of the convert and 'beliefs' about pregnant and unmarried women.

'She'll have had it by then, Gran,' said Lorraine.

'June!' cut in Mrs Brewer, as if only now discovering the name of a month she'd never heard of. '*Lovely…*'

Edward wondered when the Bailey's bottle would come round again.

They had had it all out, the afternoon after his notionally epic night out. He had dozed off on the beach and staggered home at about 6.30am with a splitting headache, only to find there was no milk in the fridge. Turning round, he'd stumped back out to the corner shop and halfway home discovered that by mistake he'd managed to buy more coffee instead of more milk. At that point he gave up and ducked into Café Bacchus, where he downed multiple espressos, returning to the flat some time after noon and straight into a row. If she'd forgotten to take a pill, Jules explained, it was really and truly a mistake – an accident. 'Was it buggery!' Edward had told her. 'I thought you didn't believe in "accidents".' She was in league with her sister, he went on. By then Jules had started to cry, which perversely made him even angrier. 'I'm bloody fed up with it!' he shouted, and then he shouted a bit more and kicked the fridge and then Jules locked herself in the bedroom. After half an hour he knocked softly on the door and asked her to come out and have a cup of tea. 'Let's go for a nice walk along the seafront,' he suggested, and he heard the door unlock. As they passed the old bandstand he held her hand and asked gently when she wanted to see the doctor to discuss the options. '*Options*?' said Jules, with wide, red-rimmed eyes, and Edward explained, causing another explosion of tears, until eventually, unnerved by the hostile stares of several old ladies and couples pushing prams, he gave in. 'Spilt milk,' he sighed, thinking aloud, and Jules started to cry again.

When they got back to the flat he told her that he needed time to clear his head. His mind felt thick and heavy. He had made some important decisions on the beach last night, but what were they? Then two days later he woke to the sound of retching in the bathroom. Jules had her appointment at the doctor's that morning and looked so weak and ill that he took the day off and went with her.

'I'm not overly concerned,' said the doctor, stroking his chin. 'Yet.'

'Yet? Can you tell me what that means, precisely?' asked Edward. They'd been there half an hour already and he was infuriated by the doctor's coy manner and the fact of his time being wasted.

'Let's see,' said the doctor, riffling noisily through his papers again before raising his head to gather them up, priest-like, in the beatific beam of his smile. *They think they're gods in white coats*, Edward thought, hating the man for his leisurely, passive-aggressive air. The doctor would have a selection of such smiles: saccharine and soft-centred, like the chocolates you spat back in the box.

'Can Mum take some time off work, put her feet up a bit more?' said the doctor.

'I don't know, can she?' he snapped back. There was an insult concealed in the question and he felt almost hysterical with annoyance. 'You're the expert. You tell me.'

'I think so – we can manage that, can't we, Edward…?' said Jules meekly.

'Splendid,' said the doctor, rubbing his hands together. 'In cases like this, it's helpful if we can support each together through the process, isn't it?' He smiled his horrible smile at them again. *Dr Crippen*, Edward thought.

'Christ on a bike,' he told Jules as they left the surgery, 'it sounds like therapy.'

'Well,' replied Jules, 'I've been meaning to talk to you about that…' The aggravation, Edward decided, it was never-ending.

After their tiresome afternoon at the Brewers', Jules went straight to bed. Half an hour later the phone rang. Edward sighed, knowing who it was and knowing that if he didn't answer it would only ring again five minutes later.

'Oh, it's you,' said Lorraine flatly when Edward picked up, it being her habit to sound surprised when he picked up his own phone.

'She's gone upstairs to rest,' he said, hoping Lorraine wasn't planning on coming over. Not that she or anyone else would ever think to alert him in advance, or ask first if he minded. Nowadays the doorbell rang without warning and in she'd march, squaring up to him, circling him like a boxer in a ring, before parking herself on his sofa or shutting herself in the dining room with Jules. What did they get up to in there, he wondered, whispering and giggling? 'She's helping me with the computer,' Jules had protested when he'd asked why Lorraine insisted on coming over five nights a week. Frequently she was already there when he got home from work: repeated incursions, an occupying army of one, with Jules as his very own Fifth Columnist. He would hear Lorraine's grating voice as he pushed open the front gate, the

375

braying laugh that set his teeth on edge. He sensed that their female chatter stopped abruptly when they heard his key in the door, and felt the women's eyes on him as he entered the room, Lorraine thinking up something to criticise or jump on him about – some trivial issue of baby accoutrements or empty cupboards or items Edward had neglected to buy at the supermarket on his way home. 'I'll get her to ring you when she gets up,' he told Lorraine. There was a short silence in which he could almost hear her thinking up something unpleasant to say. Amazing, Edward thought, how she managed to infuse even silence with reproach – a skill she would have honed on her long-suffering husband.

'You shouldn't disturb her if she's sleeping,' she said.

'I wasn't going to,' he replied. Subtle or crushing comebacks appeared to go over her head, so he didn't bother any more. 'Try her back in half an hour if you prefer.'

'I'd rather call *her* back, if you don't mind, Edward,' she replied nonsensically, as not for the first time it occurred to him that in Jules's sister the world's psychologists might uncover some rare species of narcissist, skilled at what the Americans termed 'crazy-making'. This, Edward decided, holding the phone an inch or two from his ear, would account for her hands-off parenting and her children's ragbag collection of ADHD, dyslexia, 'learning disabilities' and sundry other modern ailments. 'At this moment in time,' Lorraine continued in the convoluted language of a train station announcement, 'I'm cooking tea.'

'As am I,' he replied tersely, '*at this moment in time*. So I'll let you go.' His tone risked drawing fire, Edward knew, but he was too tired to care.

'She needs her rest, you know,' Lorraine went on. 'Although obviously no one expects *you* to understand how tiring it is, being a mother-to-be...'

Edward remembered that Freud thought morning sickness was the woman's effort to vomit up the man's baby, and was tempted to share this information with Lorraine. But he could imagine her being perversely pleased about it, seeing this, too, as somehow all Edward's fault. 'Yep, so you've said,' he agreed, with as much flippancy as he could muster. It was like being the target of some cack-handed but pestering sniper. And how telling, he thought, that, despite Lorraine's perpetual lecturing about Jules's welfare and how unfathomably dreadful it was being pregnant, she never offered to help, never offered to do some shopping or to cook a meal. With Jules out of action those duties had fallen to him, and he was having trouble keeping up with it all. He waited.

'*By the way*,' said Lorraine right on cue, after another long silence that he couldn't be bothered to fill, 'our mum found your ring next to the sink after you left.' *And there it is*, Edward thought. Because there was always something with Lorraine, some mal-intent or motive *other* than the actual welfare of her sister. Was she going to make something of it, Edward wondered, this non-event with the ring?

'Goodness, did I leave it there?' he said with exaggerated interest. 'So kind of you to let me know. I'll let you go, then, thanks so much, bye bye,' he chirruped, and rang off without waiting for her to reply. If she wanted to play that game – well, he wasn't playing. *You've got the watches, we've got the time*, said the Taliban, but he had no time for an insurgency – either to wage or to counter one, and certainly no time for Lorraine and her clumsy threats and war of attrition. He wondered if she had been disappointed to get Edward on the phone instead of Jules. Had her goal been to surprise Jules with news of the discarded wedding ring? Or was Edward the intended target all along? After he got round to mending the garden shed, he decided, and when she finally pushed him over the edge into serial-killer territory, Lorraine would be his first victim, lured with the promise of a fifty-five-inch television that fell off the back of a lorry, knocked over the head with a brick, sawn into pieces and the bits chucked in the sea. As he took the phone off the hook he pictured the body parts, grey and bloodless and slowly sinking beneath the English Channel. He studied the ring finger of his left hand. He couldn't honestly say he'd noticed the ring was gone. There was no telling white line on his skin to alert him to its absence – and this, Edward thought glumly, was testament to spending his summer indoors, in the office or shut in the house, caught in an endless cycle of working and cleaning and cooking and washing-up, while Jules was on bed-rest upstairs.

He went into the kitchen and opened the fridge. Empty. His new duties included filling it, and he had meant to pop into the supermarket on the way home on Friday, but he had got off the train in such a fog of exhaustion that it had completely slipped his mind. There had been more cutbacks at work. Half the staff were doing the work of the other half and all leave had been cancelled. There was to be no more 'skiving off' at 5pm or claiming immunity to last-minute assignments, so that Edward frequently found himself on the late train, not halfway home and already fretting like some harassed and careworn housewife about how to get to the supermarket before it shut and having the dinner dished up on time. How ever had his mother managed it? The supermarket would already be shut, Edward thought; he'd have go to the corner shop. He needed a cup of coffee first – and a quick splosh of revitalising own-brand scotch. Upstairs the bedroom door opened and he heard Jules pad across the landing. He slipped the bottle back under the sink behind the cleaning things – *operation aborted* – and waited. He heard the toilet flush, and a minute or so later Jules appeared at the kitchen doorway in her dressing gown, rubbing at her eyes like a child.

'Was that Lorraine?' she yawned. 'Sorry, I fell asleep.'

'S'all right,' he told her. He'd been enjoying these few minutes to himself, Edward realised, pottering about in the kitchen. 'Want some tea? I'm having coffee.' He was reaching for the cafetière later and later these days.

'Lovely,' said Jules. 'What did she say?'

'Your sister? Nothing much. The usual jaw-dropping advice about you taking it easy,' he added. '*All my fault*, etcetera.'

'That was nice of her,' said Jules without apparent irony, sinking down on to a chair. He stared at her, but she was listlessly picking leaves off the dried-up remains of a Busy Lizzie plant.

'Joke,' he said finally.

'Pardon?'

'Joke. Sarcasm. *I was being sarcastic.*' And bitter, Edward thought to himself. Jules was slow on the uptake these days; their wires were perpetually crossed.

'I'm sure she was only trying to help,' she replied.

'That's a pile of old wank,' he observed shortly. 'Unless you define "help" as ringing at all hours and barging in to inspect the bathroom and point out all the cobwebs.' He took a breath, tried to slow his heart rate. Why was Jules never on his side? He hated all this bickering, but couldn't seem to help it; it was as if Lorraine was always in the room with them.

'I don't know what you want me to do,' Jules responded, her lower lip quivering. 'Can't you just *try* to get along with everyone?'

'*Try*?' He couldn't believe what he was hearing. 'Don't make me laugh. It's all I do these days, try to get on with your bloody family. Why don't they *try* and get on with *me* for a change?' Jules said nothing. 'Well? How about that?' *And we're off!* Edward thought. How wretched they were, these flare-ups, like the last sparking embers of resistance on the forced march towards boredom and domestic hatred. If they weren't at each other's throats their conversations had a flat, lacklustre quality, and he felt himself having to wrest the subject away from the twin obsessions of baby clothes and buying furniture. Last week, in an unheard of adventure, they had gone out for an Indian meal, only to sit in silence like one of those couples Edward used to feel sorry for. He thought of his mother, who was always ready to lob the conversational ball back over the net. Until recently he hadn't realised how much he had relied on her for conversation, for her lively wit and the quickness of her mind. Not only had he loved his mother, but he had liked her. Seeing an interesting article in the paper – on politics, science, literature, it never mattered what – he used to look forward to hearing her point of view. Since her death all these events and bits of news had seemed to accumulate, with no one to discuss them with, which left him feeling violently sad. 'Look,' he said, seeing Jules's eyes fill with tears, 'let's just drop it, all right?'

Happy Meal appeared and began pushing around his legs. He bent down to pick him up but the cat turned away and went to sit pointedly by his food bowl. Both Jules and the cat, Edward realised, were staring at him in expectation. Had Jules fed him today? Since taking early maternity leave, this was her only job. Lacking her usual routine, and lost in some mysterious fog of women's hormones, how often did it slip her mind?

'Did you feed him?' he asked. Jules had got up and was staring into the fridge with a slack-faced expression.

'Yes, of course I did,' she replied, turning. 'Why?'

'He looks hungry, that's all.' He was aware of sounding peevish and accusing, but, as with the allegedly missed pill and the morning sickness and the chronic exhaustion, some distrustful part of him thought of Jules's pregnancy as a trick hatched with Lorraine to trap him. In his darkest, most paranoid moments he found himself wondering whether he could trust her any more.

'He always looks like that,' Jules observed, returning to the table with a packet of rice cakes. 'He had food when we came in, while you were parking the car, and this morning when I got up.' *Whenever that was*, Edward thought uncharitably. He understood that Jules wasn't lounging on the sofa in front of the telly all day eating bonbons, but she made little effort to rouse herself. When she had taken leave from the school it had been agreed she would do some part-time work from home, marking homework on the computer or whatever. Edward didn't envy her, stuck inside reading essays by halfwits and future petty criminals. He felt guilty that she had to work at all. But, as he'd explained more times than necessary, every penny of their savings had been eaten up by a hefty mortgage, and they desperately needed the cash. And then there was Facebook, Edward thought wearily. Too often these days he arrived home hungry and tired to find Jules – or Jules and Lorraine – sitting at the computer transfixed by strangers' babies and photos of people's half-eaten dinners. Obviously, no one could accuse Edward of being a Luddite. Technology had its place. But the idea of voluntarily putting yourself through any version of social media was beyond him – and also, Edward thought, watching Jules pick lethargically at a loose bit of thread on her dressing gown, beyond the pale when he found himself working all hours of the day and night to pay the mortgage and put food on the table. At first he had weighed the cost of having a word with her about it, but he'd let it be. In Jules's hormonal state any comment would be asking for it, like dipping your hand into a bucket of piranhas.

'Are we still going out for pizza tonight?' said Jules. This plan had completely slipped his mind. Jules had recently enacted a *date night* once a week, another of her tedious efforts to encourage *couple-time*, a cringeworthy phrase no doubt picked up from *Byways to Oblivion* or *Footsteps to Futility* or whatever it was she was obsessed with these days. '"Couple time"?' he had joked when Jules first mentioned it. 'Sounds like a crap porn site. Not that I'd know what one was,' he'd added, only half-jokingly. For months he had been listening to her bang on about *manifesting your desires* and *productive grieving* and *living joyfully with grief*. Once – and only once – after finding the wretched book while hoovering under the bed, he had looked into the matter, leafing surreptitiously through its pages while in the bathroom Jules vomited steadily into the toilet. Inside he had discovered a fresh and copiously bookmarked hell of spiritual pretensions, of *accepting fear of love, evolved loving* and *couples: learning playfulness*. He'd almost run in and shoved his head down the toilet with her.

'Pizza, you're right. But if you don't fancy going out ...' he said amenably, observing Jules's slumped posture and baggy eyes.

'I feel too fat to go out ...'

'Don't be daft.'

'I am, though. I'm as big as a bloody elephant. Look at my thighs.' Jules demonstrated for him, pinching at the fabric of her jeans, and he felt a stab of pity for her and for the state she was in.

'It's fine by me,' he said. 'I mean *I'm* fine – not going out. Not that your thighs are fine.' He backtracked. 'Not that they're *not*…fine, *obviously*…' he blundered on, but Jules's face had already crumpled. 'Jules, sorry…I'm sorry, that came out all wrong.' *Mucked that up*, Edward thought, and swore silently at himself – and at Lorraine, who had had a hand in this, as she did in almost everything else. Early on in Jules's pregnancy Lorraine had exhorted her sister to 'eat for two'. After this had followed two months in which Jules had joyfully gobbled up anything she could lay her hands on, at which point – wonder of wonders – Lorraine had changed her tune. One memorable miserable Sunday afternoon at the Brewers', she had remarked in her usual tone of manufactured caring that everyone understood that Jules *would* be tired, of course she would, because of 'the weight'. *You should know*, Edward had thought savagely, but the damage was done. The next day Jules put herself on a diet, and roped Edward in as 'support'. Aside from their once-a-week date/treat night, the project required endless (and expensive) trips to the health shop. One month in, Edward was starving, and Jules looked much the same as before.

'Well, I do have a few bits to do on the computer…' said Jules, who had stood up and seemed to have recovered. He watched her take the dying Busy Lizzie over to the sink and put it down. Did she expect him to water it? She was like those people who offered to help with the washing-up, but merely ferried everything over to the sink and left it there.

'For school, I take it..?' he asked.

'Yes,' said Jules, turning. 'Why?'

'No reason,' he said, smiling.

'Essays and things,' she said. 'I can heat up some soup or something for myself later on.'

'Righto.' *No need for the grim corner shop, then*, thought Edward. *Small mercies.*

'What will *you* eat, though?' Jules paused at the door.

'Oh, I'll manage,' he said. This suited him fine. He was now free to shove a box of something salty and non-organic into the microwave, to sit and fester and savour an entire evening alone in front of the telly with the cat. He closed his eyes for a moment. There was nothing more luxurious.

After the final two episodes of a *Battlestar Galactica* marathon and two Nicolas Roeg films, back-to-back on Channel 4, he watched the closing credits go up and felt overcome by an unaccountable feeling of loss and dislocation. He changed the stations aimlessly for a while with the hope of distracting himself, but discovered only repeats of cooking shows and something featuring a gruesome band of Chelsea Sloanes. He turned it off, but the blackness of the screen seemed to engulf him and he switched it back on again. Jules had never liked the cinema, he remembered, even when they'd had the time and the money – aeons ago, so it seemed to him now – for such extravagant outings. He ran through the channels again and found himself in the middle of a programme about the construction of the Empire State Building. Hadn't Isobel mentioned having a partial view of it from her apartment? He wondered what his sister was up to this evening. He looked at his watch and worked out that in New York it would be early evening – Isobel would be galloping off on some jaunt, out at a party or with her boyfriend or taking in a film herself. Although she would be at the cinema proper, he thought, not stuck at home on the sofa. She had been on his mind a lot. He had been meaning to write and tell her about the move and Jules being pregnant, but he barely had time to wipe his own arse these days, let alone sit at the computer and draft out a coherent response to all her emails. He had managed to carve out only a few minutes, here and there, to reply to her messages. They provided some light relief, breezy, with the odd little snippet about her life. He had been careful to let her know he wasn't deliberately ignoring her, explaining – without delving into the complexities of recent events – that he had rather a lot on his plate, but that he hoped that she was all right and that they would speak soon. He was surprised to realise that he missed her – the ease of conversation, the shared jokes, and possibly some sense of shared history. He had forgotten how funny she was, how clever with words, and her refined appreciation for the absurd. In that way, Edward thought, as the Empire State Building rose floor by floor into the New York sky, Isobel was like their mother. He had made a decision to hold out the olive branch, when he had time, to build some new rapport with his sister and become some sort of family again. One obstacle was not knowing how to talk about his life as it was without coming off like a miserable git. Part of him felt obscurely embarrassed by the situation as well, like a pensioner taken in by a Ponzi scheme. At some point – he couldn't recall quite when – the emails had started arriving further apart, their contents more sparse. *P.S. Don't worry about replying if you're busy!* Isobel had added at the end of one, and it had occurred to him that she herself was busy, wrapped up in work and her social life and her friends. Of course summer, Edward had heard, was the time of year when New Yorkers disappeared off to places like the Hamptons.

As the TV announcer sounded the goodnight, he recalled the other, less offhand P.S., which Isobel had appended some months ago, and which, if he was honest, had unsettled him – though he knew that it probably shouldn't have – *Thinking we could spread Mum's ashes some time soon? Christmas, maybe? Have to decide where… Thoughts?* He kept meaning to write back, but then it was as if he'd blinked and it was August and somehow he'd still not got round to it. He was ashamed to admit that it was only last week that he'd made the sombre drive over to the crematorium to collect their mother's remains – 'cremains', the woman on the phone cheerfully termed them. He had received a third stern letter in the post, forwarded from their old address, threatening to 'dispose of the remains of **M. VERNOM** in the appropriate manner' if they weren't collected within seven days. After Edward had signed for them, the attendant reached through the scratched plastic partition and pushed a garish nylon purple carrier bag towards him. What was he supposed to do with it? Walking through the car park he had struggled with how to carry it – whether to hold it from the handles, swinging it like a shopping bag, or cradle it gently in his arms in the way it perhaps deserved. In the end he gathered the handles halfway down and felt the sharp corner of a cardboard box bumping against his thigh all across the car park like something purchased from the Apple store. He couldn't bring himself to look inside. Back at the house he had gone straight upstairs, pulled the ladder down, and pushed the bag as far into the loft as he could stretch his fingers.

Clearly, Isobel felt differently about their mother's remains. His sister would have other questions too, about the hospital and the past and who knew what else. Having Isobel in his life again, Edward realised, would mean having to provide an answer to all of them.

When at last he dragged himself up to bed he set the alarm, got under the duvet and listened to Jules's even breaths. With his new status as a raging insomniac, the concept of sleeping right through the night appeared faintly absurd. He had developed a half-formed idea of needing to make the most of these days, miserable and sleep-deprived as they were, before the even more miserable and sleep-deprived ones that lay ahead in the New Year. For the first eighteen months, Gareth had helpfully informed him, you were up every two hours 'if you're lucky'. Beside him Jules let out a soft snore and he marvelled at this: the ability to simply shut yourself down like a computer. Hormones, Edward decided, and wondered whether Jules would hear the baby crying when it needed its nappy changed at 3am, or whether even this job, too, would fall to him. Jules still held on to the notion that as soon as the baby was born the joy of fatherhood would overcome him and blot out all his doubts, but he wasn't convinced. When and if he fell asleep at night, these and other anxieties he was able to hold back during the day came rushing in like floodwater under the door and he would wake, flailing for air.

Quietly he switched the bedside lamp back on, angling it downwards and away from Jules, and took his book from the bedside table, his boss's hefty biography, which Edward and his colleagues felt duty-bound to read, despite their workload, in a desperate strategy to fend off redundancy. After fifteen minutes he found himself reading the same paragraph over and over again, and he put the book aside and lay staring at the ceiling. Its surface was uncannily smooth and featureless. It gave him an empty feeling, this negation of character, of individuality. 'It's been refitted with all mod cons!' the estate agent had announced in July, having promised a tour of 'the property' as soon as the renovations were finished. 'You'll notice there's an open-plan feel,' she informed them as they followed her up the stairs, waving her hand at the hollow modern doors, at the 'Tuscany-inspired' bathroom tiling, and lastly – almost, but not quite, the last straw for Edward – at the kitchen, where the 'old-fashioned' cabinets had been ripped out and replaced with oak-veneer MDF. The whole house – the exterior, the doors and doorposts, the skirting boards, the walls and the fireplace (blocked in) – had been painted a blinding, glossy white. *God help me*, Edward had thought to himself, *it's so much worse than I imagined.* 'I expect you'll be looking to build an extension,' the estate agent had suggested. 'No,' he told her. 'We won't.' Later he would recall his own bewilderment and sense of disbelief, and the cheap clonk-clonk sound of the agent's red court shoes on the 'autumn-hued' dining room floor as she led him and Jules through the pair of plasticky-looking sliding doors which had magically appeared where the dining room window used to be, and into what used to be his mother's garden. A stark expanse of white paving stones covered the entire area, while at the far end, next to the fence, Edward could just make out the thinnest band of grass and a few stumps where her beloved apple trees used to stand. Only one remained, leaning sclerotically against the old shed. The 'space' was 'ideal' for a barbecue, the estate agent chattered on. 'A barbecue!' echoed Jules, turning to him in apparent wonderment. 'We can have my whole family round…'

'Seconds of fun,' he muttered.

'I think it takes a while to cook on a barbecue, actually,' Edward heard the estate agent tell Jules as he turned and walked away from them.

At 6am he gave up and decided to make himself one of Jules's herbal tea concoctions. A bit mimsy, Edward thought, herbal tea, and, even if it wasn't the horse-tranquillising-strength he required, its warmth was comforting and with a bit of luck – *and if Jules didn't need anything, and if Lorraine didn't ring, etcetera, etcetera* – he might fall away afterwards into a light doze until 10am or so. He put on his slippers and went downstairs, retrieving the papers from the front step on the way. In the kitchen he held the kettle under the tap. After several weeks, Edward thought, he still couldn't get used to the cooker being on the wrong side and never failed to graze his hip on the murderous little corners of the granite kitchen island. He had yet to make up his mind whether this monstrosity looked more like a sarcophagus or something on which you'd perform a post-mortem. Like a large and belligerent party guest, the thing took up virtually the whole kitchen. He dropped a bag of what looked like hay but was labelled 'Midnight Dreaming' into his cup and took the papers into the dining room. In less than twenty minutes the sun would rise, but if he shut the ugly vertical blinds Jules had ordered online and got installed last week he could pretend it was still dark. He stood for a moment looking out at the hulking turquoise-enamelled barbecue contraption parked next to the fence, a would-be wedding present from Jules's family. Even in poor light, the paving stones gave out a poisonous and radioactive glow. Above him, in his mother's former bedroom, the future nursery waited silently for its new occupant. He had lobbied hard for the box room, which was his as a child and whose diminutive size had made him feel secure and safe. After he left for university the room had become filled with papers and junk, and it was currently full of his mother's unpacked boxes, transported to their flat and then brought back to Danecroft Road when they'd moved in. He didn't feel ready to go through them and had instead proposed moving the boxes into Mary's old bedroom or up in the loft.

'Edward, I'm sorry, but the back room is much more suitable for the nursery,' Jules had told him, momentarily channelling Lorraine in some firm, tight-lipped way that Edward found rather alarming.

Ironically, on that occasion, Lorraine had been on Edward's side. 'Oh, please,' she'd said. 'The bloody baby won't know what size room it's in, will it? Put it in the box room and make the larger space into a *media* room,' she told Jules. 'Or you can use it for guests and such.'

'No, I don't think so, Lorraine,' replied Jules. 'I'm sorry, but the back room's nicer and it has views over the *garden*.'

'*What* garden?' Edward had snapped. 'What view?' Until then, he had let them get on with it, tuning out of yet another of their tiresome plans and discussions. No one said anything, and after a moment the women simply returned to their discussion without him.

He picked up his tea and left the window to go in search of Happy Meal. Except to do his business, the cat, too, shunned the garden. He called its name in a low voice and it came pattering towards him from the warm spot under the hallway radiator. Why did people speak of cats as users and chancers? Edward thought. He would never understand it. The animal appeared in his dreams lately and they had long, fascinating exchanges in which the cat offered advice and wisdom, none of which Edward managed to recall upon waking. *Animals*, he thought, as the cat purred, *they never let you down*. They didn't grow up to disappoint or betray you. They were always, and could only be, themselves – innocent and unsullied by base human impulses.

'It's just you and me now, mate,' Edward told the cat as it went to sit by its food bowl. 'And we'll have to bugger on as best we can.'

August

Delete Is Your Friend

The silly things you think about when you're on your own, thought Julie, going into the kitchen to make a cup of coffee. Although they had lived there for several weeks now, the house had held on to its familiar-yet-unfamiliar atmosphere so that she still found herself tiptoeing about as if she weren't, in fact, in her very own home. If she needed to use the facilities while Edward was at work she made sure to leave the bathroom door ajar because, however carefully and quietly she pulled it to, she seemed to hear the answering echo of another door, up in the loft above or rising from under the floor. 'Just an old house, pet,' her mother said, 'not like ours.' Was it normal, Julie wondered, this lonely feeling that shadowed her from room to room? Their flat had been chock-a-block with their belongings, but Mary's house had swallowed them all up. What the house really needed was more furniture. That was if Edward would shift himself for long enough on a Saturday morning to get to Home 'n' Wear.

In the fridge she found an empty carton of milk and experienced a little wave of irritation, struck by the idea that Edward was so strict about some things, while about others he behaved as if he couldn't care less. There was always something amiss or out of place. She'd come downstairs in the morning to find the cat up on the kitchen island licking at something, or the coffee machine left on and a cheese-encrusted plate in the microwave. Men made messes, her mother said, that was just how they were. Was it, though? Julie wondered. Could men really sit in front of the telly half the night and eat all the muesli, but never think – not even once – to buy more? Was it really something in Edward's make-up that prevented him from giving the oven a scrub or having a wipe over the top of the cooker after he'd used it? Julie wasn't so sure. On a number of occasions she had tried – as authentically and non-judgementally as possible – to address the issue, but he always got so defensive.

She filled the kettle and listened to the sound it made, an intensely hollow noise she didn't recall ever hearing in their old flat. Looking at the situation positively, a soothing herbal tea instead of coffee with milk would mean fewer calories, Julie decided, as, too late and without thinking, she snapped the kettle lid shut and heard another, quieter snap echo back to her from elsewhere in the house, from the living room, or from upstairs – as usual she could never quite place where. 'Stop,' she said to herself, pulling at and letting go the elastic band she kept on her wrist for exactly this purpose. *Snap!* It stung – a little – but with practice it stopped you worrying about things you couldn't control. Out in the hallway she opened the drawer under the phone table and took out the packet of custard creams. For the sake of the baby she and Edward had both gone sugar- and alcohol-free some weeks ago, but Edward was being very lax. Julie certainly wasn't the only one who'd noticed, especially on Sunday afternoons. Her thighs were actually rubbing together at this point, while, in her jeans, each day her bottom seemed to strain more uncomfortably against the seams than it had the day before. Was it time for elasticated waists? She had always prided herself on maintaining a neat figure, but there was no denying she had put on more weight than was called for. Inadvertently catching sight of herself in the mirror, or even thinking of the weighing scales, made her feel worse. And yet, Julie thought, shutting the drawer, on the path to personal realisation and self-development it was essential to be good to yourself. Which was how, she supposed, she had got into the bad habit, mid-morning, if she was up, of allowing herself a little something – a pre-lunch custard cream – and if she was feeling tired – which let's face it, Julie thought, was most days – another at 3pm when she sat down to watch *The Donna T. Show*. It was only a bloody biscuit. And wasn't guilt an unproductive feeling? 'Stop,' she told herself, and gave the elastic band another flick. Quickly, before she could change her mind again, she opened the drawer and took the packet and went to settle herself with her tea at the dining room table. How much nicer the room was, she thought, with the modern sliding patio doors and Mary's ugly old yellow forsythia chopped down. Despite what Edward said, the patio was so much more pleasant than their old garden at the flat, which had been a burden more than anything, with its grass and its nosy upstairs neighbours always hinting about using it for parties. Edward disagreed, obviously. She would never understand why he objected to buying Danecroft Road, Julie thought, taking a biscuit from the packet, and why he had to be so *negative* about all the improvements. The house was so much lighter and brighter – you could practically feel the positive energy pouring in through the large picture window and into the lounge. And the location was so much better than that of their old flat – and far nicer, obviously, than Lorraine and Declan's neighbourhood, which as their father had pointed out last Sunday was overrun with criminals and benefit cheats.

She ran her teeth under a thick layer of cream and managed to gnaw off the bottom layer of biscuit in one, satisfying piece. Would she allow herself one more before returning the packet safely to the drawer? Didn't she deserve a treat? Just one more little one, Julie decided, watching Happy Meal skulking about after a bird. The view of the patio not quite perfect, it was true, because of Mary's rotten old shed, but this was a temporary eyesore which would be dealt with as soon as her father found someone to pull it down for a reasonable price.

Edward showed little interest in making their house a proper home. He had refused to have 'any more dealings than necessary' with Mr Modin, or even properly view the house before the sale was finalised. 'I know what it fucking looks like,' he had replied nastily when she'd asked him to meet the estate agent for a 'walk-through' last June. It wasn't until right before moving day in July that he had finally consented to come round with her for a viewing. The estate agent, a very knowledgeable woman, had demonstrated all the amenities, although Mr Modin had already given Julie a private tour, confiding that he'd had brand new fixtures and fittings installed to attract *a better class of buyer*. She'd been astonished how different the house looked. Gone were the old-fashioned tiles, the draughty windows and rickety floors, while the kitchen – she and Mr Modin agreed – looked fit for a chef. Edward had had little to say as the estate agent took them through the house, though she had expected that the patio at least would be a nice surprise. Or that he wouldn't care one way or the other. But Edward had taken one look and stormed off with a rude comment, leaving Julie cringing with embarrassment having to make up an excuse and finish their business alone. She had found him sitting morosely in the car.

'What a cock-up,' he'd said, as she got in. 'And the garden, what was he bloody thinking? It looks like a fucking graveyard.'

Edward's language was not improving, Julie thought, and this was another thing that would have to change once the baby was born. 'Young couple with a baby on the way, you don't need all that aggravation,' was her father's opinion. 'What's a real man want with a garden anyway? It's women's work, faffing about with flowers. I'm not having any daughter of mine grubbing about on her knees in the dirt when she's in the family way.'

'What's the matter with people?' Edward had continued. 'And all that white everywhere. It looks like a fucking operating room.'

'What's the matter with people?' her father said, 'spending hours and hours digging up weeds and mowing the grass when it all grows back again two weeks later? I ask you...' Her parents' own garden was paved, front and back, with a small border along the side where her father had recently put in some radishes. Last week, in the middle of the night, someone had pulled them all up, and knocked one of the lions off its column. It lay in pieces on the pavement. 'Gyppos,' her father explained, though there were no gypsies round the area that Julie knew of.

'The ground's nice and level,' she'd offered. 'We'll be able to put up a swing-set.' Edward had stared through the windscreen with a fixed expression. Couldn't he look on the bright side for once? 'For our child,' she added, wondering if he'd heard, 'when he or she arrives.'

'Yep,' Edward had replied sourly. 'Bully for him or her.'

He had been like this for months.

It was in early June, in the brief gap of hours between the morning sickness and the chronic exhaustion, when at her sister's urging Julie had reluctantly made the drive over to Mary's old house and turned down Danecroft Road. 'I wouldn't feel comfortable living in Mary's old house,' she'd told Lorraine, who as usual was being so *definite* about everything: about the cement-mixer and the scaffolding and the large *For Sale* sign posted outside.

'What's your problem, Julie?' Lorraine had replied. 'I've had to listen to you complain about wanting a proper house. *Haven't I?* And here's your chance, and you're not interested? *Unbelievable.*'

It was true, Julie had explained, that Edward had already agreed that they might – *in theory* – need a bigger flat, but relations between them were still strained and she couldn't face any more unpleasantness.

'Well, you know best,' Lorraine had said sarcastically. 'But if I were you I'd ring that Modin guy up and make him an offer he can't refuse. You have to think of the baby. It's still cheaper than where you are now, so it's an investment,' she'd added with her usual air of expertise. 'And the housing market's collapsed, so he'll be dying to get rid of it.'

Julie had long ago given up trying to understand how her sister knew about such obscure matters, and simply accepted that, as with almost everything else, her sister knew what she was talking about. She had remembered how, on the Monday after Mary's funeral, she had dropped off Mary's keys at Mr Modin's office. Thinking back, there had been several broad hints about Danecroft Road and what was to be done with it, but at the time, what with Edward being so difficult, she hadn't really taken it in. At the same time *Pathways to Possible* had got her mind very much focused towards the positive, and so, feeling extremely nervous and apprehensive, she had gone into her bag and fished out the thick white card that Mr Modin had handed over at Mary's funeral. His executive secretary had put Julie through at once. She told him she'd been meaning to get in touch to thank him for his tasteful sympathy card. 'The card you sent Edward, with the picture of the weeping willow?' Did Mr Modin remember who she was? He seemed a bit lost. 'When Mary passed away?' she added, and Mr Modin said that of course he remembered and asked how Edward was faring 'after his sudden bereavement'. Yes, it *was* a shock, she agreed, so very sudden (and over a month ago, Julie thought to herself). She told Mr Modin that they were expecting a baby. 'A little one!' he said, and offered his 'sincere congrats'. There was an awkward pause, during which Julie had forced herself to wait. 'I wonder, might Edward by any chance be looking about for something bigger?' Mr Modin said at last. 'Because after much *soul-searching* on the part of yours truly I've had to put poor Mary's old place up for sale.' Did Edward fancy a pop round to see all the new improvements? Or might he perhaps interest Julie herself in a little tour? 'Be nice to keep it in the family going forward,' he went on. 'And don't you worry, we've put in all mod cons. You won't know the place.'

Since the business of buying and selling houses wasn't something Julie had any experience with, it was decided that Mr Modin would ring Edward first thing in the morning, but would not let on that he and Julie had already spoken. 'I would be ever so grateful,' she said, and Mr Modin had sounded pleased.

'I know your game,' he replied. 'My lady wife is the same way.' Julie could feel him leering and twinkling at her down the phone and she held it away from her ear for a moment. 'That's how all you girls work: let us think it's all our idea.'

The conversation was all going exactly as Lorraine said it would, Julie thought. She could hardly believe it. 'You don't want to look *too* keen,' her sister had warned, 'he *is* a man. And once Modin's rung him you'll have to keep the pressure on. He's got another think coming if he thinks he can do a runner on you, or try something funny. He's got to pay the price.' *The price of what?* Julie had wondered.

She tipped another custard cream out of the packet. Relations between them had been touch and go, but the notion of Edward's actually leaving had not occurred to her in some while. And certainly not since they'd got married and bought the house. And if their relationship wasn't yet completely back to normal, Julie reflected, watching the cat sniff closely at a tree stump, she no longer lay awake all night in terror of a *rift*.

Mr Modin had done as he'd promised and left a message for Edward the following day. Edward had made no attempt to call him back, though, and whenever Julie brought it up he had declared moodily that the subject was 'off limits'. At the very end of June she and Lorraine had driven over to Danecroft Road again and seen that the *For Sale* sign was still up 'like a bleeding neon message from the universe' and she had rung Mr Modin again and asked if he wouldn't mind trying Edward one last time. Later that week Edward did finally ring him back, but with a deliberately low offer that everyone knew he would never accept. And then, to everyone's surprise – 'most of all Edward's', Lorraine had observed tartly – Phil Modin had accepted Edward's offer, and, just like that, within three weeks Mary's house was theirs.

A single crumb remained at the edge of her saucer and Julie realised that she'd almost polished off a whole packet of custard creams without even realising. How did it keep happening? She would have to drag herself out to the shops and find more before Edward came home. Meanwhile there was a whole hour to fill until lunchtime. Might she allow herself another quick check of Facebook? Like her eleven o'clock custard cream, the computer was a comfort these days, a means to occupy herself during the long hours when Edward was out at work. The other day, she remembered, when Mr Modin had popped in on one of his unannounced visits – 'Just checking up on you and the little-one-to-be!' – she had actually felt quite pleased to see him for a change. Still, it was preferable to being at school, Julie thought, opening up the computer. She had been diligently practising wealth visualisations each morning so that she wouldn't have to return to the school ever again.

Facebook had become a job in itself, keeping up with the photos and comments and 'Likes' and trying not to offend people if you forgot to 'Like' something they did, or wrote the wrong comment on their timeline. There were other puzzles, most recently whether you were obliged to post a photo of your womb for everyone to see. Your insides were – *imho* – the most private of private parts, weren't they? Her aunt in Coventry kept posting requests for pictures of the ultrasound and was getting quite stroppy about it, and then the rest of her family – her cousins and uncles and aunts – had all joined in. Now, every time Julie signed into her page, a rolling list of messages and little winky faces greeted her. It made the hours fly by.

In the last half-hour, Julie saw, two invitations had popped into her inbox – one inviting her to join Lorraine's local sexual predators watch group, and another from Jaydn inviting her to join his Megamos Crypto fanclub, which she seemed to recall was something violent with cars. She deleted both. A flashing message on the right-hand side caught her attention. How strange, she thought, that the advert should appear less than two hours after she'd sent Lorraine a message saying how especially puffy and bloated she was feeling today. Facebook seemed to be brimming with such coincidences, Julie realised – what *Pathways to Possible* termed synchronous opportunities – almost as if it knew what you were thinking. The advert flashed at her. *Lose 10 pounds in 5 days, The* Natural *Way!* She looked more closely. *Sacred Body, Body Perfect – Lose Weight and Create Wealth Using Lessons from the Infinite* seemed to be written by the same people who had written *Pathways to Possible* – or the P2P Method as it was known in all the online workshops she'd signed up for. A less evolved person would dismiss this as a mere coincidence, but to a personally realised individual, Julie decided, it was clearly a sign. Was there any reason the universe *shouldn't* use Facebook to send its messages? *Hurry! Limited time offer*, the advert flashed urgently, £39.99 – Only £49.99 for the whole kit. Includes a free DVD and seven powdered meals! HURRY!!! Offer expires in 30 minutes – and before it could disappear Julie clicked on it. It sounded like a bargain. And for only £12.99 extra *Sacred Body, Body Perfect* could be gift-wrapped and delivered overnight and be here waiting for her first thing tomorrow. Why not? Julie thought. She clicked across to another window to place her order, and came face to face with Edward's inbox.

Her first instinct was to pretend she hadn't seen it, to close the window and go and make herself some cheese on toast or have a slice of cake, a last treat to celebrate starting her diet the next day. She had never before pried into Edward's private email. Isobel's letters didn't really count. Her eyes drifted down the list of messages, past the one inviting Edward to *Meet a Chinese Lady* and the offer of a *VIP Pass to Meet Local Pussies* (one cat was quite enough), and caught on one in particular. *Chat?* it suggested, from someone named *IsoVer77*. *That again,* Julie thought to herself. *No secret who that is.* She'd had no idea Edward and Isobel were exchanging emails. Not that they wouldn't, she thought, or couldn't – except that Edward almost never mentioned Mary any more, let alone Isobel. Should she have a peep at Isobel's message, just in case? Occasionally, *to achieve the path of rightness,* you were asked to make difficult choices. Her fingers hovered over the pad, and then, almost as if they had a life of their own, selected Isobel's message and pressed.

As the page flashed and changed, and the message appeared, Julie realised her mistake: the message had been listed in bold font – which meant that Edward hadn't yet read it. Which meant, Julie realised with horror, that when he next checked his inbox he would see that it had been opened – and not by him.

The phone rang. Lorraine.

400

'What do you mean, a "mistake"?' said Lorraine when Julie told her what she had found. 'It's a bloody gift!'

'I'm sure you're right,' Julie replied, wishing she hadn't said anything now, and told Lorraine that she had to run. Her sister would insist on poking her nose into her business.

Still, recalling the *Pathways to Possible* 'no accidents' rule, she located the already opened, and safely not-bold, messages in Edward's mailbox.

They read much the same as Isobel's letters. *Hi, there – how's things?* began a recent one. *Mum's 4-month anniversary coming up next month. Thought we could have a chat?* She clicked on the 'sent' folder and saw that Edward's replies were brief, often many weeks apart. One in particular, sent to his sister in June and typed in all lower case, struck her as especially abrupt: *hello – all well here. work very busy. hope all well w/you. E.* Too lazy to press Shift, Julie thought, and scrolled down to Isobel's original message, sent a few weeks before, which was markedly shorter than her previous ones: *Hiya – Just checking in!* she began, followed by an unkind comment about someone at work and how *unbearable* the hot weather was. *Be brilliant to hear all your news*, it finished. *No need to reply if you're busy! I.* Julie felt herself yawning. Was it lunchtime yet? Isobel's emails were as boring as Isobel herself. She was sorry now for letting Lorraine's suspicions get the better of her. Her sister was still convinced Isobel meant business, that if Julie wasn't careful Edward would go running over to America to 'evade his responsibilities'. Truth be told, though, she felt a bit sorry for Isobel, whose messages Edward obviously couldn't be bothered to reply to. What time were her emails sent? Julie wondered. Was she ahead of them in New York, or behind? Declan, apparently, sent texts and rang all his women between 11.30 and midnight, when he pretended to take the dog out for its last walk. 'He doesn't know I know,' Lorraine had said ominously, 'but he will soon.' One day, Declan really would cheat on Lorraine, Julie thought, and her sister would have only herself to blame.

She stared out of the window and watched Happy Meal moving about near the shed. She had no intention of rifling any further through Edward's emails. There was that one sentence she hadn't quite looked at, though, at the bottom of one of Isobel's messages. One of her annoying 'P.S.'s, probably nothing. Just to be sure, she returned to the most recent email, about having a chat, and felt herself go hot and cold.

P.S. What we discussed about New York – you're welcome to come any time.

Was Isobel joking? She couldn't believe it. It was happening again. Except that this time, Julie thought, Edward had responsibilities – a wife, and a child on the way. Isobel must know he couldn't go jetting off on his own. Or did she know, and not care? Or did she know and was doing it on purpose? But why would she write such an awful thing when it wasn't true? *Unless*, Julie thought, beginning to feel slightly unwell, Edward had told his sister otherwise. A wave of nausea hit her and she had to sit down. Once more she made herself read through the message, which said nothing about 'you and your wife' or 'you and Jules' – but 'you'. Meaning Edward. Without Julie. What had they 'discussed' together? Had they 'discussed' Julie? And did Edward complain about her to Isobel? Did he tell her how fat she was, or that their relationship wasn't what it used to be? Did Isobel know all their private business? Isobel would have been all sweetness and light and understanding, she thought bitterly. And now Edward was going to leave her and make his escape to America, just as Lorraine said he would.

As the computer's cursor blinked and waited she took calming breaths and tried to think what to do next. Her phone buzzed. A text from Lorraine. *FYI, delete is yr friend.* She had no time for Lorraine's enigmatic messages. In the eyes of the law Edward was her husband. But if he disappeared off to America, how would Julie ever find him? Who would pay the mortgage? How would she feed and clothe their child? Edward's own father had run off, she remembered, and never been heard from again. Lost at sea was how Mary had preferred to put it, but Julie had read between the lines. *Pathways to Possible* warned how easy it was for people to repeat the mistakes of their parents without even realising it. Was history repeating itself? Would Edward abandon his family, just like his father? And what if their child was a girl? Would it end up like Isobel?

She stared at Isobel's words and asked herself, for the first time, whether it was enough to visualise positive outcomes. She went to Google and typed in *time in new york. Minus 5 hours*, the answer shot back. Isobel sent her messages at night. She thought of Edward hurrying out of the shower at 6am, forgetting his tie, spilling his cereal, rushing for the train – and not checking his email. Not until the evening, and even then – or so it appeared – sometimes not at all. When Edward woke up, Isobel was just coming home. Julie could see her, high up in her skyscraper, arriving home after some party, kicking her shoes off on to the floor … the steady 'tap-tap-tap' as she typed out poisonous messages to Edward with her perfectly manicured fingers. *Bloody Isobel.* She remembered the handwritten scrawl and stupid doodles and could almost hear Isobel's voice, drawling on about finding her brother a 'cool' job and 'an awesome apartment'. When they moved from their flat, she had put Isobel's letters away in a safe place. Apparently this wasn't enough.

Within seconds Julie made a decision. Quickly she went back into Edward's *Sent* folder and scrolled down to his curt lower-case message, dated a while ago. *Perfect*, Julie thought, pressing C for copy, thankful to have picked up so many useful computer tips from Lorraine. Working slowly, so as not to make a mistake, she went back into Isobel's most recent email and pressed *Reply*.

What would Mary think?' The thought seemed to appear from nowhere, making her hesitate. Since moving to Danecroft Road she had found herself asking this question at odd moments. *What would Mary think? Or, What would Mary do?* Not that she owed Mary anything, Julie thought, or that Mary's opinion mattered any more. When she first joined the P2P online workshop she had come across the term *karmic debt,* and, if Julie had long ago learned to forgive herself, it wasn't hard to imagine Mary hovering about on the spiritual plane watching her, watching for opportunities that would let Julie make amends. It was no accident, she thought, watching Happy Meal pace along outside, tail twitching, that their *karmic values* – hers and Mary's – were now perfectly aligned. *Intentions plus time.* Julie had nothing but time, and so, for that matter, did Mary. Neither of them wanted Edward going off to America, or for selfish Isobel to interfere with his happiness.

For a moment she pictured Mary looking down from wherever she was, with the approval Julie had always craved. Then she returned to the screen and continued her work – *mine and Mary's,* Julie thought, *our work together,* as she pasted part of Edward's old message to create a reply to Isobel's newest one. When she was finished, she sat back and read the result: *bit busy but all well. hope you're all right. speak soon. E.* It certainly had a ring of authenticity, Julie thought, as she pressed *Send*. Then, with Lorraine's text in mind, she went back and located the message in Edward's *Sent* folder and clicked on 'delete forever'. She did the same with the one in the inbox. *Boom, click – done*, she thought. And, just to celebrate, helped herself to one more custard cream.

11

Christmas Eve

The Photograph

She had been waiting for the woman in the window to
stand up or turn her head. *Another one for the crazy box*,
Isobel thought. Even so, she needed to make sure. A small
movement to the left or right would offer a clearer view.
Until then she couldn't risk leaving the window unattended,
not even for a moment. She hadn't noticed the woman until
today, which was too weird to be a coincidence, seeing
as she lived in the apartment directly opposite. The city
made you acutely aware of your neighbours' lives from
afar – of parties and TV-watching, of arguments and thrown
objects, of movings-in and movings-out and cigarettes
puffed thoughtfully on the fire escape. With the Christmas
holiday here, it was only now perhaps that Isobel had a
chance to notice her, and register the particular set of her
shoulders, the hair that was fluffy and fine in that familiar
way, the colour a shade located somewhere between grey
and blonde…

In the background a television flashed images. Who watched TV at two o'clock in the afternoon? Certainly not her mother, Isobel thought, hoping none of the neighbours were watching her stare into one of their windows. And yet, if some unforeseen mistake or misunderstanding had occurred last May, stranger things had happened. Hadn't they discussed Poe's 'The Premature Burial', she and her mother? In Victorian England a little bell was threaded down into a grave, allowing the mistakenly entombed to ring for their nearest and dearest the second they woke up. 'Terrifying,' Isobel had observed. 'Imagine the panic!' 'For whom?' her mother had replied.

Last month she had typed *50 Danecroft Road* into Google Earth and been astonished to spy her mother's potted geraniums in the front garden. Heart racing, she'd zoomed in and found her wellingtons standing next to them. *What was going on?* In a panic she'd rung Melissa, who had assured Isobel – 'Seriously, Izz?' – that the image would be years out of date. She found herself searching the faces of random strangers in the street. Once or twice she had even followed one. Melissa would never understand this either, which was why, Isobel thought, as the woman across the way continued to gaze stubbornly at the television, she would never tell her, just as she would never reveal how, each night when she got home from work, in some fruitless, idiot way she opened the mailbox and still expected to find an airmail envelope with its neat handwriting and her mother's name printed on the back in blue biro. Once, she had rung her mother's number and hung up after half a ring, fearing that she wouldn't answer and, equally, fearing that she would. 'The Monkey's Paw', Isobel thought, as across the street from her the woman turned and bent down, as if to pick something off the floor next to her chair, and Isobel saw that she was too short, the profile all wrong. *Not her.*

Does Edward ever think these things? Isobel wondered. *And, if so, does he tell anyone?*

She stepped back from the window. Now what? Her bosses had closed the office until the New Year and fled for the warmer climes of St Barts, and for the first time Isobel found herself wishing that they hadn't. The city was muggy and humid, more like midsummer than Christmas Eve. Along the centre of Park Avenue stood a line of dead Christmas trees, brown carcasses extending from 96th to 23rd Streets, their needles blown in the warm breeze into small drifts across the crosswalks. No one had thought to turn off the heat in her building and she'd had the air-conditioning on full blast for close to a week. As usual, right after Hallowe'en she had folded all her lightest clothes away for the winter. The closet was tiny, so when she had first moved in she had gone out and bought plastic containers, filling them with her off-season clothes and jamming them under the bed. She had positioned the bed 'just so' to take advantage of the apartment's best and most unlikely aspect, which was a clear and perfectly framed view of the Empire State Building. She didn't care for its new pulsing gaudy LED displays. She barely glanced at it any more. But when it glowed in classic white, bright and clean in the night sky, and on rainy days, appearing and disappearing in wreaths of clouds, it still had the power to make her heart beat a little faster. She would miss it when she was gone,

She didn't regret the decision she had made. She had lived with the city so long, and felt so entwined in its buildings and streets, that she was too close to really see or appreciate it in the way it deserved. The enchanting, random, crazy things still happened. That hadn't changed. But she had come to expect them, so that, in a way, her life here had become utterly predictable. London, almost too far away to see at all, was a risk she was ready to leap at.

She went through all the plastic containers three times before realising that the shirt she was looking for might be stashed in the closet inside her empty suitcase. Right up until last week she had held on to some hope of going to England for Christmas. *Home for Christmas*, thought Isobel, as with some twisting and tugging she managed to pull the suitcase out from under a jumble of sweaters and winter coats – like the title of some mawkish romcom. She unzipped the main compartment and saw the shirt's frayed edge poking out. As she tugged at it, an object fell on to the floor and rolled away from her. She picked it up and turned the small black canister over in her hand. How odd, Isobel thought, that she'd almost forgotten about it. She checked her watch. Almost three o'clock. Did she have enough time?

Pushing the canister deep into the front pocket of her jeans, she grabbed her keys and let herself out of the apartment. The building's dinginess felt so much worse at Christmas, Isobel thought, the light in the stairwell contriving to appear simultaneously dim and harsh, the walls sweaty-looking, the floors daubed with nameless smudges and stains. Its delicate hexagonal tiles, some missing, most about to come unstuck, made her think of the bottom of an empty swimming pool. And yet the rent kept climbing. Many of the building's tenants were recent immigrants, sad-looking men willing to double or triple up in tiny studios. They cooked a lot and chattered loudly in foreign languages, moving in one day, and out the next. The front door that didn't lock, the mailboxes that didn't close, the floors that were never cleaned – she wouldn't miss any of it. Outside, the sky glowered the same colour as the stairwell, a fluorescent milky white that managed to be dull and intensely bright at the same time. She put on her sunglasses and walked east towards Madison Park, where yesterday, cutting through after work, she had caught the whiff of her mother's perfume on a passer-by. The fragrance had seemed to hit the back of her brain before she was even conscious of it, blooming as an all-enveloping cloud that contained her mother's smile and voice and everything about her. And then, as suddenly as it appeared, it vanished. Time snapped back into itself and Isobel found herself once again walking through the New York evening and the city had felt darker and emptier than it ever had before. On Radio 4 this morning they were forecasting snow tonight in the south of England, from Hampshire as far as Kent. They had used to love the snow, she and Edward, and she had decided that this would be a fun excuse to ring him, armed with something to talk about and a way to avoid the elephant in the room – which was their first Christmas without their mother, the first time without buying her a present, and so on. When it came to it, though, she couldn't bring herself to put in his number, certain then that she would be bothering him. She'd sent her Christmas card weeks ago, at the end of November. She'd told him that she was thinking of moving back, in fact was almost definitely moving back. *What do you reckon?* she wrote. Taking her therapist's advice, she had been honest about her feelings, saying that they were family and all each other had. Maybe it was time to be in each other's lives properly, she said, not living with half the world between them. She had even signed off by telling him to say hi to Jules. The post always took ages this time of year so she had also emailed, gently hinting that she had no plans for Christmas. Edward hadn't replied. Or rather, a few days later he had sent her an email saying that he was going to spend Christmas 'quietly' with Julie's family. She had taken the hint and said no more.

She found the park buzzing with people. Tourists queued up for the outdoor café while children swarmed over the latest sculpture and dogs twitched hopefully at the local squirrels. On days like this, the city had a small-town feel. And New York *was* a small town, Isobel thought, taller than London but more compact, bounded on either side by rivers. Unlike in London, you could see its edges. These were the days when she felt less certain, as if, in response to her decision to leave, New York beckoned with a melancholy glamour, while London emerged as grey and unwelcoming. She wondered what Edward was up to today. Had he bought a tree? She imagined him unpacking the Christmas decorations box and unwrapping the ornaments, before she remembered – of course – that he was spending it with Julie's family. No doubt, since their mother died, Julie's parents would have taken him to their bosom and Edward would have made them his own, showing up at their door with the perfect tree as Julie slid trays of mince pies into the oven, smiling and smiling. To be fair, she had thought a lot about Jules, and decided that she might have been too hard on her. More than likely it was not that Julie's heart was as cold and hard as a pebble, but that she was just scared of saying the wrong thing. As Melissa had pointed out, it was pretty far-fetched to imagine colourless, mousy little Julie as being Isobel's arch-enemy or some brilliant mastermind of deceit.

She checked again that the canister was still in her pocket. Why had she wasted her thoughts on someone so innocuous? Another idea for the crazy box, she decided, cutting neatly through a snarl of foreign students on 23rd and Broadway, only to be blocked by another herd of them standing patiently at the crosswalk. Out-of-towners, Isobel thought, launching herself into the street before the red *Don't Walk* man counted his way down to zero. All down Fifth mall-walkers spread themselves across the sidewalks, meandering gang-like, huge sweatshirts full of flesh swaying en masse like vast ships, while faster-moving pedestrians darted and slid between them like tiny fish. She passed a collection of families lined up three-deep in front of a store window. Amid snowy scenescapes and train dioramas, mechanical dolls, dressed in their Sunday best with furs and hats and scarves, moved stiffly while non-denominational 'Happy Holidays' music tinkled out emptily on to the sidewalk. That was something New Yorkers wouldn't appreciate, Isobel thought: the fact that she went through the city trying to spot the word 'Christmas' in a single shop window, the tally so far being zero. This evening she would make some mince pies. Take all the books and nail polish out of the oven, put on Radio 4, and listen to some Christmas carols. This would involve a trip down to Myers of Keswick, Isobel remembered, where, a little after Thanksgiving, she had gone down to see what they had in stock for Christmas. A proper shop with a real counter, as opposed to a 'store' in the American sense, Myers was where homesick expats tormented themselves with British foodstuffs. She had wandered along shelves groaning with puddings and pickled onions and boxes of Quality Street and After Eights until the woman behind the counter had asked if Isobel was looking for anything in particular. Feeling like a shoplifter, she had fled. Then, on 14th Street, she had experienced a panicky and stranded moment at the top of the subway steps. The mechanics of walking down them felt totally beyond her, the fear of falling so strong that it brought tears to her eyes. She had walked back, letting her path be dictated by the *Walk* and *Don't Walk* signs, feeling unmoored and impermanent and inexplicably upset by the encounter in the shop. Back at the apartment she had switched on BBC America and found a bog-standard stately-home murder mystery which had brought another lump to her throat. Disgusted with herself, she'd flipped it off again. Because it was one thing, Isobel thought now, as she crossed 18th Street and successfully dodged a gaggle of girls in identical jackets and high-heeled sheepskin boots, to listen to the Shipping Forecast and keep a comforting Radio 4 voice burbling along in the background – anyone could come over a bit melancholy over 'squally showers' or a storm that was 'moving quickly eastwards and losing its identity' – but it was another matter entirely to sit on the wrong side of the Atlantic all agape at some make-believe American theme park version of Ye Olde England with its garden fêtes and cream teas and elderly lady detectives. Had she become American? Isobel wondered. Or had she, after all this time, finally become British?

After her mother's funeral she had brought back to New York only what she could carry – a few keepsakes – not much, and not enough. In the time since, her memories had become insubstantial and vanishingly few, worn and faded like old photos, with corners that broke off in her hands. What she wouldn't give, Isobel thought, to be able to gather them up like Humpty Dumpty and put them all back together again. To have a complete, 3-D image of her mother as she had been, sitting in her deckchair, for instance, the complete sequence of her facial expressions and the precise ways in which she moved her head as she leaned in to tell Isobel something about one of the flowerbeds. Only fragments remained, the images stuttering and pixelated like a message transmitted from deep space. In unexpected moments, frequently before sleeping or waking, she might catch a glimpse of the whole person, before this too dissolved, like a reel of film burning up on screen.

Why was it so hard to remember her? The only explanation, the certainty that had been circling her mind for some while, was that she had not paid enough attention to her mother when she was alive. Before she'd left England she had thrown a small farewell party for her friends, but she had no recollection of her mother or Edward being among them, and presumably they weren't invited. Why? She had never given it much thought, but she knew the answer. She had wanted to draw a line under her old life – the school, the hospital, the hotel; to look ahead and focus on the future – her own future, and all the tasks that had to be gone through to get there. In short order she had handed in her notice, given up her tenancy and sold her stuff at a car boot sale, counting down to the departure itself, her one-way ticket from Gatwick to JFK, bought and paid for and safe in her purse. The rest, the entirety of her life up until that point, was just background.

And she had indeed left her life behind, Isobel thought, shedding her old life as carelessly as a rich woman shrugging a fur coat on to the floor. *You grab hold of life*, her mother used to say. And yet it had never occurred to Isobel, as her mother's daughter, to return the compliment or give credit where credit was due. She might have replied that it was only what she had been taught, that it was a gift and that she was so very grateful for it. The idea had never once entered her head. *You grab hold of life*. She had been in love with this image of herself, Isobel thought, but, as she continued down Fifth, glancing at each passer-by, without hope, and just in case, she wondered if it wasn't the very definition of selfishness – and whether that, after all, wasn't how her mother had really meant it.

Friends had told her to think carefully about moving back. Alcoholics, decreed one, called it *taking a geographic*. 'Wherever you go, there you are.' Isobel had no time for this. She had ignored the same would-be well-intentioned warnings twenty years ago. 'You should write greetings cards,' she replied. Moving on, moving forward. Could you really turn your back on the past and everything that was behind you? She recalled Edward's stricken look when their mother's coffin was brought in, and, minutes later, the mask replaced, his demeanour inscrutable, neutral. Perhaps, during their week at Danecroft Road, he had forced himself to get along with her in order to keep the peace. And then, with Isobel back in New York, he had pulled down the shutters and resumed his normal life.

'Hello, English! Long time.' The photo shop's Yemeni owner grinned at her. 'You are travelling again?'

He had forgotten her name long ago, Isobel thought, just as she had forgotten his. Not that this seemed to matter; he was always pleased to see her. If you believed all the Kodak adverts, since she'd moved to the city the shop had processed almost all of her significant memories.

'Nowhere special,' she replied. 'Just some family photos. I was hoping to get them developed before you guys close for Christmas. For the holiday,' she added hastily.

'Your family, all good?'

'Yes, fine, thank you.'

'And you need today?'

'I do need today. If that's okay?'

There was only one photo that she actually *needed*, Isobel thought. The photo would serve as proof of something, she felt sure – and it felt important to have it in time for Christmas.

By the time she returned to the shop it was almost dinnertime. Stores were already pulling down their metal gates while panicked shoppers scurried along the street laden with bags and packages, phones pressed to their ears. This time, the owner did not come up to the counter but cast Isobel a nervous sidelong glance and retreated farther into the back. That was kind of weird, Isobel thought to herself, but then she must look a bit of a sight, flip-flopping in wearing a ratty old Clash T-shirt and scuffed jeans. Through the open metal shelves of photo paper and actors' headshots she watched him conferring with two other staff members – a man, and a woman who normally came over to greet Isobel and whom she assumed to be his wife. They always had something nice to say about her photos – the cack-handed, crooked horizons of East Africa, the bizarrely murky summer vineyards of New Zealand. At first she had found this all a bit rude and intrusive, this commenting on her private business. In England, she was sure, everyone pretended that the person developing your photos never saw them. If they made it obvious that they had, you would say nothing, but would in future go elsewhere. But this didn't bug her any more. In fact, Isobel realised, she'd been quite looking forward to their comments today, which would be followed by a little conversation in which she would put the photos into context for them.

The three heads had drawn closer together in an intense huddle, like football players plotting their next play. The wife glanced over, and quickly away again, and made some gesture – hands thrown upwards, palms open – to the husband, who looked down and shook his head, whether in anger or refusal Isobel couldn't tell. What was going on? Had they lost the film? What an *idiot* she'd been not to tell them to be extra careful, she thought, as the skin on her face started to prick with anxiety. As the seconds ticked by she began to feel inexplicably guilty, as if waiting for a customs officer to finish going through her suitcase. Behind her the door opened and another customer entered, setting the wind-chimes tinkling. In the sound Isobel thought she could discern a jarring and discordant quality, as if whoever made them had hung the wrong shape cylinders.

The shop owner returned to the cash register holding a thin packet in his hand.

'Great!' she said, smiling. 'Thanks for getting them done so quickly.' The man gave a curt nod but said nothing. He rang up the price and wordlessly, without meeting her eyes, thrust the packet across the counter. She paid quickly and left.

First she took a shower and put on her sweats, then she made a big pot of peppermint and ginger tea and settled herself on the bed. She would skim over the pictures from last Christmas, when she had begun the roll. The shop's owner had asked when she *needed* the photos – *needed*, not wanted – and this was exactly right. There were the plain facts, she supposed: the flight, the hospital, the mortuary, fish fingers with Martin and Sean. There were her mother's belongings, and pathetic little Jules, and the evening with Edward at the pub. Then the boxes, and more boxes, and the funeral and their mother's friends, the inn and the rain. The actual details were almost impossible to recall, she didn't know why, though she tried not to think of the strangers who would have moved into Danecroft Road after they closed it up for the last time. Other details remained even more occluded and mysterious, so that she had lain awake wondering whether after her fall their mother had been conscious and whether she had known what was happening to her and whether she was frightened. Finally she had gone online and looked up 'brain aneurysm'. If death had not been instantaneous, Isobel had decided, unconsciousness almost certainly had been. She had taken comfort in her own last memory, understanding, as the mortuary assistant observed, that she and Edward were lucky in ways others often weren't – those *other* people, she thought, who had burned into their memories the vivid horrors she and her mother had so enjoyed scaring themselves with.

Carefully she unglued the packet of photos. Between the journey down from Heathrow and the start of the week proper would be the exact photo she was looking for. If she had doubted her mother's love these past months, if she had questioned their relationship and tortured herself about the letters, about her very last moments with her mother the camera would not lie.

The second she got the packet open and looked inside it was obvious someone else had already gone through it, and had done so several times. The shop's owners were meticulous about presentation, so it was unsettling to see that for the first time her pictures were out of chronological order. Carefully, she laid out each one face-down on the bed and slowly started to turn them over. Last Boxing Day preceded Christmas Eve, while two had been put back, as if in haste, upside down like bad omens in a Tarot deck. Where was the shot Jules had taken of Isobel and Edward outside their mother's favourite bric-a-brac shop? She passed over a bizarre and inexplicable photo of a brick wall, and felt the anticipation build inside her. *The image of the beautiful sleeper, the peaceful countenance.* Like a lucky rabbit's foot pushed deep into a pocket, Isobel realised, recalled occasionally but mainly forgotten, the photo had sustained her and kept her going. She *needed* to see it, to witness again the delicate sleeping figure from a watercolour, inviolable and complete.

She turned over a blurred, rainy scene from last Christmas, her mother standing on the station platform, her hand raised in a wave – of greeting? Isobel thought. Of farewell? *Waving or drowning.* Was this the last time she had seen her alive? She turned the photo back over, wanting the answer to a question that had nagged at her for months, but there was no time stamp or indication on the back. Was it the day, Isobel wondered, that her mother waved her off to the airport? Or the day she'd met Isobel off the train from Gatwick? Or the day she'd caught the train to see Francesca and her mother had come along to the station 'just for the walk'? Which one was it? she thought. And what did it mean that she could not even recall this one crucial event? The thought was still occupying her as she continued along the line of photos on the bed, turning them over one by one, so that, when the image she was looking for appeared, she was completely unprepared.

She lay on the bed for some time afterwards, listening to the air-conditioning, watching without seeing the tiny, winking red light at the top of the Empire State Building. Outside, the traffic roared distantly and she tried to imagine it was the sound of the sea. 'You have your memories. That's how our loved ones live on,' friends had told her, as if the dead were alive and well somewhere. But they never asked what her memories actually were, and so Isobel had never shared them. Instead she had developed a ritual each night, before going to sleep, of conjuring up a single one. Now the same image was repeating over and over, but irrevocably altered, the photo replaying in an unstoppable loop. While it had remained hidden in her camera, the illusion had held. Like any magic trick, Isobel thought, it had worked because she had wanted so much to believe it. Perhaps this was why she had put the camera out of her mind. She had done her part, as had Peter, who was a professional, after all.

There was no sleeping figure from a watercolour, no misty dreamer with her peaceful countenance. In her place was someone she barely recognised, no longer a human being but a thing, the person she had known and loved utterly gone. No sleeping figure, thought Isobel, no airmail letter, no misunderstanding – not then and not ever, only the flat unreality of death. The final proof. For so long the photo had hovered almost unseen in her mind, and with it the suggestion, the hope, however absurd, of being able to hear her mother's voice again, or watch her drink a cup of coffee, or any one of a thousand other actions and resurrected gestures, mundane and miraculous, that Isobel had seen in her mind and marvelled at, a world that had lived as if in three dimensions right under the surface of her own. This imaginary world was so fully realised that she had found herself anticipating it in odd moments, and, as with any future event, imagining the where and the how and the what-it-would-be-like – and yet, Isobel realised, never once accepting that it could never come to pass. Absurd make-believe, she thought, not so different from being able to step back into the mythical land of Blitz spirit and *Mrs Miniver*, of Pinewood and Elstree and *lashings of ginger beer*. Phantom England. Another world that had never been there in the first place. At last she understood the impulse for what it was: the hopeless wish to be transported by some magical process back to childhood. To sleep in her old room, to wake and hear the muted chatter of the radio in the kitchen, to go downstairs and find toast in the toaster and her mother there with coffee in the pot, later to wend their way through town by way of the tea rooms, coming home tired and happy, to dinner and the telly and a big bar of chocolate afterwards, knowing they could do exactly the same thing the next day – which was, Isobel realised, a fantasy she had lived in real life, and less than twelve months ago. Except this wasn't quite true, was it? Her mother hadn't wanted her there any more than did Edward, whose virtual silence could not have spelled the message out more clearly. He had tried to tell her twenty years ago and she hadn't listened then either. She had spent time wondering if returning now, after all these years, when her mother was no longer there, would be the ultimate insult, the ultimate betrayal. But the question was moot. The letters merely underlined a truth she should have accepted long ago. They were the proof that wasn't needed.

Her phone buzzed. 8.30pm. She tossed the phone on to the armchair and switched her pillow to the cooler side. *People have their own lives.* Like her shoddy, insufficient memories of their mother, Isobel thought, what remained of her in Edward's mind would have faded with neglect, the bits left to moulder into dust, the dust caught by the smallest draught, the draught dispersing it into the wind. *Etcetera.* She had grown sick of her own whining. The clichés were right. 'It is what it is.' 'Life goes on.' The past was a place you could not get at, which could never be pried out from under the present or held up to the light or seen fully or experienced again as it truly had been; while the future was vast and terrifying, never to be glimpsed over the horizon, the arrow of time absolute and inviolable. She turned the pillow back over and remembered a dream from last night. She had been standing in a garden, surrounded by gorse and rhododendrons and wild flowers, the lawn mown into pathways between them. She had had the feeling that it was an English garden, or a garden in England, but the walls were too high to see over.

In a few hours it would be Christmas Day. In another week the New Year would arrive, one more segment of time ending as another clicked into place. Her mother had fallen out of the world and it had raged on without her. 'Time heals', everyone said, but the accumulation of minutes and days and months didn't heal. They only made it more and more obvious how *gone* somebody was, while it left you, the last person at the party – the pity party – standing there in your silly paper hat feeling sorry for yourself long after everyone else had said their goodbyes and gone home. A fragment of conversation floated back into her mind, an echo from a conversation with Melissa. She had been feeling silenced by Melissa's belief, the implication that Isobel, like a contrary and wilful child, was somehow intent on *not* believing. 'But she doesn't *live on*,' she had told Melissa, 'in my memory, or anywhere else.' They had been discussing this, on and off, for some time, and it was making her feel more and more hopeless. The *past* was where the dead 'lived', Isobel said, though even that word was a stretch. She had thought of her mother, the fast-diminishing figure in the rear window, a child left at the side of a road. 'I hear you,' her friend had said, leaning towards her, forehead puckering in concern. 'But don't you *feel her presence*?'

Now, through the dull, white-noise roar of the air-conditioning unit, Isobel heard a ticking, clicking thing, some insect brought to life by the heat. She tried to listen through the sound, beyond the noise of the traffic, ears pricked and primed, dog-like, ready for the smallest sound, a whisper or a sign. There was only the uneven hum of the traffic, and the heat as it seethed and pushed, and leaned into the windows, and beyond it, a deeper silence that buzzed and whined in her ears.

Christmas Eve

The Bridge

Somewhere a child was crying. He ran through the empty house trying doors, cupboards, windows, but they were all sealed – moulded and convex, reversed in some obscene way that appalled him, as if the house had been turned inside out and cast as a replica in clay or rubber. Shapes slithered and rippled under the walls, threatening to crawl out. In the pitch-black kitchen the granite island had reversed itself and become a gaping hole in the floor. He gripped the edge of the cooker and inched around it, petrified of falling in. When the wall appeared under his fingertips he almost cried out with relief, but when he felt his way to the back door he found only a rectangular indentation – the doorknob a perfect, ungraspable hollow. The child's whimpering was coming closer. He tried to flatten himself into the space, and lowered his eyes so the whites wouldn't show, and woke to the sound of his own tears.

Dreaming in clichés again, Edward thought, as the gloom of the bedroom emerged and took shape around him. The desperate pounding of his own heart receded, replaced by the sound of Jules's steady breathing. How had he not woken her? The silence of the house offered little relief. Wretched as they made him feel, the dreams had a substance to them that the real house lacked. This was not what he had expected when they had moved in last July. He had feared the place would overwhelm him, the sounds and smells of a previous and lost world seeping through the walls. He had braced himself for an onslaught of sentimental memories: his younger self darting through the rooms, the past running before him, up and down the stairs and through the garden, his mother calling them in for bath night, dishing up fish fingers and chips in her flowery pinny. He needn't have worried. Modin's renovations and gallons of white paint had put paid to that. The house and its features had been scrubbed clean away, like a corpse dissolved in lye, its old sounds and smells absorbed as completely as if the rooms had padded walls. The notches and pencil marks on the doorpost where he and Isobel used to squabble over who was taller had been sanded away, while in the kitchen the warm, splotchy old lino had realised its dream of becoming a kitchen from a TV decorating programme. He had taken to wandering the house at night, pausing occasionally to wonder how he got there and to gaze in desolate stupor out of the windows. Sometimes, moving from room to room, traversing the dead spaces, he felt as if he were swimming across a night-time, glass-smooth pond. So quiet, Edward would think, so empty of colour or sound, the real house buried underneath, lost to him. He wished now that he'd taken the time to properly remember the place before it was gone, perhaps cataloguing its contents in some manner before clearing everything out. He turned his pillow over and thought about this process and what it would have entailed: making a note of where each piece of furniture and each object was placed, and where they were in relation to one another, like someone who knows they're going blind. *I should have taken photos*, Edward thought. Another thing he had failed to do. During waking hours, the few that he spent in the house, listening for Jules to call out or traipsing back upstairs to fetch her something from the bedroom, he would suddenly get the sense that the sounds he made were not quite real – the creak of the banister, his footsteps on the landing, caught in the air, landing at his feet like dead sparrows.

He studied Jules, her mouth slightly open, features relaxed. *The sleep of the just*, Edward thought. He barely felt real himself these days, less a human occupant of the house than a smudge or a fleck of dirt. Only rarely, in some half-lucid state, on the edge of sleep or after a few too many, did he catch the echo of happier times, some imaginary play of light and shadow, carefree and innocent, like the ripple of leaves against the summer sky. He glanced at the clock. Only eleven. How could that be? In some atavistic and hopeful way, because it was Christmas Eve, he had turned in early. Now he was wide awake. He eased himself out of bed and noticed that Jules had placed his share (hers were pink) of the horrible His 'n' Hers slippers next to the bedside table. When they arrived last week he had shoved them a fair way into the back of the wardrobe and assumed that would be the end of them. But here they were, Edward thought, their unplanned sojourn amongst his ratty old trainers only serving to bring out their lurid purple sheen and emphasise the golden 'family crest' machine-embroidered across the front. The slippers were another needless internet purchase he couldn't abide the sight of. He kicked them under the bed.

Out on the landing he stood for a moment and listened. Silence. No sounds of hooting cars or drunken posses of teenagers. Unusual silence, thought Edward, even for Christmas Eve. He went downstairs and went to the kitchen window. *Snowing!* Actual snowflakes, dense and fat and fast-moving, were flattening themselves, kamikaze-like, against the glass. There was no snow in the forecast, or perhaps this year he'd forgotten to check. The snow had arrived silently and without warning in the hours since he'd gone to bed, accumulating on the window sill in a thick, tantalising crust. With some notion of seeing if he could knock the snow off in one go, he went to open the latch, before remembering that there was no latch any more. The window had been double-glazed and sealed – 'to keep the weather out', the estate agent had informed them when they moved in.

He bent down and took the bottle of single malt from its hiding place under the sink, purchased last night on the sly after deciding he ought to treat himself for Christmas to the 25-year. The bottle had cost more than he wanted to think about, Edward thought, but how else was he expected to get through tomorrow? They were 'hosting' (her words) Jules's parents and the whole wretched brood, including Lorraine, who had offered to come over early 'to help', and her rowdy litter of children. Every time he thought about this, sharp little darts of anxiety jittered through his chest and he wondered if should simply tear his heart out now and be done with it. There would be no Christmas Truce for Lorraine, Edward decided, taking a tumbler from the shelf. Too many evenings he would arrive home to find her sizeable bulk installed on their sofa watching television or sitting whispering at the computer with Jules. For a number of months, during the spring and summer, Jules had seemed to focus every fibre of her being on him, her whole existence seeming to orbit his, her only desire being to scrutinise, to scrape at his edges with her fingernails and peel them back to pick at what lay underneath. He had found it a painful and unnecessary process – and yet, Edward thought, somehow, over the course of a few more months, he had gone from having almost nowhere to pick his nose unobserved to feeling like a spare part, a ghost in his own house. He couldn't decide which was worse.

He cupped his hands to the window and peered out into the garden. In October the last apple tree had succumbed to an obscure wasting disease, its branches turning blackened and shrivelled. He couldn't bring himself to have it chopped down, and he saw now that in the snow it had come into its own, standing out sharply against the fence, dignified and defiant. He took the bottle and his glass and went into the sitting room and switched on Radio 4. 'Hark the Herald Angels Sing' came pouring into the room, the final verse, Edward realised, where one section of the choir sang the descant and the whole thing rose on a crescendo of minor chords or whatever it was that, at that moment, made his heart ache with sorrow. He switched it off. Another splash of scotch wouldn't hurt, he thought, and poured himself a restrained, precious measure, two fingers, or three. His book was where he'd left it, face down on the coffee table, a collection of stories, poems and interviews about war through the ages. *War through the Ages*, it was titled, logically. He sat down and turned to where he'd left off: 'The Death of the Ball Turret Gunner', a morbid tale of a short man's death. He flicked through to another page – an interview with a captain from a British Navy frigate. Edward took another sip from his glass. He felt too restless for reading and instead got up and went over to the window and pulled back the curtains. The snow was still pelting down, flinging itself at the glass as if pleading to be let in. He took a moment to admire the Christmas tree in the half-light, its lopsided, spiky shape. His goal, on the way home a bit early this afternoon, had been to find the perfect one, and he had succeeded, doing the rounds of the three or four sellers in town, understanding that he would know the tree when he saw it, a bit crooked and broken and obviously unwanted, as was the tradition. *The tree that needed a home for Christmas*, the necessity their mother had made into a clever game. He and Isobel used to run round and round it with tinsel, he remembered, and then take turns to stand guard for the arrival of the fairy, who appeared on top of the tree every single year without fail, their mother explaining that, unlike Father Christmas, the fairy was apt to turn up at any hour of the day or night. Invariably and most infuriatingly, they never caught her in the act, but once she had been perched there for a day or two their mother would open the honey jar to show them, with mock-outrage, the faint scratch marks and pine needles, incontrovertible evidence of midnight snacks. He and Isobel were saucer-eyed. It was stunning, Edward thought, how credulous they were, how they had swallowed the story whole.

He wiped some condensation off the window and not for the first time wondered what Isobel was doing for Christmas. Catching up with his personal email recently, he saw that he had almost no emails from Isobel. He had at least expected a Christmas card. Jules asked him for his list some weeks ago and it had struck him that there was only Isobel to send to now. He had told Jules he would prefer to write the card himself, stringing together a few lines, long overdue, asking his sister what she had planned and whether she might be interested in spending Christmas with him and Jules. Last Christmas, it had been Isobel's turn with their mother and Edward had spent the entire day locked up with the Brewers – a day of total bedlam, he remembered, of non-stop noise and chaos and arguing. He recalled that over the summer Isobel had dropped a hint, a typically transparent one, about Christmas, in the email about their mother and when Edward might like to spread her ashes. *Christmas, maybe? Have to decide where… Thoughts? Talk on Skype? No worries if not!* And shamefully he had opted for not. Perhaps her not being here was for the best, though, Edward thought. If he had had some fond vision of the three of them – he, Isobel, and Jules – decorating the tree together, the reality would involve Isobel being subjected to his in-laws. And then he would have had to explain how he'd got himself into this situation in the first place. Where to start?

'You should take it back,' Jules had said when he arrived home with the tree this afternoon. He'd stopped off for a quick pint at the pub and was feeling quite festive and merry carrying his find up the path. One of its top branches was perfectly askew – 'a bit skew-whiff', his mother would have said – sticking out at an odd angle in precisely the required way. 'I don't understand,' Jules had said, her plump frame blocking the doorway, her lips pursed, legs akimbo, hands on hips – reminding him, Edward had realised, of her sister. 'Why did you have to pick that one?' she went on.

How would the explanation sound to her ears? he had thought.

'They're just trying to palm it off on you, because it's so late,' Jules said, turning her back and going inside, leaving him to laboriously nudge the thing through the door without spilling any of its needles. 'I told you to get it earlier. I'd take it back right now if I were you, before they close,' she said, as he set it down by the window.

Sod that, Edward thought mulishly, taking another gulp of scotch. And, to make sure, he'd decorate the tree tonight, *all by himself*, and then it would be too late, wouldn't it?

At some other point of too-lateness he understood that it probably wasn't the best decision, spending Christmas Eve digging through the old Christmas decorations box. He had been very stealthy yesterday, pulling the ladder down and getting it out of the loft, and concealing it behind the sofa. Now the whole lot had managed to come apart in his hands in a tinkling cloud of tinsel and glass baubles, leaving the carpet coated in a fine dusting of sparkle and old glitter – a little gift, Edward decided, for Jules to scold him over on Christmas morning. On moving day last summer he had rescued the box, quite by chance, during a last check of the flat before they left, bemused to find it sitting outside the back door among the various boxes of magazines and broken kitchen appliances there was little point taking with them. His first instinct had been to confront Jules and demand to know why, and what she was thinking – but then, Edward had decided, they had packed up in such a hurry, and it wasn't surprising if one of them had chucked something out by mistake, especially some taped-together old box that looked as if it was full of old newspapers. Jules wasn't herself lately either, the hormones, Edward assumed, making her uncharacteristically tetchy, and unpredictable in her likes and dislikes. He had thought it best not to risk setting her off. Instead he had hidden the box in the boot and niftily transferred it up to the loft as soon as they arrived. Were its contents looking a bit sparse this year? he wondered, examining the crumpled remainders. Or was it his imagination – some misplaced thread of nostalgia playing tricks on him again? He was certain there had been more things in the box in previous years, more ornaments wrapped in newspaper and 1970s-era Green Shield Stamps catalogues, more unfolding crêpe paper bells. *More of everything.* This, Edward decided, getting down on his knees, was memory for you in a nutshell. He unwrapped a miniature wooden dog on wheels, and a feathery swan with what looked like a broken neck. Fumbling with the tiny wires that attached ornament to branch, he attempted to find the right place for them on the tree. This had been his mother's forte, Edward remembered, these fiddly, artistic types of jobs. His own fingers scrabbled clumsily. The silence in the house had begun to weigh on him again, and he went over and put the radio back on. *Voices talking*, he thought, *good*. 'We have come to the end of our live broadcast for tonight…' said the announcer. 'And now a programme that was recorded last year.' Edward wondered why they had to spell this out so obviously? Was it some legal requirement, put in place to stop the lonely calling in on Christmas Eve, a stark reminder that other people had somewhere to be? He pictured the deserted BBC studios, the discarded plastic cups from the hideous office Christmas knees-up, the plastic tree blinking in the corner, the forlorn decorations sagging from the low ceilings. He was about to turn it off again, fearing the usual pre-recorded programme, some insufferable American banging on about 'storytelling', the patronising label the chattering classes ascribed to poor people's versions of events. But an English voice had piped up, introducing a neuroscientist who researched something called 'transactive memory structure'.

'People do it all the time without realising it,' the neuroscientist was saying.

'How so?' asked the host.

'Listen to a family chatting round a table at a wedding,' the neuroscientist replied. 'Families tell stories, they reminisce about past events – holidays, anniversaries, *etcetera*. If you listen, you'll notice how each member jumps in to contribute and fill in any information forgotten or "misremembered" by the other – who said what and who did what to whom and what happened next, and so forth.'

At least it wasn't some old toss about the baby Jesus, Edward thought, unwinding a string of tiny multicoloured bulbs from their column of rolled newspaper. Jules had demanded new lights this year, and conveniently he had forgotten to buy any. And neither would Santa, he thought. 'Lorraine has the ones where everything doesn't go off if one's broken,' she had announced when Edward had asked if there was some compelling reason, some actual *purpose*, to buying more lights when they already had plenty.

'Look,' Edward had explained, 'if the lights don't come on, you just have to test and replace the faulty bulbs.'

'I'd like the white lantern ones, if it's not too much trouble for you,' Jules had continued, obliviously. 'They're so much more elegant for the home.'

The old-fashioned lights were far more appealing, thought Edward, and far more charming than the humongous, circus-tent ones they flogged these days. He certainly didn't mind the fact that each bulb depended on the other for its light. There was something rather touching or reassuring about this. It was much as the lady neuroscientist claimed, Edward thought, trying to arrange the lights in some artful fashion without leaving too many gaps. Each human being connected the knowledge or information held by themselves to the knowledge held by others, and perhaps only in that way could you hope to form a complete memory – or in other words, Edward thought, pleased with himself, *make the lights come on*. 'We all know that memory is subjective,' the scientist was saying. 'However, it's important to us as a species to feel that we have the complete version – the whole story, if you will.'

He got all the lights on the tree, more or less, and arranged them in some appropriately zigzag fashion. That would have to do for now. He found an unopened box of lametta (there always seemed to be one) and draped it round the bottom, plus a few strands round near the top for the fairy. The fairy – inexplicably one-armed for the past few years – was the most important part of Christmas. *Where was she?* He returned to the box to rummage around for her but was down to the last layers of newspapers and tissue. There was no sign of her. *Christmas won't be the same*, he thought petulantly, taking a swig from the bottle. He didn't bother with the glass. Jules would not be best pleased if she found out, but he had left it on top of the television and didn't feel like fetching it. Who could blame the fairy if she too had had enough of it, Edward thought, the literal pain in the arse of sitting on a prickly tree year after year? With his mother also MIA, perhaps the fairy no longer felt obligated and had flown off, leaving him alone with the miserable dregs of Christmases past – and the Brewers, Edward remembered, the present dregs. He tipped the bottle back again. Even the cat had abandoned him. He used to look forward to coming in after work, having Happy Meal make figures-of-eight around his shins. Had his being at work so much upset the animal's own schedule? Happy Meal seemed to have grown far more attached to Jules, trotting round the house after her and plonking himself on her lap in the evenings, not Edward's.

With a length of string he affixed his favourite ornament, a green woollen Spitfire, to the top branch of the tree in place of the fairy. He switched off the reading lamp and crawled underneath and managed to get the plug into the socket with his eyes closed. Then, feeling his way back to the centre of the room, he opened his eyes. The lights had blinked silently, miraculously on, filling the room with Christmas. He felt light-headed, the carpet seeming to float sideways under his feet, as if gently lifting away from the floor, and he got back down and yanked the plug out. The room returned to darkness and he lay down under the tree. Right on cue Jules appeared, to moan about the noise and berate him about the tree and the general state of the house, and he felt his guts knotting up again. He cleared up the mess as best he could, relieved when he heard the bed creak and hoping that she wouldn't disturb him again.

There was a lot of scrunched-up newspaper left in the box and he lifted it out and sniffed hopefully, trying to discern pine, oranges or balsam, some fragrance of Christmas like the wreckage of something he could barely recall; instead he got a strong whiff of mildewed cardboard. He had asked, if not for happiness necessarily, then for contentment, Edward thought, sitting back on his heels to give his knees a rest. He assumed most people were no different, seeking refuge in the future, in the notion of a life in middle age that would pan out smoothly after a few bumps. Where had he gone wrong?

433

This unexplored yet bright and shining outcome had grown obscured, dulled by the monotony of days, so that more and more the past clawed at him and he felt himself pulled back into its undertow. Unlike the proverbial car in the rearview mirror, Edward thought, putting aside another layer of newspaper, the past was not closer, but farther away than it appeared – and gone altogether. 'Storm 10,' intoned a voice from the radio. The Shipping Forecast was promising 'squally showers' as Edward lifted out a tatty length of old tinsel, still hoping to see the fairy lying underneath. Someone, he could not remember who, said that tinsel possessed all the qualities of silver but with the added element of poignancy – but who? Edward thought, overcome by the need to know. Who said it? 'Who said that?' he said aloud to himself. Nabokov? Tolstoy? *Some poor old sod like me*, Edward decided, as he lifted out a partially crushed box of Woolworth's Christmas cards and saw beneath it a bundle of letters.

He was struck by how much he'd forgotten. Or rather, Edward realised, how much he had never read in the first place. He read the letters through again, more slowly this time. His sister's handwriting gave him pause, familiar to him even now – the 4s like scribbled As, the 8s winding up from the bottom, not the top, so that they resembled ampersands, and the 'Es' which at times looked like backwards 3s, and at others were curled like miniature snails. Where possible he deciphered the dates and put her letters into some semblance of order. He couldn't help noting that where Isobel mentioned something positive – a promotion, a better apartment, an exotic holiday – she seemed to put it down to luck or in the next line counter it with something negative. Was this for his benefit, Edward wondered, so that that he wouldn't feel envy or think that he had made the wrong decision? How pitiful the letters were, he thought, like someone whistling in the dark, his sister keeping up her mundane, one-sided patter over many years and not a single reply from Edward. As time went on, her news gave way to pleas, her tone becoming tinged – finally – with a desperate, imploring quality, a sense that what Isobel wanted more than anything was for him to forgive her. He read through one of the later ones. *If we could have a talk, just 5 minutes, if only for Mum's sake.* His forgiveness! What a joke, Edward thought. There was nothing to forgive. Yet out of sheer stubbornness he had chosen to withhold this fact from her for all this time. He had taken actual pleasure in denying it, he realised, this one, stupid thing that meant the world to her. 'We don't want you here,' he had told her. 'Edward, don't...' their mother had said as Isobel ran from the room. 'I won't have it. She's my daughter. This is her home as well as yours.' And in that moment he had hated their mother too – for favouring Isobel, for letting her get away with it when he could not.

This was, Edward supposed, another lie he had told himself. She had tried to reason with him, asking him to at least *talk* to his sister and sort things out. 'No, thanks,' Edward said. Faced with this obstinacy, she had taken to dropping Isobel's name into their conversations in a manner that he found infuriating. Then the letters began to arrive, one after the other, and he and his mother developed a routine. On Fridays he would come down from uni on the early train to find an airmail letter sitting on the table next to the phone. On Sundays, as he said goodbye, he would point to the envelope and say simply, 'Thanks but I won't be opening that.' Never more, never less. God help him, Edward thought, he had prided himself on this, this adult feeling of disdain, the flawless act of rejection. The following week the letter would be joined by another. 'You might as well stop bloody leaving them for me,' he said once, but the letters kept coming and the pile grew. 'Please, Edward, just open them.' And one day, 'I'm the only bridge between the two of you, and once I'm gone…' a statement that, at the time, Edward had dismissed as his mother's self-pity. And there was the day he shouted in her face and made her cry and sent her running into the garden to get away from him. And then the letters got further and further apart until, at some unremembered point, they stopped altogether. By then, not speaking to his sister had become a habit like anything else. It felt normal not to think about her, and when he was forced to, such as when she was visiting their mother, it was easier to stay away.

What on earth were the letters doing in the Christmas decorations box? For all he knew, they had been sitting there for years and he'd been none the wiser. While it was his job to brave the spiders in the loft, it was his mother's to unpack the box and hang the decorations. Mary was, Edward realised, the only person who could have put them there. He considered this. His mother was an odd combination of direct and indirect. And this would make an awful and apt sort of sense – if she had assumed, quite correctly, that the box was the one thing Edward would keep with him after she was gone. This would mean, Edward realised, that she planned for him to find them during his first Christmas without her, a punishment that seemed unnecessarily cruel.

He got up and fetched his glass over. Had Isobel known how their mother felt about her leaving for America? Now, in his heart of hearts, he was certain that his sister had no idea. If he had cursed himself for eavesdropping on his mother's phone conversation with her cousin, it was because if there were a way to un-hear it he would have followed Isobel over and would be there right now. None of that was anyone's fault – not Isobel's for going, not their mother's for letting her, nor for feeling the way she did and keeping it a secret. But for what happened afterwards, he thought – for the pain he caused them both – the fault was all his. Who could blame their mother for leaving Isobel's letters in the one place she knew he would find them? As a solution it was simple and elegant, a posthumous indictment of his own folly, delivered at Christmas, which was, after all, the worst time for surprises. About his treatment of her last May he had asked Isobel for her forgiveness, toiling over the letter accompanying his Christmas card to find the right words, acknowledging that he had not been kind during that last week before the funeral. The time had passed in a blur of stress and exhaustion, but he recalled being high-handed, dismissive of her efforts and, at the inn afterwards, of her as well. Somehow, Edward thought, emptying the last of the bottle, this final snub was the worst thing of all. After Isobel's transparent hints and her offers to stay, how very adroitly he had dodged her, pretending to be a bit farther gone than he was. True, he had been weary from the day and its peculiar social obligations. And, if he was honest, somewhat hurt that Isobel had chosen not to sit with him at their mother's service – though in light of his treatment of her this complaint was, Edward thought, a bit rich, wasn't it? Beyond co-ordinating the arrangements that week, he had not given her much thought, and this too was deliberate. When the day of the funeral had arrived he had told himself that, Isobel being Isobel, she would have plans with friends afterwards and plenty to occupy her. This wasn't true either. Isobel had had no plans and she had told him so the day before. His assumptions were made for convenience's sake, to preserve his view of his sister, Edward thought, and his own bitterness towards her. When she'd left, pensive in her inherited scarf, for a brief moment her bright, worried expression had reminded him of their mother's. *And yet*, Edward had written, *as your brother I did nothing to stop you, and for that I am truly sorry*. He understood that this could never be mended and never be made right – but he hoped that Isobel could forgive him. He had spent hours on it, filled five sheets of airmail paper, and placed them inside his Christmas card for Jules to put in the first post the next day.

He went to the front door and yanked it open. Freezing air rushed in, bringing with it a thick, moving scrim of snow, the countless flakes blown upwards and sideways. He squinted out into the whiteness. Where the road was, he could just make out their car, hunched on the kerb like a large animal under a blanket. *It's settling!* he thought, and the phrase seemed to bring back all the excitement and wonder of childhood. He watched the snow land on the dustbins, coming down properly now – 'movie snow', Isobel used to call it, unfeasibly thick and powdery, and falling steadily. He tried to picture the green things sleeping under the concrete in the back garden, the hard earth like any winter place, the lively shoots and bulbs biding their time before bursting through again, the daffodils as early as February, the tulips in April, and in June their mother's beloved strawberry patch and the dog roses flowering along the fence. In his hands were Isobel's letters and the remains of the box, the whole lot barely held together by a bit of old ribbon. *Too late*, Edward thought, going to the dustbin and pushing them down inside. He'd missed the boat, and the boat had sailed without him. He couldn't blame Isobel for her silence, his words, after all this time, being too little and too late. He bent down to scoop up a handful of snow from the doorstep. Who could he tell, Edward thought, about its soft marshmallow consistency, the cold miracle of the stuff in the palm of his hand? Earlier, making dinner, he had reached down to scratch his leg only to find, for the briefest moment, that it wasn't where he thought it was. An idea had popped into his head, like one of Jules's text messages with a half-smiley emoticon attached: *Brain tumour?* it said hopefully. *And there it is*, Edward thought, as water leaked between his fingers in thin, icy drips – the feeling that he had nothing, and rather a lot of it.

In the kitchen, for old times' sake, he opened the fridge and wedged the snowball into the freezer. Lying down on the sofa for a moment to rest his eyes, he found himself standing at the edge of the sea. There was no moon, and yet he found he was able to gaze out and down through the waves into immeasurable depths, further down than even the fishes would venture. She was there, as he knew somehow that she would be, her outline visible, floating a few inches above the seabed, arms by her sides as if confined to a hospital bed, pressed down by water and starched bed linens. There were objects strewn around, lifting gently and rhythmically off and back on to the seabed – her sunglasses, a single glove, a coffee cup perched surreally in its saucer. He opened his eyes and the scene vanished. *I must have dropped off*, Edward thought, and could have sworn she was there with him in the room, as if the adverts had come on and she'd popped out to the kitchen to make a cup of tea. The house was silent. Whatever it was that had made his mother uniquely herself, her spirit or her essence – and there was no word, Edward thought, but for the thing itself – she had felt so undeniably *here*, her presence here in the room, vivid and detailed and real. More and more lately, this was something he could not summon. Even as he tried to catch hold of it, the feeling, the certainty was already fading, slipping farther and farther away. He felt himself listening for the sound of the kettle whistling, the clack of cups in the kitchen, but nothing moved.

He stared at the empty whisky bottle and heaved himself up into a sitting position. Behind him was the ghost window, which long ago he'd consigned to an overactive imagination, to childish *Scooby-Doo* fantasy. At the time he and Isobel had been so sure. 'Friendly, or at least semi-friendly,' she had called it, when they compared notes, agreeing that the ghost or spirit – the *presence* – appeared as a small blur in your peripheral vision and drew back the moment you turned to see what it was. The ghost was independently witnessed by them both, and on different occasions, and there was some proof in that, Edward thought: the promise of another world, beyond human perception or understanding, a place not subject to the whims of time, unknowable and yet there all the same, independent of his personal beliefs. Their mother had invoked the Holy Ghost each night as she tucked them in. If the phantom was truly there, Edward thought, if he and Isobel had really seen it, if only once, didn't this call all his beliefs – or lack of them – into question? And if it had been there only once, couldn't it come back? *Going mad*, Edward thought, flicking his eyes behind him as if trying to trick the thing into emerging from its hiding place. He waited. Nothing stirred. He tried again, gathering every fibre of his mental strength, to suspend his disbelief, to summon the ghost and make it appear it in some movement or flicker as he turned back towards the window, and saw only his own face, a faint blur reflected in the glass. Above him the ceiling creaked and he started. Jules. Out of bed again. He had forgotten she was there. For a few minutes, Edward realised, he had forgotten that his wife even existed. With some difficulty he got himself up and took in his surroundings – the shreds of ragged tinsel and old cardboard littering the floor, sofa cushions flung about, the room in complete disarray. *What was he doing?* There was nothing to see in the window. Of course there wasn't. The past was dead, and everyone in it long gone. *Spilt milk.*

He was still here, though, wasn't he? *Am I?* Edward thought, considering this. To be here and be alive, to possess the blessed luxury of wondering and thinking and complaining, of eating and drinking and planning your time, however inconsequential – that was a privilege, wasn't it? You could spend your life regretting the past, Edward thought, hankering after your other self, enjoying some parallel world that was not the result of your own choices in this one. There was still time: he had a clear opportunity to correct the mistakes of the past, so didn't he owe it to himself – his future self, his child – to try? You had only to project yourself into the future and look back at the decisions you were making right now, sitting here on your sofa, Edward marvelled, and everything became so clear. The solution was staring him in the face and had been for a long time. It wasn't rocket science. Better to throw the dice, he thought, to collapse the wave function and find out what the future held, to take a chance and know that you'd done everything you could, than fail to and always wonder 'what if'. That was what his mother believed. For fuck's sake, Edward realised, she had even sent him a reminder! A gift in disguise – which he had promptly chucked in the bin – *Merry Christmas!* He would speak to Jules, and he would bridge the gap with his sister directly. There had been postal strikes on and off throughout December and it was possible his card had never arrived. If he had managed to lose Isobel again, if she wanted nothing to do with him, at least he wouldn't be left forever wondering. He had been so short-sighted, guilty of a lack of imagination, looking only outwards and in the process missing the things closest to him and right under his nose, the people and places that were the most precious. 'Cannot hear for noise of steam,' Edward thought: the last message from the *Titanic*.

Upstairs the toilet flushed and he heard Jules sigh as she crossed the landing. She hadn't had it easy this year either. Bullied by her sister, harangued by her family, miserable and fat and pissed about by her own hormones. Yet the shameful way Edward had stuck her in the middle, between him and Lorraine, leaving her struggling to keep the peace… At times, bickering with Jules about some random thing, he would experience a weird flicker of paranoia, as if the scenery were being quickly and quietly moved around behind him. Yet why would Jules, of all people, have anything but his best interests at heart? More evidence, Edward thought grimly, that he had made a cage of his own beliefs and let his insecurities take over. He had allowed himself to doubt the person closest to him, as he had with Isobel, ascribing to his wife motives or intentions that didn't consider the real person underneath. If her response played out in the pathetic desire for a new sofa or dining room table, who could blame her? And there was something sad about that, wasn't there? Edward thought. As if his wife were trying to fill the terrible gap that Edward – if he had had any sense – should have stepped into months ago instead of trying to make it all go away. What would his mother have to say about his behaviour? Edward thought, as for the first time it occurred to him that his father had done almost the same thing, finally abandoning his family and starting a new life, and a new family, elsewhere. *I didn't ask for this*, Edward thought, *this life I never wanted, and yet here we are.* Jules hadn't tricked him, he understood that now. She was doing her best, and Edward might consider having some faith and following her example. He could continue to marinate in self-pity, or grow up and make the best of it. His choice. All of it. *A new start*, Edward thought, staring in disgust at the empty whisky bottle, a new year to fully take up his role as a husband and father, in which – it shouldn't be forgotten – the family name and his genetic legacy, such as it was, would be assured. He had never been one for New Year resolutions but that would change too. He would get himself back to work and in the evenings do up the nursery. At the weekend he would fix up the old shed, and come the spring start on the flowerbeds in the front garden. He would get himself back to the gym! He would have the paving removed in the back garden and replant all his mother's favourite plants. And Jules would return to work, and they would manage, wouldn't they? They would manage well enough. There were worse ways to live. They would have a good enough life. He took the empty bottle into the kitchen and threw it into the recycling bin. He had wasted so much time pissing about and feeling sorry for himself. There was no way to know what the future held, but only one way to find out. He would grab hold of life, Edward thought; he would throw the dice and see what came up. *What an adventure!* The decision made, he felt elated, brimming with optimism. This was his time, his chance, his and Jules's and their child. Time to pull his socks up and put his shoulder to the wheel, just as his mother had done. And first thing tomorrow, Edward decided, making his way upstairs to give his wife the good news, he would phone Isobel.

Horses

For some time she had been waiting for Edward to hit rock bottom and bounce back up again. In fact, she had rather hoped it would be in time for Christmas. But Christmas was tomorrow, and, as she had told Lorraine only this morning, there he was, still down there. Obviously, Julie thought, there were other things to be thankful for. '*My* dining room,' she would chant softly to herself as she went from room to room, putting out a hand to touch a door or a wall, '*my* kitchen, *my* bathroom,' because *Pathways to Possible* had said to create a mantra and this was hers. In the kitchen she ran the tap and filled up the kettle and it came to her that, in a funny way, she didn't mind it any more, the peculiar feeling in the house, the sense – not that common any more – of being watched or followed. She had made peace with Mary's rooms – *my* rooms, she reminded herself – with their unexplained echoes and odd creaking noises. After all this time, Danecroft Road finally felt like her own.

The kettle rumbled and she took down a mug from the shelf and put it on the countertop – which was, Julie noted with pleasure, still shiny and new-looking. Elsewhere, behind or above her, under the floor or behind the wall, someone set down their own mug with a soft answering clonk. If only Edward would get over to Home 'n' Wear. She wasn't asking for the bloody world, was she? Declan and Lorraine bought their new settee at Home 'n' Wear, and Lorraine said it was in a proper mall like the one they'd visited in Florida – modern and well lit, and so much nicer than that ugly 900-year-old church that used to sit in the same spot. Julie had brought the issue up again with Edward last night, the need for a new settee – and a new bedroom set, for that matter. As usual he had turned this into a row. 'Fine,' she had told him, 'have it your way,' and for the rest of the evening they had watched television in silence.

She popped a Daytime Yearnings teabag into her cup, added boiling water, waited two minutes and then topped it up with cold, the steam causing her to sneeze as from somewhere else, above perhaps, in the room that was no longer Mary's, someone else sneezed too. 'Bless you,' she murmured, and took herself into the dining room to look through the bumper Christmas issues of *Château Style* and *California Kitchen* magazines which she had been saving for a treat. *Ring in the New Year and Ring in the Changes! Antiqued gold – a modernising and confident option for all your living space needs.* The special pull-out paint section showed a dining room extension in Colour Me Softly and an en-suite guest bathroom in Positively Pink. Definitely a mood-lifting and healing hue if ever she saw one, Julie thought, taking a sip of her tea. She must remember to cut the pictures out later and put them in her special folder. Not that she didn't *appreciate* the elegant white that Phil Modin had chosen *throughout*. And if Edward insisted on making his not very funny or clever jokes about needing sunglasses in the house, well, white was so much cheerier than those depressing pondwater greys and greens that Mary had favoured. They'd been at Danecroft Road for almost six months now and it was time for a change. An accent wall, she had suggested to Edward, in the nursery, something bright? 'Never enough, is it?' he had snapped at her as somehow the discussion moved on to a row about cutlery.

She closed her magazine and made an effort to refocus her thoughts away from Edward's harmful energy, towards the patio where – she couldn't help noticing – the cat was once more squatting down under the dead apple tree, trying out a few turns of his behind. She tapped her knuckles sharply on the glass and was gratified to see the animal look up cautiously and move away. In the middle of winter perhaps things did look a bit bleak and bare outside, of course they did, but whose garden didn't? Edward couldn't leave the subject alone, and in Julie's opinion at this point he was just doing it to get at her. *Get over it already*, she felt like saying. Their garden certainly didn't resemble 'a fucking brutalist fucking graveyard', or whatever it was Edward called it. Why could he never let go of anything? She sighed and opened her magazine again. The neatly paved area was so much more pleasant than the barely controlled jungle Mary had cultivated, crawling with insects and rife with unsanitary conditions. It wasn't natural, was it? And didn't everyone want a garden they could be proud of when company came round? Everyone except Edward, apparently. Next summer, with some colourful items of garden furniture in bold tones, and assuming Edward shifted himself and got the barbecue going, the garden would look as refined and elegant as any of the ones in *Château Style*.

She saw that Happy Meal had moved only a few feet farther away and that once more his backside was skimming the ground in narrowing circles. She leant forward and rapped on the glass for a second time, the chair creaking ominously under her weight as the cat looked away into the middle distance, at nothing in particular, with a vacant expression that reminded her of Edward's whenever she asked him to run an errand. Until recently, the cat's response had been to turn his back and continue with his rehearsals, and then simply do his business right in front of her. It was behaviour that made her think uncomfortably of school, Julie realised, and the cruelty of children who went out of their way to taunt or ignore another child. 'Go!' she called through the glass, surprised by the sharpness of her own reaction. This time the cat looked directly at her, scratched stubbornly at the concrete for a few seconds, and stalked off towards next door's garden. *Yes*, Julie thought. *Very good*. Happy Meal was learning.

She got up and went into the kitchen. Where to start? The thought of all the things she had to accomplish by tomorrow was overwhelming, and she leant against the kitchen island for a moment to gather her thoughts. There were dinner and place settings to mull over, and the fridge and the cupboards to go through because Edward couldn't be trusted to follow a simple shopping list and buy the correct items. Her father had offered to get the show on the road with a 'Roman roast' tomorrow. 'What's that when it's at home?' Edward had asked derisively – and rather ignorantly, Julie had informed him, considering he had actually been there when they all watched it being made on TV last Sunday.

'It's a chicken inside a duck inside a goose inside a pig,' she had said. Or was it a lamb? She was too distracted to remember just now. Either way, her father would be bringing the meat side of things, so Edward didn't have to bother himself.

'Fill your boots,' he had suggested.

'What if we just did a turkey inside a goose?' she'd offered – very generously, she thought, since any change in the recipe could ruin the whole meal – and the whole day itself. For everyone. It was only a little bit of meat; did he have to be so obstinate about his vegetarian diet at Christmas?

'Do what you like,' Edward had replied. 'I'll heat up a Chinese.'

She placed her cup in the dishwasher and considered whether it was at that moment, when Edward had turned and stumped off down to the pub for the third time that week, that she had finally been worn down by the months and months of negativity and bad feeling. How many times had she offered to help with his personal growth and spiritual development? Even though *Pathways to Possible* warned that going too far in the other direction with people could turn you into an 'enabler'. Was it true? she had wondered. Could you make people worse by helping them too much? The idea had been new, and at first not obvious in how it worked, but in light of Edward's recent behaviour it made a funny sort of sense. If she 'enabled' Edward in his unhealthy choices, Julie thought, opening the fridge, she would only cause him to make more of them. And if Edward couldn't – or wouldn't – be helped? If he wasn't interested in mindful communication or trying to jump-start his joy – even just to please his wife – maybe it was time to do as the book advised in such cases and practise self-compassion. If you wanted to get serious about creating your authentic identity, you had to put yourself first, whether this meant socialising on your own with other like-minded souls evolving on the path to personal fulfilment and joyousness or claiming your right to a better income, a gourmet kitchen, or a larger and more comfortable home. *This* was what it meant to be *truly* unselfish and authentic, because it allowed your loved ones their own freedom and right to self-determination. And *this*, Julie thought, searching the fridge and seeing that the three bottles of pinot grigio she put in there two days ago were no longer there, meant giving your loved one the freedom to hit rock bottom.

Except of course that hadn't happened either, had it? No. She had pictured Edward like a cork, pushed down into a bowl of cold water, and then released, to pop back up again, restored, new again – his old self. Not that Edward was ever a *bubbly* sort of person, Julie thought, opening the overhead cupboards. No one would ever say that about Edward. But he never used to go out of his way to embarrass her, to belittle her in front of her family the way he did now. With some difficulty she bent down and peered into the cupboard under the sink where last week she had found a half-empty bottle of whisky hidden behind the bleach and immediately disposed of it. Whereas Julie had done everything she could to give Edward what he needed, whereas she had supported him in everything he did and thought and felt or was interested in – he went out of his way to ignore her wishes and undermine her. And there was nothing clever or funny about that, was there? Happy Meal appeared at the window and she let him in. Then again and to be fair, Julie thought, as the cat brushed his tail around her ankles, she had found herself caring less and less these days what Edward did, thought, felt, or was interested in. His criticism and cutting remarks, together with his neglect of their relationship and his own health, simply didn't *stick* with her any more. Not like they used to. In more private moments – ones she had barely confessed to herself, let alone Edward – she found herself comparing her present feelings to the ones she used to experience, which felt strangely old and outdated, like a skirt from her youth that no longer fitted. It was all very complicated, Julie decided, finding a half-empty bottle of red wine in the back of the fridge, and certainly not *ideal* – and yet, when she thought about it, there was something … *interesting* about this new feeling – or lack of one – that she couldn't quite put her finger on. She lifted the bottle out of the fridge, sniffed gingerly at the neck and tried to think of the exact word that described how she felt about this new feeling, this *new-old* feeling. Sadness? Fear? Boredom? *Was it boredom?* Yes, Julie thought, but not only that. She emptied the vinegary wine down the sink, gave the bottle a rinse and chucked it into the bin, and decided to give the microwave a scrub. Inside she found the Christmas food shopping list Edward claimed to have mislaid the day before, scrunched up on the revolving plate in a little ball. *Well, that's just typical*, she said to herself. Lorraine was making a Sweet Potato Pot Roast, a recipe from *Big American Chef*, and it was *extremely important*, she had told Edward, that he pop to the shops to get the bag of muscovado sugar that the recipe required. He could not manage even that one simple task, while half of what he *had* managed to come home with he had put, as per usual, in *completely* the wrong place. Did he do it on purpose? It would be just like Edward to try and ruin Christmas, Julie thought, returning to the fridge to pull every single item out. She thought back to the night Mary passed away, when Edward had taken the cat and slunk off to the settee. Hearing him release his emotions through the door had seemed to her like a hopeful sign of things to come, of Edward sharing his inner-self feelings and being ready to achieve authentic intimacy. *Weak*, her father would call it – and had, Julie remembered – this past September, after she let slip that her tiredness was due less to her pregnancy than to the fact that months after Mary's passing, when a normal person would have moved on in an emotionally healthy way, Edward still woke her up whimpering in his sleep. 'Well, you're stuck with him now, luv,' her father had replied. *But was she?*

It was only after she had cleared out the *whole* fridge and gone through *every single one* of the cupboards, after she'd rung up to ask if Lorraine would mind popping to the supermarket for the various items Edward had deliberately forgotten and after she'd wrapped the presents for all her nephews and nieces and seen to her father when he dropped off the goose and the turkey (which they might as well keep outside on the patio, he told her, seeing as the weather had turned nippy) – it was only after *all this unnecessary work* that Edward decided to make his entrance, with a ridiculous broken tree and a bottle of whisky sticking out of the inside pocket of his overcoat. *Was he joking?* She knew about the drinking. They all did. And the fact that he was only pretending to go to the office every day. Last week an unpleasant woman from HR had rung the house with all sorts of questions, asking to speak to Edward, who she seemed to think was on temporary leave from work owing to stress. Redundancy and twelve months' salary was one option, she explained. Which explained Lorraine's story about seeing him sitting in Five Eyes Pizza during daylight hours, Julie had thought. But Edward was at least still leaving the house every morning, and the alternative was to have him under her feet all day, so she had decided to have a think about it and say nothing for now. That tree, though, that was going too far. How many times had she asked him to get a nice artificial one? But she was too tired, after her long day, to care, and was in bed by nine.

She woke some hours later alone in bed and lay there trying to work out what had woken her. She got out of bed and went to the top of the stairs to listen. Predictably, the radio was blaring in the lounge, and she decided that if Edward had drunk his way through the bottle of Bailey's her father had left, there'd be nothing for it, even if it was Christmas: she would have to have words. 'No fucking food in the house,' she heard him mutter. 'And whose fault is that?' she whispered into the dark hallway. Going back to the bedroom, she checked a few messages on her laptop and thought about Isobel, who in the weeks leading up to Christmas had been satisfyingly silent. In their correspondence – another unpaid job, Julie thought – she had taken a leaf out of Lorraine's book. Sensing that Isobel needed an immediate reply, for example, she made sure to take her time. And, when she did write back, Julie made sure not to answer Isobel's questions or comment on any of her news. Edward's messages were, after all, brief and to the point. And this was yet another personal sacrifice she would never get credit for, she thought, all those hours she had put in at the computer to protect Edward from his sister. Edward – the actual Edward, that was – rarely mentioned Isobel any more, and never Mary. Meanwhile her email strategy was doing the trick. Isobel's emails were shorter and less frequent, as if she was walking on eggshells. When a message did arrive, Julie focused on the positive aspects of the experience – such as being able to see for herself Isobel having to literally mind her Ps and Qs – which felt extremely *validating*, Julie discovered, and gave her a real sense of achievement. For a while she had found herself not quite trusting this new, respectful, tiptoeing Isobel. Was it really that simple? she had wondered, fearing that Isobel knew and was just playing with her like a cat with a mouse – 'playing the long game', 'boxing clever', all those phrases of Edward's that nowadays made her want to scream. And then, less and less did she feel that little flare of anxiety rise up in her chest, like the gas catching on the cooker, and this was what told her that Isobel was, in fact, none the wiser. Isobel's last email, in which there was no rabbiting on about the usual rubbish, and no taking issue with Edward's lack of response, had been at the end of November. *Hiya, Just checking in. Nothing much to report here. Figuring out plans for Christmas. Not much going on this year, I guess.*

Izzy. Izzy, Julie had thought, dear Izzy was like a broken record, and not a very good one. When she felt enough days had passed, she read back over the message and typed back: *hi – we're not doing much either. spending it quietly with Julie's family. they're being very kind. still very busy with work. hope you're well. E.* Her fingers had taken on a life of their own; she scarcely had to think about what to write. She had pressed *Send* and felt weirdly excited, almost feverish with empowerment.

There was that one dicey moment, of course, early in December, when Edward had announced that he was sending his sister a Christmas card. He had sat down to write it at the dining room table, painstakingly scratching out his words as if doing homework. Several versions were torn up before he finally sealed the envelope and handed it to Julie to post the next morning. He didn't even ask nicely, Julie remembered, merely assumed that she would drag herself out of bed and out of the house first thing the next morning, and into the cold to queue up at the post office behind all the benefits cheats. It was too much. She waited until Edward had passed out on the settee and then ripped open the envelope and got halfway through all the rubbish about Mary and Christmas fairies and inviting Isobel for bloody Christmas, before losing patience and tearing the thing into little pieces. She ran the bits under the tap and flushed the whole soggy lot down the toilet where, funnily enough, she had almost but not quite disposed of Isobel's own Christmas card, which had arrived just hours before and which she had stowed in her underwear drawer. That day she had felt the satisfaction of a job well done. But what she didn't feel – and hadn't for ages, Julie realised, fastening her dressing gown to go downstairs, was even the tiniest speck of guilt.

She found Edward in the dark, lying on the floor under the tree.

'I couldn't sleep,' she told him, switching on the overhead light. 'He or she was kicking again.' He appeared to look past her and she saw that the tree was newly looped with several ugly strands of ancient-looking decorations. A woman's voice blared out of the radio. 'You'll wake the neighbours,' she said, going over and turning it off.

'Snowing...' observed Edward.

'What's *that*?' she said, pointing to the half-empty bottle of whisky, on its side under the coffee table. *Hopeless*, Julie thought, *trying to get through to him when he's in this state – like talking to a child.* Practising active listening with your partner was all very well, but when an individual was this toxic it was advice better applied to yourself, surely, and to listening to your own needs and desires for a change.

'Christmas drink? Have one,' offered Edward. 'On me,' he said, and laughed in that way he knew she hated: a short bark, like a sea lion at the circus.

'I'm not drinking at this moment in time,' she told him. 'As you well know.' *There's nothing funny about alcohol*, Julie wanted to say, *where you're concerned*. But she took the opportunity to demonstrate that she was a better person by changing the subject. 'My mother gifted us brand new decorations this year,' she reminded him. 'Don't you remember? They're in the nursery.' Edward stared blankly at her and made no move to shift himself off the floor. 'Are you going to pretend you didn't see them?' she said. Her mother had chosen a very tasteful and modern selection of metal ornaments, green and red Father Christmases and reindeer and Swedish horses. Edward had called them 'revolting slave-labour tat', whatever that was, though as per usual it was hard to know these days what Edward was thinking or

what he meant. 'And where did these ... *things* come from?'
she said, indicating the tree lights.

'Charity shop,' said Edward.

'Really?' She watched him grope blindly down the side
of the armchair next to the tree. The lights sputtered to life.
They looked exactly like Mary's old lights, but they couldn't
be, could they? She'd got rid of them last summer – put the
whole box of Mary's horrible old decorations out the back
with the rubbish.

'I asked you to get the white ones,' she said.

'Forgot,' said Edward. And then, chuckling to himself as
if in on some private joke of his own imagining, 'These are
vintage!'

The lights seemed to glimmer at her for a moment in
some dull and reproachful manner and she sighed. 'I can see
that. Can they go any brighter?'

'I don't know, can they?' said Edward.

She folded her arms and waited. He didn't reply.

'Fine,' she said and turned to leave. She had woken up
feeling a bit peckish and now she was busting for a wee as
well. 'But next year we'll have an imitation tree like I asked
for,' she said. Edward had made it clear how he felt about
artificial trees when she had pointed out the very attractive
ones at Home 'n' Wear, which were perfectly realistic but
came without all the bother and hoovering up for months
afterwards.

'Snowing,' Edward repeated, staring glassily at the
window. It was like talking to Jasmyn. *It's just snow*, Julie
thought. *What's so bloody fascinating about it?*

'It had better all clear up by the morning, that's all I
have to say.' She watched Edward turn a small Christmas
tree ornament in his hand, and then keep turning it, over
and over and over again, like a lunatic. She had planned to

announce the news about Lorraine and Jasmyn earlier, but had decided it could wait until tomorrow.

'I'm leaving him,' her sister had announced yesterday.

'Who? Declan?' Julie wasn't a bit surprised. 'Have you told Mum and Dad?'

'Like it's any of their business,' said Lorraine, 'but I told them last night.' Six months ago she would have felt stung by not being the first to know, Julie realised, but all she felt was mild interest. 'They thought you might let me and Jasmyn stay in your spare room for a bit?'

Julie said nothing. She had learned that the best way to deal with bullies was to let them wait and respond only in monosyllables. She let the seconds tick by. 'Mmm,' she said finally. 'To be honest, Lorraine, I'm not sure if that's going to work for me.'

Her first impulse was to say that it was extremely inconsiderate and selfish of Lorraine to spring this on her at Christmas. And yet, something told her she ought to consider the idea. She had enjoyed not having to clean and cook and shop the past few months, and, although she'd been doing her wealth visualisation exercises like mad, they still couldn't afford a nanny or an au pair. What if there was someone else? Someone who was here when Edward wasn't, who would pay some rent and nip to the shops and change the baby's nappy or make Julie a cup of tea when she needed to put her feet up. Which she would, obviously, Julie thought, after she'd given birth to him or her. Having a baby took it out of you. Rent money and help round the house would mean the difference between being at home with her child, Julie thought, or facing the teachers back at the school. They agreed that at first Lorraine would bring only a few of her belongings, moving in on a temporary 'emergency basis' on Boxing Day, and fetching the rest of their things over in the New Year. The baby could have the box room, as Edward originally wanted, and Lorraine and Jasmyn would take Mary's old bedroom. He could hardly complain about that, could he? She would break the news during Christmas dinner, when Edward, who claimed he found it humiliating rowing in front of her parents but did it anyway, wouldn't be able to say no.

'I'm ...' said Edward.

She waited, keen to get back upstairs and work on her list of New Year resolutions. Again he seemed to stare past her. '*Drunk*?' she suggested.

'That too,' Edward answered nonsensically, fixing her with a watery stare.

At which point, she made a decision. A surprisingly easy choice to manifest, Julie would think later, after she had gone upstairs, fetched Isobel's letters from their hiding place, and, without Edward even noticing, placed the letters back exactly where she had found them, in Mary's decorations box.

After some calming breaths out in the kitchen, taken to suppress her excitement, she made a last check of all the doors and windows, and took herself back up to bed with four slices of wholegrain toast and a cup of Midnight Dreaming tea. Some while later she heard the back door being unbolted and what sounded like one of the bin lids being slammed shut. There was a quiet knock at the bedroom door. 'Yes?' she called, caught between tiredness and annoyance at being interrupted. 'What is it?' Silly question; she knew very well what it was, because it was the same thing at least twice a week now. Edward was standing at the doorway, swaying slightly, with a stupid grin on his face.

'I've been thinking ...' he said. 'And I realise now that ...'

How long would it take this time? Julie thought impatiently, trying not to look too interested. These conversations Edward had with himself about the meaning of life and death and all the rest of it – she'd heard it all before. There was the bit where he said that he'd 'realised a few things', and that bit near the end where he said he was going to 'take up his role', or whatever it was. 'Or something,' Edward said, his forehead wrinkling, and she realised that he had already reached the in-between part, which was so incomprehensible that sometimes even Edward appeared to get lost. Something about gambling? Or was it ghosts? She couldn't be sure either. Her father was the same way, reaching the bottom of the bottle and suddenly coming over all sober and full of ideas. The other night had been especially embarrassing, Edward having informed her that he was 'turning over a new leaf', and, when Julie agreed that yes, that would certainly be very nice, he had stared at her with such a comic expression of gratitude and expectation that she couldn't help herself: she had to put her hand to her mouth and run into the bathroom, overcome with the giggles. She had sat on the toilet, listening to Edward apologise and tap on the door, and waiting for the crying to start. Now, after a few minutes of nodding politely, vaguely trying to piece together what he was saying and whether there might be, as he always claimed, something 'different this time', she was overcome by a feeling of injustice and fury. How *dared* he impose himself on her precious private time? Why was she forced, in her own home, in her own bedroom, to listen to them, these drunken ramblings, these lists of promises that Edward would never keep?

But she took a deep breath and felt the tension trickle away. There was no point in focusing on it or getting het up. Edward never remembered any of it in the morning. As she tuned his voice out it struck her that it was like turning down the volume on the TV, and seeing Edward clearly for the very first time. *What was that film he and Mary used to drone on about*, Julie thought – *the one where they pull a curtain back and you see that little man standing behind it?* She stared at him in faint wonder. Shirt askew, eyes red and puffy, Edward looked like a rough sleeper. She remembered looking out of the bedroom window at three one morning, and seeing him on his knees in the front garden sobbing. *What next?* she had thought. Couldn't the doctor give him something? Did she need to have him sectioned? She had shut the curtains, put in her earplugs and gone straight back to bed – and just prayed the neighbours hadn't heard.

'…and I was thinking about my sister,' she heard him say. 'Reading over some of her old letters and things. I don't know…' He looked confused, doubtful, as if waiting for Julie to say something. 'And then I was thinking as well.' Another pause. 'That, if it's a girl…we can call her Mary.'

'What?' *Mary?* Was this one of his stupid jokes?

'Or Isobel,' Edward continued affably, not catching her expression. 'Either way, really.'

'*Mary…Isobel?*' she repeated.

He looked extremely pleased with himself, as if he'd won a prize or discovered how to use the potty. Was she expected to congratulate him? 'Mary-Isobel…' he repeated, trying the name out, brightening. 'Yes! Mary-Isobel. Why not? See? We can still agree on something, can't we?' he went on. 'Something to be grateful for, and—'

'Why don't you call her?'

Edward looked surprised. 'Who? Isobel?'

'Yes. Isobel.' She gestured to the bedside clock. 'It's only eight-thirty there…'

'Oh.' He looked curiously at her for a moment and down at his watch. 'You're right, actually. Yes, I should. No use putting it off, is there?' His whole posture seemed to relax

459

for a moment, and she thought he looked happier than she'd seen him look in ages. His gaze wobbled back towards the window, where the snow was pelting down harder, unpleasant and cold. 'I can tell her about the snow,' he said.

'I'm sure she'll be very excited,' said Julie.

'Anything you need from downstairs?' he asked, turning back at the doorway.

'We're fine,' she told him. 'But I'm not sleeping well, so maybe you can sleep down on the settee again tonight.' She put her glasses on and opened up her laptop. 'You can leave the door open,' she said.

'Yes,' Edward said. 'Yes, of course. I understand,' he said, and shambled off downstairs.

A few minutes later she heard him leaving a message with his mobile and his landline numbers. Minutes later the landline rang and she let him answer it. She could hardly bother herself to move, but out of curiosity she went outside on to the landing to listen. How easy it was, Julie thought, seeing Edward at the bottom of the stairs with the phone pressed to his ear. Having his sister in his life again would be very nice for him, she thought, until it wasn't. He and Isobel had never got on, Edward said it himself, and people like them didn't change. So it wouldn't last...but it would last long enough for Julie. Some breathing space, an opportunity to fully affirm her New Year plans.

'...or I could come to you,' Edward was saying brightly. 'Yes, it's been a while, hasn't it? I'll have to check with Jules but I'm off all next week...last-minute, I know...'

There's an idea, Julie thought. The courts wouldn't look kindly on abandonment. And if she placed Isobel's Christmas card on the mat when the post resumed after Boxing Day, it might give Edward an extra little push in his sister's direction. Really, Julie thought, going back into the bedroom and closing the door, her sending Edward on a little adventure to foreign parts to have his midlife crisis could not be better timed. He had chosen his own path and manifested his own reality. Was it her problem, or her responsibility, or her *fault*, if he chose to drink himself to sleep every night? She had done her utmost to help him achieve a higher, more soul-centred lifestyle, based on compassion and empathy. Ultimately, trying to light the lamp of someone's soul simply burnt out your own. If Edward couldn't be bothered to hit rock bottom and bounce back up again, he could walk his pathway to impossible alone. What other choice was there? But mainly, Julie decided, she certainly wasn't going to end up poor and alone like Mary. Let Isobel deal with him. Julie had tried, and she had had enough.

She eased herself down on to the bed, adjusted the reading light, and returned to her notes and her list. In January she had scheduled Mr Modin – Philip – whose 'dear lady wife' had developed cancer and was having a long decline in a hospice. 'Your friends and your health is all you've got,' he'd informed her, which was why, as a token of their new friendship, he had signed Julie up for twenty-four sessions with his trainer, designed for the expectant lady. At first she had found it all a bit inconvenient, Philip's constant popping in to Danecroft Road. But he had been so helpful, and now that he was attending the gym every day and wearing those nice suits she had begun to see him in a completely new light. He wasn't that old, she had informed Lorraine – and he was a gentleman, underneath. Not to mention a self-made man, a real entrepreneur, with property investments all over the place, including Spain and France. They talked about everything. Philip asked her opinion on all sorts of matters and listened intently to her answers. In return, sitting in the kitchen over many cups of Afternoon Splendour, he had offered up a good deal of useful information about Isobel, whom he'd known since she was a child and whose mental health issues – 'poor thing' – had caused everyone such terrible problems. She had gone back and reopened Isobel's letters and this time seen them for what they were: Isobel was not conniving, Julie realised, she wasn't clever enough for that, but, like her brother, she was rather sad and desperate.

In the first week of January, Philip's new seafront property would be finished. 'An area where people think they're better than us, but they're not,' Lorraine had remarked jealously. Since his wife – *sadly* – was not in a fit state to leave the hospice, he'd be 'ever so grateful' if Julie would come over and advise him on the interiors and the décor and suchlike. She was so good at that sort of thing. And the place needed a woman's touch. He would send her a taxi. But he would understand, Philip said, if she was too busy. Poor man, Julie thought, it was the least she could do, with his wife so ill and, the way things were going, likely to be gone by the spring. They'd never had children, and perhaps it wasn't meant to be, Philip had said; and though she said nothing Julie wondered if he understood that people could bring cancer upon themselves. Had he mentioned how lucky Edward was to have her? he asked. Was Edward providing properly for her and the baby? At that point Julie had felt obliged to tell the truth and had to admit that no, in actual fact Edward was having some difficulties at work. Well, if there was anything Philip could do for Julie – who he felt sure was 'a very talented woman underneath' – and 'for the little one, obviously' – she only had to say the word. After all, what else was he going to do with it all, his 'legacy'? It was what poor Mary would have wanted, he told her, for him to watch over her only grandchild. They'd had long discussions about *Pathways to Possible*, and Philip had told her it was his firm belief that creative individuals should be supported. He was encouraging Julie to launch her own business, an online 'start-up' that they had decided to name 'Future Perfect', which with only a credit card would dispense advice online along the idea of P2P, but classier and more evolved. He would be only too happy to contribute. 'To an angel investor like myself, it's just good business,' he had assured her. Nowadays, if she caught him looking her up and down, or looking away quickly, she accepted this for what it was – not judgement or criticism, but an appreciation of her talents. Recently, when she was showing him the nursery and the new paint samples, his hand had strayed towards her bottom, and Julie had found that she did not mind this as much as she'd thought she would.

She continued down her list of 'New Year Manifestations'. What about Declan? With Lorraine leaving, she felt rather sorry for her sister's future ex-husband and really should take him over a casserole or something nutritious and healthy to eat. Maybe in the spring, Julie decided, after the baby was born and when she had her body back. She deleted his name from January and pasted it a little way down, to March – *which reminds me*, Julie thought, *a workout is one thing, but I'm certainly not lugging the baby halfway down the road every time I want to leave the house.* Her father had finally found someone to put the concrete down in the front garden for a good price – so while they were at it, Julie thought, adding both items to the list, they could pull down Mary's old shed. That should be scheduled sooner rather than later.

Other than that, Julie decided, this year she would focus on herself and her own needs for a change. It was so important to take a loving and non-judgemental attitude towards yourself and your important life decisions. *Imagine a lake, Lake You. Jump in and take a long, lazy swim.* As she thought this she became aware of a new feeling, one that seemed to rise up from beneath the old-new, bored and fed-up one: a long, steady pulse that seemed to grow bigger and bigger and more insistent – a feeling, Julie recognised, that was as sharp and alive as the old feeling, but unfamiliar, more exciting. *My house, my child, my new life. Possibility* – the word seemed almost to *vibrate* with promise, filling her with a sense of happiness and anticipation, as if a long-cherished ambition had finally taken shape. Everything was a spiritual opportunity, a *pathway to possible*. You only had to wish hard enough to make it so. Because being successful and happy in life all came down to faith, Julie thought, as her head sank blissfully into the pillow. Happy Meal appeared at the side of the bed, miaowing softly. She patted the duvet and he sprang up lightly beside her and dropped something small and shiny on to her lap. 'Another little present?' she asked. 'Is that for me?' The cat purred contentedly and curled up in the space behind her knees. She picked up the shiny offering between her fingers, examined it briefly – a single, gossamer thread of tinsel – and dropped it into the wastepaper basket. She really must make a note to remind Edward to have a proper go round with the hoover in the morning, and make sure to poke the nozzle under the bed. Sleep was coming, a thick descending layer, she could feel it, and the certainty gave her a feeling of immense calm, as if her body, her whole self, were a great balloon rising on a warm cushion of air. A thought occurred to her – one last item for the list, Julie realised, before she could start her new life, before she gave herself over to sleep. From now on, it was her child who would need her most, not Edward. He or she deserved the best start in life, every advantage, and was depending on

Julie to make that possible. She closed her eyes, and made a last wish. *A baby boy*, she thought, and pictured the thought as a snowflake, and watched the snowflake drift delicately down the stairs, float through the letterbox, and out into the snowy world beyond.

Acknowledgements

My editor, Myriad's inspirational publisher Candida Lacey, took a chance on me, and I'll be forever grateful for her commitment and enthusiasm. I was exceptionally lucky to work with Linda McQueen, whose editorial expertise and remarkable good humour have improved the book in more ways than I care to admit. Special thanks to Domenica de Rosa, who believed in the book from the earliest, (s)crappiest draft, and cheered me on at every opportunity.

My thanks always to my brilliant mum, Anne, who was all for having adventures...

MORE FROM MYRIAD

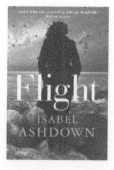

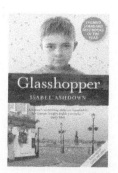

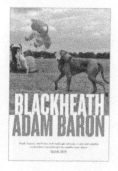

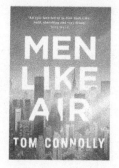

MORE FROM MYRIAD

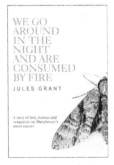

MORE FROM MYRIAD

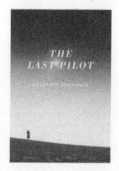

MORE FROM MYRIAD

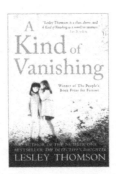